The
Wronged

Kimberley
CHAMBERS

HARPER

Harper
An imprint of HarperCollins*Publishers*
1 London Bridge Street
London SE1 9GF

www.harpercollins.co.uk

This paperback edition 2015
2

First published in Great Britain by
HarperCollins*Publishers* 2015

A catalogue record for this book is available from the British Library

ISBN: 978-0-00-752176-0

Typeset in Sabon LT Std by Palimpsest Book Production Ltd, Falkirk, Stirlingshire

Printed and bound in Great Britain by Clays Ltd, St Ives plc

MIX
Paper from
responsible sources
FSC™ C007454

The Wronged

Sunday Times #1 bestselling author Kimberley Chambers lives in Romford and has been, at various times, a disc jockey, cab driver and a street trader. She is now a full-time writer and is the author of ten novels.

Join Kimberley's legion of legendary fans on Facebook/kimberleychambersofficial and @kimbochambers on Twitter.

Also by Kimberley Chambers

Billie Jo
Born Evil
The Betrayer
The Feud
The Traitor
The Victim
The Schemer
The Trap
Payback

In memory of my dear friend Pat's husband.
Harry Fletcher
1946–2014

ACKNOWLEDGMENTS

Huge thanks to the wonderful team at HarperCollins. Getting to number one with *Payback* was an incredible moment and I owe you guys big time.

A special mention for my fab editor Kimberley Young, my wonderful agent Tim Bates, publicist Louise Swannell, Sue Cox, Sarah Ritherdon, Rosie de Courcy and Mandasue Heller.

Also Katie, Claire, Adam, Sarah, Oli and Tom.

I can't thank the supermarkets and stores that sell my books enough.

And last but certainly not least, my readers. It is all down to you lovely people that I achieved my dream. A number one *Sunday Times* bestseller! Who would have ever predicted that? Certainly not my parents and school teachers, that's for sure lol xxx

PART ONE

The first duty to children is to make them happy. If you have not made them so, you have wronged them. No other good they may get can make up for that.

Charles Buxton

PROLOGUE

Christmas Eve 1985

'We drive you from us, whoever you may be, unclean spirits, all satanic powers, all infernal invaders, all wicked legions, assemblies and sects. I demand you leave Queenie and Vivian alone. Allow them to live in peace and happiness. In the name and by virtue of our Lord, Jesus Christ, Amen.'

'Amen,' Queenie and Vivian said, glancing at one another. Both were thinking the same thing. Father Patrick was pissed.

'May you be snatched away and driven from the Church of our God and from the souls made in the likeness of God, and redeemed by the precious blood of the divine lamb. Most cunning serpent . . .'

'I think that's enough now, Father,' Vivian said, stopping the man in his tracks. She'd never been one for religious jargon and her and Queenie weren't even Catholic.

'But I haven't finished the exorcism yet,' Father Patrick bellowed, spraying both women with his precious holy water.

'Me nerves are jangled, Father. Let's all have a brandy, eh? You can finish the exorcism after I've told you my story. You don't even know what's happened to my family yet,' Queenie said. It had been Fat Beryl's idea to invite Father Patrick round. She swore by the man's power to ward off evil spirits, and after the terrible time Queenie'd had of late, she was game to give anything a go.

Grinning when Vivian handed him a very large glass of brandy, Father Patrick encouraged Queenie to open up to him. Queenie didn't need much prompting. She quite liked spilling her guts to a man of the cloth, even if he was a Catholic pisshead.

Father Patrick listened with a sympathetic ear as Queenie told him about Roy, Lenny and Molly's demise. 'That's very tragic, Queenie. Let's say a prayer for the three of them.'

Queenie squeezed the man's arm. 'No. You haven't heard the half of it yet. This year has been a real bad 'un, hasn't it, Viv? Three members of the family we've lost. Gone in a puff of smoke one after the other. One of 'em even got chopped into pieces, God rest his soul. Loved that boy, I did.'

His complexion whitening, Father Patrick urged Queenie not to gabble, and to start from the very beginning,

'Well, I've already told you about Roy, Lenny and Molly. Molly was the last of those to die. Murdered in 1980 she was, bless her. Now I'll tell you the story of everything that's happened since . . .'

CHAPTER ONE

Autumn 1980

Whitechapel was a close-knit community, especially amongst the old school who had been born and bred there, and the brutal murder of the three-year-old child had left a bitter taste in everybody's mouths.

Thankfully, the police had caught the killer. But with the murder still fresh in people's minds, parents were much more vigilant than they had been, and many a child was not allowed to roam the streets as freely as they had before Molly Butler's death.

Little Molly had been no ordinary child. She was the daughter of the infamous Vinny Butler. With Ronnie and Reggie Kray banged up, Vinny and his brothers now stood at the top of the East End's criminal ladder, along with the Mitchells from Canning Town. On the day of the funeral service, the grounds around the church were mobbed with people who had come from far and wide to pay their respects. Most of the local English shopkeepers had shut down their businesses for the day, and even though villains from across the river usually steered well clear of the Butlers' turf, Vinny recognized many faces from South London as the black limousine drove slowly through the crowds.

Molly's final journey was a mournful yet stunning sight. Two white horses pulled a glass coach through the streets of Whitechapel, past the club that the Butler brothers owned, then on to the church. As the family filed in, bystanders bowed their heads and murmured their condolences to Vinny's mother, Queenie, and her sister Viv, showing them the kind of reverence that had once been reserved for Violet and Rose Kray.

The service was extremely moving. There was barely a dry eye in the church when the pianist began to play the golden oldie, 'You Are My Sunshine'. Shortly before her untimely death, little Molly had performed the song in a talent competition at a holiday camp in Eastbourne. With her angelic looks, blonde curls and bubbly personality she had received a standing ovation from the crowd and taken first prize.

The most poignant moment of the day though, was when fourteen-year-old Vinny Butler bravely stood at the front of the church and read out a poem he had written for his little sister.

'I miss you more than words can say,
and blame myself every single day.
As your big brother I should have protected you more,
But I fell asleep and you walked out the door.

'I hope that God will take good care of you,
and love you as much as your family do.
Life will never be the same without you, Molly,
and I hope you are playing in heaven with your favourite
    dolly.

'That wicked boy who took you away,
will pay for his evil sins one day.
Until that time I want you to know,
that me, Dad, Nanny, Auntie Viv and Uncle Michael all
    loved you so.

'Rest in peace my beautiful little sister, from your big brother, Vinny.'

When the emotional teenager returned to the pew to sit alongside his family members, not a single member of the congregation sensed anything was amiss. Why would they?

The only person inside that church who knew the police had arrested the wrong boy, leaving Molly's killer still at large, was young Vinny Butler.

How did he know?

Because he was the one who had put his hands around his little sister's neck and cold-bloodedly throttled the life out of her.

CHAPTER TWO

Queenie Butler poured herself a large sherry and sat on the pouffe in front of the fire. Her sons kept offering to buy her one of those gas fires that were now all the rage, but Queenie was totally opposed to the idea. There was nothing as homely as the sight and smell of a proper coal fire.

'Bleedin' nuisance,' Queenie mumbled when her doorbell was pressed repeatedly. It couldn't be Vivian. She only lived next-door-but-one, had her own key, and had just popped out to get some fish and chips.

'You OK, Queen? I must say, that was a lovely send-off for your Molly, God rest her soul. Those beautiful white horses and the glass coach must have cost a fortune,' Nosy Hilda pried.

'Hilda, I'm not in the best of moods, love, and I certainly don't wanna talk about the funeral. The amount of tragic deaths my family have suffered, it would've been cheaper for us to open up our own poxy parlour. Now is there anything else I can help you with?'

'Well, the reason I knocked is, I just popped in the Grave Maurice. You know I like me odd glass of Guinness.'

'Can you cut to the chase, please,' Queenie snapped. She

had never been one to suffer small talk with the neighbours. It bored the arse off her.

'Your Brenda's inebriated in the Maurice with some bloke, and Tara and Tommy are sat outside with a guy.'

'Guy! What guy?'

'A stuffed Guy, as in Fawkes. They're being a bit rude, Queen, so I thought you should know. They aren't asking for a penny for the Guy, they want a pound. Then when people won't give them the money, they're threatening to set your Vinny on to them. Well, Tara is anyway. I heard her say it to Mr Patel and old Mr Arthur.'

To say Queenie was livid was putting it mildly. She had always classed such behaviour as begging and had given her boys such a clump when she'd caught them sitting outside the train station doing the same when they were nippers.

Queenie grabbed her coat and front-door keys. Brenda was her only daughter; twenty-six years old now, but still the bane of Queenie's life. The girl was an embarrassment, especially when she had alcohol inside her. She must have inherited an alcoholic gene from her father. That useless old bastard had spent more hours pissed in his lifetime than sober.

'What you gonna do? You won't tell Brenda it was me who told you, will ya? 'Cos I don't want no trouble, Queen. I only knocked because I was worried about those kiddies.'

'I'll bastard well swing for her, Hilda, that's what I'll do,' Queenie spat as she marched off down the road.

'Oh, and before I forget, Queen, Lil got taken away in an ambulance earlier. Had a stroke, by all accounts. Big Stan told me she looked dead as they wheeled her out.'

'Any more fucking joyful news?' Queenie mumbled under her breath. Lil was in her nineties now, lived in the house between hers and Viv's, and both had been dreading the old girl croaking it because they didn't want new neighbours. Talk about it never rains but it pours.

Vinny Butler took off his tie and suit jacket and stared at his reflection in the mirror. With his six-foot-two frame, piercing green eyes and jet-black hair, Vinny had always been a striking-looking man. But since Molly had been so cruelly taken from him, he'd lost weight, and felt far older than his thirty-five years.

Vinny sat on his bed, put his head in his hands and wept. Apart from during the actual service, he had kept his emotions pent up all day. Molly's send-off – unusually for anything involving his family – had gone without a hitch. The wake had been held at Nick's, the restaurant that Vinny part-owned in Stratford. Even with all the tables and chairs removed, there hadn't been enough room to accommodate the mourners. The club would have been a far more appropriate venue had circumstances been different and Molly had not been snatched from there.

No parent expected to outlive their kids, especially when they were as young as Molly had been. Her death would haunt Vinny forever. With her curly blonde hair, big green eyes and infectious personality, Molly had been the light of Vinny's life. He'd loved that child more than he had ever loved anybody. On the day he'd found out she was dead, part of him had died with her.

'You OK, Dad? I've just been crying as well. I will always blame and hate myself for what happened. I know I never played with her much, but I did love her and I really do miss her,' Little Vinny lied.

Vinny patted the bed and when his son sat next to him, he put an arm around his shoulders. With his dark hair, bright green eyes and tall build, Little Vinny was most certainly a chip off the old block. 'No point keep beating yourself up, boy. Not gonna bring Molly back, is it? I was proud of you today when you stood up and read that poem. Not an easy thing to do in a packed church.'

'So, you don't blame me no more then?'

On the day Molly went missing there had been a flood in the club cellar. Vinny had left his son in charge of Molly while he went downstairs to sort it out, but the boy had fallen asleep. The main door of the club had accidentally been left open and it still wasn't known if Molly had wandered outside or her killer had entered the club to abduct her.

'No. I don't blame you. There's only one person to blame and that's Jamie cunting Preston. He'll pay for what he did one day. As soon as he's released, I'll be there waiting for him. An eye for an eye, son. Always remember that.'

'I'll help you kill him, Dad. I'll be old enough then.' Little Vinny shook his head. 'I still can't believe it. I mean, Jamie is your half-brother. I suppose that makes him my uncle, doesn't it?'

Vinny's relationship with his father Albie had always been strained, and there would certainly never be any bridges built now. Jamie Preston was the result of an affair his father had indulged in many moons ago, and none of his family had even known the evil little shit existed until he had been arrested for Molly's murder. To say Vinny had been shocked was an understatement. He'd thought an old enemy of his was the culprit, and had beaten Bobby Jackson so badly that he was still in hospital, unable to communicate with anybody. 'Let's go downstairs and get a drink, eh, boy?'

'Can I have a cider, Dad?'

'Yeah. Course you can.'

Little Vinny could not help but smirk as he followed his father down the stairs. Life was so much better now his dad's bird Joanna and Molly were no longer around. It was like it used to be when he was younger. Just him and his old man.

Molly's mother, Joanna Preston, was back at her parents' place in Tiptree. She'd left the moment the funeral was over, unable to face the prospect of the wake, not with the Butlers lording it as if they were royalty, surrounded by all their gangster pals. Her only friend in that family was Michael's wife, Nancy, who'd accompanied her home. Michael was nowhere as bad as his brother, but even so Nancy had had a lot to put up with and the two women had supported one another when the Butlers closed ranks. Both of them had been livid when Little Vinny had been allowed to stand up in church and read that poem, and even more angry when he had failed to mention them.

'Thanks for seeing me home, Nance. I couldn't have got through today if it wasn't for you. Seeing Vinny again made me physically sick. I can't believe I was ever in love with the bastard. I bet he told that horror of a son of his not to mention us in that poem. I know the way his evil mind works. And did you see his face when I asked him for Molly's doll? The way he was smirking when he said I couldn't have it because he'd put it in her coffin. I don't believe him. He didn't even have the guts to identify his own daughter's body, so why would he have gone anywhere near her coffin? I bet he has the doll indoors. The police told me they gave it back to him last week.'

'Vinny's hateful, Jo. He always has been.' Nancy wrapped an arm round her friend's shoulders and gave her a hug. 'I don't mean this to sound horrible, but I reckon your dad was right: Vinny targeted you purposely because he knew you were Johnny Preston's kid. I mean, if he loved you even a tiny bit he would never have treated you the way he has since Molly died. He has been a total and utter pig. If you ask me, you're well rid of him.' Seeing that Joanna was about to start crying again, she added softly: 'I'll have a word with Michael about the doll. He might be able to find out where it is.'

The doll in question had been Molly's pride and joy. Vinny had bought it for his daughter and named it after her. The little girl had taken Molly Dolly everywhere with her, wouldn't go to sleep unless the doll was tucked in beside her of a night. The bedraggled, rain-soaked doll had been found a quarter of a mile away from where Molly's tiny body was located. The police reckoned Molly had dropped it as her killer led her to her death.

'How you getting on with Michael now?' Joanna asked, making an effort to take her mind off Molly and the funeral.

'He's been fine since I moved back in. Been very attentive towards me and the boys and we've had some nice family days out. We even went to the zoo last week. Sorry. I'm being thoughtless now, aren't I?'

Joanna squeezed Nancy's hand. 'Don't be daft! Even though Molly isn't here any more, I still want to hear about those boys of yours. Actually, I've got some news for you, some good news for once, but you must swear that, if I tell you, you won't breathe a word to a living soul. My mum and dad didn't want me to tell you – I think that's why my dad was a bit offish with you earlier. He thinks that if I tell you, you'll tell Michael.'

'As if! Spit it out, I'm dying to know. Have you met a new man?'

Joanna shook her head. 'That day I saw Molly in the mortuary was officially the worst day of my life. I thought today was going to be even worse, until this morning.' She gave a teary smile, swiping away the tears that were running down her cheeks. 'Talk about every cloud has a silver lining, Nance.'

'What you going on about, Jo? You've lost me.'

'I'm having another baby.'

Rather than choke, Nancy spat her mouthful of wine back into her glass.

Feeling ever so weary, Queenie Butler put on her nightdress and slippers and went back downstairs. It had taken her ages to settle Tara and Tommy down, but both were now thankfully asleep.

'They OK, Queen?' Vivian asked.

Queenie nodded. 'Took 'em a while to get off to sleep after I told them about the kids who got stabbed outside Bethnal Green station after asking the wrong geezer to give 'em a penny for the Guy. I think I might've frightened 'em.'

'What you on about? I don't remember any kids getting stabbed outside Bethnal Green station.'

'Neither do I.' Queenie managed a wicked grin. 'But I had to come up with something that'd put them off begging, didn't I?' She sank into her chair with a sigh. 'You wait until Brenda rears her drunken head tomorrow. You should have seen the state of her. Had her tongue stuck down that bloke's throat in front of everybody in the pub, and he was a lot older than her. Talk about embarrass the family. Vinny and Michael won't be too pleased when they find out. Bound to hear about it, even if I don't tell 'em.'

Vivian tutted disapprovingly. 'Who was he?'

'No bloody idea. Knowing Bren, she probably picked him up at the wake. Acting like a whore, she was. I tell ya, Viv, I'm disgusted with her. She's her father's daughter all right. As for them poor little mites upstairs, I hate to think what's gonna become of them with her as a mother.'

Vivian pursed her lips. 'Tara and Tommy will turn out

OK. It's Little Vinny you should be worried about. His poem and crocodile tears did not fool me one little bit. Molly would still be alive if it wasn't for him. A clone of his father if I ever did see one.'

After being totally lost for words, Nancy Butler had now composed herself and was trying to think of a polite way to burst her friend's bubble.

'You don't seem very happy for me, Nance. I thought you of all people would be thrilled. I can't believe my mum and dad advised me to have an abortion after everything I've been through. As much as I love my parents, I need to get my own place. I feel smothered, living with them.'

Nancy leaned across the table and held Joanna's hand. 'Please don't take this the wrong way, Jo, but your mum and dad do have a point. If you keep the baby, Vinny is bound to find out at some stage. I can fully understand why you are so desperate for another child. I would feel exactly the same. But do you really want or need the aggravation of looking over your shoulder to protect that child for the rest of your life?'

Joanna snatched her hand away and glared at Nancy. 'So, what exactly are you trying to say? That I should get rid of it?'

'I don't know what I'm trying to say, Jo. All I know is, if you keep the baby, Vinny is bound to find out about it.'

'No, he won't! Apart from you, my parents and my brother, nobody will ever know where I live or that the baby even exists. Unless you tell Michael.'

'Oh, Jo, I would never betray your trust, you know that. I love you like a sister. I'm just worried you'll never be rid of Vinny, that's all. I am happy for you, honest I am.'

'I should hope so too! No child will ever replace Molly, Nance, she was a one-off. But at least I have something to look forward to now, a future. As for Vinny, my dad reckons he'll be put in prison for a very long time after what he did to Bobby Jackson. Dad said the police have been desperate to lock Vinny up for years and they won't be lenient with him.'

Nancy forced a smile and tried to pretend she was happy for her friend, but inside she was worried sick. The police could lock Vinny up and throw away the key, but it still wouldn't stop him claiming Joanna's baby. But after everything the poor girl had gone through, how could she destroy her hopes of happiness by telling her that?

Back in Whitechapel, Vinny and Michael Butler were having a heart-to-heart about the future of their business. As a mark of respect, the club had not reopened since Molly's death over a month ago, but Michael expected that to change after the funeral. However, Vinny had different ideas and had just dropped the bombshell that he wanted to sell up as soon as possible.

Michael knocked back his Scotch. He had to be diplomatic due to the circumstances, but wasn't about to be walked all over. After all, he was joint owner of the club. 'Look, Vin, I can fully understand why you don't want to open up again, but I need the dosh. You've got other income from whatever you get up to with Ahmed, but I bloody well ain't. I've got the boys to think of and Nancy.'

Vinny sneered. 'Playing happy families with Nancy again, are you? When you gonna clock on that she's a psycho, drags you down and you'd be far better off without her?'

'Probably the same time you clock on Ahmed's a wrong 'un. Look, bruv, I don't want a war of words with you, but now is not the right time for us to sell the club.'

'Yes, it is. We could start afresh, invest our money in a new venture. Bill Evans opened one of them posh wine bars up town last year. Raking it in, he is. I saw him the other week in a brand spanking new Rolls-Royce. It's had it round here now, Michael, and we aren't ever going to get all the custom back we've lost. I watched the news last night: unemployment at an all-time high. We need to go where the money is.'

'Have you forgotten that you're looking at a long stretch inside?' Michael asked. Vinny had been charged with GBH with intent for the attack on Bobby Jackson and had been told by his brief to expect a lengthy custodial sentence.

''Course I haven't forgot. That's why I want to set the ball rolling now. We can be long up and running before my trial starts, then you can be earning fortunes for us while I'm away. No way I'm ever gonna work here again, Michael. I'm sure the place is fucking cursed. First the fire, then the shooting and now Molly. Whitechapel's finished for us. There's nothing here for us any more.'

As Vinny topped their glasses up, Michael mulled over his brother's words. Vinny did have a point, but selling up was still a big ask. 'I'm going to open up again this weekend. You don't have to be here. Let's see if we've lost any more custom and we'll go from there.'

'Have you not listened to a word I've said, bruv? I told you I wanna get rid. Never forget if it wasn't for my business brain you would currently be earning a oner a week fixing poxy cars. I set this place up with Roy's help, not yours. So what I say fucking goes, understand?'

The sound of the buzzer stopped it turning into a full-scale argument. Vinny stood up, strolled towards the entrance and gave his brother one last warning as he did so: 'If you refuse to sell, best you have the readies to buy me out, Michael. I'm sure Ahmed would jump at the chance of becoming my new business partner if you're too dense to think ahead.'

Fully expecting to see his mum, his son or Ahmed, Vinny's smug expression was soon wiped off his face when he saw six Old Bill on the doorstep. 'What do you mob want?'

DI Smithers stared Vinny in the eyes. 'Vinny Butler, you are being arrested on suspicion of murdering Bobby Kenneth Jackson. You are not obliged to say anything unless you wish to do so, but whatever you do say will be taken down in writing and may be given in evidence . . .'

'Bruv, ring my brief,' Vinny yelled. 'I have just buried my daughter, you unfeeling bunch of cunts,' he spat, smashing his fist against the wall.

Hearing the commotion, Michael ran to his brother's side. 'What the hell's going on? Vin ain't done nothing wrong. We've been at Molly's funeral, and only just got back from the wake.'

While Vinny struggled and cursed as he was handcuffed then slung in the back of the meat wagon, DS Townsend took Michael to one side. 'Unfortunately for your brother, Bobby Jackson passed away earlier this evening.'

Michael sank to his haunches in shock. This change of circumstance was bound to mean that his brother would have to await his trial in prison.

'I am sorry for your family that this happened today of all days. I can only imagine how tough Molly's funeral must have been for you all,' Townsend said. Vinny aside, the DS felt no hatred towards the Butler clan. During the investigation into Molly's death he'd got to know the family a bit better, and Michael in particular struck him as a decent bloke.

When Townsend walked away, Michael went back inside the club. He rang Vinny's brief, left a message on his answerphone, then poured himself another large Scotch. No way did he want to see his brother behind bars, but at least now Vinny was in no position to force the sale of the business. He was going to be the one calling the shots for a change.

Growing up as Vinny and Roy's younger brother had not been easy for Michael Butler, but with Vinny liable to be banged up for the foreseeable and poor Roy brown bread, this truly was his time to prove all the doubters wrong, Vinny included. And prove them wrong he most certainly would.

CHAPTER THREE

Little Vinny sat up and put his head in his hands. He had an awful hangover and an uneasy feeling in the pit of his stomach. His best pal Ben Bloggs should have been at his side today, but he'd not been coping as well as he had since Molly's death, spending all his time holed up in his bedroom. Every time Little Vinny had tried to persuade Ben to go out somewhere he'd made excuses, saying he didn't feel well, and he'd rather stay in that squalid pit he called home. But when Little Vinny called at the Bloggs' place this morning so they could go to the funeral together, Ben's junkie mother told him he'd gone out last night and hadn't come back. Now Vinny was worried. He'd thought he could handle Ben, slip him a few quid, keep him in glue and cider, make sure he understood that if he went to the police and told them he'd looked on while Little Vinny strangled his baby sister to death, they would both be in big trouble. After all, Ben was the one who'd taken her from the club, even if he only did it because Little Vinny told him they were going to make her disappear for a few hours to teach his dad a lesson. Surely Ben wouldn't have the guts to grass him up . . . would he?

'Vin, we need to talk,' Michael said, barging into the bedroom.

'Whatsa matter?' Little Vinny asked, alarmed. He could tell by his uncle's face that something was terribly wrong, and his first thought was that Ben must have blabbed. If he had, then Little Vinny would have no option but to turn the tables and tell the Old Bill that Ben was the one who'd abducted and killed Molly. If need be, he'd tell them his pal had always shown an unhealthy interest in his little sister.

Little Vinny cleverly managed to hide the surge of relief he felt when his uncle explained the situation. 'When will me dad be allowed home?'

'I'm not sure. Your dad only got bail in the first place because Jackson was still alive. Now he's dead, it might change things.'

Face etched with fury, Little Vinny leapt up and kicked the door. The whole point of getting rid of Jo and Molly had been so he could have his dad all to himself again, and now he'd been taken away. 'If my dad gets banged up, who am I gonna live with? Can I live with you? I promise I'll be good.'

Having just got things back on track with Nancy, Michael knew there was no way he could let Little Vinny move in with them. His wife had made it perfectly clear that she was no fan of the wayward teenager; she even blamed him for what had happened to Molly. 'I'm not sure there's room at mine for you with the boys, Vin. But, let's not jump the gun, eh? Your dad has a good brief and might even get bail yet for all we know. Now I want you to do me a favour. Get yourself washed and dressed so we can go and tell your nan and Auntie Viv the news. Then, later, I want you to help me get the club ready to reopen. If your dad don't get bail, I am really gonna need you to be my right-hand man. Do you think you can step up to the mark?'

'Will I get paid more money?'

'Yeah, but only if you work really hard.'

Little Vinny managed a grin. 'You got yourself a deal, Uncle Michael.'

Having had an awful night's sleep, Vivian got up before the larks and took a stroll down to the newsagent. It wasn't even daylight yet, but Viv knew the papers would be left outside the Patels' shop.

About to pass Fat Beryl's house, Vivian froze as she heard the words, 'Please don't. I really don't want to. I'm not that type of girl. You're hurting me. Stop it.'

'You've let me buy you drinks all night and you've been shoving them big titties of yours in my face. I know you want it,' a male voice hissed, trying to force his rock-hard todger down the back of her throat. The more they knocked him back, the more it turned him on.

Whitechapel had changed over the years. Many residents were afraid to walk the streets at certain times, but not Vivian. Nobody messed with her family, which was why she marched fearlessly down the alleyway.

'Get off her, you dirty bastard,' she bellowed, smashing her handbag over the back of the man's head.

The man leapt up. Had it been light, he would have recognized Vivian, but unfortunately for him it was dark. 'Jealous are ya? Want some an' all?' he taunted, waving his hard-on in his hand.

Trying to whack his cock with her handbag, Vivian screamed, 'I'll have you shot, you dirty cunt.' Realizing the woman was scary and old, the man expertly tucked his penis inside his trousers and bolted.

'Heard of the Butlers, have ya? You disgusting nonce. I'm Vinny and Michael's aunt. Watch your back. Your days are numbered,' Vivian shouted, but to no avail. The man was already out of earshot.

The poor girl was trembling, so Vivian crouched next to her and switched on her emergency handbag torch. She hadn't got a good look at the man's face, but could guess what the dirty bastard had been doing. She was actually shaken up herself. That was the first dingle-dangle she'd had waved at her in donkey's years.

'I can't go home. My dad will kill me,' the girl sobbed.

'You're Billy Higgins's granddaughter, aren't you, pet?' Vivian asked. She'd once courted Billy in her younger years and had often kicked herself for ending the relationship. Billy was still handsome, with a full head of hair. He was also a very wealthy, well-respected villain. A far better man than the arsehole she'd ended up marrying.

'Yes, I'm Janey. You can't tell my granddad though.'

'Why don't you come home with me, Janey? I'll make you a nice sweet cup of tea and we'll call the police. This man needs to be caught.'

'No! My parents will kill me. I lied to them, you see. I told them I was going out with a friend. My dad says I'm too young to have boyfriends.'

'OK. No police. But please come home with me. You can tell me what happened there, then we'll work out what to do next. You can't stay here, lovey. I know your granddad very well. A lovely man. I'd never forgive myself if I left you here all alone.'

'OK.'

Nosy Hilda could barely contain her excitement as she knocked at Queenie's front door.

'What the hell do you want this early in the morning? Oh, don't tell me, I think I can guess. Has Lil died?' Queenie asked in the most sarcastic tone she could muster.

'No. I saw her niece as she was going to work and it

looks like Lil might pull through,' said Hilda, oblivious to the sarcasm. 'I just wanted to say how sorry I was about your Vinny. Must have been a terrible shock for you that Bobby died. I mean, who'd have thought he'd croak it, after all this time.'

'Vinny! Bobby! What do you mean?' Queenie asked, the colour draining from her face as the realization started to kick in.

'Bobby Jackson. He died yesterday. They arrested your Vinny for murder last night and carted him off in a police wagon. Didn't you know?'

'No, I bastard well didn't,' Queenie hissed, slamming the door in Hilda's face.

It was in Hilda's nature to have the last word. 'Sorry to be the bearer of bad news,' she trilled through the letterbox. 'I'll be off now then.'

As soon as Janey said her attacker's name was Pat and described what had actually happened, Vivian knew who the culprit was. One Eyed Harry had told her only last week that he'd been released.

Tall, dark and handsome, Pat Campbell was the local sex-pest, playing on his looks to entice young girls to go out with him. He had a foul reputation for not taking no for an answer. He'd been getting away with it for years before one of his victims finally went to the police, and even then all he got was a slap on the wrist, a measly eighteen-month stretch.

'Thank you so much for your kindness, Vivian. I don't know what I'd have done otherwise. And thanks for allowing me to use your phone to ring my friend and my mum.'

Urging the seventeen-year-old to sit next to her on the sofa, Vivian squeezed Janey's hands. The girl had been adamant about not involving the police, and Vivian had reluctantly gone along with it, not wanting to see the poor kid forced to relive the whole thing in court and probably end up being branded a slag for having gone out on a date with the bugger in the first place.

'Are you sure that he never actually did you-know-what to you?' asked Viv when she'd finished helping the girl clean herself up.

'I'm positive,' said Janey, pulling on the fresh pair of tights Viv had given her. 'I've told you everything, honest. It was disgusting when he tried to put his thingy in my mouth. You won't call the police after I leave, will you? I'm afraid they'll say I led him on, that I've only myself to blame.'

'I've given you my word, sweetheart. Old Bill are useless anyway. They should have banged him up for a lot longer than eighteen months, filthy bastard. They call him Pervy Pat round 'ere – one young lady he attacked said he got so excited his dingle-dangle felt like a gun rubbing against her.' Seeing Janey shudder at the image, she quickly changed tack: 'What goes around comes around, luv. I can assure you that you did sod-all wrong and that dirty bastard will get his comeuppance. I'll make sure of it – that's another promise.'

Ahmed Zane popped the cork and grinned like a Cheshire cat as he did so. He'd been totally gobsmacked when he had rung the club earlier and spoken to Michael. His initial shock had soon turned to elation though. This was karma at its very best.

'Do not keep me in suspense any longer, Ahmed. Tell me, what has happened?' Burak demanded.

Ahmed handed his cousin a glass of champagne and held his own aloft. 'To Vinny Butler, who has now been arrested on a murder charge.'

'What!' Burak exclaimed.

Laughing like a hyena, Ahmed chinked glasses with his cousin. 'Bobby Jackson died yesterday. It couldn't have happened at a better time either, what with Carl on the loose, eh?'

Burak agreed. Carl Thompson had been the guy Ahmed had hired to help set Vinny up, but that plan had gone pear-shaped. Carl knew too much and needed to be found and silenced.

Ahmed topped up his and Burak's drinks. 'Can you imagine how difficult it will be for Vinny to cope in prison? I think he will go insane, especially so soon after Molly's death. I must ask for a visiting order so I can experience his misery in the flesh.'

Burak smirked. 'Wouldn't it be funny if Butler ended up in Broadmoor?'

Ahmed laughed. 'Now that would be hilarious.'

Mary Walker knew her daughter well enough to know she had something on her mind. 'Why did you go back to Tiptree after Molly's funeral? Not been rowing with Michael again, have you?' Mary pried.

Nancy sighed. She had promised Joanna that she would not tell a soul about her pregnancy, but she was so worried about her friend, she had to tell somebody. 'Boys, go and play in the garden for five minutes,' Nancy ordered.

Adam and Lee immediately stood up, but Daniel didn't. He stared at his mother and in an insolent tone said, 'No. I'm watching *Rainbow*.'

'I beg your pardon! Do as your mum says now,' Mary insisted.

Daniel glared defiantly at this grandma. 'No. It's cold outside.'

Fuming at the way her eight-year-old son had been

behaving of late, Nancy yanked him up by the arm and dragged him into the hallway. 'Now put your coat on and get in that garden.'

Knowing when she spoke through gritted teeth his mother was at her angriest, Daniel grinned, 'Make me.'

With his jet-black hair and bright green eyes, Daniel had certainly inherited his looks from his father's side of the family. So had Adam. In fact only Lee looked anything like Nancy, yet he was Michael's son from another relationship.

'I am sick and tired of your cheekiness and I will not put up with it any more,' Nancy said, punctuating her words while slapping her son repeatedly across his backside and legs.

Realizing he had pushed his mother too far, Daniel mumbled 'Mad bitch' before scarpering into the back garden.

'I told you that me and your dad had noticed a change in Daniel's behaviour, didn't I? Good job your father isn't here. I'm not going to tell him or your brother this latest episode,' Mary said.

Nancy was trembling with a mixture of rage and fear. At times like this her son reminded her so much of Little Vinny, it truly scared her. 'I'll kill him, Mum, if he carries on like that. You'd think the telling off I gave him after he beat up that boy at school would have taught him a lesson, but he's becoming more of a handful every day. Adam's fine and so is Lee, so why does Daniel feel the need to play me up? I am going to tell Michael to reprimand him when I get home. Perhaps being forced to go to bed early, or not being able to watch TV for a week might teach the little sod some manners.'

'Was that what you wanted to speak to me about – Daniel?'

'No. It's Jo. Mum, if I tell you something, you must swear to me you will never repeat what I say to another living soul.'

'Of course not! I'm your mother. If you can't trust me, who can you trust?'

'Jo's pregnant again and she says she's keeping the baby. Her parents have tried to talk her out of it and so have I, but she won't listen. That bastard Vinny is bound to find out somewhere along the line, then it will all end in tears for poor Jo. I just know it will.'

Queenie Butler was thoroughly annoyed. Not only had Michael not had the decency to inform her the previous evening of Bobby Jackson's death and Vinny's arrest, he now had the cheek to tell her that, if the worst happened, it was her duty to look after Little Vinny!

'My duty! Why is it my duty exactly, Michael?'

'Because you're his gran. Who else can he live with if Vinny don't get bail? Nancy hates him, so he can't stop with me. I guarantee he'll behave himself. I'm gonna keep a proper close eye on him from now on, and he'll be working with me full-time at the club. He's a good—'

'I'll stop you right there, Michael, before you waste any more breath. I got lumbered with Little Vinny once before, remember? And look how that turned out. He ruined my bleedin' conservatory, robbed the Patels' shop and constantly ran rings around me. Never again, boy. I'll be fifty-four next month and I really don't need the stress, thank you very much.'

Shocked by his mother's coldness, Michael tried one more time to make her change her mind. 'Mum, this is Vinny's son, your first-born grandkid we're talking about, not some stranger. Where the hell will he live if Vinny gets banged up, eh? Do you want him living round the Bloggses' house?'

'I couldn't give a shit where he lives, and even if he was Prince Charles's son, I wouldn't change my mind. No way is that little bastard ever living with me again, Michael, and that's final!'

Little Vinny knocked on the Bloggses' front door. 'Any news yet?' he asked Ben's dishevelled-looking whore of a mother.

Alison Bloggs shook her head and then burst into tears. 'I don't reckon he's coming back. He nicked my money and puff, and he's never stolen off me before. I'm clucking. I've got no readies to score with, and I can't go out to work of a night 'cause Ben's not here to look after the little 'uns. I'm gonna go to the police to report him missing. Will you keep an eye on the kids for me for half an hour?'

Immediately alarmed at the mention of the police, Little Vinny took some money out of his pocket and handed it to Alison. 'Don't bother going to the Old Bill yet. They ain't bothered about lads like Ben, and I'm gonna search for him again later. If anyone can find him, it'll be me.'

'What's the money for?'

'So you can score and straighten yourself out.' Vinny handed Alison another tenner. 'Get a couple of bottles of cider as well, eh? I'll keep you company for a bit. Between us we can make a list of where Ben might be. The filth are mugs, they won't find him.'

Staring at the money in her hand all Alison could think about was her next hit. She kissed Little Vinny on the cheek. 'You're a good boy, you are. I'll be back in twenty minutes.'

Little Vinny breathed a sigh of relief. He had to find Ben before the police did, that was for sure. His pal was obviously not in a sound state of mind and the chances were if the Old Bill got to him first, Ben would be capable of blurting out anything.

No way was Little Vinny going down for Molly's murder,

and if that meant spending a couple of hours with Ben's horrid mother to ensure she was too out of her nut to call in the Old Bill, then so be it.

Nancy Butler looked at her husband in annoyance. She had just spent the past ten minutes telling him how worried she was about Daniel's behaviour, and although Michael had promised to have a chat with their son, he seemed far more concerned about his other family – as per usual.

'I don't want you to just have a chat with Daniel, Michael. I want you to punish him and set some boundaries for the future. He is going to go off the rails if you don't sort him out, and I will not have him ending up like Little Vinny. Daniel reminded me so much of him when he was insolent earlier, it really did frighten me.'

Michael sighed. Like most women, Nancy could make a crisis out of the smallest of dramas. 'Look, I've said I'll talk to Daniel, OK? Give me a break, Nance, for Christ's sake. I've just told you that Vinny's been re-arrested and is up on a murder charge, and all you can do is moan about Dan wanting to watch *Rainbow* rather than play in the fucking garden. As if I haven't got enough on my plate right now, what with trying to sort out somewhere for Little Vinny to live and getting the club reopened this weekend. Money is running low and we can't live on shirt buttons.'

'Little Vinny is not living here, so don't even bother asking me that one. As for you reopening the club, if Vinny ends up in prison, does that mean you will be working all hours? I barely see you as it is and the boys need their father around more now they're getting older.'

'Nance, I have not even been in twenty minutes and you have done my swede in already. Nag, nag, nag. You should record yourself and listen to it sometime. You might teach yourself a thing or two.'

When Nancy started to cry, scream and shout, Michael stormed out of the house.

Back in Whitechapel, Queenie and Viv were discussing Pervy Pat. Both were in agreement that he needed to be dealt with.

'There you go. Drink it in one,' Queenie ordered, handing her ashen-faced sister a brandy. 'I wish I knew where that dirty bastard lived now. I'd go straight round there with me meat knife and chop that diseased todger of his off. Bad enough he assaulted that poor girl, but fancy offering you a portion of helmet pie an' all. He'll rue the day he ever uttered those words, we'll make sure of that. Vinny'll sort it if he gets bail and if he don't, Michael can do the honours. Did you actually see his, you know?'

'It was dark down that alley, but I did sort of see it. Big and slippery like a fucking snake. I feel sick even thinking about it. I don't wanna talk about it no more today. I need time to get over the shock. Tell me about Bren.'

Brenda had only just turned up to pick up her children and Queenie had given her daughter a right earful.

'I can't believe she reckons this geezer is the one, Viv. Got to be something mentally wrong with her. She only met him yesterday.'

'She's always been one to dive in head first, hasn't she? I wonder if he's a looker?'

Queenie shook her head in despair. 'He's in his forties if he's a day, Viv. I saw him. Looked a proper pisshead, he did – reminded me of Albie. Why the silly cow would want to take up with someone like her useless father, I do not know. I'll have to get Michael to find out who he is and have a quiet word in his ear. The silly little mare was even talking about moving in with him. Reckons he's got a big house. Probably a poxy old bedsit somewhere by the looks of him. I swear, pound signs is all my Brenda sees these days.'

'Did he look bedraggled?'

'No. He was suited and booted, but I know a plastic gangster when I see one,' Queenie replied, snatching at the phone on the very first ring. 'OK, Michael. Yep, I'll be there, don't you worry. All right, pick me up at nine. What did the brief say about his chances of getting bail again?'

Vivian hated one-way conversations. 'Well?' she asked impatiently, the second her sister ended the call.

'Vinny's been charged with Bobby's murder. He'll be appearing at Bow Street Magistrates' Court in the morning. His brief reckons his chances of getting bail again are practically non-existent.'

Margo and Anthony Warwick had two major passions in life. One was mountain climbing, the other rambling, and today they were thoroughly enjoying their first-ever trip to Hainault Forest.

Decked out in hiking boots and carrying a big stick, Anthony crouched down to examine something that had caught his eye. 'Look, Margo, it's a vole. Such tiny creatures, but so adorable, aren't they? Look at its little heart, beating fast. It's scared.'

Margo was about to bend down for a closer look when something in the trees caught her eye. Her heart started beating faster than the vole's. Unable to stop herself, Margo let out a deafening scream.

It was then Anthony looked up to see the dead boy hanging from a tree.

Little Vinny was out of his nut. Alcohol, puff and glue were all he usually indulged in, but Ben's mum had just encouraged him to have a go at what she called 'Chasing the dragon'.

Because he was only smoking something brown on a bit of foil, Little Vinny had not expected it to knock him for six like it had, but he felt wonderful, as if he was floating on air.

'Don't bother searching for Ben now, Vin. It's dark. Stay here with me for a bit. I've enjoyed your company today. You can search for Ben again in the morning,' Alison said, putting a hand on Little Vinny's thigh.

Little Vinny nodded. He usually despised Alison, but that stuff he had smoked had made him feel so happy, he now thought she was OK.

'Can I ask you a personal question, Vin?'

Unable to speak properly, Little Vinny nodded.

'You ever had a blow-job?'

Little Vinny shook his head, then grinned when Alison put her hand inside his tracksuit bottoms. When she bent her head and put his erect penis in her mouth, Little Vinny shut his eyes. The heroin, combined with having his cock sucked for the very first time, felt like he had literally died and gone to heaven.

CHAPTER FOUR

Michael Butler was awoken in his marital bed by his wife kissing him gently on the lips. 'It's half six, Michael, and you said you wanted to be up at the crack of dawn. I'm going downstairs to make you a decent breakfast. You're going to need it with the day you've got ahead. And if you want me to come to court with you, the offer's still there. My mum can take the boys to school.'

'Nah, you're all right, babe. I've got to find Little Vinny, then pick my mum up by nine. I appreciate you offering though. Means a lot.'

Nancy smiled. After their argument yesterday, she had been ready to pack some stuff and take the boys back to her parents' house once again. But a good talking to from her mum had made her change her mind.

'Nance, you know you're always welcome here, but you can't keep uprooting them boys every time you and Michael have a cross word. All couples argue. That's life, and what you've just told me isn't even that bad. As much as we all dislike Vinny, Michael must have a lot on his mind if his brother is facing prison. He's got that club to run and all sorts. You should be supporting your husband, not rowing with him. Please don't think I'm having a dig at you, love, but I do think you need to grow up a bit for the sake of your sons. That's probably why Daniel has been playing up so much, truth be known. Poor little sod needs stability, not you moving out every other month. If you're that unhappy with Michael, then get a bloody divorce. You can't keep changing your mind every five minutes. Either make a go of your marriage, or make a clean break.'

Some home truths were exactly what Nancy had needed to hear, and after a few tears, she'd immediately rung Michael at the club to apologize and beg him to come home. Michael had accepted her apology, but had told Nancy he would have to stay at the club as there was nobody else to look after his nephew. However, when Little Vinny had failed to show his face by ten, Michael had surprised her by coming home. They'd then made love.

'Your breakfast is ready, Michael. Boys, time to get up now,' Nancy shouted up the stairs.

Michael walked into the kitchen accompanied by their eldest son. 'Go on then. What you got to say to your mum?'

Daniel stared at his feet. 'I'm sorry I was rude to you yesterday. I promise I'll be good from now on. I will also ring Nanny Mary and say sorry to her.'

Nancy smiled as she bent down and hugged Daniel to her chest. Her mum was right. The boys needed a settled environment and they needed their father.

Vinny Butler sat down opposite his brief. Being locked up was making him feel insane. Molly was on his mind constantly. When he was awake, all he could think about was how scared she must have been and how he had let her down. And when he was asleep, she was still alive in his mind and he could see her pretty face as if she was right there beside him. He could even hear her talking to him. When he woke up and remembered that his daughter was dead, it was mental torture at its very worst.

'Colin, you have to get me bail. I know I'm gonna do bird over Jackson, but I can't do it right now. It's too soon after Molly. I need to get my nut straight and prepare myself. I'll go off my head if they put me in prison while I'm not strong enough to cope.'

Colin Harvey sighed. He was the most sought-after brief among the London gangland fraternity, which was why Vinny had requested his services. 'Vinny, I will do my very best for you. But I cannot make you any promises. The police opposed your original bail, and they have even more of an argument now Jackson is dead. There is one thing I can assure you though: if the decision does not go in our favour today, I will take your appeal to the Old Bailey. With everything you have been through, nothing is impossible.'

Vinny put his head in his hands. He wasn't stupid, and knew by the way his brief had tried to dress his words up that he was doomed.

Little Vinny rested his chin on the edge of the lavatory seat. He hadn't stopped spewing since he'd arrived back at the club in the early hours of this morning, and he had no idea whether it was the heroin he'd smoked that was making him so ill or the thought of that disgusting toothless whore sucking his penis.

'Vin, you upstairs, boy?' Michael shouted.

'Yeah. I'm ill. I think I've got a bug.'

Michael ran up the stairs, took one look at the state of his nephew hugging the toilet and jumped to his own conclusion. He could smell the alcohol fumes and Little Vinny's eyes looked glazed. 'You been puffing and drinking, boy?'

'Yeah. I'm sorry. It won't happen again,' Little Vinny promised. Anything was better than admitting he had chased the dragon with Alison Bloggs, then allowed her to suck his John Thomas and spunked in her mouth.

'Where did you go? I waited here until ten for you. Was you with Ben?'

Little Vinny's eyes filled with tears. 'No. I was on my own. Ben's still missing, Dad's going to prison. Nobody wants me to live with them, and I still keep thinking about Molly. It's all my fault she's dead.'

Michael rubbed his nephew's back as he retched again. His heart went out to the boy. 'You got to stop blaming yourself for your sister's death, Vin. You'll drive yourself doolally if you don't. That little cunt Jamie Preston is the one who snuffed Molly's life out, not you. Your mate Ben is bound to turn up soon. Probably wanted a break from that monster of a mother of his. As for your dad, what will be will be. But you'll never be homeless, I can promise you that. Us Butlers stick together. You know the score.'

'But who am I gonna live with?'

'I don't know yet. We'll worry about that once we know your dad's fate. He's up in court today and I know he would want you to be there. Why don't you jump in the bath while I pop round the cafe and get you something to eat? A couple of greasy egg and bacon rolls will sort that hangover of yours right out.'

'I don't think I'm well enough to go to court, and I really don't feel hungry.'

'You'll be fine, trust me. Put your smart suit on. Gonna look well bad if you don't show your face. Don't worry if you feel sick on the way, I'll tell your nan and Auntie Viv you've had a bug, OK?'

Little Vinny sighed. Why should he go to court? His family were always banging on about sticking together, yet no one wanted him. About to argue his point, Little Vinny decided against it. If his Dad was going to prison, he needed to keep on the right side of his Uncle Michael. 'OK. I'll put me suit on.'

After trying on five different outfits, Queenie Butler decided to wear her smart apple-green skirt suit. The colour suited her bleached blonde hair and bright red lipstick.

Deciding to add her big gold cross for luck so she could hold it and silently pray while waiting for the verdict, Queenie studied herself in the full-length mirror. 'Not bad for nearly fifty-four, if I say so meself,' she mumbled.

Having recovered from her shock at seeing a rock-hard todger the previous day, Vivian put her key in the lock.

'Cooey, Queen. I'm ready. Shall I make us a cuppa or would you prefer a sherry to settle your nerves?' she shouted out. She was only going to the court hearing to support her sister. As far as she was concerned, Vinny could rot in prison after what he'd put her through.

Queenie picked up her handbag and marched down the stairs. 'I'll have a cuppa, but put a large brandy in it. How you feeling today?'

'Fine. I saw Lil's niece when I went round for my paper this morning. She reckons Lil might be home next week and said she's gonna move in to care for her full-time. Nice of her, ain't it? And it saves us the worry of being lumbered with new neighbours.'

Queenie pursed her lips. She didn't much care for Lil's niece. 'Well, she's no bloody beauty queen, is she? Her arse looks like the back of a bus and as for the face . . . Never gonna get a husband that one, so she might as well move in and look after her poor aunt. At least it will give her a purpose in life.'

'Aw, Queen, you are awful,' Vivian chuckled.

'Well, no point beating about the bush, is there? Best to say it as it is, that's my motto. 'Ere, that's Michael just pulled up outside. I'll drink me cuppa, then we'll make a move.'

Ahmed and Burak were standing outside Bow Street Magistrates' Court smoking.

'Did you tell Michael that we would be here today?' Burak asked.

'No. I thought it would be a nice surprise for him and his witch of a mother.'

Burak chuckled. 'Mumma's broomstick has just arrived by the looks of it.'

After a terrible journey, with Michael having to stop three times because her grandson felt sick, Queenie Butler was not amused to spot Ahmed. 'What's he bastard-well doing here? I don't want him in the courtroom. It should be family only.'

'Ahmed's all right, Nan. He's dad's best mate, so he's gonna want to show his support,' Little Vinny said.

Queenie glared at her grandson. 'You keep your opinions to yourself, you. Stomach bug, my arse. Pissed last night, more like.'

'Mum, please don't kick off. We're all here for Vinny and that's all that matters,' Michael hissed.

'I'm not. I'm here for your mother's sake,' Vivian mumbled.

Ahmed nodded. 'Good day to you all. Burak and I felt it only right to show our faces. Vinny has been through so much and he needs his friends at a time like this. I just hope he is freed.'

Ignoring Ahmed, Queenie grabbed her sister's arm and marched straight into the court. She had never liked that Turk from day one and in her opinion he'd been a bad influence on her son. It might have been Vinny driving the car on the night Lenny died, but if it hadn't been for Ahmed encouraging him to take drugs in the first place, Viv's son would most probably still be alive. Queenie had always worn rose-tinted spectacles when it came to her eldest, and this new theory she'd come up with suited her. Anything was better than hating and blaming her own flesh and blood.

Nancy and Joanna had been on the phone for the past half an hour. Joanna seemed in pretty good spirits overall, and Nancy suspected this was entirely due to her pregnancy.

'So have your mum and dad said any more about the baby, Jo?'

'No. It's as though they are trying to pretend I'm not pregnant. Perhaps they are hoping I will miscarry or change my mind about an abortion.'

'I doubt your mum and dad would wish a miscarriage on you, mate. They're obviously just worried in case Vinny finds out. Have you thought about where you are going to move to yet?'

'I shouldn't have to move far at all if Vinny gets sent down today. Our child will more than likely be a teenager by the time that bastard is let out. I am never going to tell my baby who his or her father is. Imagine having to tell your own kid their father is a murderer! It's too awful for words. You haven't told anyone, have you?'

'No. Of course not,' Nancy replied. Jo would be angry with her if she admitted she had told her mother.

'Good. I'd better go now. My mum's calling out that lunch is ready. I never skip a meal now I'm eating for two again. Promise me you'll ring me as soon as you hear the verdict, Nance. I so hope the authorities lock him up and throw away the key. Vinny is scum and I cannot believe I ever fell for him or his bullshit in the first place.'

The magistrate was a woman and when she bellowed the words 'Bail application rejected,' Vinny went ballistic.

'You fucking witch! I hope you've got kids and one of them gets murdered, you old cunt,' he screamed, thrashing about and trying to smash up the court.

'Do something, Michael. He's gonna get himself into even more trouble,' Queenie cried.

Visibly upset as his father was wrestled to the ground and then handcuffed, Little Vinny bolted from the court.

Ahmed and Burak kept straight faces but were secretly elated. The police had urged the magistrate to remand Vinny in custody until his trial. Their argument was, now that Vinny had been charged with murder they had serious concerns that he could and probably would abscond, given the chance. They had even hinted that he might disappear abroad.

Overwhelmed with the urge to howl with laughter when Queenie began to batter a policeman with her handbag, Ahmed knew it was time to leave. He grabbed Burak's arm then shouted, 'Stay strong, Vinny. Keep your chin up and I will visit you very soon, my friend.'

After dropping his mum and aunt home, Michael headed straight back to the club with Little Vinny. He had a bit of a dilemma on his hands now. His nephew had to be found a place to stay where he would be safe and someone would keep an eye on him. Michael could think of only one solution: his father. But whether Albie would consider moving back to Whitechapel was another matter.

'So where am I sleeping tonight? Ahmed said he will look after me if I have nowhere else to go.'

Michael looked at his nephew in horror. Over his dead body was he letting Ahmed take care of the boy. The buzzer stopped Michael from replying. 'Go and answer the door, Vin. And unless it's Paul, Pete or family, do not let anybody in.'

Little Vinny opened the main club door and was horrified when a tearful Alison Bloggs lunged towards him.

'Get off of me, you slag. Touch me again and I'll kill you.'

'It's Ben! He's gone. My Ben has gone, Vin,' Alison screamed.

Little Vinny felt the hairs stand up on the back of his neck. 'Gone! Whaddya mean gone?'

Michael stormed into the foyer. 'I've had enough poxy drama for one day. What's with all the shouting, eh?'

Alison Bloggs let out a racking sob and sank to her knees. 'He's dead. My Ben's dead. He hanged himself from a tree in Hainault Forest. Why did he do it, Vin? Why?'

Feeling sick, light-headed, shocked and at the same time shit-scared, Little Vinny turned on his heel and ran.

Over in North London, Vinny Butler was struggling to cope with his new surroundings. After being literally dragged from the court he had been driven to Pentonville Prison – or the Ville, as it was known in the circles Vinny mixed in – and forced to undergo a strip search.

It had been the most humiliating experience of Vinny's life and, after kicking off big style during it, he'd been put on suicide watch and slung in a cell on his own, on what he could only imagine was the 'nut-nut wing'. It had to be as he seemed to be surrounded by a load of loonies who were continuously screaming and shouting.

Hearing the Glaswegian in the cell next door yelling for methadone yet again, Vinny leapt off his bunk, ran to the door and began kicking and punching it in frustration. 'I swear to you, if you don't shut the fuck up, you Scottish shitcunt, I will cut your tongue out that big mouth of yours and ram it straight down the back of your throat.'

The Glaswegian chuckled. 'I'd like to see you try, you cockney prick.'

Absolutely seething at being defied and laughed at, yet unable to do anything about it, Vinny crouched in the corner of his cell, put his hands over his ears and rocked to and fro. He had promised himself on the way here that he would allow himself to think of anything or anyone other than Molly. That was the only way to stop himself going totally insane and he knew it. As an image of his daughter's beautiful face flashed through his mind, Vinny turned his attention back to the Glaswegian and tried to build a picture in his brain of what the tosser would look like. He then made a vow to himself. Whoever the Jock was – and he would make it his mission to find out – he would carry out his threat and mutilate the fucktard.

Little Vinny was drunk, distraught, tired and cold. Ben Bloggs had been the only true friend he'd ever had and now he was dead. Why was it that everybody important in his life was taken away from him? First his mum, dying of an overdose when he was only five. Now, on the same day his dad had been sent to prison for Christ knows how long, Ben had been found hanging from a tree.

As he crawled into what he and Ben had always referred to as their 'special place', Little Vinny had tears rolling down his cheeks. He wasn't stupid. He knew Ben's death was partly his fault. His pal had been a shadow of his former self ever since Molly's demise, but having inherited his father's genes, Little Vinny preferred to blame others rather than himself.

'I'm gonna miss you so much, Ben. We had so many laughs together, didn't we? Who am I gonna ride up and down on the District Line with now? I blame your whore of a mother. If you hadn't had such a shit upbringing and home life, you would still be alive. I'll make sure that slag pays for the way she treated you. That's the least I owe you, pal.'

Staring at the spot where he had brutally throttled the life out of his three-year-old sister, Little Vinny began to cry. 'I am sorry, Molly. I blame your mum and our dad for making me do what I did. When you was born, nobody wanted to know me any more, and I hated you for that. I suppose I was jealous.'

Full of self-pity, Little Vinny wiped the tears from his eyes and clambered to his feet. Taking one last look around, he made a vow to himself that this would be the last time he'd ever visit this spot.

CHAPTER FIVE

'You're late,' Queenie informed her youngest son.

'Give me a break, Mum. I've been running around like a blue-arsed fly since Vinny got bird. Why have you summoned me round at this time of the morning anyway? I've only had four hours' sleep.'

'We'll get to that in a minute. How d'ya think Vinny's coping? He sounded very stressed when he rung me yesterday. I'm ever so worried about him, Michael. Why didn't he want me to come with you today?'

'Probably because prison's no place for a lady. And it's no good asking me how he's coping because I won't know until I visit him, Mum. You're the one he's been phoning, not me,' Michael hissed. It was a week to the day since Vinny had been refused bail. To say Michael was miffed that his brother had not bothered to contact him once in that time was putting it mildly.

'Why you so ratty?'

'Because I've got a lot on me plate.'

'Like what?' Queenie enquired.

'Like the club's takings are in freefall, plus I've got my wife on my case the whole time because I'm having to sleep at the club to keep an eye on my nephew because no other bastard will do it.'

Knowing Michael's words were a dig at her for refusing to take on the responsibility of minding Little Vinny, Queenie quickly changed the subject. 'Still won't talk about what happened, your Auntie Viv. Traumatized she is, I can tell. I mean, having a big dingle-dangle waved at her at her time of life could've killed her, Michael. What a shock for the poor woman,' she elaborated.

'Bang out of order, Mum. And as I promised, I'll pay Pervy Pat a visit. I haven't forgotten, just haven't had time yet.'

'Best you make time and pay him a bit more than a quick visit now, boy. Janey came clean to her family and Billy Higgins keeled over with a heart attack. Had angina for years, the poor bastard. Been rushed to hospital and is in intensive care. Your Auntie Viv's in pieces, as you can well imagine. She's always held a torch for Billy. Pervy Pat needs to be dealt with, Michael, before he gets the chance to pounce again. Shame Vinny's not around. He'd have sorted it in no time. Don't want people taking liberties while he's at Her Majesty's pleasure.'

'Vinny ain't the only person round 'ere that's capable of dealing with stuff, Mother. I do happen to be a Butler as well, you know. I'll sort it ASAP, all right?'

Queenie nodded. 'That'll be great comfort to Auntie Viv, boy. She's very depressed today and we don't want her going down that road again, do we?'

Little Vinny felt physically sick as he approached the Bloggses' abode. Letting that toothless junkie suck his cock haunted him nearly as much as throttling Molly.

Awoken from her drug-induced sleep, Alison Bloggs began screaming obscenities at the top of her voice. She stopped the moment she stuck her head out of her bedroom window and got a glimpse of her visitor. 'Oh, it's you, Vin. Wanna come in? Got any booze or puff on ya?'

Little Vinny stared up at the whore with hatred. 'No I don't, and no I ain't. I wanna give Ben a good send-off. My Uncle Michael's gonna pay for it.'

'Bit late. Ben was buried yesterday, I think.'

'Whaddya mean, you *think*!'

Alison Bloggs shrugged. 'Some geezer turned up 'ere the other day and said they were burying him.'

'Didn't you even go to the funeral?' Little Vinny asked in astonishment.

'I weren't well. They took all me other kids away, Vin. Suicide is a selfish way out. Ben left me right in the shit. Come in, boy. Makes me feel better, your company.'

Pausing only to retch his guts up all over the pavement, Little Vinny ran off as fast as his legs would carry him.

'How's it going, bruv?' Michael asked diplomatically. His mother had made him promise to tread on egg shells during the visit as she didn't want her number-one son any more upset than he already was.

'I'm having a wonderful time, Michael. It reminds me of being back at Kings Holiday Park.'

About to order his brother to drop the sarcasm, Michael bit his tongue instead, leaned forward and, using a code they'd worked out over the years for when there were eavesdroppers in the vicinity, told him what Pervy Pat had been up to. Since the day Queenie had told him about Viv's ordeal, Michael had been having him watched. It turned out the nonce was a creature of habit: every night, regular as clockwork, he frequented the same two boozers. He was working up to telling Vinny how he planned to deal with the bastard when his brother cut him off.

'How dare that cunt behave in such a way to Auntie Viv! I take that as a personal insult, don't you? So what ya gonna do about it, little bruv? Only, it weren't that long ago you nearly shit yourself over a cow mooing the night we sorted Clever Trevor,' Vinny taunted. Since a very early age it had fallen to him to solve any problem his mother or family might encounter, and he hated the fact that he was helpless in the Ville while scum like Pervy Pat roamed his turf. His little brother had always been a reluctant participant in any heavy violence and he didn't trust him to take over the reins in his absence – not that he had any choice in the matter.

'I ain't no mug, Vin, so please don't treat me like one. I'll look after the family, and put it this way, I'm the only fucking guardian your son has at the moment. I'll sort Pervy Pat, don't you worry. And while I'm at it I'll restore our club to its former glory days. We're losing money hand over fist at the moment, but I have a plan.'

'What you on about?' Vinny sneered.

Sick of being treated like a lackey, Michael forgot all about his mother's earlier warning and came right out with it: 'I'm thinking of turning the club into a disco. Times have changed over the years and we need to move with 'em. Nobody wants to see live singers these days. I just know I can earn us a fortune by changing things. Trust me on this one.'

The only thing that kept Vinny from reaching across the table and punching his brother was the thought of ending up in solitary confinement. Instead he leaned across the table and hissed, 'You listen to me, Billy Big Bollocks. That club is my baby, always has been and always will be. Therefore, I decide what's what. You get my drift? Defy me, Michael, and I swear on my life I will make sure you live to regret it. Now, do we fucking understand one another?'

*

46

In the depths of Hainault Forest, Little Vinny was stoned, drunk and extremely morose. He had no idea of the exact spot where Ben had hung himself, but just being there made him feel close to his mate.

Annoyed with himself for doubting Ben's loyalty, Little Vinny felt he needed to get a few things off his chest. 'I loved you, pal,' he shouted into the trees. 'I weren't really gonna tell the Old Bill that you had an unhealthy interest in Molly. I did think about saying it, but only because I thought you might've grassed. I should've known better. You were a top lad. No way would you ever snitch on me.'

Wishing more than anything else in the world that Ben was still alive to reply to him, Little Vinny put his head in his hands and wept. He'd been helping out his Uncle Michael at the club, but he couldn't really move on with his life just yet. Too much had happened in a short space of time and his head was a complete mess.

Crouching down as if in prayer, Little Vinny made a vow to his pal: 'I'm gonna get revenge for you, Ben. I know how much you loved your brothers and sisters, and I'll make sure they don't suffer like you did. You deserved so much more in life than the shitty cards you were dealt. I know you never killed yourself because of Molly. It was your junkie slag of a mother that drove you to it. Well, I'm gonna sort her out for ya. It's the least I can do after everything you did for me.'

Pete and Paul had been friends with Roy Butler at school. Back in the sixties when Roy and Vinny had first opened the club, both men had jumped at the chance to work for the Butlers and had remained loyal ever since.

Officially, they were bouncers, but Pete and Paul had always been willing to help out in an unofficial capacity if need be. Even so, they were both gobsmacked when Michael Butler summoned them in for an afternoon meeting and demanded that they kidnap Pervy Pat that very night.

'It's a bit rushed, isn't it, Michael? We'll need time to sort out an alibi and prepare properly,' Pete warned.

Though neither of them said it, it wasn't the suddenness that worried them or even the order itself, it was the fact that Michael was the one issuing it. Although he'd been part of the set-up for years, Vinny had always been the one in charge of dealing with that side of things.

Desperate to make an impression, Michael Butler stood firm. 'I've already sorted out our alibi plus a van, and we already know Pervy Pat's movements. Billy Higgins is one of our own and that nonce-case needs to be stopped once and for all,' Michael insisted. He didn't mention his aunt's ordeal, as his mother had ordered him not to tell anyone, other than Vinny. 'Nosy bastards round 'ere will have a field day if they find out Viv got offered a portion of helmet pie,' she had spluttered. Seeing the doubt in his employees' eyes annoyed Michael. 'Not being funny, lads, but Roy is dead, Vinny is banged up for the foreseeable, so I'm your boss now. You in or out?'

Paul and Pete exchanged glances. 'We're in, boss,' Paul confirmed.

Queenie Butler was not in the most patient of moods. She'd done her utmost to cheer her sister up, but Vivian was still as miserable as sin. Viv had got over having a todger waved in her direction. They'd both roared with laughter over that last night. But she'd now gone into meltdown over Billy bloody Higgins. A man she'd barely spoken to for years.

'I should've gone with my instinct and called the police, Queen. If I'd accompanied Janey to the station, she'd have had no need to blurt it out to her family. She didn't want to tell 'em, but obviously they guessed something was wrong. It's my fault Billy's fighting for his life.'

Queenie gritted her teeth. If her memory served her correctly, Vivian hadn't shed this many tears over poor Molly. 'For Christ's sake, snap out of it, Viv. It's terrible what happened to Janey, but no real harm was done – he only tickled her with his stick, and she's barely family to us, is she? As for Billy, he's been living in Rainham for donkey's years with a heart condition. Been in and out of hospital many a time.'

Shocked by her sister's outburst, Vivian retaliated: 'You can be a very cold-hearted person at times, Queenie. Has anybody ever told you that?'

'You need to get a grip, love, or you'll end up in that loony bin again if you're not careful. I spoke to Michael earlier and he's promised to deal with the matter sooner rather than later, OK?'

Vivian nodded. Ensuring Pervy Pat got his comeuppance was the least she could do for Janey and Billy.

Having waited until it was dark, Little Vinny put the hood up on his jacket and checked nobody was about as he tapped on Alison Bloggs' front door.

'I'm so glad you're here, Vin. I've been feeling really depressed.'

Ushering the ugly whore into the hallway, Little Vinny handed her the bottle of vodka he'd stolen from the club. 'Get that down your neck. It'll make you feel better,' he urged.

'D'ya want me to suck you off again?' Alison volunteered hopefully. She wasn't used to gifts unless she gave something in return.

'Maybe later,' Little Vinny lied. 'First I want you to drink that and tell me everything that's happened.'

Alison began to greedily slurp the neat vodka while describing how Social Services had turned up earlier in the week and taken all her children into care.

'They're stopping me child allowance, Vin. How am I gonna manage financially?' Alison whined, clearly far more concerned about losing the money than having her kids taken away.

Little Vinny sipped his cider and smirked as Alison's eyelids began to droop. He'd bought a score's worth of Temazepam off a local dealer and emptied the liquid from the capsules in the vodka bottle.

Putting on an identical pair of Marigold gloves to the ones he'd throttled his sister with, Little Vinny waited until Alison had drunk most of the vodka before plonking himself next to her on the stinking threadbare sofa.

'That you, Vin? What you doing?' a sleepy Alison slurred.

'I'm doing what I should've done a long time ago. Snuffing out your miserable existence, you waste of fucking space.'

'What?' Alison mumbled, eyelids drooping.

Little Vinny took the razor blade out of his pocket. 'Rot in hell, slag,' he hissed, as he slashed first Alison's right wrist, then her left. He then took great pleasure in watching the blood and life seep out of her body.

Patrick Campbell aka Pervy Pat was not a stupid man. He'd experienced more in his twenty-five years than most blokes had in a lifetime.

Left in a public toilet as a newborn baby, Pat had no idea who his actual birth mother was. He'd then been shunted from one children's home to another before being fostered by Lena and John at the age of ten.

John had been a nice man, had encouraged him to take up sport. Lena, however, was a bitch. When John had a heart attack and passed away, Pat had been led a dog's life, both physically and mentally, thanks to Lena. Well aware that he was now notorious among the locals, since his release from prison Pat had taken to going further afield in search of prey. Pretending he was some big shot usually got him what he wanted these days without a struggle.

Rubbing his hand up and down his latest victim's back, Pat was rather pissed off when she informed him that she had no intention of leaving with him, no matter how much he flashed the cash and promised her a good time.

'Your loss, sweetheart. There's plenty more fish in the sea,' he said, turning away.

What Pervy Pat didn't realize as he sipped the last of his brandy and sang along to Black Slate's 'Amigo' was that outside the Fanshawe Tavern a rather unpleasant surprise was waiting for him.

Parked up behind Patrick Campbell's car, Michael Butler was becoming rather impatient at being kept waiting. 'I thought you said he always left this boozer before ten.'

'He did the other nights, Michael, but we've only followed him a few times, remember,' Pete reminded his boss.

'Give us that torch. It's as black as Newgate's knocker out there,' Michael ordered.

All three men were sitting in the back of the van while keeping a watchful eye out the front window. 'Don't start shining torches. We don't want to bring unwanted attention to ourselves. No way can we miss him parked 'ere,' Paul warned.

'So what's occurring exactly, Michael? We need to know our alibi,' Pete said.

'Our alibi is a game of poker at the club. Us three, plus Nick, the Kelly brothers and Jimmy Elliot. The others are all back at the club as we speak. I've told 'em to answer the phone and say I'm in the middle of a card game if anyone buzzes or rings. I've also told Nick to make two outgoing phone calls to my mum and dad, just in case the phone records are checked. I'll wise my parents up on what time I supposedly called when I get back.'

Seeing Pete and Paul glance worriedly at one another, Michael grinned. 'Like two rabbits caught in the headlights, you pair remind me of. Chill, for fuck's sake. I know you're thinking I shouldn't have involved Nick 'cause he has Old Bill in the family. But that makes for an even better alibi, if you get my drift. Anyway, we're not committing murder, just gonna teach Pat what happens to perverts.'

Pete stood up and leaned over the passenger seat. 'Speak of the devil.'

Pat Campbell's pride and joy was his Jaguar XJS, so his first thought when he was grabbed from behind by two men in balaclavas was that they were after stealing his car. 'Get off me, you shitbags,' he yelled, desperately trying to break free from their grasp.

Seconds later, Pervy Pat was smashed over the head with a hammer by a third man, then dragged into the back of a van.

Little Vinny was in high spirits as he strolled back towards the club. Today had been a good day. Visiting Hainault to pay his respects to Ben had made him feel much better about himself, and killing Alison was the icing on the cake. If Ben was looking down from heaven, Little Vinny knew he'd be relieved that his brothers and sisters would no longer have to suffer the hardship he had. At least in care the poor little bastards would be bathed, fed and clothed properly.

The spring in his step left Little Vinny the moment he put his hand in his pocket. His keys were missing.

Patrick Campbell had no idea where he was being driven to, or who'd abducted him. The bang on the head had left him dazed and confused, and he couldn't see a thing because a sack of some kind had been placed over his head and tied up around his neck.

'Where am I? What's going on?'

Michael Butler grinned at Pete as he supplied the answer: 'You need a little operation, me old mucker. Did you know that poor young Janey was a pal of mine's granddaughter?'

'Operation! But I'm not ill. And who the hell is Janey?' Pat mumbled through the sack.

Pulling the sharp carving knife out of the bag of goodies he'd brought with him, Michael ordered Pete to tie their prey's arms up.

'What you gonna do to him?' Pete asked, alarmed. He and Paul had been under the impression they were just going to teach the nonce a valuable lesson.

Michael Butler had never been as cold-blooded or sadistic as Vinny. Even Roy had got off on violence more than he had. However, now that he had been left in sole charge of the Butler empire, Michael knew he had no choice other than to do what he was about to.

The man's screams were horrendous when Michael unzipped his trousers and began hacking wildly at his penis.

'Jesus wept! He's gonna die and we're all gonna be up for murder now,' Pete hissed.

Chucking the severed penis out of the window as though it were no more than an unwanted pork sausage, Michael ordered Pete to shut the fuck up and told Paul to take the next turn off and stop the van as soon as the coast was clear.

Ten minutes later, the cockless, unconscious pervert who'd wronged Auntie Viv was lying on a grass verge in Aveley, while Michael and his henchmen were on their way back up the A13 towards London.

Little Vinny was in a complete panic. It wasn't just his old house keys on the keyring, the bunch his uncle had entrusted him with for the club were on there too.

He'd had them when he went into Alison Bloggs' place, so they must have fallen out of his tracksuit bottoms while he was sitting on her shabby sofa. In his stoned, drunken stupor he'd been so elated at killing her that he'd forgotten the most important thing of all: covering his tracks.

Not knowing how to dig himself out of the hole he'd got himself into, he tried to get hold of his uncle and then Ahmed. When that failed he was at a loss. Having made his way back to the club he decided his best option would be to hide in a doorway opposite the club and wait for Michael to show up.

'Got any drink or money, Sonny Jim?'

Little Vinny startled at the sight of the dishevelled old tramp peering in at him. It occurred to him that this doorway was probably the vagrant's spot, and the last thing he needed was the guy kicking off and drawing attention to him. He held out his bottle of cider. 'Here, have this.' Then he reached into his pocket for his last fiver and handed him that too.

'Bless you, my boy. May God take good care of you,' the tramp said, before walking away with his gifts.

Slumped in the doorway with his head in his hands, Little Vinny decided he had nothing to lose by putting his own faith in the big man above. 'Please, God, I swear, if you help me out of this situation, I will never drink, take drugs or do anything else bad ever again,' he mumbled.

The Wronged

When his Uncle Michael suddenly appeared, as if ma-terializing out of nowhere, for the first time ever Little Vinny truly believed that it paid to be nice to people.

PART TWO

Just as you cannot understand the path of the wind or the mystery of a tiny baby growing in its mother's womb, so you cannot understand the activity of God, who does all things.

Ecclesiastes 11:5

CHAPTER SIX

Summer 1984

Queenie and Vivian had always been creatures of habit, and for the past few years they had fallen into a regular Saturday routine. First they would travel down to Plaistow Cemetery to tend to the graves of Roy, Lenny and Molly. Then they would visit their dear old mum's plot in Bow before popping home, getting dolled up and heading off to the Roman.

Roman Road market was most certainly the place to be these days, especially on a Saturday. The trendy stalls and shops attracted women done up to the nines, not just from London but Essex and the surrounding counties as well.

At fifty-seven, Queenie was three years older than her sister. Both women wore their hair straight, shoulder-length and bleached blonde, and they had often been mistaken for twins. Neither lacked confidence. The heavy foundation they applied helped cover up their wrinkles, the bright red lipstick thickened their naturally thin lips, and the high heels they wore made them look much taller. Queenie was only five foot two, Vivian five three, but in their eyes they looked far more glamorous than all the younger dolly birds the Roman seemed to attract.

Vivian nudged her sister. 'Look at the bleedin' state of that! Talk about mutton done up as lamb.'

Queenie craned her neck to see who her sister was referring to. 'Gordon Bennett! She's got to be in her fifties. That ain't a skirt, it's more like a wide belt. If you look close enough, you can see what the old trollop had for breakfast this morning. Fancy walking about showing your muff at her age! Got no class these women, have they?'

About to reply, Vivian unfortunately caught her heel in a hole in the pavement and fell flat on her face.

Queenie crouched down. 'You all right, Vivvy?'

Within seconds, Vivian was surrounded by concerned shoppers and stallholders. Steve, who sold fruit and veg, gathered up Viv's shopping bags. 'You OK? Let me help you up, darling.'

Being the aunt of such notorious nephews often had its advantages, but right now Viv wished she was anybody but herself. The story of her stacking it would be all round Whitechapel by this evening and her nosy neighbours would probably dine out on it for months. 'Poxy bastard shoes. Me heel snapped off. Show's over, people,' Vivian spat, as she scrambled to her feet.

'Have you hurt yourself?' Queenie asked, her face full of concern.

Hobbling towards her sister with one shoe on and one off, Vivian grabbed Queenie's arm and hissed, 'I'm fine. Let's go to the pub.'

Michael Butler grinned as he finished counting the previous evening's takings. His brilliant business brain had proved all the doubters wrong. He was literally raking it in.

When Vinny had first got banged up, Michael had gone

along with his wishes and kept their club as it was by sticking with the singers, comedians, live bands, etc. But when the takings had dipped even more, he'd had no choice but to move with the times. His mother and Vinny had been appalled. But Michael had stuck by his guns, and his disco idea had taken off almost immediately.

The club now opened four nights a week. Thursday, Friday and Saturday nights were aimed at the youngsters, and on Monday evenings Michael had come up with an over-thirties' night. He and his staff privately referred to it as 'grab-a-granny night', but it had proved a massive success. The only thing from the past that Michael hadn't got rid of was the strippers on Sunday lunchtimes. They attracted perverts from all over and perverts spent good money.

His two old stalwarts Pete and Paul remained as invaluable as ever, but it had been Little Vinny who had proved to be the biggest asset to Michael at the club. His nephew was now eighteen and unrecognizable as the scruffy skinhead delinquent he'd once been. The lad worked like a Trojan, had a great business brain, and as a result Michael had added a commission-based bonus on top of his wage.

To say Michael had been surprised by the change in Little Vinny was an understatement. He'd been convinced his nephew was a liability, especially after the night when he'd returned to the club after chopping Patrick Campbell's cock off to find out the stupid kid had killed Alison Bloggs and left his keys in her house.

Doing what any decent uncle would have, Michael had broken into the property in the middle of the night to rectify Little Vinny's mistake. Thankfully, he'd found the keys within seconds and made a speedy exit, leaving Alison's body where it was.

Both he and Little Vinny had got away with their crimes.

The police had concluded Alison's death was an open-and-shut case of suicide. As for Pervy Pat, he'd survived his 'operation' and after a spell when his story was on the front page of all the national papers as well as the London press – it wasn't every day a geezer had his manhood chopped off on the A13 – he'd slunk off, disappearing without trace.

Michael had just finished locking the takings in the safe when the phone rang. The minute he heard his drama queen of a wife ranting at him hysterically down the line, his good mood evaporated. His sons were a handful, especially Daniel. But boys would be boys and, as per usual, Nancy was making a mountain out of a molehill. So what if they'd had a ruck with some lads from the opposing team while playing football? That's what lads did, and Michael was glad his boys had inherited his genes and stuck up for one another and themselves. 'Nance, I really can't be dealing with this right now. I'll have a word with the boys to-morrow, OK?'

'No, Michael. It's not OK. I told all three of them to go to their room and stay there, but the only one who made a move to obey me was Lee. Daniel just laughed in my face, then dragged Lee and Adam out the door with him. I have no idea where they are now, so you really need to take a break from that bloody club of yours, and put your family first for once.'

'It's three in the afternoon, not the morning, Nance. Lee's twelve, Dan's eleven and Adam is nine. They're hardly toddlers, are they?'

'No, more's the pity. Definitely got your family's genes though. I despair for their futures, Michael.'

Feeling his hackles rise, Michael took a deep breath. No way would he still be with Nancy if it weren't for the fact the boys needed a mother. 'You need to take a reality check,

Nance. The only one of my sons who has never brought the police to our door is Lee – and Denise gave birth to him, not you. If you're searching for bad genes, why don't you take a butcher's at your own side of the family, eh? Your mum's top drawer, bless her. But your father and brother are two of the biggest arseholes God ever put breath in.'

Little Vinny parked up in Cardigan Road, closed the roof of his white Ford Cabriolet, and sauntered towards the market. His life was pretty decent these days, apart from the odd flashback that disturbed his sleep now and then.

The July sun was scorching, so Little Vinny took off his T-shirt and slung it casually over his right shoulder. Checking out his reflection to ensure he had not messed up his carefully gelled hair, he was aware of a few admiring glances from younger and older females as he continued his journey.

Sammi-Lou Allen grinned as she spotted her boyfriend from afar. He was so handsome and at six foot tall he stood out even in a market full of people. With his jet-black hair, piercing green eyes and cute turned-up button nose, it really had been a case of love at first sight for Sammi-Lou. The fact he ran a nightclub and was Vinny Butler's son was just an added bonus.

Putting his arms around his girlfriend's waist, Little Vinny treated her to a short but passionate kiss. Sammi-Lou was the seventeen-year-old daughter of multi-millionaire Gary Allen, who owned Allen's Construction. Five foot five, with beautiful blonde hair, a voluptuous figure and big chocolate-coloured eyes, it had been a case of love at first sight for Little Vinny too. Before Sammi he had played the field. The club turning into a disco and him being classed as management had enabled him to take full advantage of the young birds who flocked there in their scantily dressed droves – and take advantage he most certainly had.

'What do you want to do first? Shop or eat?' Sammi asked excitedly. Unlike her ex-boyfriend, Little Vinny was as passionate about shopping and fashion as she was.

'Let's grab a bite to eat. Not sure I'll have time to shop today. My nan rung me as I left home. My aunt took a tumble earlier and she's twisted her ankle. They're in a boozer along the road here and I said I'd pick 'em up at four.'

'Aww. I hope your aunt is OK. Her and your nan make me laugh so much. My dad's organizing a big party at our house for my mum's fortieth. All your family are invited. My mum can't wait to meet Viv and Queenie. I've told her so much about them.'

Little Vinny felt a shiver run down his spine. He had been with Sammi just over six months now and had met her parents twice. Both times Sammi's little sister had been present, and it had really freaked him out. The child was seven, had blonde curly hair and reminded him of how Molly might look now. Worse still, her name was Millie. 'I won't be able to get time off work, babe, if the party is at a weekend. I have a club to run, you know that.'

'But it's only one night, Vin, and I want you there with me. Surely you can take one Saturday off?'

Desperate to change the subject, Little Vinny clasped his girlfriend's hand and smiled. 'I'll do my best. Speaking of parties, you looking forward to Charlene's tonight?'

Sammi grinned. 'Yep, but I'm only staying a couple of hours. I'll be at the club with you by eleven.'

Little Vinny grimaced. As much as he thought the world of Sammi-Lou, ever since she had passed her driving test and her dad had bought her a brand-new Mini, she had taken to showing up at the club every single Thursday, Friday and Saturday night. 'Sam, it's your best mate's eighteenth. You can't sod off after a couple of hours. It's not right.'

'But I like spending Saturday evenings with you, and waking up with you on a Sunday morning.'

'Yeah, I know you do, and I like it too. But because I thought you weren't coming to the club tonight, I invited some old school pals of mine down. We're gonna have a game of cards with Uncle Michael and a couple of his mates once we lock up. I can't cancel now, it's too late,' Little Vinny lied. He didn't even have any old school friends. The only pal he'd ever had in those days was Ben.

'OK. If you don't want me there, I won't come,' Sammi said, her eyes brimming with tears.

Suddenly feeling as suffocated as a Doberman locked in a two-foot cage, Little Vinny took his girlfriend's hand and steered her into Beau Baggage. He knew it was one of her favourite shops. 'Let's not argue. Pick out whatever you want and I'll buy it for ya.'

Vinny Butler finished his hundred press-ups and decided to have a rest before starting his sit-ups. At least six times a day he exercised vigorously. In prison you needed something to focus the mind on.

Thanks to his smart-arse brief and brilliant Queen's Counsel, Vinny had literally gotten away with murder. The prosecution had tried to portray him as some kind of monster, but the jury had clearly been touched by Molly's untimely death, and all he'd ended up with was an eight-year stretch for manslaughter. Bobby Jackson's family and friends had gone apeshit when the murder verdict was read out as 'not guilty'. Jackson's lunatic of a mother had even lunged at Queenie and then been dragged from the court kicking and screaming.

Having already spent over a year on remand before his trial, Vinny should have been up for parole soon. It was usual to serve only half your sentence if your behaviour

was good. Unfortunately for Vinny, he'd had a few altercations with other lags over the years, and as a result the
authorities had argued he should not be released yet. His
brief, however, was on the ball and had told Vinny that,
providing he stayed out of trouble, he was sure he could
get him parole in the next year.

Lying on his bunk, Vinny stared at the ceiling. He was
by far the most respected inmate in the Ville now, and so
he bloody-well should be – after all, he was *the* Vinny
Butler. It hadn't been easy, getting his head back together
after Molly's death, but once he'd made his vow not to
think or speak about his daughter, he'd started to get back
to his old self. It had been tough, and even now he couldn't
stop Molly appearing in his dreams, but he refused to shed
a tear. Only weak men cried, and if prison had taught
Vinny anything, it was how to be mentally strong.

He checked the time; his brother would be here soon. It
was a prospect that gave him no pleasure. Relations between
himself and Michael had become somewhat strained ever
since he'd been banged up. Right at the start they'd had a
bust-up over Little Vinny's living arrangements that kept
them from speaking to each other for nine months. Vinny
had expected his son to move in with Michael, and had
gone ballistic when his brother had instead rented a house
opposite his own and allowed Little Vinny to live in it with
their arsehole of a father. In Vinny's eyes, Molly would still
be alive if his old man hadn't fathered an illegitimate child
with that slag Judy Preston.

When Michael disobeyed his wishes and turned the club
into a disco, it had led to even more friction. It grated on
Vinny that his brother had been right and he'd been wrong.
Even though it was earning him big bucks, he'd rather the
disco had failed. Anything would have been better than
having to eat humble pie.

In Vinny's opinion, the success of the venture had gone to Michael's head. According to Ahmed, he was now swanning around Whitechapel in a brand-new red Porsche convertible like he owned the fucking area. He'd gotten far too big for his boots, and Vinny would have liked nothing better than to bring him down a peg or two.

Resisting the urge to punch the wall, Vinny took a deep breath and did his sit-ups instead. He had no idea why Michael had insisted on visiting him today, but he'd be glad when the visit was over.

Standing in the queue to be searched, Michael Butler smiled politely at a blonde who seemed unable to take her eyes off him. He was used to lots of female attention. His boyish good looks and charm attracted all types.

The blonde walked over to him. 'Hi, I'm Wendy – I've seen you in the Blind Beggar. I'd just like to thank you for getting rid of you-know-who. He attacked me many moons ago and I'm so glad I never have to bump into him any more.'

Rumour had spread around the East End that Michael was responsible for Pervy Pat's little accident and subsequent disappearance. Billy Higgins had recovered from his heart attack, then died of another six months later, and Janey had since moved away from the area. Far too wise to ever admit his involvement, Michael nevertheless enjoyed the notoriety. Even law-abiding members of the community looked upon nonces as vermin, and he was now seen as some kind of local hero.

After politely telling the blonde she must have mistaken him for somebody else, Michael allowed the screw to search him, then sauntered into the visiting area.

Vinny faked a smile as his brother approached. 'What the fuck's that?' he asked, pointing at Michael's new ring.

'What's it look like, Vin?'

'Something you nicked out of a bender's jewellery box.'

Knowing Vinny was being his usual facetious self, Michael decided two could play at that game. 'Treated meself up at Hatton Garden, bruv. Look at the quality of that diamond. It's flawless. Bought this Gucci watch an' all. Thank God I had the foresight to turn our business around, eh? Would never have been able to afford such luxuries otherwise. If we'd stuck with those live singers like you wanted us to, I'd have been wearing a Swatch by now,' Michael chuckled.

'You have what is referred to in medical terms as short-term memory loss, Michael. Have you forgotten how you cried and threw all your toys out the pram when I marched in that shitty garage and told your old boss you couldn't be his tea boy no more? You'd still be working there if it wasn't for me taking the initiative.'

Smirking, Michael laughed out loud. 'I doubt that very much. Got more of a business brain than you'll ever have, that's for sure. What I've done to the club speaks for itself. The proof is in the pudding, brother dearest.'

Vinny was not amused. 'If you've come 'ere just to give it the big 'un, bruv, you might as well fuck off now. I really ain't in the mood after the morning I've had.'

Sarcastic tone immediately changing to one of concern, Michael asked what had happened.

'Jay Boy's brother's been killed, and I heard some Jock cunt laughing about it earlier. He's so gonna get it. It's the same mouthy prick who gave me stick when I first arrived. He's only been back in 'ere a week. I'm gonna shut him up for good this time,' Vinny hissed, before glancing around to check nobody was earwigging.

'Sorry to hear that. I know how close you are to Jay Boy. Be careful though. You don't wanna get more time added on your sentence.'

'I'm gonna have a word with Jay later. He'll be out before me and he needs something to look forward to. I'm gonna offer him a job at the club.'

'Erm, aren't you forgetting something? We're partners, remember?'

'Don't start larging it again, Michael. The mood I'm in, I'll smash you right across this room in a minute.'

Michael stood up. Vinny would never change. He was a regular Jekyll and Hyde. 'I'm gonna tell Mum we had a pleasant visit and you're sending me another VO real soon. Best you say the same if you don't wanna upset her. Oh, and I'm happy to trust your faith in Jay Boy and employ him. Perhaps in future though you should ask me rather than tell me. It's much more polite and professional.'

'See you, you flash cunt. I've got people keeping an eye on you. So watch your back, big man,' Vinny bellowed.

Michael held his hands out and pretended they were shaking. 'I'm terrified, bruv. Honest I am.'

Losing it completely, Vinny leapt up to punch Michael's lights out and was quickly restrained by the screws.

Having spent the afternoon drinking brandies in the Rose of Denmark, Vivian could now see the funny side of her little tumble. 'Trust me, Queen, never gonna live down the shame, am I?'

Queenie chuckled. The sight of Vivian cursing, while hobbling down the Roman with one shoe on and the other in her hand had been comical and attracted some weird looks from passers-by. 'I felt sorry for that nice lady who works in Ashby's. She only asked if you were OK and you told her to mind her own fucking business. How we meant to queue up in there for our meat and salt-beef sandwiches in future, eh?'

Vivian roared with laughter. 'I'll go in and apologize to

her next week. Silly question to ask though. If I was OK, I would hardly be limping along the road like a lame dog with one shoe in me sodding hand, would I?'

'Oh, Viv, you are a case. How's your ankle now? It's definitely swollen. We'll get a bag of frozen peas on that when we get home.'

'Can't feel no pain – the alcohol must have numbed it. It's more painful looking at these poxy slip-ons you bought me. That's the last time I'm sending you shoe-shopping. I look like silly-girl-got-none. Hope we don't see anyone we know as we walk to the car.' She checked her watch. 'What time did you say Little Vinny was picking us up? Ring him and ask if he can bring a balaclava with him so I can't be recognized in me new shoes.'

Her sides aching from laughter, Queenie urged her sister to behave herself.

Little Vinny was horrified when he arrived at the pub to find both his nan and aunt inebriated and giggling like two silly schoolgirls. He was clean as a whistle these days. Did not drink, smoke or take drugs.

'What the bleedin' hell do you look like? And why you got your jeans rolled up and those silly dark glasses on? Not sunny in here, is it? It's a pub,' Queenie tutted.

'And he's topless. I think me and you should walk in a boozer one day baring our top halves, don't you, Queen? I mean, if you've got it, why not flaunt it? And if that skinny bag of bones has it, then so have we.'

Even though he knew full well he looked a cool dude in his rolled-up faded Levis, white Lacoste trainers and Porsche sunglasses, Little Vinny felt his face go red as he caught a couple of birds and a geezer looking his way and laughing. His nan and aunt had loud enough voices when sober, let alone when drunk. 'Yous two wouldn't understand fashion. Come on, we're going.'

'Don't be so rude. You've not even bought me and Viv a drink yet. Put your top on and get up the bar. We'll both have a brandy and lemonade,' Queenie ordered.

'Aw my gawd, Queen! He's wearing pink. Take the T-shirt back off again, Vin. You look like a poof!' Vivian guffawed.

Noticing the two birds and bloke on the next table laugh at him again, Little Vinny saw red. He ran towards the male, grabbed him by the neck and slammed his head against the wall. 'You wanna be careful who you take the piss out of, you soppy-looking prick. I am Little Vinny Butler, son of *the* Vinny Butler, and I can easily arrange your funeral.'

Aware that his cellmate was trying to stifle his sobs, Vinny Butler walked over to his pal's bunk and rubbed his back. He'd calmed down now, although Michael had pissed him off immensely. 'Let it all out, Jay. Far better out than in – trust me, I know.'

'I feel such a fucking dick crying, Vin, but I loved my bro so much,' Jay wept in his broad Scouse accent.

Jay Boy Gerrard was an up-and-coming boxer who had only just turned pro when he'd ventured down to London for a pal's stag night. Undefeated as an amateur, the future looked bright for Jay Boy until he'd got involved in a drunken brawl. One punch was all it had taken Jay to kill his victim. It hadn't been his intention, but unfortunately the lad had fallen backwards, smashed his head against the edge of a kerb and died instantly.

Jay had been given a five-year sentence, and was looking forward to his imminent release. He and his brother had planned to set up their own boxing gym, but that dream was over now. His brother had been stabbed outside a boozer in Kirby last night and was dead. 'I don't know what I'm going to do, Vin. My bro's a legend in Liverpool.

I don't want to go back there now. If I do, I'll be reminded of his death everywhere I turn. I can't believe he's gone and I'm never going to see him again. It doesn't seem real.'

Knowing exactly what his mate was going through, Vinny gave the lad a hug. Jay was fourteen years his junior. They had been sharing a cell for the past two years and Vinny cared for the bloke like a brother or a son. Jay had most certainly brightened up his time inside, which was why Vinny wanted to repay the favour. 'Listen, mate, why don't you stay in London and work with me? You can work at the club. I'll see to it you get treated with respect and paid good dosh. Then, when I get released, you can be my main man.'

'Really! But what about your bro?' Jay asked. He was well aware of the friction between Vinny and Michael as his cellmate often spoke about it.

'Don't be worrying about Michael. He will do exactly as I tell him. Whether he likes it or not, I'm the boss. Always have been and always fucking will be.'

The man apprehensively entered the plush office. His boss could be a real tyrant at times and he hoped he wasn't in any trouble. His last task had proved anything but fruitful.

'Sit down.'

'Sorry I had a wasted trip, boss. I tried my hardest to track him down, honest I did.'

'I know. Which is why I'm putting my faith in you again. I have an address of a nightclub in the East End of London. There you will find a man called Michael Butler. I want photos, movements; dig up as much as you can on him. I even want to know when he takes a shit. Understand me?'

'Clearly, boss.'

CHAPTER SEVEN

Joanna Preston clapped as the rendition of 'Happy Birthday' ended. She bent down next to her daughter. 'Make a wish, darling, then blow out the candles.'

'What's a wish, Mummy?'

'It means think about something you want. Why don't you wish for that little fluffy white kitten you saw last week, eh?'

Ava did as she was told, then squealed with delight seconds later when her granddad handed her a small cardboard box with the kitten inside. 'Can I call it Bagpuss?' Ava asked. She loved to watch TV and the videos her nan and granddad brought her, and *Bagpuss* was her current favourite.

Deborah Preston picked up the kitten and chuckled. 'Seeing as she's a pretty little girl, just like you, I think we can come up with a nicer name than Bagpuss. Why don't we make a list of names, then you can choose which one you like the best?'

Standing with her hands on her little hips, Ava Preston shook her head in defiance. 'No, Nanny. I want to call her Bagpuss.'

'She's a case, isn't she? Talk about three going on

thirteen,' Nancy Butler joked. Ava was nothing like Molly in any way, shape or form, and Nancy still couldn't decide whether that was a good omen or bad. With her mop of curly blonde hair and sweet nature, Molly had been a replica of her lovely mum. Ava was far more of a little diva, and with her jet-black hair there was a definite resemblance to her father.

'Stroke her, Nancy,' Ava demanded.

Nancy smiled as Ava climbed on to her lap. She wondered if the reason she'd not bonded with her as much as Molly was because she saw Ava far less frequently. Since Joanna had moved deeper into Essex to a small village called Tillingham, they only met up once a month at most. It was difficult to speak on the phone regularly too. To prevent Ava's existence from becoming known to the Butler clan, Joanna insisted that Nancy only ever call her from a phone box.

'Why don't you ring your mum, Nance, and ask if the boys can stay with her tonight? It's been ages since we've had a proper catch-up, and my mum and dad are staying over anyway, so they'll look after Ava. There's a nightclub not too far from here that the locals call the "Four Views" which has a good disco on a Saturday night. Please say yes – we'll have such a giggle.'

Nancy sighed. She hated asking her parents to have the boys overnight these days. Her father was always so bloody critical of their behaviour, especially Daniel's, and she was sick of having to defend her sons, especially when she knew the criticism was justified. 'Oh, I dunno, Jo. I promised my mum I'd pick the boys up by nine.'

Joanna squeezed her pal's hand. Even from their infrequent conversations, she knew that Nancy had been down lately and could do with having some fun. 'Don't be so boring. It will be a laugh. When was the last time you let your hair down, eh?'

Nancy could not remember the last time she'd even had the chance to let her hair down. Michael might refer to the club as work, but at least he was still out socializing. She wasn't. She was stuck indoors being a mother to three boys, one of whom didn't even belong to her.

'Sod it!' she said, the decision made. 'Pass me your phone, Jo.'

Ahmed Zane was living his dream. Having used a massive chunk of the money he'd earned through drug importation to build a fine hotel in Turkey, he had just enjoyed a luxurious stay in his homeland and flown back first-class. On arrival, he headed straight for the restaurant he co-owned with his cousin in Tottenham.

Burak was both surprised and pleased to see Ahmed. 'What are you doing back so early? I thought your flight was not until Wednesday.'

Ahmed led his cousin into the office. 'I heard some very interesting news, Burak. Hence my early return.'

'What? About who?'

'I think I have learned something that will fuck Vinny's head up big time. In fact, it will probably explode when he hears!'

'Tell me,' Burak demanded, his tone overloaded with impatience.

Ahmed smirked. He and Vinny Butler had once been the closest of friends, but the car crash that killed poor Lenny had put an end to that. Ahmed could have forgiven Vinny for crashing the car. What he could not forgive was that his so-called best pal had dragged his unconscious body from the passenger seat and belted him into the driver's seat, leaving him for fucking dead and framing him in the process.

Vinny's excuse was that he'd thought Ahmed was already dead and panicked, but Ahmed was too cute to fall for that old chestnut. Vinny's actions had been callous and calculating. A panicking man would have just legged it without stopping to move bodies and see to it that someone else took the rap.

Burak slammed a glass of Scotch on the table. 'Why do you always do this, Ahmed? You half tell a story and then you fucking stop.'

Ahmed chuckled. 'Chill, Burak, chill. Tarkan Smith rang me at the hotel. He had some exciting information regarding Johnny Preston. Apparently, Preston is working at a car lot in Wickford for somebody that Tarkan knows well. It also turns out that Preston has a young granddaughter who he is very cagey about. He never even mentioned the child's existence until he was seen out with her. Now why would Johnny be trying to keep her a secret, eh?'

'You think the kid could be Vinny's?'

Ahmed grinned. 'It looks that way. When Preston saw his boss in the restaurant, he said the child was not related to him, but then she called him "Granddad". Apparently the mystery child has jet-black hair and green eyes. Sound like anybody you know?'

'Sure does. Vinny will go mental if he finds out Joanna had another kid by him and kept it a secret. He'll be climbing the walls in his prison cell.'

Ahmed had been surprised and annoyed by how well Vinny had coped with being incarcerated. He'd had a few altercations with fellow prisoners and had seemed very depressed when he first got banged up, but since then he'd taken it all in his stride. Obviously Vinny had no idea how much Ahmed loathed him. He still thought they were pals – the mug.

'Exactly, Burak. Which is why, first thing tomorrow, I shall be hiring the best private detective money can buy.'

*

Over at the Walker household, Donald was becoming more embarrassed and angry by the second. Out of all of the days to play up, his grandsons had chosen to do so in front of Christopher and Olivia.

'Stop acting stupid. Eat your dinner before it gets cold,' Mary ordered.

Aware of her discomfort, Daniel giggled and flicked a pea at Lee, who in turn flicked one back that missed Daniel and hit Mary instead.

'Right, that's it! If they can't eat like normal human beings, put their dinners in the bin,' Donald bellowed.

'Not hungry anyway,' Daniel replied, defiantly pushing his plate away.

'I'm not hungry either,' Lee said, copying his brother as he always did.

When his nan took their plates away, Daniel leaned towards Adam. 'I dare you to knock Olivia's drink all over her.'

'Nah, Dan. We'll get in trouble.'

'I'll give you a pound if you do it,' Daniel urged.

Seconds later, Adam stood up, pretended to stumble and did as he'd been asked.

'You stupid clumsy child! Go and ask your nan for a cloth. I am so sorry, Olivia,' Donald said in a mortified tone.

Christopher leapt up. 'It's OK, Dad. Most of the drink went on the carpet anyway. I'll clean it up.'

Nudging Lee with a silly grin on his face, Daniel decided to go one better. 'Why is your nose so big, Uncle Christopher?' he asked innocently.

'Mary! Get these children out of my sight before I do something I truly regret,' Donald screamed.

Back in Whitechapel, Queenie and Vivian were discussing Little Vinny's violent outburst.

After threatening the poor bloke on the next table, Little Vinny had tipped over a table, thrown a chair at some people who were standing at the bar, then stormed out of the pub.

'Never felt so embarrassed since that time we got barred from Kings,' Queenie said. Kings was the holiday park in Eastbourne where Vinny and Michael had once owned bungalows.

'Got no sense of bloody humour, that boy,' Viv tutted. 'I mean, we were only ribbing him. And I'll tell you something for nothing, no way am I ever getting in a car with him again. Drove like a bleedin' lunatic. I felt right sick by the time he dropped us at the chippy.'

Queenie nodded in agreement. Little Vinny had hung around for her and Viv opposite the pub, but refused to speak to them all the way home. 'I'm gonna have a word with Michael about him. I thought meeting that pretty girl had sorted him out, didn't you? Living with Albie obviously hasn't done him any favours at all.'

When Queenie had been officially married to Albie, Vivian had hated the sight of the man. She no longer loathed him though. 'Albie isn't a violent man, Queen, so you can't be blaming him. Got your rose-tinted specs on again, aintcha? Well, let me take them off for you. There's only one person Little Vinny takes after and that's his bloody father.'

'I suppose you're right. Both got a bleedin' temper on 'em, that's for sure,' Queenie admitted begrudgingly.

Pleased that her sister had agreed with her verdict, Vivian happily changed the subject. 'How's your Bren? You heard from her recently?'

Queenie pursed her lips. Since her daughter had moved to Dagenham to live with a bloke fourteen years her senior, contact had dwindled between herself and Brenda. 'Nope.

No matter what time of day I ring up, she's never in. Out on the piss all the time with that tosser, if you ask me. It's Tara and Tommy I feel sorry for. Must be raising themselves – and probably running riot, poor little mites. Do you think me and you should pay Bren another visit? Just to check the kids are being looked after properly.'

Vivian shrugged. Tara was twelve now, Tommy seven, and the last time Queenie had dragged her over to Dagenham for an unexpected visit, both kids had been happy enough and looked well-fed and dressed. Brenda and Dave had seemed content enough as well. 'If you want my honest opinion, I don't see what you're gonna gain by us keep poking our trunks in. Even if you think the kids are unhappy, you ain't gonna want custody of 'em, are you? Brenda and Dave are both pissheads, so they're well suited. And at least Dave takes Bren out, Queen, unlike my Bill and your Albie did with us. Kitchen-sink women me and you were.'

Hearing the chugging of what sounded like a clapped-out vehicle outside accompanied by loud voices, Queenie ran over to the window. 'Aw my dear Lord! Please don't tell me this is our new neighbours.'

Vivian hobbled over to the window. Their old neighbour, Lil, had croaked it a few weeks back. They'd seen the council popping in and out a few times since, and had been expecting new neighbours to arrive any day now. Not at nine o'clock at night though, in a poxy old Transit tipper truck. There were two women, a man and a couple of boys.

'Blimey, Queen. D'ya reckon they're gypsies?'

'No idea what they are, but I don't like the bleedin' look of 'em.'

'We did say we'd be happy to get anyone other than Indians,' Vivian reminded her sister.

Seeing the youngest lad, who looked about twelve, stick

two fingers up at her, Queenie did the same back, then shut the curtains. 'I'd prefer Indians any day of the week to that motley-looking crew. Trust our luck, Vivvy. I reckon God must bastard-well hate us at times, I really do.'

When 'Relax' by Frankie Goes to Hollywood began to blare out of the speakers, Joanna grabbed Nancy's hand and dragged her off the dance floor. 'Let's get another Malibu and pineapple. My feet are killing me in these shoes.'

'That bloke is still staring at you, Jo. He's ever so handsome, don't you think?'

'I'm really not interested, Nance. Vinny's put me off men for life. I'm quite content being a single mum, thanks very much.'

'You can't allow Vinny to ruin your life, Jo. You are stunning, you've got a heart of gold, and you deserve to find true love. Oh my God! I think he's coming over. Please don't be nasty to him. He just might be Mr Right.'

Little Vinny was not in the best of moods. He'd had a row with his girlfriend earlier, which was probably the cause of him kicking off in the Rose of Denmark. Now his uncle had just informed him that his father's cellmate would be working at the club in the near future. 'Why didn't you say no? What's he gonna be doing here? We don't need any more staff.'

'Jay's brother has been murdered, and the lad is in bits. He can't face going back to Liverpool by all accounts. I dunno what he'll be doing yet, but to be honest Jay can only be an asset to the business. He's a good-looking bloke and the birds will love him.'

Little Vinny hated Jay Boy Gerrard. He'd seen him when visiting his dad and thought he looked a flash bastard. His father was always banging on about what a great lad Jay was and that pissed Little Vinny off immensely. He got the distinct impression that his old man would have preferred Jay as a son. That was why he hadn't bothered visiting the prison for the past six weeks. 'I don't wanna work with Jay, Michael. There's something about him I don't like. You better tell my dad it's either him or me.'

'Don't talk wet. You're my right-hand man. Jay will either work as a bouncer or behind the bar, that's all. He isn't going to have a position of importance.'

'He will if my fucking old man has anything to do with it.'

'Vin, I half own this club. Your dad might think he's still the overall boss, but he ain't any more. It was me that turned this gaff into a disco and made a huge success of it. Therefore, I can promise you that Jay will just have an average job, OK?'

When the DJ put on Wham's 'Wake Me Up Before You Go-Go' Little Vinny stormed into the office. Sammi-Lou was a massive Wham fan and she loved this song.

Staring at his uncle's bottle of Scotch, Little Vinny undid the lid. He had not touched a drop of alcohol since that drunken, drug-fuelled night when he'd thought his dead sister had paid him a visit. Molly had been wearing a white gown and her eyes were bulging with terror in the same way they'd looked as he'd throttled the life out of her. He still wasn't sure if he had seen her ghost, but he preferred to think that his mind was playing tricks on him.

Neither his father nor Michael had any idea that Little Vinny had visited brothels and snorted cocaine with Ahmed in the past. The Turk had been a massive support for him since his dad had been banged up and, even though they'd seen far less of each other recently, Little Vinny knew that if he ever had a problem Ahmed was the man to turn to.

Little Vinny took a sip of Scotch but immediately spat it on to the carpet. He might have had a bad day today, but he quite liked the new him. Alcohol was evil. All it did was remind him of bad things.

He picked up the phone and dialled, and to his relief it was his girlfriend who answered. The last time they'd had a row, her dad had picked up the blower and all but threatened him.

'You OK?' he asked. 'Didn't you go to your mate's birthday bash?'

Not wanting to admit that she'd been crying periodically ever since they'd parted in Roman Road earlier, Sammi pretended she was just getting ready to go out.

'Well, I'm missing ya. So if you fancy coming to the club later, we can cuddle up in bed,' Little Vinny suggested.

When Sammi-Lou told him she'd be there by midnight, Little Vinny smirked. He had his pretty girlfriend firmly in the palm of his hand and he liked that very much.

Over in Pentonville, Vinny tipped the wink for the fun to begin. He'd arranged for Andy Tucker and three of his cronies to be paid a bullseye each for kicking off at the appointed hour.

'You can fuck off,' Tucker bellowed. 'We ain't going back to the cell. We should be allowed to watch *Match of the Day*.'

One of Tucker's pals threw a chair across the room and a moment later all hell broke loose as other inmates joined in.

'Let's do it,' Vinny urged Jay Boy.

Jock McIntyre was in shock as Vinny dragged him out the TV room. Nobody heard his cries for help though. The screws were too busy trying to stop a full-blown riot getting under way and the prisoners were busy arguing and fighting amongst themselves.

'Check nobody's coming, Jay,' Vinny ordered, before clumping Jock repeatedly in the stomach.

Jock, who weighed less than ten stone, doubled up and fell to the floor groaning in agony.

'All clear,' Jay said, after checking both ends of the corridor.

'Quick, hold the cunt's arms down,' Vinny urged.

'Get off me. I'm sorry if I've upset you, OK?' Jock cried.

'Not larging it now, are ya?' Vinny spat. He would've loved to cut Jock's tongue out, but didn't have time. He pulled the razor blade he'd melted into a toothbrush handle from his sock and as quick as a flash, slashed a reasonably straight line across the Scotsman's mouth.

As Jock screamed in agony and fright, Vinny muttered, 'Grass, and I swear on my dear old mum's life, next time it'll be your throat.'

Thirty seconds later Vinny re-entered the TV room. With a quick nod to old Frank, the screw guarding the door, he rejoined the fracas.

Enticing a screw into his pocket had been a smart move on Vinny's part. He'd always known it would come in handy at some stage.

Queenie and Viv were happily gushing over how radiant a heavily pregnant Princess Diana looked when they were disturbed by the doorbell ringing.

Queenie pursed her lips. 'This better be my Michael, or he'll have some explaining to do.' Her son had not been in touch since the prison visit and Queenie was not amused.

'There you are! Been ringing your bleedin' club all evening. Why didn't you pop in earlier, like you promised?'

Michael Butler gave his mother a kiss on the cheek. 'I'm

sorry. I've just had a manic day. Little Vinny said Auntie Viv had an accident. Is she OK?'

'I'll live,' Viv shouted from the living room.

'Don't keep me in suspense then. How did the visit go?'

'Good. Vinny was in high spirits,' Michael lied.

'Did you build bridges, like I told you to? And don't lie to me, 'cause I'll find out the truth.'

'We didn't need to build bridges, Mum. We're brothers at the end of the day.'

Beaming from ear to ear, Queenie hugged her youngest son. 'That's what I like to hear. Us Butlers stick together through thick and thin, always. Well, apart from me and your father, of course,' Queenie chuckled.

'I'd better get back to the club, Mum. I left Little Vinny in charge.'

'I want a word with you about him.'

'Not now. It was busy when I left.'

'OK. But I need to ask you a favour, boy.'

Not another one, thought Michael, but as his mother pursued him down the path he had no option but to nod.

'I'm worried about Tara and Tommy. Dave isn't a good influence on our Brenda, you know. I think you should pay him a little visit.'

'And do or say what?' Michael asked.

'Well, I don't know, do I? You and your brother are the men of this family. Just do or say what you did to Pervy Pat that time. I was so proud of you when he scarpered. So was Vivvy.'

Michael looked at his mother in disbelief. 'Brenda's a pisshead, Mum, and until she gives up boozing, she'll always end up with one of the Daves of this world. Pat was a nonce. Big difference.'

*

Johnny Preston read the letter once more, then put it in his trouser pocket. He was dreading having this conversation with his wife. However, he had promised there would be no more secrets between them and he meant it. Since he'd got out of nick and married Deborah for the second time, their relationship had gone from strength to strength. There was no way he would jeopardize that by hiding things from her.

'Can we talk, babe? Sit down a minute.'

'Whatever's the matter?' Deborah asked, alarmed. She could tell by the look on her husband's face that it wasn't going to be good news.

'It's Jamie. My mum's been visiting him in Feltham and she swears blind that he didn't kill Molly. He wrote me this letter. Read it,' Johnny urged.

Deborah's eyes filled with tears. It was coming up to four years now since Molly had been brutally murdered, yet the memories of that torrid time were still very raw to her. Ava had filled the gap in her life to a certain extent, but she would never replace Molly. No child could. 'I don't want to read it, Johnny. Jamie must be guilty. The police aren't bloody stupid. Please don't tell me you are thinking of visiting that treacherous murdering scumbag?'

'I have to, Deb. I need to find out the truth.'

Deborah shook her head in pure disbelief. 'Joanna will go crazy when she finds out. And what is visiting that vermin going to solve? Not going to bring Molly back, is it?'

'It will solve whether that little fucker is lying or not, Deb. And there is no need for Jo to know. If need be, I will tell her afterwards.'

'And you don't think he's going to lie to you, Johnny? He lied to his nan and the fucking police.'

'As soon as I look him in the eyes, Deb, I will know the truth. Trust me on that one.'

*

Mary Walker kissed her sleeping granddaughter on the forehead, then hugged her son and daughter-in-law. Christopher and Olivia had got married in 1981 and little Janine was now eighteen months old. 'Keep safe at work, won't you, son?'

Christopher raised his eyebrows. He was twenty-seven now. A detective sergeant in the drugs squad at Arbour Square. However, his mother still treated him as though he was some rookie. She never let a week go by without phoning him at least three times to make sure he was still alive and had not been harmed in the line of duty.

Donald followed his family into the hallway. 'I do apologize once again for the behaviour of the boys. I shall punish them all personally in the morning; I can assure you of that.'

Rather than upset his mother, Christopher mumbled, 'Boys will be boys.' He was not at all surprised that Nancy's sons had turned out such horrible little bastards. What else could you expect, with Butler blood running through their veins?

When he was a kid, Christopher had witnessed Vinny Butler stab a man to death outside his nightclub. Vinny had then threatened and blackmailed him into keeping his mouth shut. Once the police had got involved, Christopher, despite being absolutely terrified, had told his parents the truth. That very same evening they'd done a moonlight flit from their beloved café in Whitechapel.

'Bye-bye. Drive safely.' Mary stood on the pavement waving him off. She was dreading going back inside the house because she knew what was coming next.

Donald's face was like thunder when she walked back through the door. 'I don't know about you, but I have never felt so humiliated in all my life. What must Olivia have thought? I do hope she doesn't tell her parents. As for Christopher, he deserves a medal for holding his temper.

Talk about show us up! Adam knocked that drink over Olivia on purpose – I saw him do it. And as for Daniel asking poor Christopher why his nose was so big . . .'

Donald shook his head. 'I truly wanted the ground to open up and swallow me. Even Lee played up, and he's usually the best behaved out of the bloody three. I shall teach them all a lesson in the morning, Mary. That cane I keep in the shed will be put to good use. Words and threats are meaningless. Such behaviour warrants corporal punishment.'

'Please don't overreact, Donald. Yes, they were very naughty and I felt ashamed too. But you can't be caning them. Nancy'll go mad, and what do you think Michael will say? Anyway, it wasn't Adam or Lee's fault – Daniel was the bloody instigator. He's forever egging the other two on. I overhead him dare Adam to knock that drink over Olivia, and he kept getting Lee to wake Janine up. I'll have a word with Nancy tomorrow. She most certainly needs to chastise them more, especially Daniel.'

'They will not be welcome back in this house, Mary. Not until they have learned some manners. If you want to see those boys in future, you can visit them at Nancy's. After tonight's debacle, I totally wash my hands of all three.'

Little Vinny grinned as his girlfriend took her dressing gown into the bathroom. For some strange reason, Sammi-Lou would never get undressed in front of him, and Little Vinny found her shyness quite a turn on.

Obviously it was Sammi's natural beauty that had first attracted Little Vinny to her, but the fact she was no slag like most of the other girls he'd met had cemented their relationship. Sammi admitted that she'd slept with one lad before him, but it had been a serious relationship, not a one-night stand. It had taken Little Vinny six weeks to get her into bed.

When Sammi-Lou turned the light off and slipped under the quilt, Little Vinny kissed her then tried to ram his cock inside her as quickly as possible.

'No. Not yet,' Sammi whispered.

'What's up?'

Sammi-Lou said nothing as she began to kiss Little Vinny's neck and chest. Her best pal Charlene was currently dating a twenty-five-year-old and their sex life sounded far more exciting than hers. As much as Sammi loved and fancied her boyfriend, he was a bit of a 'Wham bam thank you, ma'am' merchant. There was no foreplay like Sammi had been used to with her ex, and although she pretended otherwise to Charlene, since she'd been with Little Vinny, Sammi hadn't had a single orgasm.

As his girlfriend's lips moved down his stomach towards his penis, Little Vinny froze. That toothless slag Alison Bloggs had been the first bird to put her mouth round his todger and she would most definitely be the last.

Feeling suddenly nauseous, Little Vinny roughly shoved Sammi-Lou's head away from her destination and leapt out of bed. He pointed a finger at her. 'Don't you ever fucking do anything like that again, understand?'

Sammi-Lou burst into tears. 'I was only trying to make you happy. I'm sorry. I thought you'd like it.'

'No, I don't like it! Only whores do stuff like that,' he hissed, a twisted expression on his face. He then stormed out of the room leaving Sammi-Lou sobbing her heart out on the bed.

CHAPTER EIGHT

The man breathed a sigh of relief as he laid eyes on Michael Butler. His boss would be pleased. At least this trip hadn't been a complete waste of time, like the last.

Clicking away with the specialized spy camera, the man wondered what this task was all about. Usually his boss was very open about such matters, but this time his lips were well and truly sealed.

As Michael Butler sauntered down the street like he owned it, the man smirked. Whatever plans his boss had in store for the cocksure-looking Michael, they wouldn't be pleasant, that was for sure.

Deborah Preston stared solemnly out of the car window. Just over a week had gone by since Johnny had told her he planned to visit Jamie in Feltham and she'd thought of little else since.

'Cheer up. Jo is gonna think something's wrong otherwise.'

Deciding to have one last attempt to make her husband change his mind, Deborah gave it her all. 'If you loved me as much as you say you do, Johnny, no way would you be putting me through such heartache. I've not slept or eaten properly all week. I just don't understand how you could even consider being in the same room as that animal. It doesn't make sense to me. Won't you feel the urge to stick a knife straight through his heart? Because I know I fucking well would.'

Realizing his wife was near to breaking point, Johnny parked up and took her in his arms. 'I need to visit Jamie for my own peace of mind. See what he's got to say for himself and watch him squirm. I owe it to Molly.'

Huffing and puffing, Albie Butler dragged another crate of mixers into the bar area.

'Dad, you look like you're gonna keel over. Sit down and I'll get you a drink. The bar staff can finish that off.'

At sixty-four, the years of heavy drinking and chain-smoking had begun to take their toll and nobody was more surprised he was still alive than Albie himself. 'No, boy. I like to earn my keep, you know I do.'

Not one to take no for an answer, Michael put an arm around his father's shoulders and made him sit down.

Albie grinned when Michael plonked a pint in front of him. He enjoyed pottering about at the club doing odd jobs five days a week. It made him feel useful, something he'd never felt in all the years he'd been married to Queenie.

As a young man, Albie had been handsome, full of life and could have had his pick of women. Queenie had done all the chasing and, after a whirlwind romance, Albie married her. Life was good until Queenie fell pregnant. From the moment Vinny was born, things had gone from bad to worse. Vivian was always at their house, and Albie was pushed to one side. No wonder he'd ended up a drunken womanizer. Queenie had only ever wanted sex to make babies, and Albie had spent more nights sleeping on the sofa than in their marital bed.

'What's up, Dad? You having a Dorothy moment?'

Albie sighed wistfully. He'd found love with a woman in later life. Dorothy was a wonderful lady who'd restored his faith in the female of the species. They'd been so happy living in Ipswich at his brother Bert's house, until she'd passed away suddenly. 'Sort of, boy. I wish I'd have married Dorothy instead of your mother. Then we could have spent many more happy years together.'

Michael sat down next to his father. He knew exactly how Albie felt. His own romance, with a model called Bella, had been short-lived but truly unforgettable. Michael had ended it for the sake of his boys, but he had never forgotten the stunning brunette who'd stolen his heart. He'd even tried to find her once, but had been told by the new tenants that Bella had moved to New York. Nancy had no knowledge of the affair. The only people who did were his dad and Vinny.

Hating to see his old man down, Michael playfully punched him on the arm. 'If you hadn't married me mother, then I would've never existed. Thanks very much, Dad.'

Albie smiled. Unlike Vinny, who'd once beaten him up so badly he'd ended up in hospital with broken legs and ribs, Michael had been a wonderful son. 'I'll never forget how kind you've been to me, boy. But I do worry what will happen when your brother gets out. He ain't gonna want me working here, is he?'

Michael gritted his teeth. He could foresee many problems on the horizon when Vinny got released, but was determined to stand his ground. 'You leave Vinny to me. Your job will be safe, I can assure you of that. I ain't Michael the kid brother any more. I am Michael the fucking adult and Vinny's going to have to accept that.'

Vivian was sitting on a deck chair in Queenie's back garden, reminiscing about the past. Kings Holiday Park in

Eastbourne had been such a big part of their lives, until Vinny started a ruckus that got them barred from the clubhouse.

'Do you remember that time you got pissed and tried to snog Des O'Connor, Viv? And you used to have the hots for that Mick who ran the amusement arcade.'

Vivian laughed. 'Talk about pot calling kettle! You might come across all prim and proper, but I know you fancied Ray King. You used to act all silly every time he pulled up in his Rolls-Royce. And what about the time you embarrassed yourself outside the launderette?'

Queenie felt her cheeks blush. Ray King had been the owner of the holiday park, and even though she'd most definitely had the hots for him, she'd never admit it, not even to Viv. Hurriedly she changed the subject: ''Ere, look – it's that thing that killed the bird I found earlier. Look at its eyes. They're evil,' she said, pointing at the ginger-and-white moggy who was sitting on the fence staring at her.

About to remark that the cat's eyes reminded her of Vinny's, Vivian bit her tongue. 'It's called Chester. I heard her next door calling it yesterday for its grub,' she said. 'I bumped into Nosy Hilda round the shops this morning and she filled me in on the set-up. That ain't her old man living there, it's her brother. The other tart is his wife. Them boys are hers though. Little sods they are, by all accounts. Hilda said they took the right piss out of Mr Arthur the other day 'cause he was wearing his war medals. And they've already been caught stealing off the market. Her name's Shell. The boys are Kurt and Brad. I can't remember the others' names, although Hilda did tell me.'

'Shell! What, as in a bleedin' sea shell? That's all we need, two little tea-leaves living next door. What's the betting they try to burgle us while we're up the Roman one Saturday?'

'I think we should knock there, Queen. Let 'em know exactly who we are. They need to show a bit of respect. Their music system must be right next to my lounge wall. I couldn't even hear me *Brookside* properly last night. They were playing that black man's music again. I'm not putting up with that.'

'It's Bob Marley.'

'Oh, is that her brother's name? I could have sworn blind Hilda said it was something different.'

'No. It's Bob Marley records they keep playing, you daft bat.'

About to ask who the hell Bob Marley was, Vivian gasped as the cat leapt off the fence and grabbed a little robin by its throat. 'Oh, my giddy aunt! Do something, Queen.'

Queenie picked up her hoe. She loved birds and welcomed them into her garden with the lovely bird table that she hung food from on a daily basis. 'Get away, you ginger-and-white bastard,' she screamed.

As the hoe came towards him, Chester fled without his prey. Queenie bent down and saw the terrified bird take its last breath. 'We won't be lowering ourselves by knocking there, Viv. I need a brandy to calm my nerves, then we'll ring Michael. He can do the honours. I must bury this bird first though. Poor little mite.'

Ahmed and Burak were on their way to the Butlers' club. Sunday lunchtimes were when the strippers performed and Ahmed liked to pop in at least twice a month as he knew Michael did not like him.

'Any more news on the kid?' Burak asked.

'I rang the private detective yesterday, but it went on to answerphone. If he does not get back to me in the next day or two, I will sack him and hire the guy that Tarkan recommended.'

'Please say if you think I am speaking out of turn, Ahmed, but I am bemused why Tarkan suddenly wants to be your best buddy. He's had no dealings with Vinny, so has no reason to hate him like we do. I find it slightly suspicious that he has found what is supposedly Vinny's daughter, yet could not find that prick Carl Thompson when he turned out to be such a fucking liability to us.'

'What are you trying to say? That Tarkan warned Thompson that I was trying to kill him? No way, Burak. I have known Tarkan for years and he wouldn't dare cross me. Us Turks stick together.'

'Tarkan's half English,' Burak reminded his cousin. 'So, what is the point of our visit today? To wind that flash wanker Michael up again?'

'No. Little Vinny rang me twice in the week. He seems extremely upset that his father's cellmate will soon be working at the club, and I think he's fallen out with his girlfriend as well. This is the perfect opportunity for us to entice him into our clutches again. Then on a drunken night out, I shall accidentally drop the bombshell that his daddy killed his mummy.'

Burak chuckled. He could never understand why his cousin hadn't just killed Vinny off years ago instead of waiting to have his revenge. But Ahmed was a complex character at times, and loved nothing more than fucking people up mentally.

As Ahmed laughed and joked, he had no idea that his cousin had been spot on in his estimation of Tarkan Smith. He was not the loyal friend Ahmed thought he was at all.

Ye Olde White Harte in Burnham-on-Crouch overlooked the quay where the boats and yachts were moored. The late-July weather was glorious and Johnny was thankful that not only had his wife cheered up, his daughter seemed on top form as well.

'Why you not eating your dinner, Ava?' Johnny asked, stroking his granddaughter's dark glossy hair.

Ava protruded her bottom lip as she often did when bored. 'Don't want it. Can I go and play?' she asked, pointing at two children who were skipping nearby.

Joanna looked around. Ava was a very bright child for her age. Her elocution was good and she often asked unusually intelligent questions for a child so young. She could even tell the time, and recite the alphabet in twenty seconds flat. 'Is it OK if my little girl plays with your children?' Joanna asked the couple on the table behind.

When they agreed and Ava left the table, Joanna turned to her parents. 'I've got something to tell you.'

Deborah grinned. She knew what was coming. Her daughter looked radiant. 'You've met a new man, haven't you?'

'It's early days, Mum, but he seems very nice. He's totally different to Vinny.'

Johnny was not so delighted by the news. 'Who is he? Where did ya meet him?'

'I met him when I went out with Nancy last weekend. His name's Darren, and he's divorced with a four-year-old son. We've not been out on a proper date yet, but we've spoken on the phone a lot and I met him for a coffee yesterday. I aim to take things slowly, of course, but Darren does seem really genuine.'

'You're hardly a good judge of character when it comes to geezers, are you, Jo? Look at the last one you fell for,' Johnny pointed out.

Annoyed that, having lectured her earlier about the need to lighten up, her husband now had a face on him like a smacked arse, Deborah ordered him to go to the bar to get some more drinks. 'So what does Darren do for a living, love?' she asked the moment he was gone.

'He's an estate agent, Mum, in Chelmsford. I never thought I would allow another man into my life, but we've spoken for hours every night on the phone this week and Darren's really nice. It gives me something to look forward to when Ava goes to bed. He makes me laugh and he seems a loving dad. I'm a bit nervous about going out with him alone, so do you think it would be a good idea to take the kids with us? Darren suggested we take them to Colchester Zoo next weekend.'

Johnny chuckled as he plonked the drinks on the table. He'd overheard the back-end of the conversation. 'You're so gullible. How do you know that Vinny hasn't tracked you down because he found out about Ava, eh? Darren could be working for him for all you know.'

Seeing her daughter's happy mood suddenly deflated, Deborah was livid. 'What the hell is wrong with you, Johnny? If anybody deserves to find happiness, it's our Jo. Do us a favour and go for a walk, will you? Ava wants an ice cream, so you can take her with you.'

Johnny grabbed Ava's hand. Perhaps he was a bit over-protective now. But he had every right to be after the Vinny debacle. Like any decent father, all Johnny wanted was the best in life for his daughter.

'Granddad, pick me up. I don't want to walk.'

Grinning at his cheeky granddaughter, Johnny did as she asked. What Johnny did not realize, as he held Ava above his head until she squealed, was that the private detective Ahmed had hired was snapping away behind him with his camera.

'It's hot and noisy in here. Let's go outside and have a chat,' Ahmed said, putting an arm around Little Vinny's shoulders. Burak was enjoying himself watching the strippers and Ahmed knew there was far more chance of the boy opening up to him if they spoke alone.

Eyes like a hawk, Michael followed his nephew. Approximately eighteen months ago, Little Vinny had gone off the rails for a while. He'd taken days off sick, looked like shit when he had turned up, and Michael was sure by his eyes he'd taken some kind of drug. Ahmed had been hanging around a lot at the time and even though Little Vinny had sworn blind that he'd not been spending time with Ahmed outside the club, Michael wasn't so sure. 'Where yous two going?' he asked, grabbing his nephew by the arm.

'Outside to cool down a bit. You really need to invest in some more of them fans that hang from the ceiling, Michael. It's like a sweatbox in here,' said Ahmed.

When Michael walked away looking none too happy, Ahmed smirked. Once outside in the fresh air, he began to sow his seed. 'What's all this about your father's cellmate starting work here then, Vin? You sounded well pissed off on the phone.'

Little Vinny explained the situation.

'Well, I can't say I blame you for having the hump. I bloody would too. There is a very close bond between your dad and Jay. Whenever I visit your old man or he writes to me, he is always praising the lad. I think your dad sees him as a second son. He must have big plans for him if he wants him to work at the club though.'

Feeling extremely agitated, Little Vinny glared at Ahmed. 'Whaddya mean, big plans? Has my old man said something to you? Only I'm the one that's made a success of this club with Michael. He said it was taking peanuts when my fucking father was in charge.'

Ahmed put a comforting arm around Little Vinny's shoulders. 'No. Your dad has said nothing about his plans for Jay to me. I shall be going to visit Vinny soon, so will have a quiet word to see what I can find out. That's just between us though.'

'Of course. Cheers, Ahmed. I've worked my bollocks off for the sake of this business and if my old man gets out and puts that cunt Jay above me in the pecking order, I will tell him to shove his job where the sun doesn't shine.'

'When is Jay due to arrive?'

'Soon. He got released from nick a few days after his brother died and travelled up to Liverpool. I think the funeral was on Friday, so I dare say he'll turn up this coming week.'

'I'm always on the end of the phone if you need me. What I reckon you would benefit from is a bloody good night out. How about we go up West in the week? Burak and I have found this great club. Everybody shags one another. You get some proper wild women in there, let me tell you,' Ahmed chuckled.

Little Vinny shook his head. 'I can't be going places like that now I'm with Sammi-Lou. She'd kill me if she ever found out.'

'How's it going with Sammi? From what you said the other day, I got the impression the two of you had had a falling out.'

Ever since the blow-job moment, things had been strained between himself and his girlfriend, and Little Vinny knew she had the hump with him as she'd spent the weekend in Clacton at her friend's parents' caravan. 'It's going OK. She's a bit full on at times, but I do love her, I think.'

Ahmed laughed. 'You're only eighteen. Far too young to know what true love is. You should be playing the field. You need to have many girlfriends to find the one. Then when you do, you marry her.'

Little Vinny respected Ahmed, but no way was he taking

relationship advice from him. Ahmed had married an English lady called Anna who he had two children with. He was rarely at home though and fucked anything that breathed. 'You know you just mentioned a night out. Well, it's Sammi-Lou's mum's fortieth next Saturday. Her dad's got a massive gaff in Essex and they're having a big party. Sammi told me to invite all my family, but Michael said he can't leave the club and my nan and Auntie Viv won't go. Will you come with me? I've only met Sammi's parents briefly a couple of times, and her old man makes me feel a right div, to be honest – and I won't know any bastard there.'

Ahmed grinned. This party would be the perfect opportunity to get Little Vinny back on the booze and into his clutches. 'I would be honoured to accompany you, my friend.'

Queenie Butler was that fuming, she slammed the phone down on her youngest son. That was the difference between her Vinny and Michael. Instead of laughing at her like Michael just had, Vinny would've been round like a shot.

'Well?' Vivian asked.

'He told us to knock there ourselves. He said, "That'll be the day I get into an argument 'cause a cat killed a bird." He reckons it's nature.'

'Why didn't you tell him about the bloody music, Queen? I can hear it through the wall now. They're playing it again.'

'Let's have another brandy, then we'll knock there. Talk about if you want anything done, do it your bleedin' self. Eight bastard hours I was in labour with my Michael, and what thanks do I get, eh? None.'

Singing along to 'Three Little Birds', Shell Baker put the paintbrush down and cracked open a can of lager. She'd been arsehole lucky to get this house after her sons Kurt and Bradley had got her evicted from their previous property in East Ham. Thankfully for Shell, her mate Dawn worked for Tower Hamlets council and had managed to pull a few strings.

Family and friends meant everything to Shell, which was why she'd invited her brother Karl and his wife Melissa to move in with her. They'd been living in a poxy old bedsit that was full of mould and damp, and stood far more chance of getting their own place via Tower Hamlets council than Newham.

When somebody started ferociously hammering on her door, Shell's first thought was that it was the Old Bill again. Then she reminded herself that Kurt and Brad were currently upstairs painting their bedroom, so couldn't have got in any more trouble since yesterday.

She opened the door to find her new neighbour on her doorstep, lips pursed and hands on hips, glaring daggers at her.

'That ginger and white thing belong to you?'

'If you're talking about a cat, yeah, that's my Chester.'

'Best you stop your Chester coming into my garden and killing my birds then. Murdered one right in front of us this morning, didn't he, Viv?'

'Yeah. Poor little robin was terrified,' Vivian added.

Shell looked at the two women like they'd just arrived from another planet. 'You are joking, right?'

'Do I look like I'm bastard-well joking? I spend a fortune every week on seeds and nuts for them birds. Breaks my heart to see them getting ripped to pieces.'

Shell burst out laughing. 'Karl, Mel, you gotta come and listen to this,' she shouted. Her brother and sister-in-law were in the lounge.

'Not going to hear you over that racket, are they? And that's another thing we wanted to talk to you about. If you think we're putting up with that shit blaring through our walls, you've got another think coming. Do you know who we are?' Vivian asked indignantly.

Holding her crotch because she was chuckling so much she was afraid she might wet herself, Shell burst into the lounge and gestured for Karl and Mel to follow her into the hallway.

Queenie and Vivian were appalled. They weren't accustomed to being laughed at. People were usually too scared to say a bad word to them, let alone take the piss.

'Meet our neighbours,' Shell guffawed. 'They've asked me to tell Chester not to go in their garden and kill the birds. Now do you want to tell him, or shall I, Karl? I think there's more chance of Chester listening to you. He understands you better than me.'

When the brother and sister-in-law also burst out laughing, a red-faced Queenie started to wag her forefinger. 'You'll be laughing on the other side of your faces once my family gets to hear about this, let me tell you.'

Hearing the commotion, Kurt and Bradley appeared. 'Shut up, you mad old bat,' Kurt told Queenie.

'My grandson will deal with you, you little shit. As for the rest of yous, watch your backs. I am Queenie Butler. Mother of *the* Vinny and Michael Butler who run this fucking area.'

Still laughing, Shell replied, 'And we're *the* Bakers. Nice to meet you. Now piss off!'

When the door was slammed in her face, Queenie felt faint. 'Hold me arm, Viv. Get me back indoors. I need another brandy.'

Feeling satisfied with his day's work, the man dialled the all-important number.

'Well?'

'Found him boss. I took plenty of photos that are already on their way to you. I have an address of a house where I believe his wife and sons live. Do you want photos of them too?'

The boss slammed the paperweight against his mahogany desk. 'Did you not understand my orders? I want photos of every fucking thing Michael Butler has contact with. Even his cunting pet dog.'

The man apologized and ended the call. If he were a betting man, he'd put his house on Michael Butler being dead this time next week.

CHAPTER NINE

Nancy Butler prodded her husband. 'Michael, wake up. That was my mum on the phone. Freda Smart is seriously ill, so I'm going to the hospital. Will you look after the boys today?'

Squinting at the radio/alarm clock, Michael was annoyed he'd been woken up so early. 'Freda Smart's a mad old bat and her fucking grandson dumped my sister while she was pregnant, in case you'd forgotten.'

'I know that, but Freda was really kind to me when I was ill in hospital, Michael. She hasn't got anybody else to visit her,' Nancy retorted.

'I've got to go to work today, so the boys will have to come with me.'

'I don't want them going to the club. Can't you have the day off and take them somewhere else?'

'No. I can't. Now stop rambling on and let me get some poxy kip.'

Mary Walker was unusually quiet throughout the journey to the hospital.

'You OK, Mum?' Nancy asked.

'I just hate going back to Whitechapel, love. Reminds me of our old café. Do you remember the interior, Nance?

103

You probably don't, as you were still quite young. Beautiful, that café was. I was heartbroken when we had to walk away from it.'

'I remember the red tables and chairs and the jukebox,' said Nancy, patting her mum's arm. 'I don't like coming back here either. It reminds me of Molly.'

'I wonder who's living in Molly's old house now?'

Nancy shrugged. 'I think Michael sold it to an Indian family. Let's hope they have more luck there than poor Jo did.' Vinny had instructed Michael to sell the house via a phone call from prison.

'I hope poor Freda knows who we are. She must be in a pretty bad way for the hospital to ring me so early. Shame, isn't it, love. Must be awful, not having any family to call upon at a time like this.'

Watching her mother struggle to get out of the car, Nancy issued a warning. 'It'll be you in hospital next if you put on any more weight, Mum.'

Mary sighed. She only weighted eleven stone something, but looked bigger because of her five-foot frame. Donald was a whole foot taller than her and when they'd met she'd been ever so petite with a tiny little waist. 'Thanks for that, Nance. It's not easy to lose weight at my age. You're lucky 'cause you're taller than me and still young.'

'Mum, you're fifty-two not seventy. Your sweet tooth is the bloody problem, not your height or age.'

'Has Michael upset you this morning, dear?' Mary asked knowingly.

Nancy nodded. 'I asked him to take the boys out some-where for the day, but he's taking them to work with him instead. It gives me the heebies, them going anywhere near that club after what happened to Molly. The place is jinxed.'

Mary linked arms with her daughter. 'Try not to worry too much. The boys are far more capable of looking after themselves than poor little Molly was. They'll most likely all be working there when they leave school anyway, Nance. So you might as well get used to it.'

Having prepared themselves for the worst, Mary and Nancy were surprised to see Freda propped up against a pillow reading the newspaper. She didn't look well though. Her skin and the whites of her eyes were the colour of egg yolks.

'Thanks for coming at such short notice. I really do appreciate it,' Freda said, before explaining her cancer was back and was now terminal.

Nancy squeezed the old lady's hand. 'Surely there must be something the doctors can do? Isn't there any treatment they can try?'

Freda shook her head. 'Riddled with the bastard disease, I am. Even spread to my liver now. Once it hits your vital organs, that's it – curtains.'

Mary had tears streaming down her face. She'd first met Freda back in 1965. Freda had barged into the café in Whitechapel one day to warn her and Donald how dangerous the Butler family were. At the time, Mary and Donald had dismissed her as some nutty local scaremonger. But Freda had been spot on. Over the years she'd become a valued friend and she would be sorely missed.

'Now stop all them tears. I'm no spring chicken, so I can't complain. I've had a decent innings. Open that drawer, Nancy. I wrote a list out last night. The doctor reckons I ain't got long left, so I need to get my affairs in order. You don't mind helping me, do you? I've no one else I can trust.'

Nancy forced a smile. 'Of course we'll help you.'

Michael Butler had just ordered himself and the boys some breakfast when his mother and Auntie Vivian marched into the café like two bulls in a china shop.

'There you are! I was ringing the club continuously last night and couldn't bloody get hold of you. I rung Nancy twice and she didn't know where you were. I wish some bastard would invent a phone you could carry around with you, else what's the point of having sons,' Queenie spat, completely ignoring her grandchildren.

Seeing a table full of workmen staring his way, Michael ordered his sons to stay put, then led his mum and aunt outside. 'I went out with me old mate Kev. I haven't seen him for yonks. What's the problem?'

When Queenie and Viv explained word for word about their altercation with the neighbours, Michael lit up a cigarette and inhaled deeply to calm his temper. Nobody around here dared disrespect his family. The locals were all too aware of what happened to those who did. Terry Smart, Trevor Thomas, Kenny and Bobby Jackson had all either disappeared or met a grizzly end after falling foul of the Butlers. No one else wanted to meet the same fate.

'Well? Don't just stand there like a stuffed dummy. What ya gonna do about it? Vinny would've been round there first time I asked. So would my Roy, God rest his soul.'

Michael dropped his cigarette, then stamped on it and twisted his foot as if he were snuffing out the life of a tarantula. 'Do you honestly still see me as your baby boy, Mum? Or that fresh-faced David Essex lookalike that birds used to chase down the road in the seventies? Or do you just see me as the weakest link of this family? Not up to Vinny's standards perhaps?'

'I didn't mean it like that. It was you who sorted Pervy Pat, so I know you're more than capable. I just meant that Vinny would've straightened them bastards out like a shot.'

Michael smirked. 'Well, thanks for the vote of confidence, but seeing as Vinny is currently being detained at Her Majesty's pleasure for his swift way of dealing with things, I shall sort out this problem in my own sweet time, Mum. It will be dealt with though, I can promise you that. Now, if you don't mind, I must excuse myself as my breakfast is getting cold.'

Queenie looked at Vivian in sheer amazement as Michael sauntered back into the café. 'Saucy bastard. Who the hell does he think he is, eh? I won't be insulted like that, Viv, not by one of me own.'

When her sister went to march back inside the café, Vivian grabbed her arm. 'Leave it, Queen. Michael does have a point and I trust him to deal with those bastards next door.'

'But he totally disrespected me.'

'You were very disrespectful to him. He proved himself good and proper when he chopped that pervert's dingle-dangle off. Believe me, that boy has more brains and integrity than you give him credit for. He's a better man than Vinny will ever be, and that's a fact.'

Johnny Preston felt as sick as a dog as he queued up inside Feltham Borstal. His mother had wanted to accompany him, but Johnny had refused. He needed to do this alone.

Once searched, Johnny was led away from the other visitors and taken down the corridor. Because of who he was he'd been allowed to speak to his nephew away from the prying eyes and listening ears of other inmates and their families.

'Here we are. There will be four prison officers in the room with you for security purposes.'

'I would much rather speak to Jamie alone.'

'I'm afraid that won't be possible. The guvnor's orders, not mine. Jamie has been involved in numerous violent altercations while in our care, so the boss didn't want to take any chances. He doesn't allow many visits of this kind, so you're lucky you've got one.'

Knowing it was now or never, Johnny took some deep breaths to try to calm himself. He couldn't lose it in there, because if he did and got himself arrested, Deborah would probably divorce him.

'You OK?' the screw asked.

Johnny leaned against the wall and nodded. 'Just give me a minute.' The last time he could remember his heart beating at such a frantic pace was when he'd been plotted up outside that club waiting to shoot Vinny, and that hadn't turned out too well. He'd drunk Scotch to calm his nerves and had accidentally shot Roy Butler instead. 'I'm ready now.'

The first thing that struck Johnny as he entered the room was how different Jamie looked. He was eighteen now, full of muscle and had the body of a man rather than a teenager. His dark hair was cropped, and he had a big scar that ran diagonally from his right ear to the corner of his mouth.

'Thanks for coming, Uncle Johnny. I had doubts you'd show up.'

Johnny was sure that, had he not been in prison when she was born, had he met his granddaughter, held her in his arms, read her bedtime stories and got to know her little personality, no way could he have stomached this visit. Perhaps the reason he was able to face Jamie was because the only memory he had of Molly was a couple of photographs.

Pulling the chair out from under the table, Johnny sat down opposite his nephew. Jamie had the same piercing green eyes as Vinny, which was no surprise seeing as it was now common knowledge they were half-brothers. 'Cut the "Uncle Johnny" bollocks, and say what you gotta say. I don't wanna be anywhere fucking near you, so the quicker you spill your guts and I can get out of here, the better.'

Jamie stared directly into his uncle's eyes. 'I asked Nan to speak to you because I wanted you to hear my side of the story. I've been framed, Johnny, and you are the only one who can help me. I am so sorry about what happened to Molly. You and your family must have been to hell and back, but I didn't kill her. I swear to God, I never.'

'Pull the other leg, it's got fucking bells on,' Johnny hissed.

'What type of monster do you think I am, eh? I could never hurt a little kid. I promise you, if I'd been guilty of such a despicable act, I'd have killed myself by now. What type of cunt could live with themselves after murdering a three-year-old? Not me, that's for fucking sure.'

If it hadn't been for the four prison officers standing guard, Johnny would have lunged across the table and beaten his nephew black and blue. How dare he have the front to do what he'd done and then blatantly lie about it?

'I want to speak to the police and urge them to re-open the case. Molly's killer needs to be caught.'

Johnny looked at Jamie in disbelief. 'As if the Old Bill are gonna do that. You were caught with a bedroom full of newspaper cuttings, you'd been ripping missing posters off walls and fucking lampposts, you even rung up the cunting police station and told them you had taken Molly. You were seen sat opposite the club on the day she went missing. Have you hit your head since you've been in here? The police got you bang to rights, boy, and you know it. Now why don't you do me a favour and just admit it. It's upsetting your nan the way you keep pleading your innocence. You're making her ill.'

Eyes brimming with tears, Jamie shook his head furiously. 'No way would I ever admit to something I didn't do. It's bad enough that the whole world sees me as a child-killer when I'm fucking innocent. I'll hold my hands up to the newspaper cuttings, ripping the posters down and phone calls. That was wrong – bang out of order, in fact – and there isn't a day goes by when I don't regret it. But I was fourteen years old, for fuck's sake. And I only did that shit because I hated Vinny so much. He tried to make my mother abort me – as you well know – and I blamed him for Mark's death. That night we started the fire at Vinny's club, Mark was climbing out the window when some evil cunt pulled him back in that storeroom. It had to be Vinny or a member of his staff. I can still hear Mark's screams now as he burned to death. I could even smell his flesh being cooked,' Jamie wept. Mark had been his older half-brother and they'd been so very close.

'So you killed Molly to get back at Vinny. Is that what you're trying to say?'

'How many more times have I got to tell you, Johnny? I didn't fucking touch Molly. I never even met her, let alone strangled her. The police found not one shred of evidence connecting me to Molly's body or the area where she was found. I'd never even heard of that place, let alone been there.'

'But you admitted you were sat opposite the club on the day she went missing.'

'Yeah, I was. It would have been Mark's eighteenth that day. I was upset, which is why I bought some cider and drowned my sorrows. If I had planned to snatch Molly you don't honestly think I would be sitting opposite the club so the whole world could see me, do you?'

Johnny shrugged. 'Well, you was silly enough to do all the other stuff, so why not? Hardly fucking Einstein, are you?'

'No. But I'm no Ian Brady either!' Jamie banged his fist on the table and all four prison guards instantly took a step forward. He raised his hands in apology, took a couple of deep breaths to bring his temper under control and then continued: 'Listen, I found out something recently which I want you to tell the Old Bill. They won't listen to me, but they might you.'

'What?'

Jamie put his elbows on the table and leaned towards his uncle. 'There's a lad from Whitechapel in here. Good pal of mine. Did you know that Little Vinny's best mate topped himself around the time of Molly's funeral?'

Johnny shook his head.

'Don't you find that odd? Why would a young lad with his whole life in front of him want to hang himself down Hainault forest for no reason, eh? Guilt maybe? Word is, he was a right oddball, into glue-sniffing and all sorts. Perhaps the little weirdo couldn't live with something bad he'd done? You get my drift?'

Johnny shrugged. He was feeling more uneasy by the second, truth be told. Jamie certainly did not have the demeanour of a guilty person. Quite the opposite, in fact.

'Do you mind if I tell you what it was like in here at the beginning for me, Johnny?'

Johnny stared deep into Jamie's eyes. 'Go on.'

'Every single day I got tortured. Word got round very quickly what I was in here for, and I wasn't just branded a child-killer but also a fucking nonce-case. I was actually glad when I got stabbed in the gut then beaten so badly that I was unconscious for hours and had glass put in my food, because each time something like that happened it meant I got to stay in hospital for a bit. That was the only break I got from the bullying. Somebody even tried to set me alight while I was sleeping – got the burns on my back to prove it. And do you know the only thing that stopped me taking my own life?'

His complexion now drained of colour, Johnny shook his head.

'No way did I wanna die without clearing my name first. To kill myself would've been the easy way out and, like yourself, I'm a fighter. However, I'm off to big boys' prison soon and you can guarantee that, once I'm in there, Vinny will see to it my life comes to an end. That's why I'm so glad you came today. I wanted you to know the score, and if I'm not around to tell the tale, get justice on my behalf. Not just for me, but for Nan's sake, your family's, and most of all poor little Molly's. If Little Vinny's mate didn't do it, then Molly's killer is still walking the streets and is bound to strike again one day. Once evil, always evil, Johnny.'

CHAPTER TEN

Vinny Butler was doing some one-armed press-ups when Frank unlocked his cell. Vinny had a decent relationship with most of the screws on his wing. He caused them no grief, and they caused him no grief. With Frank, however, it was different. Frank was the one that Vinny had well and truly in his grasp.

The old screw stepped inside the doorway, put his hand down his trousers and fished out a carrier bag which he handed to Vinny. 'I'll have to bring you the Scotch later,' he said apologetically. 'My balls would've looked like King Kong's otherwise.'

Vinny chuckled. Frank was a comical and wily old bastard. That was why Vinny had chosen him to be his link to the outside world. Every week Frank would receive an envelope through the post via Michael. It covered the cost of anything Vinny required, plus fifty quid on top for services rendered. 'Cheers, pal. You're a diamond.'

'And you're a bleedin' pest. You'll get me hung, drawn and quartered one day, Butler.'

'Good. Then you can get out of this shithole and come and work for me at the club.'

Frank gave him a wink then ducked back out into the

corridor. Once he was alone, Vinny studied his new gadget. Since Jay Boy's release, Vinny had been bored shitless. He put the earphones on and flicked through the radio stations. Stopping on one that was playing the Kinks 'You Really Got Me', Vinny grinned. 'Whoever invented this Sony Walkman, I fucking love you,' he mumbled.

'What's up, boss?' Paul asked, as he and Pete sat down in Michael's office.

'I need a favour. I want you to follow a geezer for me, keep an eye on his movements. You know the score: find out if there's a regular pattern that he follows, which local he drinks in, which pals or lady friends he drops in on.'

'Anyone we know?' Pete asked.

Michael explained the situation with his mother's new neighbours. 'Nobody gets away with disrespecting my family, lads. Don't worry, I'm not going to do anything too severe. But I need to let this Karl Baker know exactly what and who he is dealing with.'

'When do you want us to start following him?' Paul asked.

'Tonight. Take it in turns, if you want, but you're probably better to work together, otherwise you'll be bored as fuck. Don't worry about the club. Me and Little Vinny can manage that. We never get any trouble on grab-a-granny night anyway.'

Pete nodded. 'OK boss. We'll park up near your mum's house about six-ish.'

Hearing the scrape of chairs signalling the end of the meeting, Daniel, Lee and Adam stopped earwigging at the door and scarpered in the direction of the toilets. All three had clearly heard their father say that Shell Baker's two sons had insulted their nan.

'Right, this is the plan,' Daniel told his brothers. 'Soon as Dad comes out of his office we're gonna tell him we're bored and we want to go out to play. Then we'll head round Nan's and see if we can spot those boys.'

Still only nine years old, Adam wasn't quite as clued up as his older brother. 'What we gonna do when we find them?' he asked innocently.

Daniel gave Adam a gentle tap around the head. 'Beat 'em up, you div, what else?'

Nancy had hoped that a bite of lunch in the pub would lift their mood, but it wasn't doing the trick.

'I can't eat, love. I'm really not hungry,' Mary said, putting her knife and fork down and pushing the plate away.

'Freda would hate us to be moping about, Mum. And think how pleased she will be when we pop back to the hospital and tell her what Mrs Bullock said.'

Mary forced a smile. One of Freda's main concerns had been the welfare of her two cats. Mrs Bullock, who lived opposite Freda, had been taking care of them since she'd been in hospital and had now agreed that the cats could live with her permanently.

Freda's other main concern was Dean. She was adamant that her grandson must not attend her funeral. If he did, there was every likelihood that the Butlers would be there waiting for him. They'd never forgiven him for running out on Brenda; the fact she was an absolute cow and had made his life hell was no excuse in their eyes. When you married a Butler, you were stuck with them until they decided they'd had enough of you.

'I'm dreading ringing Dean, Mum. How do you word something like this?'

'He already knows about the cancer, love. Freda said she'd told him.'

'Yeah, I know that. But it's still awkward, isn't it?'

'Just try to be upbeat. Tell Dean that we went to see his nan and she was her usual bubbly self. Say she's in no pain, that type of thing. Whatever you do, don't tell him she looks yellow and we've been asked to carry out her final wishes, 'cos then he'll be round like a shot. The whole point of your calling him is to make sure he doesn't visit her or turn up at the funeral. Freda knows what good friends you and Dean were and she feels he'll listen to you.'

'I'm not very good at lying though, Mum.'

Mary squeezed her daughter's hand. Nancy was soft and took after her, whereas Christopher was very much like his father. 'You won't be lying, darling, just playing down the truth a bit. And you'll be doing it for a very good reason: it's the dying wish of a lovely lady who has been good to us.' There was a tremble in her voice as she added, 'I only hope you can convince Dean to stay away. Because if you don't, I'm afraid the Butlers will see to it we'll be burying him too.'

'What's up, boy? You seem quiet today.' Albie was worried about his eldest grandson; it wasn't like him to be moping around the place.

'Sammi-Lou is being really off with me. I've got a feeling she's going to pack me in.'

Albie put an arm around Little Vinny's shoulders. Since they'd lived together, they'd become close. 'Perhaps it's for the best, lad. A handsome boy like you could have your pick of the ladies, and you want to play the field before you even think of settling down.'

'How old was you and me nan when you met?'

'I was twenty-three, your nan sixteen. We were married within a year, and then your dad was born the year after. It was all too much too soon, Vin. Times have changed and people don't settle down so young. Back in the olden days you had to get wed just to get your end away.'

'Really?'

'Yeah. Don't get me wrong, there were a few that put out. I remember losing my virginity up against a tree to Marjorie Hopkins. All the blokes had her, but no decent girl back in my day would have sex before marriage. You've got it made in this day and age, which is why you should take full advantage of it.'

'Don't you like Sammi-Lou?'

'I think Sammi's a lovely girl, Vin. But she reminds me of your nan the way she turns up round home and here all the time. Your nan was like my bleedin' shadow. Everywhere I looked, there she was. She was pretty back in the day though. Looked like a film star, she did.'

Little Vinny chuckled. He couldn't imagine his nan ever being pretty and was about to crack a joke about his granddad's eyesight when the buzzer sounded.

'I'll get it. It's probably Michael's boys,' he said.

'All right, kidda? Michael about?' Jay Boy asked Little Vinny.

'Who you calling a kid?' Little Vinny spat. In his navy Lacoste round-necked jumper and faded jeans, Jay Boy looked much cooler now than he had on the inside. He also had muscles in all the right places, which pissed Little Vinny off no end, because regardless of how much he ate, he could never gain any weight or muscle.

Jay Boy chuckled. Vinny had told him to expect this kind of welcome off his son, so he was well prepared. 'Kidda's a saying from where I come from. We speak differently to yous cockneys. Your uncle about, is he?'

'Michael's in the office with his accountant. He said not to disturb him. What's with the case?' Little Vinny asked.

'You not spoken to your dad lately?'

'No.'

'Your old man wants me to stop at the club, keep an eye on the gaff, like. He said you once had a fire and he hates it when nobody's here through the night now. Don't worry. He's given me permission to use his bedroom. I'll unpack me stuff now, eh?'

Absolutely fuming, Little Vinny marched into the office. 'Michael, you better get out here, now!'

After a soothing brandy, Queenie Butler had now calmed down and was chatting to Vivian about Princess Diana. Staunch royalists, both women were extremely excited that the princess was nearing her due date.

'I reckon she'll have a girl this time, Queen. I might pop in Corals and have a bet on the name.'

'Nah. I reckon it's gonna be a little brother for William, and I have a hunch Charles and Di will call him George.'

'If it's a boy, wouldn't it be lovely if they called him Leonard after my Len? Prince Leonard has a lovely ring to it,' Vivian said wistfully.

About to reply, Queenie was disturbed by the doorbell. 'Bleedin' nuisance. Who is it, Viv? Can you see?'

Vivian peered through the curtain. Both she and Queenie hated visitors. 'They're standing too close to the door. Tell 'em to sod off, whoever it is.'

Queenie opened the front door and was dismayed to see Michael's three boys on her doorstep. Since Molly had been so cruelly taken from her, Queenie had neither the patience nor desire to play the doting grandma. That little girl had been truly special, whereas the boys were right little bastards. 'What do yous three want?'

'We just wondered if we could sit in your garden for a bit, Nan? We've been playing football and we're thirsty,' Daniel lied. He'd actually heard voices coming from next door's back garden and wanted to get a closer look at the boys he planned to attack.

'Wait there and I'll get you some lemonade and choc ices,' Queenie said.

'Why don't Nan ever let us in her house?' Adam asked.

At that precise moment, a door slammed and Daniel spotted his prey. 'Sod Nan – come on, let's follow 'em.'

'I think they're older than us, Dan. The tall one definitely is,' Lee warned. He didn't particularly fancy a confrontation with older lads. It was far too dangerous.

'Dan, let's go back to Nan's. I want me choc ice,' Adam pleaded, chasing after his brothers.

'Yeah, let's go back, Dan. It's not fair on Adam,' Lee urged his brother.

'Stop acting like a pair of girls. There's three of us and two of them. Oi, I wanna word with you,' Daniel yelled, running towards the two lads.

Fourteen-year-old Kurt and twelve-year-old Brad chuckled as the stupid kid began issuing threats. 'Go home to your mummy before you get hurt, little boy,' Kurt mocked.

'I'm a Butler, you mug. You really don't know who you're dealing with, do you?' Daniel retorted, before letting fly with his fists.

As a proper scrap broke out, Lee had no choice but to join in. Daniel was getting battered.

Petrified, young Adam stood rooted to the spot.

Another perk of having the screws wrapped around his little finger was the amount of phone usage Vinny was allowed. He still queued up with the other inmates to make some calls, but Frank would often take him out the cell so he could ring his family or friends in private. They'd got caught by the governor once, and Frank had told him that one of Vinny's family was ill and the call was an emergency.

Today, for the first time ever, Vinny wished he did not have that privilege. Ahmed had something of the utmost importance to tell him, but would not spill the beans over the phone. His mother was having grief with her new neighbours, which pissed Vinny off immensely. Now Michael was giving it large, yet again.

'Where did you expect Jay to sleep, eh? He comes from Liverpool, so has no contacts in Whitechapel. He's also just come out of nick and doesn't have a pot to piss in. Anyway, what's it got to do with you? It's my bastard bedroom.'

When Michael started arguing that the club was half his, he wasn't comfortable with a stranger living there and it wasn't fair on Little Vinny, Vinny punched the wall in frustration. That was the worst thing about being banged up. The people whose lights you wanted to punch out, you couldn't. 'Don't fuck with me, bruv, because you'll regret it if you do. If it wasn't for Jay Boy, I would never have got through this sentence. I owe him, which is why I want to help him, especially now his brother's dead. What you seem to forget, Michael, is that if it wasn't for me, both you and Little Vinny would be piss poor. It was mine and Roy's brains that set up the Butler empire. You really have become a bit too big for your boots lately, and I won't stand for it.'

'What ya gonna do about it then?' Michael asked brazenly.

'I will tell you what I'll fucking do about it, shall I? We might have started out as equal partners, bruv, but when Roy died his share was transferred into my name. On paper, that means you only own thirty-three and a third per cent of our business, Mister Cocky Bollocks. Mess with me and I swear on Mum's life, I'll offer to sell my share to Ahmed. Who would you rather work with? Him or me?'

It was now Michael's turn to punch the wall. 'You make me sick to the stomach, Vinny. You've no morals whatsoever. Worked my nuts off while you've been away to make sure you've got a nice nest egg to come home to and this is how you repay me. You are one slippery cunt.'

'No, I'm not. Roy's share was only put in my name to keep things simple at the time. Providing you stop acting like Billy Big Balls, I'll change it as soon as I get out this shit-hole. I don't wanna keep arguing with you, Michael, for Mum's sake more than anything else.'

Michael sighed. 'All right. Jay can stay, providing he proves his worth. But I'm warning you, don't ever threaten me like that again. I'm not the mug you think I am.'

'Well, I'm glad we've got that sorted. And while we're on the subject of threats, you need to make sure Mum and Auntie Viv don't get any more agg. Comprende?'

'It's already in hand.'

'Good. I'll send you another VO so you can let me know the score,' Vinny replied. He would never discuss anything that could come back and haunt him over a prison phone. You never knew who was listening in on conversations.

'OK. I've gotta go now. Some bastard has got their finger stuck to the buzzer.'

Vinny grinned as he replaced the receiver on top of its cradle. He hadn't seen his brother since the last visit when it had all kicked off, but was looking forward to their next encounter. Nobody was clever enough to get one over on him, Michael included.

Deborah Preston looked at her husband in pure astonishment. Was he trying to say what she thought he was? Or were her ears deceiving her? 'Just get to the point, Johnny. I know you've been drinking. You're rambling. Why didn't you come straight home?'

'I needed a drink to deal with the shock. He's innocent, Deb. Jamie didn't kill Molly.'

Her face etched with fury, Deborah picked up the saucepan

and slammed it so hard against the kitchen counter the potatoes flew out. 'You stupid, stupid man! The police caught that evil little bastard red-handed, so how dare you sit there and tell me he's innocent. If Jo gets wind of any of this it will break her heart. I'm disgusted with you, Johnny.'

'I might be a lot of things, but stupid ain't one of 'em, Deb. Once I explain everything you'll understand. Sit down and I'll go over the visit word for word.'

Deborah stormed towards Johnny like a bull to a red rag. 'No way will you mention that murdering lowlife's name in this house ever again. I've had enough, Johnny. You never knew Molly. She was the most beautiful, enchanting little girl I have ever met and I will not allow you to tarnish her memory by sticking up for the callous cunt that killed her. Get out! Go on, piss off back to your mother's. It's that scheming old witch with her deluded theories that's caused all this. Yous two are a match made in heaven. Like mother like son.'

Michael Butler looked at his watch. It was getting late and he couldn't put off ringing Nancy any longer. His wife was going to go ballistic when he told her what had happened, he knew that much. 'Will you be OK for five minutes, boys? I need to ring your mum and find a doctor to see where your bloody X-ray results are. We've been here for over three hours now.'

Lying side by side in separate beds were Daniel and Lee. Both had taken a beating, but it was Daniel who'd come off worse. All Lee had was a wobbly front tooth, a cut lip that had needed two stitches and a headache. Poor Daniel was in horrendous pain and had also needed stitches around the corner of his left eye.

'We're OK, Dad. Go and ring Nancy,' Lee said. His own mother had died in a car crash when he was young, and even though Nancy had played the role of his mum for years, Lee would never refer to her as such. He still remembered his own mum, and also recalled that Nancy had hated him at first.

'You come with me, Adam,' Michael ordered. There was something about Daniel and Lee's story that didn't add up and he knew it would be easier to get the truth out of his youngest son.

Wincing when Daniel slyly pinched him, Adam shook his head. 'No, Dad. I wanna stay here with me brothers.'

'OK. I won't be long.'

When his dad walked away, Daniel rounded on his brothers. 'You're not convincing enough, especially you, Adam. We have to stick to the story I made up.'

'Why don't we just tell Dad the truth, Dan? That old man who helped us knew who we were, and that lady came over. If Dad finds out we lied, he'll go mental,' Lee warned.

'He'll go even more mental if we tell him the truth. Do you want to see him locked up like Uncle Vinny? 'Cos that's what'll happen, I'm telling ya. We're not kids any more, Lee. Well, I ain't anyway. I wanna sort this out myself.'

Adam felt a shiver of fear run down his spine. 'What ya gonna do then, Dan?'

Daniel sank back on the bed as a bolt of pain shot through his left shoulder bringing tears to his eyes. 'I'm gonna get better first, then decide. But they ain't getting away with this.'

Little Vinny Butler was not a happy chappy. Michael wasn't working because of some family emergency. Pete and Paul had been given the night off, and the club was absolutely heaving.

'You OK, boy? Sight for sore eyes in 'ere tonight, eh? I thought because it was an over-twenty-nines night most would be in their thirties. But I've seen at least ten women who look as old as me, and they had mini-skirts on. I can't imagine your nan ever dressing like that, or Viv, can you?'

'We don't call it grab-a-granny night for nothing. Fucking old slags the lot of 'em.'

Knowing his grandson was teetotal now, Albie pointed to his glass. 'Is that beer you're drinking?'

'Cider,' Little Vinny replied, pushing away some old trout who was singing along to Gloria Gaynor's 'I Will Survive' while wriggling seductively in front of him.

'Don't be so boring. Come and have a dance with us,' the old trout's friend said, grabbing Albie by the arm.

Years ago, Albie would've been in his element. He was sixty-four now though, and not one of the women in the club could ever hold a candle to his Dorothy. 'No thank you, love. You go and dance with your friend.'

'In other words fuck off, unless you want to get barred,' growled Little Vinny.

When the women scuttled off, Albie put a protective arm around his grandson's shoulders. As a rule, he never worked in the club of an evening and had only stayed on tonight because Little Vinny had begged him to. 'Jay will never be as important to this club like you are, boy. Me and your dad may not see eye to eye on a lot of things, but I do know he idolizes you. You're the only child he has now, therefore you'll always come first.'

'Will I fuck! Last time I visited him all he did was take the piss out of what I was wearing. You were right about me dad all along, Granddad. He's a proper cunt.'

Albie looked on worriedly as his grandson ordered more drinks. His eyes were already glazed, which was hardly surprising considering he hadn't touched a drop of alcohol for Christ knows how long.

Little Vinny kicked the bar in annoyance. He'd spent the

early part of the evening working the door with Jay, which was why he was so wound up. What was it about that cropped-haired thug with his squashed nose that women liked so much? True, most of them were old mooses he wouldn't touch with a bargepole, but it still got his back up to see every single tart that walked through the door flirting with the Liverpudlian. 'What has that wanker got that I ain't, eh, Granddad?'

'Whadd'ya mean, boy?'

'He has every bastard eating out of his hand. All the bar staff were bigging him up earlier and all the birds were swooning over him like he was that Richard Gere bloke in *An Officer and a Gentleman*. Even me old man thinks Jay's the dog's bollocks. I just don't get it.'

Albie knew exactly why Jay Boy was so popular. He'd stood on the door for an hour with him earlier when his grandson had stormed off in a huff. Like himself back in the day, Jay had the gift of the gab. He was full of charm and cheeky one-liners, and women loved that, especially if teamed with good looks. Michael was the same, and the girls had always buzzed around him like flies around shit.

'Answer me then, Granddad. What am I gonna do if Sammi-Lou fancies him as well? I'll fucking kill him if he tries flirting with her.'

Albie sighed. As much as he loved his grandson, the lad had definitely inherited some of Vinny's traits. Little Vinny was a nicer person than his father, but he had the same not-so-bubbly personality and hot temper, and like his dad he was a nightmare in drink. 'You're being paranoid, Vin. Jay is older than you, so of course he's gonna have more to say for himself. As for him being better looking and your Sammi fancying him, don't make me laugh. Every time I go out with you, the birds can't take their eyes off ya. And d'ya know why?'

Little Vinny shook his head.

'Because you look exactly like your old granddad did when he was young.'

When his grandson chuckled, Albie thought his bad mood had passed and it was safe to leave his side. 'I need a tiddle, boy. Wait here – I won't be a tick.'

Little Vinny finished his drink and was signalling to the barman for another when he noticed the bloke standing next to him at the bar. He was wearing white trousers and a Hawaiian shirt and looked a complete and utter tosser. About to start mocking the chap, Vinny felt a tap on his shoulder, turned around and froze. He hadn't seen Stephen Daniels since his school days and had no desire to.

'How's it going, Vin? Sorry to hear about Ben. No hard feelings, eh?'

Stephen was the ring leader of the gang who'd terrorized Ben Bloggs at school. The bullying had only stopped when Little Vinny had borrowed his father's gun and scared the life out of Daniels and his cronies. 'Get out my fucking club, you druggie cunt,' he snarled.

'Chill, Vin. I only said hello. I've not even taken no drugs.'

Nobody batted an eyelid as Stephen was dragged past them. The punters were far more interested in chucking themselves about to Black Lace's 'Agadoo'. It was the latest silly chart craze.

'What's going on?' Jay Boy asked.

'You fucking thick, or what? Look at the junkie prick. Do you honestly think we allow this type of clientele in our club?'

'Give me a break, Vin. It's my first night and I've been stuck out here on my own for most of it. Sorry if I didn't get a chance to check the customers' arms for needle marks.'

Ignoring Jay's sarcasm, Little Vinny marched Stephen outside the club and into the alleyway where the bins were kept. He then slammed his head against the brick wall. 'Proud of picking on Ben now he's dead, are ya?'

'Look, I don't want no agg, Vin. Let me grab me mates and we'll leave,' Stephen pleaded. Little Vinny threatening to shoot him had been the scariest moment of his life, and no way did he ever want to endure a repeat performance.

Eyes blazing with temper, Little Vinny lost it completely. 'How dare you have the front to turn up 'ere, knowing Ben was dead. I'm gonna fucking kill ya,' he yelled, grabbing an empty bottle from the bin and repeatedly striking Stephen over the head with it.

Hearing the commotion, Jay Boy quickly stepped in. He'd only known Little Vinny half a day and could already tell he was damaged goods. The kid was an idiot and nothing like his father.

'Get off me, you Scouse prick,' Little Vinny yelled, trying to break free from Jay's firm grasp.

Jay lessened his hold on the boy. 'Shut your trap, you little shit. Just do one will ya, before the bizzies arrive. I'll sort this mess out – and believe me I'm not doing it for you, I'm doing it for your old man.'

Aware that there were now a few revellers watching, Little Vinny decided to take his dad's pal's advice. He took one last look at Stephen, who was lying motionless on the ground, then legged it.

The man stood facing the hospital smoking a cigar.

When Michael Butler appeared with his three sons, the man frantically clicked away with his camera.

He felt no emotion whatsoever that the boys were surely destined to be fatherless soon. In his line of work you needed a mind of steel and a heart of stone.

CHAPTER ELEVEN

'So, how long am I gonna get the silent treatment for, eh, Nance? Or are you just planning on moving back in with Mummy and Daddy like you always do if things don't go your way?'

Blanking her husband, Nancy loaded up the dishwasher. She was furious Michael had taken the boys to the club against her wishes, and even more livid that they had got into an altercation with some older boys while roaming the streets of Whitechapel. Was Michael incapable of even looking after his sons?

'Do you know what, you were more mature at sixteen when we first started dating than you are now. Why can't you just say what's on your mind like any other normal human being would, eh? It beats acting like a sulky child.'

Nancy glared at her husband. With his thick dark hair worn lightly Brylcreemed to the side and his smart designer suits, Michael was just as handsome as he'd been the day they first got together. But there was a thin line between love and hate, and Nancy often swung from one emotion to the other. 'OK. I'll tell you what's on my mind. The more I think about it lately, the more I realize what a shit father you are, Michael. One day I ask you to perform your parental duties, and look what happens: two of our sons end up needing hospital treatment.'

'You can't blame me because a couple of older boys jumped 'em, Nance. They were bored at the club and asked if they could go out and play football. They're not fucking five any more. We can't wrap 'em up in cotton wool for ever. I know what happened is unfortunate, but that's life. They're home now, so there's no real harm done. Myself, Vinny and Roy were always getting into scraps when we were kids. It's what boys do.'

Nancy looked at Michael as if he were from another planet. How could he say no real harm had been done when both boys had stitches and one had been left with a broken collarbone? The doctor said Daniel would have to wear a sling for a month at the very least until the fractured clavicle healed. 'I really don't understand how your brain works at times. Our sons are going off the rails and you truly think that is normal. When will you wake up and smell the coffee, eh? When one of them gets stabbed, or shot, or ends up in borstal? Then again, in that family you come from, that's normal, isn't it?'

'Why do you always have to slag off my family every time we argue? My mum and aunt have been nothing but kind to you over the years. You knew what I was when we first got together, Nance. You knew exactly what you'd signed up for, so don't play the innocent victim with me. I've been a good husband to you and a brilliant father to our sons. When have any of yous gone without, eh? I even bought you a Porsche – which you refused to drive, you ungrateful cow,' Michael yelled. The car he was currently driving about in was actually Nancy's unwanted birthday present.

'You know I've never been a confident driver, so why buy me such a fast car in the first place? To make yourself look good, probably. And as for you being a brilliant father and good husband, don't make me fucking laugh! We do nothing together as a family and you spend hardly any time whatsoever with me or the boys. I spoke to my old school friend Rhonda the other day. Her husband takes her boys to judo, swimming and football. You do sod-all with ours, which is why they probably keep getting in bloody trouble. And Rhonda and her husband have regular family days out and holidays. When was the last time we did anything as a family, Michael?'

'I offered to take the boys to a boxing club last month, Nance, and you said no. Vinny was right about you. You're a definite psycho.'

She was about to retaliate when Adam wandered into the kitchen. 'We're all awake now, Mum. Can you make us some bacon sandwiches?'

Nancy snatched her handbag off the kitchen counter. 'Mummy's got to go out, but I'm sure if you ask your brilliant father, he'll be more than happy to oblige.'

Vinny Butler was deep in thought as he made his way towards the visiting area. He knew Ahmed had something of extreme importance to tell him and had been unsuccessfully racking his brains as to what that might be.

Ahmed grinned as his so-called friend sat down. He couldn't wait to see Vinny's reaction when he told him the life-changing news. 'You're looking well, my friend. Still training, I take it?'

Vinny hated being kept in any kind of suspense and had never been one to beat around the bush. 'What was it you couldn't tell me over the phone?'

'I have made a very interesting discovery on your behalf, Vinny. A very interesting discovery indeed.'

'Spit it out then,' Vinny ordered, furtively glancing around to check that nobody was listening.

Ahmed leaned forward. 'You have a daughter. Her name is Ava and she looks just like you.'

Vinny's face drained of colour. He felt as though the room was spinning around in front of his very eyes. 'Nah. That can't be right.'

'You are my friend, and no way would I drop a bombshell on you like this if there was any doubt. I even hired a private detective to—'

'Who's the mother?'

'Joanna. She was obviously pregnant with Ava when yous two split up. What an evil woman, eh? Fancy denying a child its father. She has probably told little Ava that you are dead.'

Vinny was shell-shocked. During the time they'd been together he'd done more shagging with prostitutes than he had with Jo. 'How did you find this out?'

Ahmed explained that Johnny Preston worked for a friend of a friend, and told him how Ava's existence had been stumbled upon.

'I just can't believe it. I'm still not convinced the kid's mine. Jo might have met someone else,' Vinny stated. His stomach was churning. Part of him wanted the child to be his, but he'd feel disloyal to Molly if it was. No way could he ever love another little girl the way he'd loved her. Molly had been the most special child ever.

'Ava is most definitely yours, Vinny. She's the right age and is the spitting image of you. You wait until you see the photos of her. There will be no doubt in your mind then.'

'Where are the photos? I need to see her.'

'Obviously I couldn't just walk into this visit with photos in my hand, but I can post them to you if you wish? I wasn't sure you would want me to, though. You know, in case of any repercussions.'

Vinny's head felt mashed. He couldn't even think straight. 'Does Ava look anything like Molly?'

'Apart from the bright green eyes, no. Ava has olive skin and hair like you. She's a very striking child, Vinny. It's such a shame you've missed the first few years of her life.'

'Don't post the photos. It's too risky. I want you to put them in an envelope and give them to Michael. Old Frank will sneak them in 'ere for me. Have you got Jo's address?'

Sensing that he could wind Vinny up a bit more while screwing money out of him at the same time, Ahmed shook his head. 'No. Do you want me to ask the private detective to find that out?'

'Yeah. Michael will square you up, dosh wise. I'll have a word with him and explain all. Who you told about this discovery?'

'Only Burak.'

'Well, keep it that way. I am more than fuming, Ahmed.'

Vinny was cracking now. Ahmed could see that psychotic glint in his piercing green eyes, so he decided to stoke the fire even more. 'You were a fantastic dad to Molly. The best father that child could have wished for in her short life. That's what annoys me. What right has that slag Joanna got to prevent you being the same to Ava?'

Glancing around to check none of the screws were earwigging, Vinny leaned forward. 'I'll tell you something, Ahmed. If what you're saying turns out to be true, I will kill that deceitful whore and her cunt of a father. I swear to ya, if Ava is mine, then mine she shall fucking be.'

Nancy and Mary were at the hospital again. Freda was over the moon that her cats were being well looked after and seemed happy in their new home. 'You'll never guess who turned up 'ere to visit me this morning!'

'Queenie and Viv?' Mary replied.

Freda chuckled. 'I'd have them two old bats evicted by security if they ever tried to visit me. Keep this to yourselves obviously, but my Dean came to see me.'

'Oh my God! I thought Dean was in Glasgow. Nobody recognized him, did they?' Nancy asked worriedly.

'No. I didn't even recognize him myself at first. He drove down from Scotland on his motorbike and was dressed in leathers with one of them bleedin' big helmets on. Good disguise though, I have to say.'

'Aw, I bet you were so pleased. What a nice surprise for you,' Mary said.

'I was thrilled to bits. He looks so well and I'm so bloody proud of him. He employs thirty-five men now to work for him and is minted. Just bought himself a four-bedroom house he has, showed me some photos of it. I'm so glad he got away from those Butlers and made something of his life. It just goes to show you, crime doesn't pay. My Terry would still be alive if he'd gotten away from the underworld.'

Mary squeezed Freda's hand. 'I know how you feel. Myself and Donald are ever so proud of what our Christopher has achieved. It's a lovely feeling, isn't it? Makes your heart swell.'

'It sure does. Open that drawer, Nancy. Dean left a letter in there for you. I dunno what it says, he wouldn't tell me. Shame I never had a kettle in here. I could've steamed it open. He's always held a torch for you, you know.' Freda chuckled.

Nancy blushed and put the letter in her handbag. 'I'll read it when I get home,' she said. It didn't seem fair on Dean to open it in front of her mother and Freda. If he hadn't told his nan the content, then Dean obviously wanted whatever he'd written to remain private.

'Don't take it home with you, in case Michael finds it. Dean gave strict instructions for you to read it inside the hospital then rip it up in little pieces and bin it. That boy swore to me that he'd abide by my wishes and not attend my funeral, but if that letter says any different, Nancy, then I want you to tell me. I need to be able to rest in peace.'

Nancy nodded, made her way to the nearest toilet, then opened the envelope. The letter was short and straight to the point.

Hi Nancy,

I would really like to see you while I'm down South. I'll be in the Merry Fiddlers pub in Dagenham tonight (Wednesday), tomorrow and Friday at eight p.m.

Get a cab and I will give you the money for it.

Please turn up.

Dx

PS Don't order a cab from home. Call from a phone box or somewhere.

PPS Make sure you rip this letter up.

Nancy sighed as she carried out Dean's instructions. She would love to catch up with him, but if Michael found out it would most certainly end her marriage. Decisions, decisions . . .

Joanna Preston could not wipe the smile off her face as she sang along to George Michael's 'Careless Whisper'. She'd gone out with Darren again last night. He'd taken her to a lovely Italian restaurant, then they'd gone back to hers and made love for the first time.

Unlike Vinny, who had never enjoyed kissing, Darren made Jo feel sexually desirable and wanted. He was the first man she'd slept with since Vinny and it had felt so right. Darren was loving, gentle, romantic and very eager to please. In fact, he was the total opposite to Vinny in every way imaginable.

Parking the car on her mother's driveway, Jo let herself in with her own key. 'Hi, Mum. I got you these to say thanks for looking after Ava. Darren gave me the money to buy them. He's such a gentleman. I just know you and Dad will really like him.'

Thanking her daughter, Deborah put the flowers in a vase. She hadn't told Jo that Johnny was currently staying at his mother's as Jo would insist on knowing why.

'Where's Ava?'

'Upstairs, having a nap. Been a right little madam today she has. Played me up something chronic,' Deborah complained.

'What's she done?'

'Just wouldn't stop whingeing. I hate to say this, but I reckon Ava takes after him. Molly had your sunny . . .'

'Don't say stuff like that, and don't ever mention him again, Mum,' Jo butted in. 'All kids are different. Ava's an angel compared to that boy next door to me. Horrid little rascal he is. I don't like it when you keep comparing Ava to Molly. It's not right. As for saying she's like him, that's a vile thing to say.'

Deciding a change of subject was needed, Deborah apologized and asked about Darren.

'He's just so lovely, Mum. We went to a pub on Monday night, then last night he took me to a really nice Italian restaurant. We're gonna introduce the kids on Saturday and have a family day out. We're not going to bother with the zoo now. Darren said we should make the most of the hot weather, so we're taking them to Southend for the day. Shane sounds like a nice little boy so I'm sure he and Ava will get on well. He's only a year older than her.'

'Oooh, this sounds serious. You've got a glow about you today an' all. What you and Darren been up to?'

Joanna immediately felt herself blush. She was close to her mum, but no way was she discussing her sex life with her. Nancy was the only person she had those types of chats with. 'Nothing, Mum. I'm just happy, that's all. I felt so insecure at times with Vinny, but Darren's changed all that. He's always saying nice things to me and I feel like I've finally got my confidence back. I really want you and Dad to meet Darren. How about Sunday? We could have lunch at that pub we went to last week?'

'I think your father has other plans on Sunday, love.'

'Like what? Yous two haven't fallen out, have you?'

Knowing that it would break her daughter's heart in two if she told her the awful truth, Deborah had no option but to lie.

A week had gone by since he'd last seen his girlfriend, so Little Vinny had decided to make a special effort today. That's why he'd brought her to the big Top Shop in Oxford Street and told her to pick whatever she wanted and he'd pay for it.

'All I want is this, Vin. I can't see anything else I like,' Sammi-Lou said, handing him the item she'd chosen.

Little Vinny looked at the clothing in disgust. It was one of those baggy T-shirts that Wham had made famous with the words CHOOSE LIFE printed across the front. 'What d'you want that shit for? It's naff. Why don't you pick out some nice dresses? You wanna look good for your mum's party.'

'Nah. I'm not really in a shopping mood, to be honest. My feet are hurting in these shoes and I'm hot. Let's go and get a cold drink and something to eat instead.'

Throwing the T-shirt down in annoyance, Little Vinny grabbed his girlfriend by the hand, marched her out of the shop and into a nearby pizza place. Once seated, he said his piece: 'I can't believe I've brought you all the way up 'ere to your favourite shop and you're still acting weird. If you're gonna finish with me, Sammi, then just do it, 'cause I don't need this shit any more. I might not be the perfect boyfriend, but I'll take some beating. How many other geezers my age are gonna take you shopping every week and foot the bill for whatever you want, eh?'

When Sammi-Lou burst into tears, Little Vinny felt embarrassed. Everybody was looking, including the waitresses. 'What's wrong with you? Do you wanna call it a day between us?'

'No. It's not that.'

Working out female emotions wasn't Little Vinny's strong point and he was beginning to lose his patience. 'I'm not a mind-reader, Sam, so best you just spit it out.'

'My dad's gonna kill me – and you. I'm so scared, Vin,' Sammi sobbed.

'Why?'

'Because I'm pregnant. We're going to be parents, Vin.'

The Merry Fiddlers was a big pub full of tough-looking men and Nancy had very nearly had a panic attack on arrival in case she was recognized. She'd calmed down now though. She'd also been so nervous about meeting Dean for the first time in years, but he was a lovely bloke and a complete joy to talk to.

'Same again, Nance?'

'Yes, please. I'd better be going after the next drink though. Michael will be wondering where I am otherwise.'

When Dean walked up to the bar, Nancy took the opportunity to study his appearance. He'd changed so much and aged really well. Gone was the lanky, baby-faced lad she remembered. Dean was thirty-one now and hard work had obviously improved his physique. He was also full of confidence, had a cheeky grin and was quite good looking compared to most men. Not Michael though. Much as Nancy currently hated her husband, there was still no getting away from the fact that he was the most handsome man she'd ever seen.

Dean grinned as he put the drinks down on the table. 'I've made a decision. I shall kidnap you unless you agree to stay another hour at least.'

Nancy pondered momentarily. 'Sod it. Why should I rush off? I never go out of a night. In fact, I've had no social life whatsoever since Jo moved away.'

'That ain't right, Nance. Beautiful girl like you should be out there enjoying herself.'

Whether it was the wine or because Dean was such a good listener, Nancy found herself opening her heart to him. She confided in him about her arguments with Michael and admitted how worried she was for her sons. 'They're such a handful, Dean, especially Daniel. He's so cheeky and arrogant. I'm sure it's him that leads the other two astray. Even my mum and dad have said that. It pains me to admit this, but the best behaved one out of the three is Lee, and he isn't even mine. It makes me question whether the way they're turning out is my fault. Do you think I might be a bad mum?'

Dean squeezed Nancy's hand. 'Don't be so daft. You're a brilliant mum. It's not your fault that you get no support off Michael. Surely he must be able to afford to get someone to run that club for him a couple of nights a week so he can spend more time with you and the boys?'

'Of course he can afford it, but he won't do it. I've begged him to spend more time with us as a family in the past and even though he promises to, he never does. Michael just thinks if he chucks money at me and the boys then that makes him a good father.'

'Do you still love him?'

'I could never not love the father of my children. But I also loathe him at times. He's so pig-headed when he wants to be. Michael's the old-school type who firmly believes that a woman's place is in the home, cooking, cleaning and looking after the kids while a man's duty is to provide.'

'But times have changed. Women are just as capable of holding down decent jobs as blokes are these days. I can't get my head around why a husband would not want to spend as much time as possible with his wife and kids. Then again, who am I to judge after walking out on my own family? Half of me thinks that was the best decision I ever made, but the other half thinks it was the worst. I must have been some callous bastard back then.'

It was now Nancy's turn to comfort Dean. 'No you're not. You're a lovely bloke and you left Whitechapel for all the right reasons. You'd never have been the man you are today if you'd have stayed with Brenda. And if you'd have taken the kids with you, Vinny would've hunted you down and killed you. Your nan is so proud of you, Dean, and as much as she misses you she's relieved you got away. You've no need to ever beat yourself up about what you did.'

'I do though, Nance, and always will. Not only did I walk away from my kids, I walked away from my nan – and I'm all she has. Not a day goes by when I don't think about all three of 'em, you know. When Bren got pregnant with Tommy I felt like I had no choice but to get out, because I knew if I held him in my arms my life would've been mapped out, and I'd have been stuck with Bren for ever. I wished I could have taken Tara with me. I loved her so much. Leaving her was the most difficult decision I'll ever have to make in my life, but like you say, the Butlers would never have let me have her, even though they all knew Brenda was a lousy mother and the kids would have been better off with me.'

'Why haven't you ever settled down again, Dean? Perhaps you should, you know. It might help take away the pain of the past. You'd be a great dad, I know you would.'

Dean shook his head. 'I'd rather just throw myself into work and make a success of my business. I've only ever truly loved one woman in my life and unfortunately for me she's taken. If I can't have her, I don't want nobody else.'

'Is that the girl you lived with for a while? I remember your nan telling me you were all loved up once.'

'No, Nance. That girl is you.'

Feeling shocked and awkward, Nancy stood up. 'I'd better ring a cab now, Dean. I really do need to get home to Michael and the boys.'

CHAPTER TWELVE

Unable to visit their loved ones' graves or go shopping because of a stomach bug, Queenie and Vivian decided to catch up with their weekly fix of *Brookside*. Both women were addicted to the Channel 4 soap, but they struggled to understand the Liverpudlian accent at times.

'What did Bobby just say?' Vivian asked.

'Shush. Sheila's about to have a go at him,' Queenie hissed. The Grants were her favourite soap family.

'Gordon Bennett! Not again,' Vivian exclaimed as next door's music pounded through the wall.

Queenie paused the video and leapt out the armchair. 'I ain't putting up with this no more. I'll ram that fucking stereo right up that rough old malt's arse.'

Vivian grabbed hold of her sister's arm. 'Let Michael deal with it, Queen. Unlike us, they've no class and you can't reason with scum. I've got an idea. Why don't we plug my Lenny's disco equipment in and turn it up full blast? I bet they aren't fans of Chas and Dave.'

Queenie's anger turned to giggles. When her nephew had died, Vinny had put his disco equipment and records into storage. Vivian now had both in Lenny's old bedroom, which she'd kept as a shrine to her son. 'Come on, let's piss 'em right off – "Rabbit, rabbit, rabbit . . ."'

Michael Butler was reasonably impressed with the way Jay Boy had settled into life at the club. He was already popular with the staff and customers and was very on the ball. Last night alone, Jay had barred two drug dealers and single-handedly broken up a mass brawl on the dance floor.

Michael had been furious when he'd learned that Little Vinny had dragged Stephen Daniels out the club, then beaten him up outside. He'd recently had a warning about his licence because of the amount of noise the punters were making on leaving the premises, so more aggravation was the last thing Michael needed.

Considering he'd been thrown in at the deep end, Jay had dealt with the situation superbly. He'd bunged Stephen a oner to keep his trap shut, and taken him home personally. Michael had since reimbursed Jay's money and given Little Vinny a stern talking to. However, Michael was still determined to give Jay a bigger test, if only to piss his brother off. Vinny had taken a liberty by insisting that Jay be part of the set-up, and two could play that game.

'Paul's on the phone for you, boss,' Jay shouted out.

'What's occurring?' Michael asked his doorman.

With all the bother over Little Vinny and his own boys, Michael had forgotten about his mother's nuisance neighbours, and it took him a moment to work out who Paul was talking about when he said that Karl Baker was a regular at the Brewery Tap pub in Barking. Then the penny dropped. By the time Paul finished telling him that he'd overheard Baker arranging to meet his pals in Barking this evening, Michael had put it all together. 'OK, Paul, leave it with me. Little Vinny's not working tonight, so I need you and Pete at the club. Jay can come with me. Did Karl drive to the boozer?'

'Yeah. Serving up in there he is,' Paul chuckled.

'He'll be more than serving up when I get my hands on him later. Nobody upsets my mum and aunt and gets away with it. Fucking mug.'

Johnny Preston packed the remaining few items in his sports holdall. He was dreading the conversation he was about to have with his mother, and very much doubted she would understand his dilemma.

'You hungry, son? Wanna bacon sarnie?'

'Sit down, Mum. We need to talk.'

Spotting the holdall, Shirley Preston knew what was coming. 'Please don't tell me you're not gonna go to the police now. You can't leave poor Jamie to rot.'

'I'm sorry, Mum, but I have to put my own family first. Jo's been through so much already. It's not fair on her to rake up the past again.'

'Don't try and pull the wool over my eyes, Johnny. It's that fat fucker you married you're more worried about. You said yourself when you came back from Feltham that you thought Jamie was telling the truth. So what's changed, eh? Her slinging you out?'

'I said I thought he *might* be telling the truth, Mum. I still do, but I'm not a hundred per cent sure. Don't forget, he had all those cuttings, he ripped down the posters, he was sat opposite the club the day it happened and he admits that he rung the fucking Old Bill saying he had taken Molly.'

'He was a child back then, Johnny, and a stupid one at that. But you know as well as I do that he never killed Molly. If you turn your back on that boy, that's me and you finished, son, for good.'

Tears pricking his eyes, Johnny picked up his holdall. 'I'm sorry. I've made my decision.'

'Boss, it's me. I have been watching his every move, and I have photos of his family and work colleagues now. His movements are nothing to get overly excited about. He spends most of his life inside his club.'

'Get your arse back here and bring the photos with you,' the boss bellowed.

'Is that it? Job done?' the man asked, surprised.

After last night's events, the boss was in no mood for small talk. 'Stop asking questions and just do as I fucking say.'

Little Vinny was sitting in the armchair chewing at his fingernails. Sammi-Lou's news had knocked him for six, and he'd been in a sort of a trance ever since.

Albie sat opposite his grandson. Michael had given the boy a week off work after his altercation with Stephen Daniels, but Albie was sure it was more than that preying on his mind. 'Talk to me, Vin. I'm ever so worried about you. You can tell me anything and I'd never repeat it. What's the matter, boy?'

Little Vinny put his head in his hands. When Sammi had told him the news, he'd been too gobsmacked to even discuss the subject. He'd driven her straight home in silence and ignored her phone calls ever since. He was only bloody eighteen and he hated kids. 'It's Sammi. She's pregnant, and I'm too young to be a dad. Her old man's gonna go mental when he finds out. He hates me, I can tell. What am I gonna do?'

'Oh dear. Sounds like Sammi's got you trapped, boy. I told you to be careful and use a you-know-what, didn't I?'

'They made me cock itch. Sammi said she was on the

pill and I trusted her,' Little Vinny whined. He was feeling more sorry for himself by the second.

Albie sighed. He'd grown close to the boy over the years, but could sense he was a troubled soul, which was hardly surprising with Vinny for a father. 'You're definitely not ready to be a dad, but you can't keep avoiding Sammi's phone calls. You need to be a man and tell her how you feel. She's only young as well and hopefully if you say you're not willing to marry her or settle down yet, she won't want to keep the child.'

'But say she does?'

Albie shrugged. He wasn't about to advise the kid to tell his father in case the poor girl ended up dead. He would never forgive himself if that were to happen. 'There ain't a lot you can do if Sammi wants to keep the baby, but it still doesn't mean you've got to marry her or live with her. Times have changed. You can still be a good provider and dad these days without getting yourself shackled to the child's mother.'

Little Vinny tried to picture Sammi as a mother. An image came into his mind: Sammi-Lou cuddling her little sister, her little blonde, curly-haired sister. Before he could stop himself, Molly's face flashed through his mind. Little Vinny gagged and ran from the room. How could he ever be a dad after what he'd done?

Queenie and Vivian were sunbathing and sipping a sherry to celebrate their victory. Neither had realized just how loud that disco equipment was when played in such a small room. It had literally made the walls shake.

'How funny they all pissed off out, Queen. Well, we know what to do in future. Anytime I hear them playing that Bill bloke's records from now on, I shall blast the bastards out with our Chas and Dave.'

'His name ain't Bill, Viv. It's Bob bleedin' Marley. How many more times I gotta tell ya? Anyway, I reckon it was our rendition of "Ain't No Pleasin' You" that made 'em all leave home. We weren't born with the best of singing voices, were we?' Queenie sniggered.

'Look, Queen! Where's the other one?' Vivian said, pointing at the magpie. Both sisters were very superstitious when it came to magpies; 'One for sorrow, two for joy, three for a girl and four for a boy' was an old wives' rhyme their dear old mum had drummed into them as children.

About to point out another two magpies, Queenie screamed as Chester pounced and grabbed one of the birds by its tail.

Seeing the bird struggle, Vivian covered her eyes with her hands. 'Do something, Queen. Do something!'

Grabbing a big stone from her rockery, Queenie yelled 'Shoo,' as she threw it with all her might. She then winced as Chester fell lifeless to the grass.

'Oh my gawd! I didn't mean for you to kill it,' Vivian exclaimed.

'Everything OK, ladies?' Mouthy Maureen shouted, poking her nosy head over the fence.

'Yes. Fine, thank you,' Queenie replied, snatching a towel off her washing line and throwing it over poor Chester. She wasn't much of an animal lover, much preferred her wildlife, but didn't want the whole of Whitechapel to find out she was a cat killer.

When Maureen went back indoors, Queenie turned to Viv. 'Quick, get me the shovel.'

Vivian was horrified. 'You ain't gonna cave its head in, are ya?'

'Course not! Whaddya think I am? The bleedin' thing's already dead. We just need to bury it before that lot next door get home.'

146

'Me stomach's rumbling again. I need to go to the lav,' Vivian said, dashing indoors.

Feeling guilty, Queenie made sure none of the neighbours were looking, lifted the towel slightly, and said a few words. 'Sorry, Chester. But you did shit in me garden and murder me birds. I didn't mean to kill you, though, honest I didn't.'

Chester opened his beady eyes and stared at the evil woman who had attacked him. No longer stunned, he leapt up and scratched at her scrawny face in a fury.

Vinny Butler's emotions were all over the place. Ahmed's revelation had left him shell-shocked and he'd thought of little else since. Vinny didn't know if he wanted Ava to be his or not. It would be far less complicated if she wasn't, but the more he'd dwelled on it, the more convinced he'd become that this child he'd never seen was his. Joanna was no slag, and there was no way Vinny could imagine her entering into a new relationship straight after Molly's death. Like himself, Jo would've been far too distraught to even contemplate such a thing.

There was a knock on the cell door and Frank the screw stuck his head in. 'You all right, Vin? I thought I'd better warn you that you'll have a new cellmate later today. I managed to make sure it was someone half sensible. He's an older man and his name's—'

Vinny could feel his heart pounding nineteen to the dozen. 'You got that envelope Michael gave you?' he interrupted.

'Yep,' said Frank, reaching into his pocket. 'Here you are.'

'Cheers. You get going now, mate. I need to have a butcher's at something before this new cellmate arrives.'

'Okey-dokey. Just give me a shout if and when you need anything else.'

Vinny's hands shook as he ripped open the envelope.

Gasping, he immediately knew Ava was a Butler. She had his jet-black hair, green eyes, same skin tone, and looked a lot like Little Vinny had at the same age.

Satisfied the child was his, Vinny grinned at the photo in which Ava was scowling and pouting. She looked a real character, but thankfully there was no resemblance whatsoever to Molly. Vinny doubted he'd have been able to handle such a likeness. Molly was so pretty and unique, but Ava was cute in her own way too.

It was odd, staring at a child that he'd only just found out existed, but Vinny felt an immediate connection with Ava. It was as though he already knew her and he couldn't wait until he could see her in the flesh. How dare that bitch Joanna decide that he wasn't worthy of being Ava's father? She was bang out of order, and would pay for what she'd done. Vinny would make fucking sure of it.

Karl Baker was in good spirits. Selling cannabis in boozers beat working for a living any day of the week, and he got to socialize at the same time.

His wife was cool about his choice of career, but his sister didn't know the score. Shell would probably chop his bollocks off if she knew he was keeping his stash in her loft.

Karl lit up a cigarette, then dropped it as he was grabbed from behind. 'What the fuck! Get off me,' he yelled.

'Shut your cakehole and get in that van,' Michael ordered.

'I ain't getting in no van. Is this what you want?' Karl reached into his pocket and produced a see-through bag of drugs. 'Here, take—'

Seeing red, Michael put his hands around Karl's neck and smashed his head against the side of the Ford Transit. 'Do I look like a druggie?'

Karl was used to the odd fight and reckoned he could look after himself, but there was something sinister about these two men in hooded tracksuits that had him scared shitless. 'Are you undercover Old Bill?' he asked.

Michael prodded his cosh against Karl's head. 'I'm your worst fucking nightmare, that's who I am.'

'Let's get out of here, boss. I can hear someone coming,' Jay Boy warned.

Michael handed his accomplice the cosh. 'He's all yours now. Make sure you give him a good going over.'

'Why me?' Jay Boy asked. The odd scrap with punters trying to force their way into the club was one thing, but dragging people off the streets and doing them over with a cosh was another.

'Please let me go. I won't tell anyone, I promise,' Karl pleaded.

Forcing Karl into the back of the van, Michael slammed the doors and turned to Jay. 'My brother obviously didn't describe your position of employment too well. Working for me and Vin means you also help us out if we have any little problems we need sorting. You get my drift?'

'Yes, boss.'

'What you waiting for then? Climb in the back of the van. I'll drive, and while you're doling out the punishment I'll explain to the prick why he had it coming.'

By the time the van turned into Longbridge Road, Michael Butler was grinning broadly. Karl Baker was crying and begging for mercy and Jay Boy was proving to be a dab hand with the cosh.

'Wow! This is some party – you've certainly fallen on your feet with this girlfriend of yours, Vin,' Ahmed said, suitably impressed. Hutton was not an area Ahmed was familiar with, but the house was enormous and set in at least two acres. A massive marquee had been erected in the grounds and there were waiters serving guests and a valet parking service.

'Can you see Sammi?' Little Vinny asked. He hadn't told Ahmed about her pregnancy in case he told his dad.

'Champagne, gentlemen?' a waiter asked.

Ahmed took a glass off the tray and urged Little Vinny to do the same.

'Nah. I'm gonna stick to orange juice.' Little Vinny didn't have a problem with alcohol as such. It just dredged up memories he'd rather forget and made his temper worse. There was always the chance he could blurt out something stupid in drink as well.

'Hello, Vin. Sammi's in the marquee,' Meg Allen said.

'Happy birthday. I got you this,' Little Vinny replied, awkwardly thrusting a gift-wrapped bottle of Cartier perfume Meg's way.

'Aw, thanks, love. That's very kind of you.'

'And I bought you these. I'm Ahmed, by the way, Vinny's father's best friend.'

Meg thanked Ahmed for the huge bouquet and turned away. She was immediately accosted by her husband. 'Who's that foreign-looking geezer with our daughter's boyfriend?'

'His dad's mate.'

'Why didn't he bring one of his own mates? Hasn't he got any?' Gary hissed.

'I don't know, do I? I know you're not struck on the boy, Gal, but you wouldn't have liked whoever Sammi brought home.'

'Yes, I would. And I wouldn't say I dislike him. I just find him a bit of an oddball. My mum always said to me "Never trust a man who won't look you in the eye" and that boy won't hold my gaze.'

'He's probably too scared, that's why. You're enough to scare most boyfriends off,' Meg chuckled.

Positive that Sammi-Lou's parents were talking about him, Little Vinny dragged Ahmed inside the marquee. He spotted Sammi-Lou straight away. She was on the dance floor, wearing a tight-fitting white dress.

Staring at her stomach, Little Vinny felt himself go all hot. She definitely had a slight pot belly now which he'd never noticed before, and if her father were to spot it there'd be mayhem. 'Excuse me, Ahmed. I need to have a chat with me bird. I won't be long.'

Sammi-Lou was only dancing because her friend had told her that Little Vinny had arrived. He'd been acting all weird with her since she'd told him the baby news and even though she felt lonely and worried, she was determined to act as though she didn't have a care in the world.

'Can we talk?' Little Vinny asked.

Sammi-Lou nodded, and led her boyfriend to a secluded spot in the garden.

'How are you?' Little Vinny asked awkwardly.

'OK. Not getting any morning sickness, if that's what you mean. I was thinking that tonight is probably the best time to break the news to my mum and dad. They can't kick off with all these people here, can they? And I'd rather you were with me when I told them.'

Little Vinny squeezed both of his girlfriend's hands. He was crap at saying the right thing, but knew he had to try to be diplomatic, seeing as a baby was involved. 'I do love you, Sam, you know that. But . . . we're far too young to be parents. Why don't we get rid of this kid? I'll pay. That way your mum and dad never need to find out.'

Snatching her hands away, Sammi-Lou looked at her boyfriend in horror. 'I'm a Catholic, so are my parents. We don't believe in abortion. How can you even suggest such a thing, Vinny? Doing away with our own baby would make us child-killers.'

The word sent Molly's angelic little face flashing through his mind and he could feel himself breaking out in a cold sweat. 'But it ain't even a proper baby yet, is it? It probably ain't even the size of my thumb. I'm worried about your dad, Sam. I can tell he don't like me, and if you tell him you're up the spout, he's gonna kill me.'

'No, he won't. My dad might not jump for joy, but I know once I tell him the news he'll support us. My dad's loaded, so he can easily pay for our wedding and buy us a house to live in.'

Little Vinny opened his mouth to reply, but no words came out. The mention of a wedding had obviously affected his power of speech and the only thing he was capable of mumbling was 'OK.'

Melissa Baker screamed as she opened the front door and her battered and bloodied husband fell into a heap in the hallway. 'Oh my God! Shell, come quick.'

Shell Baker knelt down next to her brother. 'Ring an ambulance, Mel. He needs to go to hospital.'

'No, don't. I don't want the filth involved,' Karl groaned, clutching his ribs. His attacker had given him a real good going over, and Michael had threatened to cut him into small pieces and feed him to the pigs if he grassed. 'Mel, get me some painkillers and a neat vodka. I'm gonna have to go to the dentist first thing tomorrow. Two of me teeth are loose and I'm in agony.'

Shell was extremely suspicious. She knew Karl had sold drugs in the past and wondered whether he was up to his old tricks again. 'Who did this, Karl? I need to know if you're in any trouble in case they turn up 'ere. I've got the boys to think of.'

'Nobody will turn up providing you keep your trap shut. And we mustn't play any more loud music, or argue with those two old cows who live either side of us. We have to be nice to them from now on.'

'What!' Shell exclaimed.

'It was them, them two old bags that organized this,' Karl said, pointing at his battered face. 'That Queenie's son is a fucking lunatic, I'm telling ya, and so was his mate.'

Back at the party, Little Vinny's non-alcohol policy had gone right out the window. Traumatized had been the only way to describe how he'd felt when Sammi started talking babies and weddings, and knocking back glass after glass of champagne had seemed the best way to deal with the situation.

The DJ was spinning mainly sixties and seventies tunes, which was not to Little Vinny's taste, but the temporary dance floor was crammed with people who were thoroughly enjoying themselves. Ahmed was one of those people. He was currently thrusting himself against some pissed-looking old tart in a green dress in time to George McCrae's 'Rock Your Baby'.

As Ahmed caught his eye, Little Vinny gestured to him.

'I've pulled. I will fuck her senseless before we leave,' Ahmed chuckled, slapping Little Vinny on the back.

'I wanna go soon. I really don't feel comfortable. It's full of old fogies and I'm sick of Sammi introducing me to people. Her old man keeps giving me the evil eye an' all.'

'Don't be so boring. Have some of this and you'll soon liven up,' Ahmed offered, pressing a wrap into Little Vinny's hand.

Remembering the lift cocaine had once given him, Little Vinny nodded and headed off to the toilet.

*

Shell and Melissa Baker were both shocked to the core. Karl was now lying on the sofa with a plastic ice-cube tray against his swollen eyes, but he couldn't relax at all. His ribs and his teeth were giving him terrible gyp.

'So, what exactly happened, Karl? I'm fucking fuming. Them old bats next door ain't gonna get away with this,' Shell spat.

What had happened was that Karl had been driven to a secluded spot, tormented, threatened, then beaten to a pulp. He could still hear Michael Butler's final words to him as he kicked him out of the van near his home: 'If you ever upset or disrespect my mother or auntie again, I swear I will bury you alive, you skinny-gutted cunt.'

'I really don't wanna talk about it, Shell. I just want you to promise me that you and Mel will behave and be nice to the neighbours in future. You need to tell the boys to stop playing loud music an' all. If you don't abide by the Butlers' rules, then I'm fucking dead meat, I'm telling ya.'

In the past when Little Vinny had snorted cocaine with Ahmed it had made him feel happy and confident, but for some reason tonight it was having the opposite effect. He felt overwhelmed with anxiety.

'Vinny, will you dance with me?' Millie asked, grabbing his hand.

Shuddering, Little Vinny snatched his hand away from the child and shook his head. Looking at the curly blonde hair, doleful eyes and sweet innocent smile, it was all he could do to remind himself that this was Sammi-Lou's younger sister, not Molly as the seven-year-old she'd not lived to become. 'Nah. Go and find Sammi,' he snapped. 'She'll dance with ya.'

Ahmed chuckled. 'Don't be so cruel, Vinny. She's only a nipper. Dance with your future sister-in-law.'

At that precise moment, Sammi-Lou appeared with some posters. 'You must see these, Vin. My dad had some old photos blown up. This is my mum when she was my age. Don't we look alike?'

'Yeah, you do.'

'And this is my mum holding me as a toddler. My hair was much curlier back then, but I was cute, wasn't I?' Sammi-Lou chuckled.

Little Vinny recoiled in horror. If he'd thought the sister was like an older version of Molly, it was nothing compared to the resemblance between Sammi-Lou and his sister. Surely this must be God paying him back?

As Ahmed was dragged towards the dance floor by the drunken woman in the green dress, Little Vinny stood helpless, wishing his stupid girlfriend would put the photos away. If she didn't, he was sure he would end up punching her.

'You OK, Vin? You've gone ever so white. I wasn't that ugly as a child, was I? I reckon if we have a girl she'll look just like me, and if we have a boy, he'll be dark like you,' Sammi-Lou giggled in her boyfriend's ear.

'Shut the fuck up! Just leave me alone,' Little Vinny hissed, pushing Sammi away. Then he ran towards his Ford Cabriolet, shoving the parking valet out of the way and driving off at breakneck speed.

CHAPTER THIRTEEN

Having laid the photos across his desk, the man studied them until he'd absorbed every last detail.

Michael Butler was a lucky man in more ways than one. What he lacked in morals, he made up for in looks. But looks could be destroyed in a instant. Especially with a fucking machete.

Michael Butler stepped out of the car and glanced around. He'd had an uneasy feeling he was being followed the other day, but he was probably just being paranoid.

Satisfied that the coast was clear, Michael made his way inside the prison. He and Vinny still weren't seeing eye to eye and the only reason he'd agreed to come today was that he guessed his brother wanted to discuss Ava's existence.

'Alright, Vin?'

'Not bad. Yourself, Michael?'

'Sweet as a nut, me. Oh, and you can tell that geezer you've got spying on me that I've clocked him.'

'What the fuck you going on about?' Vinny spat.

Michael was sure that he'd seen the same man outside the hospital the other evening that he'd also seen loitering outside the club a day or two previously. 'The tubby dark-haired geezer. Got a squashed nose.'

'You've either lost the plot, or you've been taking drugs again. Or has your new-found wealth befuddled your brain?'

Feeling a bit of a prick, Michael chuckled. 'Chill! I'm only messing with ya.'

'Look, let's try to be civilized towards one another today, shall we? Waste of a visit otherwise,' Vinny said.

Michael shook his brother's outstretched hand. 'How did ya manage to wangle a private visit?' he asked.

'I didn't. Frank did. Not sure what he told the guvnor. Family death or crisis, probably. Well? What did you think when you saw the photos?'

'I was shocked. She don't arf look like you.'

'You haven't told anybody, have you?'

'No. Not a soul.'

'Good. Keep it that way. I haven't decided how I'm gonna play it yet. I'm worried that if I confront Jo when I get out and demand contact with Ava, she'll up sticks and do a moonlight flit.'

'You should involve a solicitor. Go through the proper channels to get access. That way, if Jo fucks off, you can do her for abduction. I dunno how I've stopped myself tearing a strip off Nancy. She must have known, surely?'

'You married a wrong 'un, bruv. I've always said that. How's Jay settled in?'

'Really well. Little Vinny doesn't like him though. I think he's got a bit of the old green-eyed monster.'

'Tough shit. He'll get over it. Some son he turned out to be. Can't even be arsed to visit me. How's Mum and Auntie Viv? Did you sort their problem out?'

Michael chuckled as he explained to his brother what had happened the previous evening. 'Right weasel Karl was.

No way will Mum or Viv get any more grief after the hiding we gave him. Typical small-time puff-dealing loser.'

'Good. I'm glad you sorted it. Going back to Ava, I think you might be right about hiring a solicitor. I'm happy to do things the proper way, but I'm telling you now, if Jo gives me major grief, I'll have her done away with. That will entitle me to full custody. No court in the land will hand Ava to the Prestons over me. Especially when they hear her cocktard of a grandfather shot Ava's Uncle Roy.'

Michael thought Vinny was jesting until he looked into his eyes and saw the evil glint. 'You can't murder the mother of your own kid, Vin. She was Molly's mum an' all. That's taking things to the extreme and you'd be the prime suspect.'

About to brag he'd already got away with it once, Vinny bit his tongue instead. Only Ahmed and Burak knew that he'd organized the death of Little Vinny's mum, and that was the way he wanted it to stay.

Karl Baker now knew the full extent of his injuries. He'd had two teeth extracted and X-rays had confirmed he also had a fractured jaw and ribs.

'Did the nurses or doctors mention involving the Old Bill, Karl?' Melissa asked, as they rode home from the hospital in a taxi.

'Yeah. I told them I was pissed and had fallen down the stairs. They probably didn't believe me, but they didn't push it. Did you tell the boys not to play loud music, Shell?'

'Yeah. But whatever I tell 'em goes in one ear and out the other.'

'I need to pick me motor up at some point. It's still in Barking,' Karl said.

'Don't worry about that today. You need to get some rest,' Mel ordered.

When they pulled up outside the house, there were two very interested spectators watching from behind the net curtains of the house next door as Karl struggled to get out of the cab.

'I told you Michael would sort it, didn't I, Queen? Look at the state of him! He can hardly walk. Bent over double,' Vivian cackled.

Queenie grinned. 'Good ole Michael. That's my boy.'

Deborah and Johnny Preston had patched up their differences, but on one condition. Johnny was never to mention Jamie's name or visit him again. Johnny had agreed to his wife's demands, and tried to square his conscience by telling himself that the police were not stupid and would not have locked up Jamie had he not been guilty.

Today, Deborah and Johnny had met their daughter's new beau for the first time. As Joanna and Darren walked hand in hand with their children to get the ice creams, Deborah nudged her husband. 'Well? I think he's perfect for our Jo. Seems ever so genuine and he's got lovely manners. His little boy is cute too.'

'So far so good. I must say, I haven't seen Jo look so happy since Molly died. I just hope he don't break her heart, 'cause if he does I'll break his legs.'

'Don't say stuff like that, Johnny. Darren seems charming and I can tell by the way he and Jo are looking at one another, they're both besotted.'

'Hitler would seem charming after Vinny Butler,' Johnny mumbled.

Deborah punched her husband's arm. 'If you don't lighten up, me and you are gonna fall out again. What's the matter? Don't you like Darren?'

Johnny squeezed Deborah's hand. 'I'm sorry. Course I like Darren. He seems a decent guy. I just worry that Jo will get hurt again, that's all. It's an over-protective father thing. You wouldn't understand.'

'Shush now. They're coming back.'

Joanna plonked herself on the sand between her parents. 'You'll never guess what!'

'What, love?' Deborah asked.

Eyes shining, Joanna clapped her hands with glee. 'Darren's taking me, Ava and Shane to Spain for a holiday. I am so excited. He's going to book it tomorrow.'

Deborah beamed from ear to ear. Their daughter had found a good man this time round, and she knew it.

Telling Burak to make himself scarce for five minutes, Ahmed walked up behind Little Vinny and playfully slapped him on the back. 'There you are! I thought you'd left the country.'

'Sorry about the party. I shouldn't have left you there, but that gear freaked me out and Sammi did my head in.'

'Don't worry about me. I ended up bonking your future mother-in-law's drunken sister up a tree. She was the one I was dancing with in the green dress.'

When Little Vinny didn't even crack a smile, Ahmed put an arm around his shoulders. 'What's going on, Vin? I know something is troubling you. You can tell me anything and I would never repeat it to anybody, not even your father or Michael. Me and you are pals.'

About to spill his guts about the baby, Little Vinny clocked Michael staring his way and decided not to. 'I dunno. It's a bit of everything, I suppose. Me and Sammi have been arguing, and I hate working with Jay Boy. Even Michael thinks the sun shines out of his arsehole now. The cheeky prick had the front to order me about this morning. I ain't putting up with that, Ahmed. I feel like I've all of a sudden been demoted to the gofer, and that'll only get worse when my old man gets out, because he's obsessed with that Scouse knob-end.'

'That's not on, Vin. You're a bright lad and a good worker. I'm not fond of Jay either. He's too sure of himself for my liking. And why does everybody refer to him as a "Boy" when he's a man?'

'That was his boxing name apparently. I honestly feel like looking for another job, but I ain't gonna earn the dosh I'm earning here.'

Ahmed grinned. 'You will if you come and work with me. And you can be one of my managers.'

'Doing what?'

'What you're doing now, but in a much more trendy area and bar. Keep this to yourself, but I have just put a bid in on an empty premises in the city. I am going to turn it into one of those yuppie wine bars. That is where the money is these days, Vin. It's all about the Filofax brigade, as I like to call them.'

'My old man wants to open a bar like that. He was telling me about it last time I visited him.'

'That's probably why your dad employed Jay. I bet he will ask him to run it with him.'

Hearing Jay's unmistakable loud laugh, Little Vinny turned around. The tosser even had the elderly punters eating out of his hand.

'Don't bother looking. You're worth ten of him.'

'When will this bar of yours be open?'

'I'm expecting the offer to be accepted tomorrow, then the building work will start immediately. I already have that lined up.'

'Will I definitely be a manager?'

'Of course. My word is my bond, you know that. If you take the job, you have to promise me one thing though.'

'What?'

'That you tell your dad and Michael that you asked to work for me, not that I offered the position to you. There will be ructions otherwise.'

Smiling for the first time that day, Little Vinny held out his right hand. 'You got yourself a deal.'

Jamie Preston's thoughts were in a very dark place. His Uncle Johnny had been his only hope of justice and now that was just a pipe-dream. His nan had informed him of Johnny's decision to turn his back on him yesterday, and Jamie was so fucking angry. Johnny had known he was telling the truth, Jamie had been sure of that.

'What's up, blud? You wanna smoke to help you chill? My girl just happened to pop this in my mouth when she kiss me,' Errol Jackson joked, showing Jamie the lump of cannabis resin.

'Nah. You smoke it.'

'For fuck's sake, man. What did your nanna say to you that was so bad, eh?'

Jamie punched his right fist repeatedly against his left palm. 'You can choose your friends but not your family – that's such a true saying, mate. Cunts, that's what my family are, bar me nan. I'll tell you something now, Errol. If I make it through adult prison, when I get released I'll have some major scores to settle. My family will pay for the way they've wronged me. I'll ruin each of their lives, one by one, and that's a fucking promise.'

Gary Allen was no prude, but he was completely taken aback by what he saw as he entered the Butlers' club. Sammi-Lou had told him that her boyfriend's family ran a successful discotheque. Not a bastard strip-joint.

The club was packed with seedy geezers, leering and whooping at the six naked tarts who were writhing about on the stage, and a mixture of cigarette and cigar smoke clouded the air. Gary's eyes scanned the club in search of Little Vinny.

'Gotcha, you little shit,' Gary mumbled, as he strolled towards the lad. At six foot three, Gary was no shrinking violet and could more than handle himself.

Little Vinny literally went flying through the air as the uppercut connected with his chin. 'Nobody treats my daughter like that and gets away with it. Who do you think you are, eh?' Gary shouted, as Ahmed tried to restrain him.

Michael and Jay Boy were quickly on the scene and grabbed hold of Gary by his arms. 'What the hell's going on?' Michael demanded to know. His dazed nephew had just sat up looking rather sheepish.

Gary made a head gesture towards his daughter's boyfriend. 'That little bastard has got my daughter up the duff. Then he has the cheek to tell her to abort the child. I'll have his fucking guts for garters if he upsets my girl again, I'm telling ya that much.'

'Let's take this into the office. You an' all, Vin. This is your doing, boy,' Michael bellowed, pushing his way past the nosy punters.

Michael slammed the office door and poured a drink. 'I'm Vinny's uncle Michael, by the way. Here, get that down your neck.'

Gary Allen knocked the Scotch back in one gulp. He was that incensed, he could have quite easily ripped Little Vinny apart limb by limb with his bare hands.

'Can I have a drink?' Little Vinny mumbled, rubbing his throbbing chin.

'No, you bloody-well can't.' Michael clipped his nephew around the ear. 'Well, now you've got yourself into a bit of a pickle, ain't ya, boy? What did I always drum into you, eh? Gonna have to man up now and take responsibility for once in your life. Being a good dad is hard graft.'

Like the majority of residents in London and Essex, Gary Allen was well aware of who the Butlers were and what they stood for. So he was shocked and pleasantly surprised by Michael's bullish reaction to the news. Gary had expected a full-blown argument, not backing.

'So where do we go from here?' Gary demanded. 'My daughter's extremely upset, but insists she loves your nephew and wants to make a go of it. Personally, I think they're too young to get married. They should see how their relationship pans out first. But I'm happy to allow them to live in one of my properties – rent-free, of course. I want to give that baby the best start I can in life.'

Not only did Michael admire Gary Allen for having the front to bowl into the club alone, the geezer was also a multi-millionaire who had morals and spoke sense. 'Sounds like a plan to me. Whaddya reckon, Vin? Sammi's a lovely girl and you owe it to her to support her and your baby. I think that's a very kind offer from Gary, don't you?'

Little Vinny was stunned into silence. He couldn't believe his life was being mapped out before his very eyes and he had no say in it. Surely Michael should be siding with him instead of fraternizing with the enemy?

'Well? Cat got your tongue?' Michael asked his nephew.

Little Vinny put his messed-up head in his hands. He was sure he loved Sammi, but no way did he want to live with her and raise a child. How could he even consider such a thing after what he'd done? It was too late to turn the clock back. He was a child-killer and always fucking would be.

PART THREE

If man were immortal he could be perfectly sure of seeing the day where everything in which he had trusted should betray his trust, and, in short, of coming to hopeless misery. He would break down, at last, as every good fortune, as every dynasty, as every civilization does. In place of this we have death . . .

Charles Sanders Peirce

CHAPTER FOURTEEN

Winter 1984

Vinny Butler shook hands with the prison staff on his way out, pausing when he came to old Frank to whisper, 'You ever get pissed off seeing the inside of this shithole, you come to me for a job.' Frank had made Vinny's spell on the inside a damn sight easier than it would otherwise have been and Vinny was never one to forget such loyalty.

Frank patted Vinny on the back. A few of the screws had been a bit wary of Butler's infamous reputation, but Frank hadn't. What you saw was what you got with Vinny and Frank was going to miss him and his weekly bung. At least the man had class and was no scumbag like a lot of the inmates he had to deal with.

The December weather was freezing, the wind strong and bitter, but Vinny cared about neither as the big metal doors closed behind him. Freedom was something you just took for granted until it was snatched away from you, and Vinny intended to savour every moment from now on.

Spotting Michael, he frowned, then sauntered towards him. He and his brother were currently not on speaking terms again. 'What you doing 'ere?' Vinny snarled. 'Jay Boy said he was picking me up.'

Michael pretended to yawn. Finding out about Ava's existence had papered over the cracks for a short spell. Then he and Vinny had had the barney of all barneys when Michael had informed his brother that he was spending thousands from their business account to refurbish the club.

'Grow up, Vin. We need to at least try to get on. If us being business partners isn't a good enough reason, then let's do it for Mum's sake.'

Still scowling, Vinny begrudgingly shook his brother's outstretched hand.

'There's a shirt and suit in the motor, and I've booked us a table in Langan's at one. I thought we'd stop at your tailor's on the way, so you can order yourself a new wardrobe. Never known anybody to beef up in nick before. Lags usually lose weight, but not you,' Michael joked.

Vinny smirked as he stepped into Michael's Porsche. 'Was you pissed or on drugs when you bought this?'

Deciding not to bite back, Michael reminded his brother that he'd bought it for Nancy. 'I'll probably chop it in soon. It's a lovely drive though. I've given it some proper welly,' he added.

'Nice to know Nancy's still as ungrateful as ever. Anyone else meeting us at Langan's?'

'Nope. Just me and you, bruv. We have a lot to discuss, and it ain't all good I'm afraid.'

Queenie Butler took the sausage rolls out the oven and put the mince pies in. Everything was home-made of course. Queenie wouldn't touch that shop-bought shit with a barge-pole.

Hearing the opening bars of Greg Lake's 'I Believe in Father Christmas' she dropped her oven gloves and rushed to switch the radio off. Molly had loved that song and Queenie wanted nothing to spoil her upbeat mood. She was so looking forward to her eldest son's homecoming and wanted this to be the best Christmas ever. Time was a great healer, and if only Vivian could find it in her heart to forgive Vinny it would make her the happiest woman alive. Vinny had made a mistake in driving under the influence and it had cost Lenny his life, but he'd loved his cousin and did not deserve to be punished for what was clearly an accident. A stupid accident. God had already punished him enough by taking Molly away.

Queenie's dark thoughts were erased by her sister's arrival. 'You'll never guess what I've just seen?' Vivian teased.

'Enlighten me?'

'Them next door loading their stereo system in his van.'

Queenie burst out laughing. Since Michael had waded in with his fists and whatever else he'd used, she and Viv had barely heard a peep from their nuisance neighbours. The cat was still a bastard pest, kept shitting in the garden, but all else had been peaceful until the other night when the adults had gone out and the boys had played their music at full blast. 'Told you that rough old malt looked petrified when I pulled her yesterday, didn't I? Especially when I told her Vinny was coming home, and he had a far worse temper on him than my Michael. She went as white as my cotton sheets.'

'Serves her bleedin' well right. Shouldn't have been so disrespectful towards us in the first place,' Vivian cackled.

Having left the back door open to get rid of the condensation from her oven, Queenie froze as she heard noises coming from the kitchen. 'Did you hear that?'

Vivian nodded and grabbed the fire poker.

Queenie flung open the kitchen door and flinched in

terror as she spotted the unwanted intruder. Ever since Chester had scratched her face she'd kept her distance from the horrid creature, and here it was brazenly stood on her kitchen top eating her sausage rolls.

'Get away. Go on, shoo you bastard,' Vivian yelled, inching towards Chester with the poker.

When the ginger-and-white monster stood on its hind legs hissing wildly with an evil glint in its eye, both Queenie and Vivian screamed, then ran.

Daniel and Lee Butler were in deep discussion at the local comprehensive. Today was the last day of term, and they were allowed to wear their own clothes instead of the usual horrible uniform and bring in games to play.

Having brought Cluedo into school, Daniel made sure nobody was looking as he lifted the lid off the box. 'The Butlers are gonna do the Bakers this weekend with the knife.'

Lee stared at the flick knife in horror, then slammed the lid back on the box. 'You gotta be kidding, Dan. We can't get locked up before Christmas. Dad's bought us a Space Invader and Pac-Man machine.'

Daniel grinned. He adored his brothers, but was by far the strongest character out of the three, and thoroughly enjoyed his role as leader of the pack. 'As Dad always says, "An eye for an eye." Those Baker boys won't grass us up. They know who we are now and will be far too scared. Nobody breaks my bones and gets away with it, Lee, and I mean fucking nobody.'

Sammi-Lou Allen was feeling down in the dumps. Being heavily pregnant was no fun, neither was living with Little Vinny. Her once loving, attentive boyfriend had changed beyond recognition since she told him about the baby, and

Sammi couldn't help but think it was God's way of paying her back for her lies and deceit.

When Sammi had first met Little Vinny it had been love at first sight for her. She'd seen the way other girls looked at him, and it had made her paranoid about losing him. That was why, within six weeks of their first date, Sammi had decided to stop taking her birth-control pill. She hadn't particularly wanted a baby at such a young age, but she was determined to keep hold of her man.

That plan seemed to have backfired now though. Sammi-Lou had thought she might be pregnant many weeks before she'd bothered to do a test and Little Vinny had been furious to learn, soon after she'd broken the news, that she was already twenty weeks gone. He'd accused her of trapping him, then called her every name under the sun.

Feeling the baby kick again, Sammi sat on the sofa, put her head in her hands and wept. She hadn't admitted to her parents how bad things were. She was afraid her dad would kick off and be at loggerheads with the Butlers. Her father had kitted out a lovely three-bedroom house he owned in Harold Wood with every mod-con going so that they would want for nothing. He would go mental if he knew that Little Vinny rarely bothered coming home at nights any more, and when he did he was paralytic and abusive. She hadn't even told her parents that her boyfriend had smashed his car up and had his driving licence taken away.

When the phone rang, Sammi answered it immediately. 'Hi, Mum. You OK?'

'Fine, darling. Me and your dad will be passing yours this afternoon. We've bought some more presents for the baby. Just checking you were in.'

Lying through her teeth and putting on a brave face was something Sammi-Lou had become accustomed to recently.

'Sorry, Mum. We're just on our way out. Vinny's treating me and bubba lump to lunch in a posh restaurant up town.'

Meg Allen put the phone down, and took a deep, calming breath. Mother's intuition told her all she needed to know and she couldn't keep lying to her husband. Afraid of starting World War Three, Meg had kept her fears to herself for weeks now. But enough was enough, and as soon as Gary got home she would tell him the truth. Sod the Butlers' reputation. Her daughter's welfare came first.

Little Vinny Butler was woken up by a pair of lips around his todger. 'Fucking get off me. Whaddya think you're doing?' he yelled, leaping out of bed.

'Carrying on from where we left off earlier. What's your problem?'

Little Vinny stared at the blonde tart in disgust. She had a posh voice, and looked about thirty.

'Just get dressed and get lost. I've got a thousand and one things to do today.'

Felicity Frost-Hunter was not used to being spoken to like a piece of dirt. She was the managing director of a fashion magazine and worth a fortune, thanks to her ex-husband whom she'd recently divorced. 'Well, what a charming young man you are. Your parents must be so proud.'

Still high on the cocaine he'd been snorting until he'd crashed out in the early hours, Little Vinny was unable to control his temper. He grabbed Felicity by her long permed hair, then spat in her face. 'You know nothing about my parents, you stinking old whore. Now do yourself a favour and fuck off. You have two minutes to leave before I really lose my rag. Posh, rich slags like you are ten a penny – and don't you ever forget that.'

Startled by the evil glint in her latest one-night-stand's

eyes, Felicity Frost-Hunter hurriedly got dressed. Her ex-husband had been unable to get an erection for some time, which was probably why she'd gone a bit wild since they'd split up. If this awful experience had taught her anything though, it was that toyboys were not for her. To spit in someone's face was an absolutely disgusting act.

As soon as he heard the old slapper leave, Little Vinny yelled Ahmed's name. Receiving no reply, he wandered into the kitchen and saw the note on the worktop.

Sorry I had to get off early, Vin. You take today off, sort yourself out and catch up with your dad. I'll pop down the club over the weekend to see him myself. Always remember, what happens between friends stays between friends. I will never mention a word to your dad about any of your shenanigans and neither must you.

Bell me if you need anything,

Ahmed

Feeling more messed up than ever, Little Vinny splashed his face with cold water. He used the excuse of losing his licence for not sharing his girlfriend's bed these days. Told Sammi it made more sense to stay at a pad Ahmed owned in Camden than to be wasting money on cabs every night.

Little Vinny reached for his wallet and took out the photo of him and Sammi-Lou. It had been taken in a photo-booth on one of their early dates and they looked the perfect couple. Sammi was beautiful, and in his heart Little Vinny knew she'd probably be the love of his life. Besides, he was too dysfunctional for any other girl to put up with him.

Putting his weary head in his hands, he cursed the unborn child that was making his life a misery. He kept having nightmares that the baby was born and when he looked into the crib he saw Molly reincarnated. If it was a girl and looked even remotely like his sister, Little Vinny knew he wouldn't be able to handle it. Guilt was an evil thing to live with.

Langan's was not the restaurant Vinny Butler would have chosen to eat in today. Owned by Peter Langan and the famous actor Michael Caine, the gaff was classy, but far too poncey for Vinny's liking. Especially at this time of year. It was full of what he liked to refer to as Hooray Henrys.

Never one to miss a trick, Vinny's eyes scanned the joint. Champagne was being knocked back like it was going out of style, and it was this type of clientele that would soon be making him an absolute fortune. Vinny had kept track of the outside world via newspapers whilst banged up, and he was well aware that the yuppie brigade had now taken over London. That's why he was going to invest in a plush wine bar. Anything was better than working back at the club. He'd never wanted to be the owner of a poxy disco-theque in the first place, and the gaff would just be a constant reminder of how his beautiful daughter had met her maker.

'You OK, bruv? You seem distant. Don't be worrying too much about Little Vinny. Once he's away from Ahmed and working back at the club with us, he'll be fine,' Michael insisted.

When Michael's bad news had turned out to be concerns over his son's recent behaviour, Vinny had been relieved. He'd thought for a split second that Joanna had done a runner with Ava. 'I'm OK. Just feels a bit surreal to be free at long last. I'll have a man-to-man chat with Little Vinny tomorrow. He's been a complete mug to get that little tart of his up the spout, so if he's gone off the rails a bit, there's your reason. Gonna have to man up and be a good dad once the kiddie arrives, ain't he? I'm gonna have to clump him though. Handsome geezer like me can't be referred to as granddad at my age. It's gonna proper ruin me street cred!' Vinny chuckled.

'Your son being spotted at a whorehouse in North London out of his box at three in the morning with Ahmed ain't no laughing matter, Vin. And I'm sure he isn't living with that bird. Every time I ring up, the girl says he isn't there. Something's amiss, I'm telling you, and I wouldn't put it past that mate of yours to have got Little Vinny on the gear. Dad's really worried about him an' all. After not having seen hide nor hair of him for weeks, he popped up to Ahmed's bar in Liverpool Street to catch him at work. Dad reckons Little Vin's lost weight and looked well rough.'

'Our father's a fine one to speak about losing weight and looking rough, isn't he? Little Vinny's my son and I'll do the worrying, Michael. The boy might be on the piss, but no way would Ahmed give him gear. He has too much respect for me to do that, and he knows I'd go apeshit if I ever found out.'

'I just think the sooner the boy is working back at the club with us, the better.'

'Michael, you know full well I won't be working back at the club. I told you that when you first insisted on keeping the gaff. Don't get me wrong: I'm glad your idea was a success and I'm grateful for all the dosh you've earned us in my absence. But unless you change your mind and invest in a wine bar with me, it's definitely time for us to go our separate ways.'

Michael had felt for some time that a parting of the ways was inevitable, but he'd never have believed it could be this amicable. He'd chosen Langan's as a venue in the hope it would make Vinny keep things civilized; it seemed it was working. 'No way am I giving up the club, Vin. We don't get on like we once did and I reckon it'll be for the best if we both become our own bosses now. I've never been keen on that wine-bar idea. It ain't my scene.'

'Fair enough. As soon as I've checked with my accountant that I've received half of everything we've earned since I've been away, I'll sign the club over to you.'

'Deal,' Michael said, eagerly holding out his right hand.

Registering the elation in Michael's eyes, Vinny smirked. It was time to deliver that final blow he'd been gagging to deliver for ages. 'Oh, plus you'll have to pay me half of what the property is currently worth before I sign it over. And you'll need to sort yourself out new staff. Pete and Paul will be coming to work for me, so will Jay Boy.'

'Very funny, bruv.'

When Vinny had first guessed this was Michael's plan he'd been very hurt. If the boot had been on the other foot and it was one of Michael's kids who'd been murdered, Vinny was sure he'd have understood his brother's dilemma and agreed to sell up. Didn't being family and working together mean anything to Michael? How could he carry on working in that place after Molly's death?

'Vin, this is some kind of joke, right?'

Glad that Michael's smug look had turned to one of shock, Vinny took a sip of his drink and shook his head. 'I'm afraid not, Michael. It was mine and Roy's dosh that originally purchased that premises. Paul and Pete were *our* pals who *we* employed from day one. Jay Boy is my mate too, so all this makes perfect sense to me. You was nothing to do with the business at the beginning, was you?'

'But I was something to do with the business when we moved to the other club down the Commercial Road, then bought this one back.'

'Yes, but those clubs bought themselves through profit we'd made, Michael. You never came up with any hard cash to help buy one, did you?'

Knowing that Vinny had him over a barrel because, legally, he owned the bulk of the club, a furious Michael slammed his glass down on the table. 'You're a fucking no-good shitcunt, Vinny. Always have been and always will be.'

Clocking a table full of posh types all looking their way, Vinny turned to the gawpers and smiled. 'I do apologize for my brother's foul language. You can take this one out of the East End but he'll always be a cockney barrow-boy.'

When Michael snatched up his Crombie overcoat and stormed out of the restaurant, Vinny asked the waiter for the bill. He'd waited a long time for this moment; it was the only thing that had helped him keep his temper in check when Michael used to come swanning into the nick, giving it large. Enjoyable as it would have been to smash Michael's smug face into that visiting-room table, this was even better. His little brother had needed to be brought down a peg or two and Vinny thought he'd done it in complete and utter style.

Savouring the rest of his Scotch by swilling it around his mouth before swallowing, Vinny Butler smirked. He was not a man to be underestimated, so more fool those who tried. Anybody who wronged him would pay the price for their stupidity, and Michael was no exception.

CHAPTER FIFTEEN

Sammi-Lou was dozing when she heard the front door slam. 'That you, Vin? I'm glad you're home. I haven't been feeling well at all these past couple of days.'

'Of course it isn't Vin. He's probably waiting for you at the posh restaurant up town you told your mother you was going to,' Gary Allen replied angrily.

When both her parents marched into the lounge, Sammi-Lou was furious. She'd made her father promise that he would never use his own key. She insisted it invaded her and her boyfriend's privacy, yet here he was, standing in front of her with a face like thunder. 'What you doing? You swore to me you'd never just walk in without my permission. I will never trust you again.'

'Perhaps me and your mother feel the same about you, Sam. Why you lying to us? And where exactly is that toe-rag of a boyfriend of yours? Because if he hasn't been home for the past couple of days, he'll regret it when I get my hands on him.'

Meg grabbed her husband's arm. 'Just calm down, you're making matters worse. I want to talk to Sammi alone.'

'I have as much right to know what's going on as you,

Meg. I said that little bastard was a wrong 'un in the first place, didn't I?'

When her daughter became distressed, Meg pushed Gary towards the front door. 'Go and have a pint at that pub round the corner. Give us a half-hour at least, then come back more sympathetic. I know you're upset, Gary, but your attitude is enough to send poor Sammi into an early labour. Use your loaf, for goodness' sake.'

After storming out of Langan's, Michael was now propping up the bar in one of those poxy gaffs his untrustworthy, manipulative arsehole of a brother wanted to buy. No way was Vinny getting away with treating him like this. The money their accountant showed to the taxman was stashed in a joint business account, but there was plenty more that wasn't and if Vinny wanted to play silly games, then Michael would too.

'Yes, sir. What can I get you?'

'A brandy, mate. And make it a large one.'

Fleetingly Michael wondered whether he should seek legal advice, but immediately dismissed the idea. The club had robbed the taxman of a fortune over the years and it certainly wasn't worth opening up that can of worms. If he was going to fight Vinny, then he'd have to stand up to him like the man he now was.

About to take a sip of his drink, Michael heard a distinctive laugh behind him and nearly dropped the glass in shock. It couldn't be her, could it? Last he'd heard, she was living in New York.

Joy and Christmas spirit filled the air as Michael scanned the packed bar for the source of the laughter. People were draped in tinsel and wearing silly hats, obviously celebrating now that they'd finished work until the New Year.

He was just telling himself that his mind must have been playing tricks on him when he spotted her. She had her back towards him, but her stunning figure, long legs and flowing glossy dark hair were unmistakable. His heart somersaulted in recognition. There was no question it was her: Bella.

Nancy Butler was busy washing up when she spotted movement out of the corner of her eye. 'Oi, where d'ya think you're going?'

Daniel, Lee and Adam stopped in their tracks. 'We're just popping out for a bit. We'll meet you round Nan and Granddad's,' Daniel informed his mother.

'Oh no you won't. You're only just back in your granddad's good books and he'll be furious if you turn up late and looking scruffy. I want you all to have a bath and put on something smart.'

'Why?' Daniel spat.

'Because I bloody said so. And if you dare be rude to Uncle Christopher, Olivia or those kids, I swear you'll be grounded until the New Year.'

'Stupid cow,' Daniel muttered as he ran up the stairs. He had wanted to try and ambush the Baker boys before heading off to his nan's.

'What we gonna do now?' Lee asked. He was still very uneasy about the whole idea.

Daniel took the knife out of his pocket and hid it under his mattress. 'We'll have to do it tomorrow instead.'

'Say we accidentally kill 'em? We'll be sent to that bad boys' place and we won't get our presents,' Adam said.

'Stop being such a namby-pamby. If you don't wanna come with us tomorrow, then stay 'ere with Mum. Lee will help me.'

180

'I'm not a namby-pamby, and I do wanna come with you.'
'Well, stop whingeing then.'

Gary Allen let himself back in the house and poked his head in the lounge. 'Where is she?'

'Upstairs, packing a few things. I've talked her into coming to stay with us over Christmas.'

'So, what's been going on?'

'Vinny's lost his driving licence and they haven't been getting on too well. By the sounds of it he stays most nights at a pal's nearer to where he works.'

'Fucking little dickhead. To think I put a roof over his head an' all. Who does he think he is, treating our Sammi like that? She's pregnant and he should be here for her, end of.'

'I know. They're only kids them bloody selves. That's where the problem lies.'

'Well, he won't live to make old bones if he upsets our daughter any more, Meg. In fact, I think I'll pay that uncle of his a little visit at his club tomorrow. He seemed quite a reasonable—'

Having overhead the end of the conversation, Sammi burst into the room shouting. 'I told you not to tell him, Mum. I don't want Vinny confronted, nor his uncle. This is my problem and I want to deal with it in my own way. Dad sticking his two penn'orth in will just make things a hundred times worse.'

When her daughter began to cry, Meg put her arms around her and glared at Gary. 'Your father won't be confronting anybody, darling. If he does, he can expect my divorce papers in the post.'

Queenie and Vivian were enjoying their first mince pies of the festive season accompanied by a glass of port when there was a loud banging at the door. 'Why don't they use the bleedin' bell? If it's any neighbours wanting to pop in for Christmas drinks I shall tell 'em to eff orf. Nosy bastards only wanna see what new furniture and bits and bobs I've bought,' Queenie said, before yanking open the front door.

'OK if me and the kids come to you for Christmas, Mum? Dave's going to his mum's and I can't stand the old bag,' Brenda said loudly.

Queenie glanced up and down the road, before dragging her dishevelled-looking daughter inside. She'd obviously had a tipple and Queenie only hoped the neighbours hadn't clocked her. Whenever they asked about Brenda these days, Queenie always lied and said how well she was doing.

'What you drinking? Can I have one?' Brenda asked, pointing at Vivian's glass.

'No, you bloody well can't. Look at the state of you! Ashamed to call you my daughter, I am. You ain't arf let yourself go again, girl, since you've been with that tosspot. Where are the kids?'

'At school.'

'Can't be at bleedin' school now, can they? It's nearly five.'

'Well, they'll be indoors then, and Lauren'll be there with them,' Brenda lied. She had no idea whether her boyfriend's seventeen-year-old daughter would be at home or not.

Vivian shook her head in disgust. Tara, Brenda's daughter, was twelve, her son Tommy, just seven. 'Poor little mites. Latch-key kids.'

'What's that mean?' Brenda spat.

'What kids were called back in our day when they came home to an empty house and had to fend for themselves. You're a terrible mother, Brenda. You always was,' Queenie chided.

'Pot calling kettle,' Brenda sneered.

The sound of the doorbell stopped Queenie from clouting her daughter. 'Take her out in the kitchen, Viv, and make her a coffee to sober her up. And shut the door while I see who this poxy nuisance is.'

'Hello, Queenie. Happy Christmas,' Nosy Hilda said, holding out a card.

'There's a letterbox there. Didn't you see it?'

'I just wanted to wish you a happy Christmas personally, and I knew you were in because I saw your Brenda arrive. Is she OK?'

'That wasn't my Brenda. It was Michael's new cleaner at the club. She's doing a bit of work for me. I want the house sparkling because my Vinny comes home today.'

'I could have sworn it was your Brenda.'

'Nope. It wasn't. Now, if you don't mind, I'm busy cooking. Merry Christmas,' Queenie said, slamming the door in Hilda's face.

Bored with her father and brother droning on about Christopher's work in the police force, Nancy Butler wandered into the kitchen. 'Do you need a hand with anything, Mum?'

'No. Everything's under control, thanks love. The boys are well behaved, aren't they?'

'I brought them some games round to keep them quiet. They seem to get bored very easily. Were me and Chris like that when we were kids?'

'All kids have their moments, Nance. I was lucky with you because you were a little bookworm. Then you reached sixteen and fell in love with Michael Butler, of all people. That Enid Blyton has a lot to answer for, I can tell ya.'

Nancy chuckled. After many ups and downs, she and Michael had been getting on OK recently. Her husband wasn't the most romantic of men as a rule, so Nancy had been thrilled when he'd surprised her with an early thirteenth anniversary present and taken her to a posh manor house in the countryside. They rarely ever spent any time alone, and it had been so nice to be just the two of them. Her mum had stayed at hers to look after the boys. She'd been in on the surprise.

'So how was your dirty weekend away?'

'It was really lovely. The food was to die for, and we visited some smashing olde worlde pubs. There was even this quaint little tea shop where we ate the most gorgeous home-made scones with jam and clotted cream. You and Dad should go there one day. You'd love it.'

'You know what an old stick-in-the-mud your father is, love. He wouldn't even come on holiday to Eastbourne with us that time. I have to say, I didn't think I'd ever forgive Michael for showing up at Freda's funeral in the hope he'd find Dean there, but he's slowly redeeming himself in my eyes.'

Freda Smart's funeral hadn't been the best of send-offs. Only twenty-odd people had bothered to turn up and those included Michael, a pissed-up Brenda and her big-mouthed boyfriend, all three of them hoping to pounce on poor Dean. Thankfully, Dean had the brains to stay away. Instead he'd left it until the following week to visit his nan's grave, lay flowers and say his goodbyes with Nancy at his side.

'Look at what Michael wrote in my card, Mum.'

Mary looked inside the card.

Unlucky for some, thirteen!
　Happy Anniversary, babe.
　Love always,
　Mr Butler

Mary smiled. 'Why did he give you your card so early? It isn't your actual anniversary until Christmas day.'

'I'm aware of that – I am married to the man. Michael gave me the card early because the reservation was inside. Why do you ask?'

'No reason. Well, only that your nan used to say it was terribly unlucky to open an anniversary card early.'

Nancy sighed. 'Cheer me up, why don't you, Mum.'

Transfixed by her beauty and grace, Michael couldn't take his eyes off the woman he'd very nearly left Nancy for. Their affair had been brief but truly memorable, and Michael had often wondered about Bella over the years. Was she happy? Had she ever married? Did she have kids?

Spotting her trying to edge towards the bar, Michael waved a hand.

Bella gasped and put her hand over her mouth. She could not believe her eyes. 'Michael! Oh my God!' she giggled.

'What's so funny?' Michael asked.

'Nothing. I'm just laughing because I'm so happy to see you,' Bella replied.

Giving Bella an awkward hug, Michael grinned. 'It's great to see you too. You haven't changed a bit.'

'Neither have you. You're still the spitting image of David Essex.'

'Nah. I've aged far better than he has,' Michael quipped. 'What you drinking? That's if you've got time for a drink, of course. I know you're with some pals as I clocked you a bit earlier.'

'They're my work colleagues. I'd love a glass of champagne, please, Michael. I still can't believe it's you. Do you come to this bar often?'

'First time I've ever been in here, so our meeting must

be fate. You said you were with work colleagues. You living back in England then?'

'Yes. I've been back nearly a year.'

'Bottle of champagne over here, guv. Your finest, please,' Michael said, waving a wad of money in the air.

Bella chuckled. She'd missed Michael's cockney accent, which was so different to her own. Her parents were Italian and she'd lived in Italy until her modelling career had taken off.

'What you laughing at now?'

'The way you talk. I could never forget your accent.'

Michael stared deep into Bella's eyes. 'And I could never forget you.'

Stunned by Sammi-Lou's brief note saying she was staying at her parents' for a while, Little Vinny decided to pay a visit to Molly's grave.

Glaring at the two women who obviously thought a cemetery was no place to drink alcohol, Little Vinny asked them if they wanted a sip.

'No, thanks,' the shorter woman replied.

'Well, what you staring at me for then?' Little Vinny shouted.

When the women scuttled away, Little Vinny walked around searching for Molly's plot. He hadn't been here since the funeral, so had not seen the headstone yet.

'There you are,' he said, staring his sister's image squarely in the eye. She had a massive headstone with her photo engraved in the centre.

Having taken two fat juicy lines of cocaine before leaving home, paranoia had kicked in and Little Vinny was now fixated with the idea his sister was somehow to blame for his recent run of bad luck. 'Look, I'm sorry I killed you, Molly, but I was out of me nut. If I could change what I did, I would. You can't go on punishing me for ever though. I wanna sort my life out and be normal, and all these bad things that keep happening to me are stopping me from doing that.'

Sparking up a joint, Little Vinny sat on the edge of the grave. 'Can't you send me a sign so I know you can hear me? Anything will do, like a bird falling out the sky.'

Getting more agitated by the second, Little Vinny whacked his plastic cider bottle against Molly's photo. 'Don't ignore me, you spoilt little bitch. I wanna sign.'

Livid when a bird still didn't fall from the sky, Little Vinny glanced around. He couldn't see anybody nearby, so unzipped his trousers, flopped out his penis and pissed all over Molly's headstone.

'Oi! Whaddya think you're doing?' a voice bellowed.

Seeing a massive bald bloke ambling towards him, Little Vinny zipped himself up, picked up his cider and ran.

'Vinny, it's great to see you, mate. Welcome back to reality.' Paul was grinning from ear to ear as he shook his boss's hand and slapped him on the back.

'Is Michael inside?'

'No. I thought he was picking you up.'

'Yeah, he did. Then we parted company. What about Pete and Jay Boy, they in there?'

'Yeah. They'll be thrilled to see you. Go and have a few bevvies with 'em before the madness starts. It'll be rammed in there, give it another hour or so.'

'No. Not tonight. I haven't even seen my mum yet. Do us a favour, Paul, give the lads a shout for me. I just wanna have a quick word out here with the three of you.'

'OK.'

Vinny glanced up at the new illuminated sign. It still said

BUTLERS, but had the word DISCOTHEQUE below and silly musical notes that lit up all around it.

Sparking up a cigarette, Vinny leaned against the wall. Apart from in his dreams, Vinny had refused to allow himself to think about Molly while incarcerated. But being at the place where he lost her brought it all back to him in an instant.

'Here he is! The main man. So chuffed you're out, Vin. I've missed you big time, mate. I wanted to come with Michael to meet you, but he said you had some stuff to sort out,' Jay Boy said.

'Fuck me! That Scouse accent of yours has sped up even more since we were cellmates. You sound like you've been inhaling helium,' Vinny joked, hugging his pal.

Pete was the next to greet Vinny. 'You don't arf look well. Great to have you back, boss. Whitechapel hasn't been the same without you.'

'I just wanted to put you in the picture, lads. Me and Michael have decided to go our separate ways. He wants to keep this club and, for obvious reasons, I need a fresh start. As soon as the New Year arrives I will be searching for the right premises to open up a posh wine bar. It'll be up town somewhere. That's where the money people are, and obviously I want yous three to come with me. You'll be on more dosh than you get here, of course.'

'Count me in,' Jay Boy grinned.

'What about Michael though?' Paul asked.

'What about him? He'll have to get new staff in. Not being funny, Paul, but it was me and Roy who employed you and Pete all those years ago. Loyalty is very important in this day and age, don't you think?'

Paul nodded. 'Of course, boss. Count me in too.'

'What about you, Pete?'

Pete wasn't silly. He knew what Vinny was like and he wasn't a geezer to get on the wrong side of. He grinned. 'Yep. I'm in too. A change is as good as a rest, so they say.'

Queenie and Vivian had found a new tipple they were rather partial to. It was called Baileys and was incredibly moreish. The pair of them were singing along to Chas and Dave's 'Ain't No Pleasin' You' when Vivian suddenly got the giggles.

'What you laughing at?' Queenie asked.

'Us. We're a funny pair, you know. I can't believe we dressed Brenda up like a fucking Arab so none of the neighbours would recognize her, then shoved her in a cab. Our lives are like a comedy sketch at times.'

Queenie roared with laughter. 'I reckon the cab driver thought Bren was one of them Muslim women until she opened her drunken gob. He looked shocked to the core, poor bastard,' she cackled. 'What about the time I made Vinny and Roy dress Albie up to come round for dinner? He looked like John Wayne gone wrong when he came walking up the path. Talk about bringing unwanted attention to the door. I said to Vinny and Roy I didn't want the neighbours to recognize him, so they dressed him up like a bastard cowboy! All he needed was a bloody horse.'

'Albie had that long mac and big hat on, didn't he? I said he looked like a flasher, and I'm sure when he walked in my Lenny blurted out everything we'd said. He was a funny kid, weren't he, Queen?'

'Funny ain't the word. That boy was a legend. I know you used to get embarrassed when he got his dingle-dangle out and flashed it at all the neighbours we didn't like, but I secretly thought it was hilarious.'

'I don't arf miss him this time of year, Queen. Lenny used to love Christmas.'

'I know, darling. I miss Lenny, Roy and Molly terribly this time of year. That poor little girl's death still haunts me in my sleep. I dreamt she was standing at the end of my bed the other night, calling me, and when I woke up and realized she wasn't, I cried.'

'Perhaps her spirit came back to visit you. Fat Beryl believes in all that stuff. She goes to a medium who she reckons gets in touch with her Cyril.'

'Whaddya mean, "gets in touch"? He's been dead for over ten years.'

'Mediums can contact the dead, according to Beryl,' Vivian explained.

'What a load of old bollocks! That medium must have seen Fat Beryl coming. Probably charges her a tenner a time an' all.'

Vivian chuckled. 'There ain't much left of this Baileys. We might as well finish the bottle.'

Before Queenie had a chance to reply, the doorbell rang. 'That better not be Brenda back again, because over my dead body is she staying 'ere.'

'Don't answer it then.'

'I've got to, in case she starts shouting her mouth off,' Queenie replied, marching into the hallway and yanking open the door.

'Hello, Mum.'

'Vinny! I wasn't expecting to see you until tomorrow. I thought you'd be out partying with the lads tonight. Come in, boy. You'll catch a death of cold out there.' She ushered him through to the living room. 'Now, what do you want to drink? Scotch? A brandy?'

Unable to stomach the happy reunion, Vivian put on her

coat. 'I'm off, Queen. Speak to you tomorrow,' she said, barging past Vinny without even looking at him. Why should she acknowledge the man who'd killed her beloved son? She owed him nothing.

CHAPTER SIXTEEN

Fearing that her friends might reclaim Bella, Michael suggested that they leave the wine bar and grab a table at a nearby restaurant where it would be possible to have a proper conversation instead of trying to shout above the volume of noise in the wine bar. 'What do you fancy to eat?'

'I'm not overly hungry, Michael. Just order the pizza you want and I'll have one slice. I had a big lunch,' Bella lied. She didn't want to admit that the butterflies in her stomach were playing havoc with her appetite.

Michael took a gulp of red wine and smiled. 'When was it we last saw one another?'

'I moved to New York in the summer of seventy-seven, so it must have been just before that. How are your sons? Did you have any more children?'

'My boys are good, thanks. Daniel and Lee are both twelve now and Adam's nine. No, I didn't have any more kids. The three of them are enough to keep me on me toes. What about you? You married? Got kids?'

'I've never been married, but I do have a son. His name's Antonio, and he truly is the light of my life.'

Even though he had three sons himself, Michael couldn't

help but feel a pang of jealousy that Bella had fallen pregnant by another man. 'How old's Antonio? You still with his dad?'

'Antonio's three. And no, I'm not with his dad. We split up shortly after Antonio was born.'

'Why was that?'

'Because I found out I'd been cheated on while I was pregnant. It's no loss. Clint was an arsehole anyway. Antonio and I are just fine on our own. I can give him everything he needs.'

'Does Antonio have any contact with his father now?'

'No. What about you? Still with Nancy?'

'Yeah. We're not happy though. Like ships that pass in the night these days. I will always respect and support Nancy 'cause she's the mother of my kids, but I don't love her any more. Well, not in the way I should.'

Michael Butler was an incredibly sexy man, and as he stared seductively into her eyes, Bella looked away. Michael oozed charm, had the gift of the gab, and that, combined with his handsome face and cheeky grin, was a fatal combination. 'I should be going, Michael. I promised my au pair I'd be home early. She looks after Antonio while I'm working.'

Michael leaned across the table and put his hand on top of Bella's. 'Stay another half an hour, please? The pizza'll be here in a minute and we've still got half a bottle of wine left.'

When Michael's thumb began tantalizingly massaging the palm of her hand, Bella weakened. She never had been able to say no to him.

Ahmed Zane's wine bar was situated around the corner from Liverpool Street station. It attracted mainly city workers, which was why Ahmed was only open for business

Monday to Friday. Hordes of football fans passed through the station on a Saturday and there was no way Ahmed was going to risk his bar being smashed up by a bunch of rowdy hooligans.

Ahmed was at the bar most days. He liked to keep a watchful eye on his domain, and was usually to be found sitting in a corner of the bar smoking a fat cigar, sipping a glass of fine wine or champagne. He also liked to socialize with the clientele. It never hurt to let people know who was the boss, and like himself some of the punters were very wealthy, interesting people.

'Boss, we have a bit of a problem. Vinny's just turned up, he's very drunk and he's arguing with a couple of customers,' Mario the bar manager whispered urgently.

'Where is he?'

'By the door.'

Ahmed was fuming as he made his way through the packed bar. He had a strict policy: none of his staff were allowed to drink alcohol while working. Once the bar was closed, they could go off wherever they liked and drink as much as they wanted. He and Little Vinny often ended up going on to a club or some sordid massage parlour and staying out till all hours.

'In the office – now!' Ahmed bellowed, arriving just in time to stop a full-blown fight.

'It weren't my fault. That posh geezer barged into me, then he started giving it the large. He was taking the piss, then all his mates joined in. I ain't gonna stand for shit like that. Why should I?'

Ahmed locked the office door and handed Little Vinny a wrap. 'Snort that. It'll sober you up. This is our livelihood, Vin, so you must never turn up here shit-faced again. What's happened? You had a row with your old man?'

'Nah. I ain't even seen him. It's Sammi. I went home and

there was a note on the table. I think she's left me for good.'

'Perhaps it's for the best. I'm not sure you're ready to settle down yet. You can still be a good dad without being shacked up with the kid's mother. I only see my children a couple of times a week, yet they are happy and very balanced.'

'But I can't be a good dad. I don't ever want kids.'

'You're just scared of fatherhood and the responsibility, Vin. Once the baby's born, you'll be fine, trust me.'

'You don't understand, Ahmed. Nobody does.'

'Understand what? Look, I know there's something on your mind, so why don't you tell me what it is? A problem shared is a problem halved, and you know you can trust me. I'm your friend.'

Queenie Butler had missed her first-born dreadfully. She would have gone to see him at every opportunity, but Vinny had insisted that Pentonville prison was no place for a lady like herself and would only allow her to visit him twice a year: his birthday and hers. Even though he had rung her most days and written regularly, nothing beat seeing him in the flesh.

'There you are, love. Get that down ya neck. Nice bit of ham off the bone and fresh crusty bread. Drink that drop of Scotch and I'll pour you another. I've put some mince pies in the oven to warm up. Do you want double cream with yours? I did make some sausage rolls 'cause I know how much you love mine, but that bastard cat next door ate them. Had to throw what was left away.'

'Mum, stop fussing and sit down a minute. We've stuff to talk about.'

Queenie topped Vinny's drink up, turned the oven down, then sat on the sofa. 'Your Auntie Viv will come round one day. Difficult time of year for her, is Christmas. That's when she misses her Lenny the most.'

'Well, I know how she feels now, which is probably God's way of paying me back. Christmas Day felt like any other day in nick, but it's gonna be strange being out and not being able to watch Molly open her presents.' He took a swig of the Scotch and put the glass down. 'I was wondering, Mum. Will you accompany me to her grave on Christmas Eve? We can lay flowers for Roy and Champ at the same time. I don't think I can face going alone.' Vinny and his brothers had never referred to their cousin as Lenny. They'd always called him Champ, ever since he was a nipper.

'Me and Viv have already made arrangements to go over the cemetery on Christmas Eve. How about me and you go over there Sunday on our own, eh? Or we could go Christmas morning?'

'Sunday sounds good. I have some running around to do on Christmas morning.'

'You're still coming to me for dinner, aren't you? Michael's coming. Nancy's going to her parents, but she'll be here in the evening with the boys. You won't recognize them now, Vin. They ain't arf shot up.'

'Will Auntie Viv still come if I'm here? She couldn't get out quick enough when I knocked on the door.'

'You leave Viv to me. She'll be fine. So where's Michael? I thought yous two would be out on the lash?'

'We had words, Mum. Nothing serious, so don't worry. Michael's gonna buy the club outright I think, and then I'm gonna make a fresh start by investing in a wine bar.'

Queenie looked crestfallen. 'But you've always worked together. That's what brothers do.'

'Yeah, well you can blame Michael for that. He's known all along how I feel about going back to the club. How would he feel, having to work somewhere that reminds him of his kid's murder? I've suggested we make a fresh start, buy a new place together, but he's adamant on keeping the club. Selfish bastard he is. I'd have stood by him if the boot had been on the other foot.'

'Oh dear. I was so hoping this Christmas would be one without any bleeding problems. We've had enough drama in this family to last us a lifetime.'

Vinny kissed his mother on the forehead. 'I've got some good news for you as well. But, you have to promise me you won't breathe a word until I give you the OK.'

'You have my word.'

'While I was in nick, I found something out. Joanna was pregnant when we split up. She doesn't know that I know yet, but I have another daughter, Mum.'

Queenie put her hand over her mouth. 'Crikey! That's wonderful news! But how can you be sure the child's yours? Jo's probably shacked up with another bloke by now.'

Vinny took the photos out of his pocket. 'The dates match up. See for yourself, Ava's a ringer for me.'

Queenie gasped as she laid eyes on her granddaughter for the very first time. It was actually a blessing the child looked nothing like Molly, as that would've upset Queenie greatly. 'Oh my gawd! She could be Little Vinny's twin at the same age. Ava's a pretty name. When can I meet her?'

'Soon. Colin, my solicitor, is on the case. I met up with him after me and Michael parted company earlier. That's where I'm going Christmas morning. I know Jo's address and her parents'. I'm gonna pay 'em a surprise visit and meet my daughter. Big mistake on their part keeping Ava a secret from me. Biggest mistake they'll ever fucking make.'

Bella was in turmoil. She'd thought she was over Michael, but he was having a worse effect on her than he'd had the first time around, and she desperately needed some space to figure out how she felt about all this. 'I must go home now. It's been lovely seeing you again though, Michael. I've thoroughly enjoyed myself.'

'Me too, sweetheart. What you doing tomorrow?'

'I'm taking Antonio to a pantomime. We're off to see *Aladdin*.'

'Weren't *Aladdin* about some rough geezer who met a princess?'

'Yes, and he had a magic lamp.'

'Sod the lamp – I only want the princess.'

Bella stood up. 'It's been a pleasure, Michael, as always.'

Michael grabbed hold of Bella's arm. 'You're not going anywhere until you've given me your phone number. When can I see you again?'

'You seem to have forgotten you're a married man. I can't get involved, Michael. It's not fair on Antonio. Neither is it fair on Nancy and your sons.'

Michael stood up, held Bella's hands and stared intensely into her eyes. 'Listen, Bella, I love you, I always have. I let you walk away from me once and not a day's gone by I haven't regretted it. No way will I ever make that mistake again.'

Ahmed Zane paid the cab driver, then helped Little Vinny out of the vehicle. The boy could barely put one foot in front of the other, and Ahmed was determined to find out what was troubling him. It was something big, Ahmed could feel it in his bones.

'I was enjoying myself at that club. Why did we have to come home?' Little Vinny slurred. They'd gone up west, but were now back at Ahmed's flat.

'Because you kept knocking into people, then wanting to fight them. Rack us some gear up, Vin. I'll pour the Scotch.'

Cocaine made him want to talk until the cows came home, and it wasn't long until Little Vinny started rambling on about Sammi-Lou.

'I remember you saying once that Sammi was too full-on. I think it was because she turned up at the club every night,' Ahmed reminded the lad.

'She was full-on, but that's only because she cared. She really did love me. Now she fucking hates me. Why did she have to get up the duff, eh? It's ruined everything.'

'You're just scared, Vin. You wait until you hold your daughter or son in your arms for the first time. All your worries will be replaced by feelings of unconditional love. I know, because I've been there.'

Little Vinny downed his Scotch in one greedy gulp. 'I'll be all right if it's a boy, but I won't if it's a girl. Sammi's sister looks like Molly, and so did Sammi when she was young. That'll be a proper head-fuck and I can't deal with it.'

'I know losing your sister was very upsetting, Vin, but life goes on.'

Chewing at his fingernails, Little Vinny gave no reply. He had kept the truth surrounding Molly's death a secret for so long, the guilt was eating away inside of him. Perhaps Ahmed was right? Maybe a problem shared was a problem halved?

'What is it, boy? You can tell me anything, you know that.'

Little Vinny shook his head. 'This is something proper bad, Ahmed. If my dad found out he'd kill me. I would tell you, but I can't.'

Knowing that cocaine loosened his lips, Ahmed racked up another two fat lines.

'Your dad is no saint, Vin. He's done some real bad stuff in the past. One thing in particular plays on my mind. It's something that involves you.'

Little Vinny crouched next to the coffee table with a straw in his hand.

'What? Tell me, Ahmed.'

'I can't. Because if your dad ever found out, he'd kill me.'

'You have my word that I'll never grass you up. I swear on my unborn kid's life and Sammi's. Please tell me. I promise if you do, I'll tell you my secret.'

Ahmed held out his right hand. 'You have a deal. But if you ever betray my trust, there will be major repercussions. You understand what I'm saying, don't you?'

Little Vinny nodded.

'How well do you remember your mum?'

'I don't remember her well. But I know she was very pretty. I had a photo of her for years, but I don't know where it is now. Why are you asking about my mum?'

'Because it was your dad who killed her.'

'No fucking way! That can't be right. I was told she died from a drug overdose.'

'Yes, she did. Your dad wanted her death to look like an overdose.'

Downing his drink in one, Little Vinny slammed the glass against the table. 'But why would he kill her?'

'Because she turned up in your life. Your dad didn't wanna share you.'

'So that's a good enough excuse to kill my poor mum, is it? I fucking hate him, Ahmed. He's a cunt and I wish he'd die.'

'Tell me what has been playing on your mind now. It can't be any worse than what I've just told you.'

Little Vinny took deep breaths. He could feel his heart racing and wasn't sure if it was due to the strength of the cocaine or the news he'd just heard. 'Promise you'll never repeat it, not to anyone. Swear on your life.'

Not a believer in old wives' tales, Ahmed swore on his life.

'It was me, Ahmed. I killed Molly.'

'Stop talking rubbish! It was Jamie Preston who killed your sister. Just because you were looking after her, doesn't mean you were to blame.'

Little Vinny put his messed-up head in his hands. 'You don't understand. It wasn't Jamie. It was me. I strangled Molly. Ben Bloggs helped me abduct her, then I throttled her with my bare hands. Do you see why I can't have a daughter now? Do you fucking understand?' Little Vinny yelled.

Ahmed Zane could only sit there in shock, his mouth open wide. He'd known that Little Vinny was harbouring a secret, but never in a million years would he have expected this.

'You won't tell my dad, will you? Promise me, Ahmed. Promise me.'

Looking into the drunken, coked-up lad's eyes, Ahmed saw nothing but evil. He and Vinny had always been sadistic fuckers, but only to those who had wronged them. Molly had been a lovely kid – a helpless three-year-old who'd never hurt anyone. How Little Vinny could have been so callous as to take his own sister's life beggared belief.

'Say something, Ahmed. Fucking say something,' Little Vinny pleaded.

Trying desperately to compose himself, Ahmed put an arm around the evil one's shoulders. 'It's OK, Vin. We all make mistakes. I won't breathe a word, I swear to God. Neither must you about your mum.'

'Thank you. I know I can trust you, Ahmed. I would never have killed Molly if I'd been the man I am now, you know. I was a kid back then, and I was really jealous of her.'

'I understand. I shall nip to the toilet, then pour us another drink,' Ahmed lied.

Instead of nipping to the toilet, Ahmed dashed into his bedroom and rummaged through the drawer for his miniature tape recorder. If ever anything needed to be preserved on tape, it was Little Vinny's confession. He would play it to his father before finally killing him off.

Oh yes, revenge truly was a dish best served cold.

CHAPTER SEVENTEEN

After spending most of Saturday hanging around White-chapel without catching so much as a glimpse of Brad or Kurt Baker, Daniel insisted that they would just have to come back again the following day.

'We can't sit 'ere, Dan. It's too near Nan's. Her neighbours are bound to recognize us,' Lee complained.

'Just keep your hood up and stare at the kerb if anyone walks past. If we don't make eye contact, we won't get recognized, unless Nan or Auntie Viv clock us. If that happens, we'll pretend we've come to visit 'em.'

'Two boys have just come out of a house near Nan's. Is that them, Dan?' Adam asked.

Daniel Butler stood up. The boys had their backs to him, were walking in the opposite direction, but he was sure it was Brad and Kurt. 'Come on. Let's follow 'em.'

Vinny Butler froze as he laid the flowers on his cousin's grave. 'This ain't the headstone I bought. My name ain't on it.'

Queenie crouched down next to her son and squeezed his hand. 'Vivian didn't think it was appropriate for your name to be on there after everything that happened, so

Michael paid for a new headstone. I thought he would've told you, Vin.'

'Nah. Far too full of his own self-importance these days to bother telling me about a change of headstone. Really upset me that has, but not as much as this will,' Vinny said, walking over to his daughter's tiny grave.

The headstone was made of expensive polished marble, and set in the centre was one of the last photographs taken of Molly. It had been Vinny's idea to have a photo of his daughter ground into the marble, with cherubs either side.

Tears rolled down Vinny's cheeks. 'That's a beautiful photo of her, Mum. I'm so glad you chose that particular one.'

'That smile of Molly's must be lighting up heaven as we speak. And I bet she's being spoilt rotten by your nan, your brother and Lenny. They'll take good care of her in our absence.'

Vinny crouched down. 'You Are My Sunshine' had been Molly's favourite song, so a verse plus the chorus was inscribed on the headstone. 'Daddy loves and misses you so much, sweetheart. Life just isn't the same without you. Merry Christmas, wherever you are.'

Seeing how distraught her big, strapping son was brought tears to Queenie's eyes. She rubbed Vinny's back. 'Let it all out, boy. Better out than in.'

'I can't believe I'm standing next to my daughter's dead body. No parent should ever out-live their kids. That cunt Preston will pay for what he's done, I promise you that, Mum.'

'And he deserves nothing less,' Queenie added.

Vinny planted his lips against Molly's photo. 'You got any of them wet wipes, Mum? Stinks of piss, does Molly's headstone.'

Queenie wiped the headstone and arranged the flowers

neatly in the vase. She then stood the teddy bear and card against the headstone. 'You OK, love? It does get easier, coming here, you know. I was the same as you at first.'

'It'll never get easier for me, Mum. Brings everything back, being 'ere. Let's go home.'

Jamie Preston nodded to a couple of fellow inmates as he sauntered down the corridor. Life in Wandsworth was a different kettle of fish to what he'd experienced in Feltham. In Wandsworth, you spent far more time locked up in your cell, which was why Jamie was so chuffed that he'd got himself a job in the laundry. It helped to relieve the boredom and gave him far less time to dwell on the fact he was paying for a crime he had not committed.

Unlike some of the lags, Jamie had few visitors. A couple of the lads he'd served time with in Feltham had come to see him since being freed, but other than that his only regular visitor was his nan. His uncle Johnny hadn't been in touch since the day they'd had their heart-to-heart. Leaving an innocent man to rot on the inside was not something Jamie could ever have on his conscience, but he felt he had only himself to blame by acting like a complete and utter idiot when Molly had first gone missing. To ring up the Old Bill and lead them on a wild-goose chase was a despicable thing to do when a child was involved, and Jamie was truly ashamed of his actions.

Entering the laundry, Jamie immediately set to work. 'You all right, Drakey? You don't seem your usual self.'

Andrew Drake glanced at the screw who was meant to be keeping a watchful eye on them but instead seemed to be completely engrossed in his newspaper. 'You need to watch your back. I overheard something earlier,' Andrew whispered in Jamie's ear.

'What?'

'Well, I ain't hundred per cent sure it was about you, but I don't know any other Preston in 'ere. I heard someone say you were gonna get done over.'

Jamie smirked. Andrew Drake wasn't the brightest spark around by far, which was one of the reasons he'd taken him under his wing. The lad had been bullied relentlessly by three of the other inmates until Jamie arrived on the scene and intervened.

'I won't be a minute, lads. Got a dodgy tummy,' said Brian the screw, getting up out of his seat and dashing out the door.

'Right, you can talk now. Who did you hear say what?' Jamie asked.

Before Andrew had a chance to reply, the door was flung open. 'Get out the fucking way,' Gerry Williams ordered Andrew.

Andrew immediately did as he was told. Gerry Williams was notorious as one of the prison's hard men. Nobody defied him.

'A present from Vinny Butler,' Gerry hissed, as he slung the contents of his bucket at Jamie. 'Anyone grasses, they're dead,' Gerry warned, before legging it.

Preston's screams were horrific. Scalding water mixed with sugar was truly every prisoner's worst nightmare.

Telling the barmaid to keep the change, Johnny Preston carried the drinks over to the table. 'What you sat here for? Real men stand at the bar.'

Far too nervous to see the funny side of Johnny's joke, Darren Grant tried to pluck up some courage. He genuinely liked Joanna's parents, but was wary of Johnny.

'Come on then, spit it out. You've brought me here for a reason, haven't you?'

'Yeah. How did you know?' Darren asked.

'Because you have the look of a man who's facing his

final hours on death row. What's up? You ain't got my Jo in the family way, have ya?'

'No. The thing is, Johnny, I know me and Joanna haven't been together that long, but I really do love her. We get on so well, and you must know what it's like when everything just clicks?'

'I sure do. I worship the ground my Deborah walks on.'

'I feel the same, which is why I wanted to drag you out the house for half an hour. If you give me your blessing, Johnny, I want to ask Jo to marry me on Christmas Day. We won't rush into anything, I promise – that's if Jo says yes, of course.'

'You can't propose without a ring, or have you already took the liberty of buying one?'

'No. I would never do that without asking your permission first. I did take the liberty of finding out Joanna's ring size though. My plan was, if you gave me the thumbs up, I would go to Covent Garden to buy a ring tomorrow.'

'You're an organized man, Darren, I'll give you that much. So, what happened between you and the mother of your son? Get bored with her, did you?'

Darren shook his head. 'My ex got involved with a fella at work. The relationship ended because of that. She was a city girl, was Lorraine. Not really the family-orientated type. We wanted different things in life, unlike me and Joanna. We want the same things.'

Johnny Preston was deep in thought as he sipped his pint. He wasn't sure his daughter was ready for marriage just yet, but Darren was an honest, hard-working bloke and an enormous improvement on Vinny Butler. Darren doted on Ava too, which was also important in Johnny's eyes. And Deborah thought the sun shined out of his arse. His wife was the best judge of character Johnny had ever met.

Darren could feel beads of sweat forming on his forehead

as he waited for an answer. 'Shall I get us another drink?' he asked politely.

Johnny nodded, then waited until Darren returned from the bar before delivering his answer. 'You have my permission, but I need you to promise me two things. You wait a year at least before you book the actual wedding, and if you have any doubts in the meantime you speak to me before telling Jo.'

'I promise. But there are no doubts, Johnny. If there was, I wouldn't be proposing in the first place. Joanna's the girl I want to spend the rest of my life with. I adore her.'

'I hope for your sake, you're right. Because I swear, if you ever hurt my daughter, or Ava, I will break every bone in your body. Now, do we understand one another?' Johnny held out his right hand.

Darren shook the outstretched hand. 'Yes.'

Nosy Hilda hadn't come by her nickname for no reason. When she wasn't outdoors prying into people's lives, she was indoors peering at them through the net curtains.

Earlier, Hilda had spotted three lads she believed to be Queenie's grandsons. They had their hoods up even though it wasn't raining and seemed to be following Brad and Kurt Baker in a rather suspicious manner. Still annoyed with Queenie for lying about Brenda's visit, Hilda decided to make it her business to find out what they were up to.

She'd followed them for some distance before one of the boys paused and looked around him in a furtive manner. Quickly ducking out of sight behind a parked van, Hilda couldn't resist a triumphant little chuckle. 'You're definitely up to no good and I will catch you out! That'll teach that deceitful nan of yours to lie to me. Michael's cleaner, my arse.'

*

Burak Zane dragged his cousin straight into the office. Ahmed had rung him yesterday, said he had some earth-shattering news, then refused to reveal what it was – as per usual.

'Ask the chef to rustle me up some food, Burak. What's the dish of the day?'

'Sod the dish of the day. I want to know what's happened. I've been racking my brains and it has to be something Little Vinny said. Am I right?'

Ahmed grinned as he handed Burak the cassette. The original recording was now locked away in his secret safe at home and only he knew the combination to that.

Burak pressed the play button. The quality wasn't great, but he recognized Little Vinny's voice immediately.

'Turn it up. You'll hear something very interesting in a minute,' Ahmed chuckled.

Burak did as Ahmed asked, then gasped as he clearly heard his cousin ask Little Vinny why he'd killed his own sister. 'What the hell!' he exclaimed.

'Shush. Or you'll miss the best bit.'

When Burak heard Little Vinny say he'd murdered Molly through jealously, because his dad had loved her more, he stood open-mouthed. He was shocked to the core, could barely believe what he was hearing.

'Pause it and pour a drink. You look like you've seen a ghost,' Ahmed laughed.

'I cannot fucking believe it. I know we've done some bad things in our time, but nothing tops this. Didn't he write some heartfelt speech and read it out at Molly's funeral?'

'Yes. All about how much he loved and missed Molly. Must be a psychopath.'

'Shows you how shit the Old Bill are! They obviously didn't want the East End to be in a panic, thinking there was a child-killer on the loose, so they arrested the wrong boy. You don't think Little Vinny was lying, do you?'

'Most definitely not. Ben Bloggs helped him abduct Molly. That's why Ben hung himself. No wonder Little Vinny is so fucked up and can't handle his girlfriend being pregnant. It all makes perfect sense now. Can you imagine what our policeman friend Christopher Walker would make of this story, eh?'

'Don't be involving him again, Ahmed. Policemen cannot be trusted – as Jamie Preston being locked up for murder proves. We must deal with this ourselves.'

Ahmed smirked. 'If you ask me, we should enlighten Vinny sooner rather than later. He might have got through prison better than expected, but no way will he be able to handle the knowledge that his own son killed poor little Molly. What father could?'

Burak shuddered. Unlike Ahmed he wasn't married, but he did have an eight-year-old son from a casual affair, and he saw the child on a regular basis.

'Come on,' Ahmed urged, 'Think how entertaining it will be to see him go to pieces. There's no way he will allow his son to go on living once he finds out, and then—'

'No, cousin, it is far too dangerous for us to play any more mind games with the Butlers. Let's just lure Vinny and his son somewhere under false pretences, play the tape, then finish them both off. They are vermin.'

Sunday was Bella's favourite day of the week. She'd recently started up her own modelling agency in London's West End, so from Monday to Friday she had to work long hours, and Saturday was often spent catching up on paperwork. Sunday was the one day of the week that she could dedicate entirely to her beloved son.

'Mummy, can I have some waffles, please?' Antonio

asked, his eyes glued to the television. His current obsession was Spiderman.

Bella planted many kisses on her son's face before heading into the kitchen. Antonio was such a loving, polite, intelligent, good-natured child. Truly a gift from God.

'Mummy, the phone's ringing again. Shall I answer it?' Antonio shouted.

'No. Let it go to answerphone, darling.'

Bella smiled as she heard Michael's voice leave another message. She'd been an easy catch the first time round, and that had brought her nothing but heartache. This time she was determined to play things very differently.

Vinny Butler eyed the new décor with a look of contempt on his face. Gone was all the classy leather furniture. The club just resembled a big open space now, with bench-style seating and shelving fitted around the walls. The worst feature of all was the wall facing the entrance. 'Butler's Disco' had been painted on it, along with stupid images of dancing people either side of the name.

'Glows of a night, that. Looks good, don't it? Michael employed some bloke to come in and paint it. Professional graffiti artist. Clever man, eh?'

Vinny treated Pete to a look of pure disdain. 'Michael wants to ask for a fucking refund. I've seen better graffiti on bus shelters round by the market. Looks cheap and nasty.'

'Looks different in the dark, Vin. Especially with the new strobe lighting Michael's just invested in. Amazing, that is.'

'The only thing amazing about this shithole is the fact I own it. Where is Billy Big Bollocks? Lording it up in the office?'

Pete nodded. He hated it when Vinny and Michael were at each other's throats. It made him feel awkward, and both he and Paul were dreading Michael's reaction when he found out they were leaving to work for Vinny.

Vinny entered the office without knocking first. 'Well, this is cosy. Room for another one?'

Albie, who had his back to the door, spilt half of his mug of tea over his trousers.

'Steady on there, Dad. Anyone would think you weren't pleased to see me,' Vinny chuckled.

'How are you, Vinny? You're looking well,' Albie mumbled.

'Yeah, I'm good thanks, Dad. I never received any of your letters while I was in nick. Must've got lost in the post, eh?'

'If you've got a fucking bone to pick, pick it with me, Vin,' growled Michael. He nodded to his father: 'Go and pour yourself a drink, Dad. I'll be out in a bit.'

'So what's it gonna be? We gonna try and have a sensible chat? Or you gonna go stomping off like a child again?' Vinny smirked.

'I didn't stomp off like a child. I left the restaurant because it was the only way I could keep myself from decking you.'

'And when exactly did you become the big tough guy, Michael? That'll be the day when you deck me, let me tell you.'

'I'm busy. What is it you want, Vin?'

'You heard from Little Vinny?'

'No. He's hardly bothered contacting me since he stopped working 'ere. Surely your mucker Ahmed knows where he is?'

'Ahmed said that, as far as he knows, Little Vinny's at home. But I've been ringing his number and can't get no reply. Ahmed's meeting me here in a bit. We're gonna take a drive down to the address. Some son he's turned out to be.'

'Perhaps he feels the same way about you as you do our dad?'

'Very funny, Michael.' He applauded mirthlessly. 'With that great humour of yours, you should be on stage doing a stand-up routine. You'd bring the house down with lines like that. And just in case you're suffering from some kind of memory loss, our father was a drunken, potless bum when we were growing up. Me and Roy had to go out thieving to help Mum put food on the table and pay her rent and bills. Whereas Little Vinny has never wanted for anything in his lifetime, the spoilt, ungrateful fucker.'

Michael poured himself a Scotch. 'Want one?'

'No, thanks. Thought any more about my offer?'

'Yeah, and I still think you're taking the piss. Have you thought any more about that promise you made in prison? A fifty-fifty share for me as soon as you got out.'

'Yes, but that was before you moved the goal posts, Michael.'

'How have I moved any goal posts? A deal's a fucking deal.'

'And I would've kept to my side of the bargain, had you not expected me to give you a property the size of this for nothing. What do you think I am? Some cunt still wet behind the ears?'

'How about if you keep a small stake in the business instead? Ten per cent is more than fair,' Michael insisted.

'Ten per cent! You've having a laugh, ain't ya! You got any idea what this property is worth?'

Michael knocked back his drink. He had plenty of dosh in the bank, but what if he and Bella wanted to make a proper go of it? Nancy had been on his earhole lately about moving the boys to a nicer area and, if his circumstances were to change, not only would he have to provide for Nancy and the boys, Bella would expect to live in luxury as well.

Vinny stood up. 'Right, you're boring me now, Michael. Get back to me when you've made your decision. Oh, and

Jay Boy won't be working tomorrow. He's coming out on the lash with me.'

'I need Jay 'ere, Vin. We've sold all the tickets.'

Vinny grinned as he turned his back on his brother. Jay Boy, Pete and Paul had been ordered to keep their traps shut, so he would save the news of their imminent resignation to ruin Michael's Christmas.

After hanging about in the freezing cold outside the Wimpy while the Bakers stuffed their faces, Daniel Butler felt the time was right to strike. He hid until the Bakers turned into a side street, glanced around to make sure the coast was clear, then took the knife out of his pocket. 'Come on. Let's do 'em.'

Hearing footsteps running behind them, Kurt and Brad were quickly on their guard. 'What do you little mugs want?' Kurt Baker taunted.

'We ain't scared of you little pricks,' Brad Baker added.

Daniel Butler was very astute for a twelve year old. He'd leared a lot from his father, incuding mimicking his tone and certain words he used when he was angry. 'Well, you should be scared, you dopey cunts,' Daniel hissed, brandishing a knife.

Kurt Baker was fourteen, older and wiser than Daniel. 'Put that away and go home, you div. You'll get us all nicked otherwise.'

'Who you calling a div?' Daniel spat, lunging towards both boys and making prodding motions like he was some fencing expert. Realising Daniel wasn't right in the head, Kurt urged his brother to run.

'Get 'em, Lee. Chase 'em, Adam,' Daniel ordered.

Frozen to the spot, Adam Butler put his hand on his crotch and promptly wet himself through fear. His mum had always warned him of situations such as this. She'd said he'd end up in the bad boy's home like his friend Denny Crookes had. Daniel Butler laughed like a hyena as Brad Baker slipped. He leapt on top of him and plunged the knife straight into the skin. Blood seeped through Brad's clothing and trickled onto the pavement.

Wishing for once she didn't have such an inquisitive nature, Nosy Hilda shook like a leaf as she crouched behind the Ford Cortina. She'd always known the Butlers had a violent reputation, but what she'd just witnessed had shocked her to the core. Daniel had only celebrated his twelfth birthday recently. What hope was there for him in life?

Vinny Butler hadn't had a chance to purchase himself a new car yet, so Ahmed had kindly offered to drive him to Harold Wood to see his son.

'I hope we don't have a wasted journey. The little shit better be in. He ain't even been in touch with my mum recently. She hasn't a clue whether he's coming to Christmas dinner or not. How's he been getting on working with you? You had any problems with him?'

'No. Little Vinny is reliable and does his job well. Not sure he's ready to be a dad yet though.'

'Tough shit. He should've thought of that before humping without protection.'

Ahmed grinned. 'You should come and see the bar tomorrow. I am holding a party there for staff and friends. I'm sure you'd enjoy letting your hair down.'

Vinny had been hurt and annoyed when Ahmed had bought his bar without inviting him to participate, therefore had no wish to see it. Investing in such a property had been his idea in the first place, and Vinny couldn't understand why his pal hadn't waited until he came out of nick so they could be business partners. 'Nah, you're OK. I've already made plans for tomorrow.'

'What you up to?'

'Going out with Jay Boy. Eddie Mitchell's popping down the Beggar for a beer with us at lunchtime. Should be a good 'un. Not been pissed since I got out,' Vinny chuckled.

'Did you keep in contact with Mitchell while you were inside?'

'No. He left a message at the club and I rung him back last night. Salt of the earth, he is,' Vinny said, knowing full well Ahmed was wary of his budding friendship with Eddie, son of the legendary Harry Mitchell. Like the Butlers, the Mitchell family had built up a fearsome reputation in the East End. They'd started out in Canning Town with a pub protection racket, but rumour had it they'd now gone into the old loan-sharking game as well. In the past the Mitchells and the Butlers had always been careful to steer clear of each other's turf, but after Molly's murder Eddie had offered his help in finding the culprit. It was a gesture that had meant a lot to Vinny.

'We're nearly there now. I think I should wait in the car. You need to spend father-and-son time alone,' Ahmed suggested.

'Michael tells me the kid's back on the booze.'

'Not at work, he isn't. I don't allow any of my staff to drink during their shifts. That's his house there,' Ahmed pointed out.

Vinny stared at the property. The area was nice and the house looked decent. 'Bollocks. His car ain't on the drive.'

What Vinny did not know as he stood pummelling his fist against the door was that Ahmed had warned his son of their impending visit.

CHAPTER EIGHTEEN

Shell Baker led her sons down the corridor. Kurt had been kept in overnight as a precaution, but thankfully his injury wasn't too serious. The doctor said he was lucky because the wound was only an inch deep and had missed the major blood vessels.

'I need yous two to do something for me,' Shell said.

'What?' Kurt replied.

'The police are coming round to ours in a bit. You're not to tell them the truth. I want you to say you got into a row with three boys you'd never seen before. Think up some descriptions between yourselves now.'

'But we told you who done it, Mum. Why can't we just tell Old Bill the truth? Daniel Butler is a lunatic, and next time he might kill someone,' Brad warned.

'Brad's right, Mum. Why should we risk getting in trouble for lying to the Old Bill when we ain't done sod-all wrong?'

'Because I bloody-well said so. They're a vile family, those Butlers, and I don't want any more grief with them. You remember when your Uncle Karl got beaten up that time?'

Kurt and Brad nodded.

'Well, Daniel Butler's father did that – just because we

217

played loud music. Can you imagine what he'll do to Karl if you grass his son up?'

Kurt and Brad glanced at one another. Both thought the world of their uncle, and would be devastated if anything bad were to happen to him. 'OK, Mum. We'll lie,' Kurt said.

Little Vinny was in the Pompadours pub in Harold Hill. Getting off his face certainly wasn't the answer to his problems, but it beat sitting indoors waiting for his father to knock again. He'd got so paranoid last night when he'd heard a car engine running, he'd hidden in the bottom of the wardrobe for ten minutes.

Kicking the leg of the table in frustration, Little Vinny rested his chin on his hands. How could he have been so stupid as to tell Ahmed about Molly? His boss had sounded fine in the few answerphone messages he'd left, but no way could Little Vinny look him in the eye just yet. That's why he'd skipped the work do today. He was still in shock after learning that his dad had killed his mum as well. Something else to mess with his head, that was.

'All right, Vin. I got your stuff. Give it a couple of minutes, then follow me outside. I'm in the blue Cabriolet.'

Little Vinny nodded. He'd only met the local drug dealer for the first time yesterday and had ordered half an ounce to see him OK over Christmas. The gear was probably cack compared to the purity of the stuff he was used to, but anything was better than facing Ahmed right now. He was too eaten up with self-pity and worry to face anybody he knew.

Queenie Butler had her hand up a turkey's arse when Michael let himself in. She liked her boys to have their own keys and come and go as they pleased. It made her feel as though they'd never really left home.

'I just saw Auntie Viv down the market, Mum. She looked a bit glum.'

'We haven't long been back from our grave-visiting duties. Viv finds this time of year very difficult, Michael. Cried like a baby at the cemetery and I had to drag her away. I think she's got the hump because Vinny's gonna be here for Christmas an' all.'

'Tomorrow is what I've come to see you about, Mum. Sorry to let you down, but I'm gonna have to give it a miss.'

Queenie was annoyed. 'Please don't tell me you're not coming because of your brother. I'll bang your bleedin' heads together before long if you don't make this silly argument up.'

'It's nothing to do with Vinny. Dad's gonna be on his own, and he gets very down this time of year an' all since Dorothy passed away.'

Screwing her nose up at the mention of the woman her ex-husband had found true love with until she'd popped her clogs, Queenie turned on her son. 'I can't believe you're putting that old bastard before me, Michael. I'm your mother, the one who spent hours giving birth to you. I'm also the one that worked her fingers to the bone cleaning them posh arseholes' houses when you were young and while your father was out drinking and whoring.'

'I know you're upset, Mum, but you're still gonna have plenty of company, unlike Dad. He ain't looking too well lately. His breathing is bad and for all I know this could well be his last Christmas. No way am I letting him spend it alone.'

'Oh, for Christ sake, invite the old fucker round 'ere then.'

'Really?'

'Yes. Ring him quick before I change me mind.'

'Thanks, Mum. You're a diamond.'

Cackling away to herself, Queenie waited until Michael was out of earshot before muttering, 'Be funny if the old tosspot kicks the bucket while he's 'ere tomorrow.'

Johnny Preston was locking up the office, when the phone rang. He'd had a couple of near misses earlier with customers buying cars as last-minute presents and dashed back in, hoping it would be someone ringing to say they'd changed their mind.

'Mum!' Johnny exclaimed when he heard the voice at the other end. They hadn't spoken since he'd refused to back Jamie.

'Don't you call me Mum. Jamie's suffering from the most awful burns. Currently in St Andrew's Hospital in Billericay fighting for his life. I hope you're fucking proud of yourself, Johnny, and I hope that fat slag you chose over your own flesh and blood turns out to be worth it. You knew that boy was innocent, yet you opted not to help him. Don't you dare show your face round here ever again – you disgust me.'

Vinny Butler got a hero's welcome as he sauntered into the Blind Beggar. Even a soldier returning from the Falklands would not have received more handshakes, pats on the back and offers of drinks.

Lapping up the attention, Vinny gave the barman three hundred quid and told him the drinks were on him until the money ran out.

Jay Boy was impressed. 'Jesus, Vin. I knew you were well known, but I didn't know you were as famous as Kenny Dalglish,' he joked, referring to his football idol.

'Come on, let's nab that table,' Vinny said, excusing himself from his fan club.

'What time you going to see Ava tomorrow?' Jay asked.

'My brief's picking me up at nine. We're gonna drive to Joanna's first. If she ain't there, she's bound to be at her parents'. I can't wait to see the lying slag's face when I knock on the door. Colin's had a load of legal-looking jargon drawn up, stating that if I am refused visitation rights, we'll be taking Jo to court. And he's threatened that she'll be arrested if she disappears with the child. That'll shit the life out the Prestons,' Vinny chuckled.

'You must be well excited.'

'Very, but I'm also a bit nervous. Gonna be strange, meeting me daughter for the very first time. I hope Ava likes me. I went out first thing this morning and bought her some really nice presents.'

'Sound. She'll love you, Vin. Do you want me to come with you for a bit of moral support?'

'Nah. I'll be fine, but thanks anyway. Colin weren't too pleased to be giving up part of his Christmas Day, but he soon changed his tune when he heard what I was paying him. Money buys anything, always remember that, Jay Boy. I'll be back early, so I was gonna suggest you meet me in 'ere at lunchtime. We can have a few beers before we go to me mum's. Bound to kick off once we get round there, it always does at some point,' he chuckled.

Jay Boy joined in the laughter. He was grateful to Vinny for the invitation; he went back to Liverpool occasionally to visit his own family, but could never spend Christmas there now. It reminded him too much of the brother he'd so tragically lost.

'Welcome back to reality, Vinny. How's it going? You're looking well, mate,' Eddie Mitchell said.

Surprised to see Harry, Ronny and Paulie as well, Vinny

leapt out of his seat and shook hands with all four of the Mitchells. 'Sit down while I shout yous up a drink. What's your poison? This is my pal Jay Boy, by the way. He was my cellmate in the Ville. Top lad, he works for me now.'

'I'll come up the ramp and give you a hand,' Eddie replied.

Chatting away to Eddie at the bar, Vinny noticed that all eyes were on them. The Mitchells were just as notorious in the East End as his own family, and now he was about to part company with Michael, Vinny would love to one day set up a joint business venture with them. Especially with Eddie. Together they would be formidable.

When they returned to the table and Vinny handed Harry Mitchell a large brandy, he was surprised when the man thrust a large envelope into his hand. 'What's that?'

'Just a little home-coming gift.'

When he saw the envelope was stuffed with fifty-pound notes, Vinny handed it straight back. 'That's a lovely thought, Harry, but I can't take it. I'm fine for wonga, and the club's done really well in my absence.'

Eddie Mitchell laughed. 'Just take it, Vin, 'cause my old man don't take no for an answer. I told him you wouldn't accept it, but he's old school.'

'I'll have it if you don't want it,' Ronny Mitchell joked.

'Honestly, it's a lovely gesture, but I would much rather you shared it amongst your grandkids,' Vinny told Harry.

Harry put his hand on Vinny's arm. 'Back in the day, when a man came out of prison a gift was always waiting for him. It's an unwritten rule for our kind. We look after our own. Believe me, I know you don't need it, but I will be very insulted and upset if you don't take it.'

Vinny took the envelope and shook the old man's hand. No way was he going to insult or upset the fucking Mitchells.

*

Bella smiled as she sat down opposite Madam Lydia. 'Thank you for fitting me in today. I thought you'd be too busy.'

Madam Lydia squeezed Bella's hand before staring into her crystal ball. She had clients come to her from all over the world, such was her unique talent for predicting their futures. Bella had been to her quite a few times in the past and even though Madam Lydia had not been planning on working today, she'd had one of her funny feelings whilst speaking to Bella on the phone and knew it was important to see her as soon as possible.

Bella could feel her heart pumping in her chest. Madam Lydia had predicted some years ago that she would meet a married man, then move to New York when the relationship failed. All of which had since come true. She'd also predicted she would have a son.

'Ah, so your visit today is regarding a man. Very handsome, dark hair, kind face. He's also someone from your past. Am I correct?'

Bella nodded.

'This man loves you. I can see his wife in the background, but she is moving away from him. That means their marriage will come to an end. Oh dear, that's very strange.'

'What's the matter?' Bella asked, alarmed.

'The wife has completely vanished.'

'What does that mean?'

'I'm not sure, but she will no longer have contact with her husband.'

'Is there a future with me and this man, do you think?' Bella asked, nervousness creeping into her voice.

'I can see lots of love between this man and yourself, and yes I can see bells, so that means a wedding is planned.'

Bella breathed a sigh of relief. Bella Butler had a wonderful ring to it and Madam Lydia had so often been right in the past.

'Oh dear, now I don't like the look of him. He has a dark shadow surrounding him. This man is sinister and is out to cause trouble for you.'

Suddenly feeling rather nauseous, Bella asked, 'What man? The one who loves me?'

'No. There is another man. He is not a nice person, not a nice person at all.'

'I wonder who that could be then?'

'I have no idea, but you stay away from him, do you hear me? Stay well away. He is not a nice person at all.'

'They're home. Look! And he's only limping. No sign of the Old Bill either. Told you Brad wouldn't die and we'd be in the clear. Yous two worry too much,' Daniel told his brothers.

'I didn't say he would die. That was Adam,' Lee reminded his brother.

'Well, that taught the Baker boys a lesson. Bet they don't mess with us again,' Daniel chuckled.

'Now they're home, Dan, let's go and buy our presents. We haven't bought one yet,' Adam said.

Daniel shook his head. 'Nah, I can't be arsed. You can get presents cheaper after Christmas. There's a sale on then. That way we can keep most of the money Dad gave us. Good idea, right, Lee?'

Rather than admit he would prefer to buy the Christmas presents for their family today, Lee just nodded. It was always easier to agree rather than disagree with Daniel.

Bella answered the phone on the third ring. 'Hello.'

'Bella, it's Michael. How are you?'

'Very well, thank you. Yourself?'

'All the better for hearing your voice. What you been up to?'

'I have just read Antonio a bedtime story. He's fast asleep now.'

'I bet he's looking forward to tomorrow. Where you spending the day?'

'Here. My parents are in London, so they will spend the day with us. What about you? Will you be at home with Nancy and the boys?'

'You're joking, ain't ya? Nancy's going to her parents with the boys and I'm going to my mum's. I told you, we lead separate lives now,' Michael said, conveniently not telling Bella that Nancy and the boys would be joining him at his mum's later in the evening.

The next half an hour was spent chatting about life in general, until Michael decided to ask the all-important question. 'So when am I gonna see you again?'

Not sure if Michael was lying about his and Nancy's stagnant relationship, Bella decided to test him. 'How about Boxing Day? My parents are taking Antonio sightseeing, so we could meet for lunch if you like?' Bella guessed it would be very difficult for a married man to make an excuse to leave his family on Boxing Day.

'Yep. That's fine. What time and where?'

After finalizing arrangements, Bella replaced the receiver and grinned. Madam Lydia had been right. She could feel it in her bones.

CHAPTER NINETEEN

'Vin, open up. I know you're in there. I saw you peep through the curtain.'

Receiving no reply, Ahmed lifted up the letterbox flap. 'I swear, if you don't open this door, I will break the poxy thing down.'

Little Vinny opened the door and Ahmed followed him into the lounge. The lad had obviously been on one of his binges. He looked awful. 'I was worried about you yesterday. Why didn't you come to the party?' Ahmed asked.

Having already prepared his get-out clause, Little Vinny hung his head in shame. 'Because of what I said about Molly. I never killed her, Ahmed. As if. I might be a bit of a lad, but I ain't no child-killer. Neither was Ben. He loved Molly, and raised his brothers and sisters while his slag of a mother was out whoring. It was her I killed. I slit Alison Bloggs' wrists and made it look like suicide. I did it to get revenge for Ben. Alison made his life hell. That's why he topped himself.'

'Why did you say you killed Molly instead of Alison then?'

Little Vinny shrugged. 'To see if I could trust you, I

suppose. I wanted to see if you'd say anything to my dad or Michael, before I confessed properly. You do believe me, don't you?'

Ahmed wasn't stupid. He knew the little shit was regretting his confession and trying to lie his way out of it. Well, two could play that game. Slapping his employee on the back, Ahmed chuckled. 'Great minds think alike, Vin. That's why I knew it was a good decision to make you my right-hand man at the wine bar.'

Confused, Little Vinny asked what his boss meant.

'I'm afraid I lied too. Your dad didn't really kill your mum. But he did kill other people. I was waiting to see if I could trust you before revealing the gory details.'

'Saying my dad killed my mum isn't funny, Ahmed. I've been thinking about it ever since.'

'Neither is pretending you throttled your little sister, Vin. So shall we call a truce?'

Relieved that his own lie had been believed, Little Vinny held out his right hand. 'Fancy a beer? Or you gotta dash home?'

'I'll have a beer. Anna and the children have gone to her parents' for the day. My religion doesn't really celebrate Christmas. New Year is when we have family and friends over and indulge in a big feast like you English do on Christmas Day. The kids love Christmas though. They got me up at six to open their presents. Speaking of kids, have you heard from Sammi?'

'Not a peep. I really think it's over between us.'

'That girl loves you, Vin, and if you care about her you need to man up and do something about it. What I suggest is we pop to a pub, have a few beers and a couple of lines, that will give you some Dutch courage, then we drive round to Sammi's parents' house. If you haven't contacted her, she probably thinks that you don't want to know. She is pregnant with your child. You need to show her you have feelings towards her.'

'What about her old man though? He's a lairy bastard and he hates me.'

'Bollocks to her old man. I'll be with you to back you up. Shame you haven't got Sammi any presents that you could take with you.'

'I have bought her presents. I did my Christmas shopping weeks ago and got her a load of stuff from Beau Baggage.'

'What you waiting for then?'

'I'll just have a quick shower and get changed before we go. I look a mess.'

'No need. You look fine,' Ahmed lied.

When Little Vinny grabbed his keys, Ahmed smirked. When the dishevelled-looking evil one turned up pissed and coked-up on the Allens' doorstep, Gary was bound to knock his lights out.

His whole body pumping with adrenalin, Vinny Butler pressed the doorbell. There was a car on the drive, which was a good sign.

'You looking for Jo, love?' a neighbour asked, as she flung open her window.

'Yes, I'm an old friend.'

'She's gone to her parents' house. Not due back until the twenty-seventh.'

Thanking the nosy neighbour, Vinny opened the passenger door of Colin's car, smirked and mumbled the word 'Bingo.'

Shirley Preston had been planning on spending Christmas with a friend, but instead was at her grandson's bedside at St Andrew's Hospital in Billericay.

'You all right, Nan? How long you been here?' Jamie croaked.

'Not long, love. You were soundo, so I didn't want to wake you. How you feeling today?'

'Sore. But I'll survive. I'm just thankful my face ain't scarred for life. I can cover up me body.' Jamie's left shoulder, chest and stomach had borne the brunt of the burns.

'What did the guvnor say when he visited?' Shirley asked.

'Asked me who did it. I told him I didn't know. Then he offered to put me in a different wing for my own protection, which I refused.'

'Why did you refuse?'

'Because it's the wing where all the nonces are kept. I can't handle being around scum like that.'

Shirley squeezed her grandson's hand. She was so desperately worried about his welfare. 'You can't go back to where you were, love. At least you'll be safe on that other wing.'

'No way, Nan. Makes me look guilty when I'm innocent. I've asked the guvnor if I can be moved to Chelmsford. I've got a few pals in there who I was in Feltham with.'

'Did he agree?'

'Not yet. He said he'll get back to me. I tell you something, Nan, and I mean this from the bottom of my heart. If I survive prison, the day I walk out those big gates, I will get even with every bastard who has ever wronged me.'

Nosy Hilda and Mouthy Maureen were indulging in a Christmas-morning tipple. Unable to keep the secret of what she'd seen to herself, Hilda had just informed Maureen.

'Oh my God! I saw Michael's boys acting suspiciously that day as well. I wasn't sure it was them at first 'cause they had their hoods up, but then young Adam turned around.'

'Lee and Adam didn't do sod-all. It was Daniel who stabbed that poor boy. I saw everything,' Hilda boasted.

Mouthy Maureen despised Queenie and Vivian Butler. She'd tried to make friends with them, but they were wrapped up in their own little bubble and couldn't be bothered with anybody but their own. Rude, common and abrupt were just three of the words that Maureen would choose to describe them.

'The Baker boys must've known who the culprit was, but I bet Shell told 'em to keep their trap shut after her brother got a good hiding that time.'

'What time?'

Hilda explained what had happened. 'I'm only speculating, but I know Queenie and Viv were moaning about the loud music. My guess is Michael sorted it for them. I mean, I used to hear the Bakers' music from my house, yet I've not heard it once since Karl got done over.'

'Me neither. Not nice people those Butlers, Hilda. I think you should tell the police what you saw. I'll back you up and tell them I saw Michael's boys acting suspiciously.'

'Don't be so stupid. Anyone who grasses that family must have a death wish.'

Mouthy Maureen smirked. 'Nobody will know it was us if we make an anonymous phone call, will they?'

Johnny Preston grinned at his wife as Ava opened her final present. She'd forgotten all about Bagpuss now, thankfully. Ava's beloved kitten had met an untimely death under the wheels of a Vauxhall Corsa.

Cabbage Patch dolls were the latest kids' craze and Johnny and Deborah had travelled miles to purchase the two they thought Ava would like best. Such was the demand for the dolls, Deborah had nearly had a fight in the shop when some deranged woman had tried to snatch the gifts out of her hands.

'Say thank you to Nanny and Granddad,' Joanna

ordered, embarrassed by her daughter's lack of appreciation.

'When you wrote that letter to Santa, you told him these were what you wanted, Ava,' Deborah reminded her granddaughter.

'But then I wrote Santa another letter at nursery and told him I wanted a dog,' Ava sulked.

'Kids, eh? So ungrateful these days. Come on, Darren. Let's go for a pint up the Anchor,' Johnny ordered, his voice tinged with anger.

When her dad and boyfriend left the house, Joanna scolded her daughter. Ava could be such a sweet child at times, but unlike Molly she wasn't perfect.

Michael Butler tapped on the window of the Blind Beggar.

The guvnor opened the door. 'Morning, Michael. Hello, Albie. Everything OK?'

'Yeah, fine. Any chance of an early drink? I realize you ain't officially open yet, but you know how mobbed I get whenever I walk in. Me and Dad just wanna quiet chat.'

'Of course, Michael. What would you like to drink? My treat, and Merry Christmas to you both.'

'It won't be a merry one for me. I'm lumbered spending the day with Queenie,' Albie joked.

Michael sat down opposite his father. 'Do you remember me telling you about that bird I fell for years ago? I was really cut up when she moved to New York.'

'Of course I do. You said she was to you what my Dorothy was to me. Wasn't her name Bella?'

'Yep. Well, I bumped into her again. Fate, it was. I had a bust-up with Vinny, ended up in some wine bar, and there she was. Now I can't stop thinking about her. I've arranged to meet her tomorrow for lunch.'

'What about Nancy and the boys?'

'The boys are all grown up now. They're more than old enough to handle me and their mother splitting up. I'm sick of living a lie, Dad. That weekend I took Nance away for our anniversary bored me shitless if you want the truth. We have sod-all in common and I don't love her any more in the way I should.'

Thanking the guvnor for the drinks, Albie necked his chaser in one. 'I'm not sure the boys will handle it very well. I think Daniel especially will go off the rails if you leave home.'

'What makes you think that? I'll still see the boys as often as I can and, let's be honest, I'm barely at home these days. Daniel's just finding his feet in life. I know he's had a few scrapes, but he isn't a bad kid.'

Not wanting to upset his favourite son, Albie smiled. 'True love is hard to find, son. I know that. Dorothy was my world and no woman will ever replace her. Go with your heart, but promise me you won't rush into anything. You've only just met up with Bella again.'

Michael shrugged. 'Can't promise you that, Dad. I've already lost this woman once and no way am I losing her again. I love her, simple as.'

Deborah Preston was busy preparing the vegetables when the doorbell rang. 'Get that, Jo. It's probably Sandy, arrived early,' Deborah shouted, referring to her best friend.

'I'll get it, Nanny,' Ava said, excitedly. She'd got to the age where she loved to answer the door and the phone. It made her feel like a big girl.

As the door opened, Vinny stared at the child. Seeing her in the flesh up close was completely different to seeing her in a photograph. She had the biggest green eyes Vinny had ever seen, and looked like a female version of him at the same age. Vinny crouched down. 'Hello, darling. I'm your daddy. Merry Christmas.'

Dropping the saucepan in shock, Deborah Preston darted towards the front door. 'Get away from her. If you don't I'll call the police.'

'Mummy said my daddy died,' Ava mumbled, unable to take her eyes off Vinny.

'Did she really, darlin'? That makes Mummy a liar then. Now, do you want to open all the presents Daddy bought you?'

Ava grinned, then started crying as her nan dragged her away.

Frozen with fear, Joanna was unable to move from the armchair. Apart from Molly's death, this was her biggest nightmare.

Vinny shoved his foot inside the door when Deborah tried to slam it. 'Meet my solicitor, Colin. He has some legal papers here for you.'

Hearing the word legal, Joanna found her bravado and dashed into the hallway. No way was that bastard having anything to do with her daughter. 'Ava isn't yours, Vinny. If she was, I would have told you. Now go away and leave us alone.'

Colin waved his paperwork in the air and cleared his throat. 'I really think we should discuss this inside. Your neighbours seem to be taking notice of events.'

Having moved from Tiptree to Burnham-on-Crouch, Deborah did not want a scene in front of her new neighbours.

'Ava isn't yours. Tell him, Mum. Tell him,' Joanna cried, when her mother gestured for Vinny and Colin to follow her into the lounge.

'Why don't you take Ava upstairs, love, while I sort this out,' Deborah suggested. She could feel herself trembling.

She knew Johnny would hit the roof if Vinny was here when he returned.

'You ain't taking my daughter anywhere. I've bought Ava lots of presents and I intend to watch her open them,' Vinny hissed, crouching down and urging Ava to unwrap his gifts.

'My Little Pony! This is what I wanted,' Ava exclaimed happily.

'Glad you like it, sweetheart,' Vinny grinned, taking the toy out the box.

'I love it, Daddy. Thank you,' Ava replied, throwing her arms around Vinny's neck.

Joanna began to hyperventilate. 'Get away from him. He isn't your father,' she screamed.

Vinny glared at the mother of his child. With her long blonde hair and blue eyes, at twenty-six Jo was still attractive, but she'd never really done it for him. He'd only got a hard-on over her in the first place to get one over on her father. Payback for Johnny shooting Roy. 'Calm down and stop talking crap, woman. Ava's the spitting image of me.'

Colin handed Deborah the paperwork. 'Mr Butler is entitled by law to have regular contact with his daughter. If you don't comply with our wishes, then we will have no option but to take the matter to court. Mr Butler was a decent and loving father to Molly and there isn't a judge or magistrate in the country who would deny him access to Ava. Especially seeing as it was a relative of yours who ended poor Molly's life. What I suggest you do is read through all my notes and I will pop back tomorrow. Is noon OK for you?'

Panicking because she knew Colin had a valid point, Deborah stared at her tearful daughter. 'Joanna isn't lying. She had a fling. Vinny's not Ava's father.'

Colin Harvey smirked at Vinny. He'd been fully expecting

this to be the Prestons' argument, which was why he and his client had arrived fully prepared. 'In that case, we shall insist Ava have a blood sample taken. I'm not sure if you're aware, but Mr Butler's blood group is a very rare one indeed.'

CHAPTER TWENTY

'Turn the telly off and put *Chas and Dave's Jamboree Bag* on, Viv. The one with "Billy Muggins" on it. Reminds me of Albie, that song. I might sing it to the old bastard after a few Baileys,' Queenie cackled.

Vivian did as asked, secretly thinking she was glad Albie was coming. She'd been dreading spending the day in Vinny's company; it made it a little easier knowing that she'd have a kindred spirit in Albie, who hated that no-good murdering shitbag just as much as she did.

Queenie found it hilarious when Michael and Albie turned up at the exact same time 'Billy Muggins' came on.

'Merry Christmas, Mum. What you laughing at?' Michael asked.

'This record. The person who wrote it must have known your father.'

The song was about a chap who was deemed simple, yet as soon as his pals' backs were turned, he'd sleep with their wives.

Ignoring the insult, Albie forced a smile. 'Merry Christmas, Queenie. Merry Christmas, Vivvy. I'm not very good at choosing presents, but I know how much you both love flowers so I got you these.'

Vivian grinned as she looked at the lovely bouquet. 'Thanks, Albie. They're beautiful. I'll nip indoors and put 'em in water.'

Queenie snatched her bouquet without a thank-you. 'Where did ya steal them from? Some poor bastard's grave?'

'Don't start, Mum,' Michael warned.

Albie stared at his shoes. He hadn't wanted to spend Christmas with Queenie or Vinny, but Michael had talked him into it. Some Christmas this was going to be.

Ahmed and Little Vinny were in the King Harold. Little Vinny had opted to go to his local rather than the Pompadours, as he had a vague recollection of being so far gone he'd fallen over in there the previous evening.

'I got you a chaser as well. Brandy is very good for calming nerves,' Ahmed pointed out.

'I don't think I should drink much more. I don't wanna turn up pissed.'

'You'll be fine. Go and have a couple of lines. That'll sober you up.'

'Nah. Let's drink these and make a move.'

'We can't go round there yet, Vin. Sammi's father isn't going to be very happy if we turn up and spoil his Christmas dinner. We should wait until after four, make sure they've eaten first.'

'I suppose you're right. I better have a line then.'

Ahmed smirked as Little Vinny walked into the toilet. The lad was far too trusting for his own good.

Johnny Preston knew something bad had happened as soon as he put the key in the lock. He'd heard Joanna shouting and sobbing from outside. 'Whatever's the matter?' he asked, directing the question at Deborah. Surely his wife hadn't slipped up and told Jo he'd visited Jamie that time?

Leaving Darren to comfort her daughter, Deborah led Johnny into the kitchen. He was going to go ballistic, she knew that, and she didn't want Jo any more distressed than she already was.

Ava, who had been to the toilet, came skipping out happily. 'Granddad, my daddy came to see me. Look at all the presents he bought me. I like them more than yours and Nanny's.'

Face drained of colour, Johnny stared at his grandchild as though he'd seen a ghost. 'What did you just say?'

It was Deborah who answered. 'Vinny's been here, Johnny. He knows about Ava.'

Johnny smashed his fist against the door. 'Over my dead body will that lowlife have anything to do with our Ava. He's wronged this family too fucking often. If killing the cunt is the only answer, then so be it.'

Queenie had already told Vivian about Ava, so it was only Albie who was gobsmacked when his evil son arrived full of the joys of spring, bragging about how beautiful his daughter was. Michael felt embarrassed. He'd meant to tell his father, but had been so wrapped up in the Bella conversation, he'd completely forgotten.

'Did you see Joanna? Was Johnny there? What did you say to Ava?' Queenie asked, thoroughly excited.

'Johnny weren't there. I reckon he was down the boozer. Jo went into meltdown, as expected, and Deborah wasn't exactly pleased to see me, the fat witch. Ava was though. You should've seen her little face when I told her I was her daddy. It was as though we had an instant bond. Loved her presents an' all.'

'Aw, bless her, Vin. I can't wait to meet her,' Queenie gushed.

'Did Jo try and pretend Ava weren't yours like you thought she would?' Michael asked.

'Yeah, but our blood group stopped that argument. Colin played a blinder. You wanna see all the legal jargon he typed up. I saw the look on Deborah's face when she glanced at it – she was shitting herself! He's popping back round there tomorrow lunchtime. Worth every penny I pay him that geezer is.'

Knowing he should show some interest, Albie piped up with a question. 'You don't think the Prestons might do a runner in the meantime, do you, Vinny?'

Vinny grinned. 'They won't get far if they do. I'm paying someone to watch 'em. Luckily for me, I was born with me mother's brains rather than yours. Now let's open the presents. This bag is for you, Mum. These are for you, Auntie Viv. Dad, we've never done presents. And Michael, I'll be giving you yours later.'

Vivian glared at her nephew. 'I want nothing from you, only my son back and I doubt I'm gonna unwrap him, am I?'

Albie was the one who followed Vivian out to the back garden. 'Don't let him grind you down, love. I know it's more difficult for you than anyone. Loved your Lenny, I did. Christmas ain't the same without him, that's for sure.'

Tears running down her cheeks, Vivian quickly wiped them away. 'How dare he buy me fucking presents when he killed my son? Feel sorry for little Ava, I do. I'll have a hundred-pound bet with you now: if the Prestons don't play ball, he'll see off that poor Joanna.'

'Whaddya mean?'

'Vinny'll kill her, that's what I mean. Might not do it himself, but he'll pay some other bastard to. You mark my words, Albie.'

Over at the Prestons', the whole family were still in shock, bar Ava, who seemed delighted by Vinny's unexpected visit.

When his granddaughter repeated herself yet again, asking if her daddy would buy her a dog, Johnny finally lost his rag. 'Get that ungrateful little cow out of my sight. She's had more presents today than some poor kids get in a lifetime, yet she still wants more. No wonder she's already bonded with that bastard. They obviously share the same genes.'

Appalled, Deborah punched her husband in the arm. 'Stop it, and get a grip, for goodness' sake. Ava's three years old, you fool. As if she understands what's going on.'

'I'm going back down the pub,' Johnny spat.

'No, you're not. I'm about to dish up dinner,' Deborah replied.

'As if anyone's gonna be hungry after the devil's turned up on the doorstep. Merry fucking Christmas,' Johnny yelled, before slamming the front door so hard it nearly flew off its hinges.

Darren and Joanna were upstairs, but had heard every single word of the argument that had been going on for the past half hour. Johnny had wanted to leave the area tonight. Deborah had refused, hence Johnny storming out.

'What am I going to do, Darren? I know my dad's idea of moving makes sense to a certain extent, but we can't keep running for ever. Vinny will hunt us down wherever we go. I know what he's capable of.'

Darren put an arm around Joanna and held her close to his chest. His proposal had gone right out the window now. Christmas was ruined and the ring would just have to burn a hole in his pocket until the time was right. 'I think you're spot on. I know you hate Vinny, Jo, and you have every reason to, but you did tell me he was a very good dad to Molly.'

'He wasn't when he left her with his useless son and she was led to her death,' Joanna argued.

'Babe, I'm sure he's just as traumatized over what happened to Molly as you are. What you have to ask yourself is could you fault him in any other way as a father?'

Joanna shrugged. 'Not really. He was a bastard to me, but worshipped the ground Molly walked on.'

Darren kissed his girlfriend on the forehead. He'd been horrified when he'd heard Johnny tell Deborah they should move to Spain. It wasn't that simple for him to just up sticks. He was very close to his parents, who lived locally, plus his nan who wasn't in the best of health. Then there was Shane. As much as he loved Joanna, he could never abandon his own flesh and blood.

'You haven't answered my question, Darren,' Joanna reminded her boyfriend.

'No need to. You answered it yourself, Jo. As you said, Vinny was a good father overall, and you can't keep running for ever. Because if you do, you're gonna run out of places to hide.'

After a hearty Christmas dinner, the Allens had just settled in the lounge to watch TV when the intercom system buzzed. Meg answered it.

'Who is it?' Gary yelled.

'Another delivery. I hope it isn't more flowers. I've run out of bloody vases,' Meg replied.

Gary Allen immediately smelled a rat. 'Nobody delivers poxy flowers at half four on Christmas Day, Meg. You and Sammi stay here. I'll deal with this.'

Sammi-Lou's ears pricked up. She had been very surprised and disappointed that her boyfriend hadn't tried to make contact with her, and was hoping it was him. 'Mum, have a look out the window. If it's Vin, I want to talk to him.'

Gary Allen opened the front door, his face as stony as

the gravel Little Vinny was having difficulty walking on. 'Get off my property now. Sammi doesn't want to see you. Look at the state of ya. My daughter's worth a hundred of you.'

Picking up the bag of presents he'd just dropped, Little Vinny waved them in Gary's face. 'I ain't frightened of you. You can't stop me seeing Sammi and giving her her presents. My dad's out of nick now and if you do try to stop me, you'll have him to fucking answer to. Ever met my old man in the flesh, have you? He'd eat you for breakfast, you mug.'

Watching events from the warmth of his car, Ahmed smirked when Gary Allen grabbed Little Vinny by the throat and smashed him against the wall. He had told the lad it would be inappropriate for him to intervene unless things got really messy, as this was a family matter.

'Dad, stop it! Please don't hurt him,' Sammi-Lou screamed, poking her head around the front door.

'How dare you turn up here pissed and shouting your mouth off? Involve your father, for all I care, I'll tell him exactly why I don't want you anywhere near my daughter,' Gary hissed, releasing his grip on Little Vinny's throat.

Wanting to impress his girlfriend and Ahmed, Little Vinny swung a right hook that connected with Gary's chin.

'Do something, Mum. Do something,' Sammi-Lou shrieked, clutching her stomach.

Meg ran out of the house, just in time to stop her husband knocking seven bells out of her daughter's boyfriend. 'Get inside now, Gary. I'll deal with this.'

'Look at the state of him, Meg. The little bastard wants castrating before he gets anybody else up the duff,' Gary spat, before obeying his wife's orders. He would stand his ground with any man, but his pint-sized old woman scared the life out of him once she got a bee in her bonnet.

'Sammi, come back. I've bought you some nice presents,'

Little Vinny shouted, as Gary ushered both his daughters inside the house and slammed the front door.

Meg Allen slapped Little Vinny hard across his face. 'Don't you ever disrespect me, my daughter or husband again by turning up here drunk, do you hear me?'

Wiping the grin off his face, Ahmed leapt out of the car. 'Come on, Vinny. It's time to go home, my friend.'

Queenie Butler loved nothing more than putting on the spread of all spreads at Christmas. Times had been hard when she and Vivian were growing up. Many a festive season they'd had no dinner at all, and on one occasion their drunken bully of a father had brought home a sheep's head that still had all the gore hanging out.

'Jesus wept, Muvver. How many more animals you cremated? At the rate you're going, Old Macdonald won't have a farm left,' Vinny quipped.

Queenie chuckled and hugged her eldest from behind. 'I know you're a big meat eater, boy, so I bought extra to make up for all those Christmases you missed. It's a relief to have you home, I can tell ya. Been far too many crimes committed round 'ere recently. Poor old Mr Arthur got mugged on the way home from the pub last week. The streets will be much safer now you're back.'

Michael was furious. Not only had he held his family together financially in recent years, he'd also sorted out any problems of a physical nature.

Vivian was none too amused either. 'My Lenny loved his meat an' all. Shame he ain't 'ere to tuck in, isn't it, Albie?'

Sensing an argument was brewing, Albie nodded then excused himself to go to the toilet.

'What's up with you?' Vinny asked, knowing full well why Michael was peeved.

'Sod-all. Why? Should there be?'

Vinny smirked. 'Of course Mum's relieved to have me home. I'm the head of the family, never forget that, bruv.'

'If it was up to you, we'd be lucky to have a fucking sparrow to eat today. Never forget it was me who turned our business around in your absence,' Michael retaliated.

'No arguing today please, boys. I want a peaceful, stress-free Christmas for once. And I'll have you both know that I'm the head of this family. If it wasn't for me, neither of you would have ever bleedin' existed.'

Aware that Vinny and Michael were still exchanging hostile looks, Jay Boy tried to break the ice. 'Would you like me to start carving the meat, Queenie? I'm a bit of an expert, I'll have you know. My first ever job was in a butcher's shop.'

The doorbell stopped Queenie from replying. She wasn't too pleased when she opened it to find her daughter standing there. 'What do you want? I told you the other day to spend Christmas with that loser you live with.'

Standing either side of Brenda were Tara and Tommy. 'Dave and Mum had a row. Then we got chucked out of Dave's mum's house,' young Tommy informed his grandmother.

'And now we haven't got no dinner. We're starving, Nan,' Tara added.

Queenie sighed. No way could she see her grandchildren starve. 'Nanny's got plenty of grub. Go in the bathroom and wash your hands, kids.'

'I should think so too. I am your daughter and they're your grandchildren,' Brenda reminded her mother.

Queenie grabbed hold of Brenda's arm as she attempted to barge past. 'I'm warning you, young lady. You get pissed and perform, you're straight out this door – and so are Tara and Tommy. Behave, or else.'

*

Over at the Prestons', the mood was sombre and the food virtually untouched.

'Where do you think Dad is, Mum? The pub only opens until two today, so he can't be there,' Joanna said.

'I have no idea, love. Probably pissed, wherever he is. Has a habit of turning to alcohol when the going gets tough, does your daddy,' Deborah spat.

'You talking about my daddy?' Ava asked innocently.

Unable to control her emotions or temper any longer, Deborah screamed, 'Shut up, Ava. You haven't got a fucking daddy.'

'You OK, Bren? Kids are getting big, eh?' Albie said awkwardly.

'No. I'm not OK. I know how pushed out you must've felt now. Mum's only ever wanted her boys. She don't ever fuss over Tara and Tommy like a grandma should, because they're my kids. No wonder I drink too much. She should be fucking ashamed of herself.'

'Who's "she", the cat's mother?' Vinny snarled, snatching the glass of wine out of his sister's hand.

'Give us that back,' Brenda yelled, lunging towards her brother.

When Vinny pushed his sister and Brenda flew into the table lamp with such force it smashed, Michael saw red and squared up to his brother. 'You wanna fight with someone, fight with me, big man.'

'Get out my face, Michael, before I knock your spark out,' Vinny warned.

'Stop it! Stop it!' Queenie yelled, standing between her warring sons.

'See what I mean, Dad? I'm lying here injured and all that old cow's bothered about is her precious sons.'

'Don't talk about your mother like that, Brenda. Apologize to her now,' Vivian ordered.

Grabbing hold of Brenda's arm, Queenie screamed, 'Get out! Go on, out my house, now! Nothing but a fucking drunken trouble-maker you are. Go on, sling your hook.'

Jay Boy looked on in amazement as Queenie Butler manhandled her daughter out the front door. Jay had thought his family Christmases had been mad back in Liverpool, but he'd never experienced anything like this one before, and couldn't help but feel sorry for Brenda's kids. They'd had the door slammed in their faces as well.

'Mum, you can't just chuck Bren out like that. It ain't fair on Tara and Tommy. Let me sort it,' Michael said.

Standing with her back against the door, Queenie shook her head vehemently. 'This is my house, Michael, therefore I make the rules. I warned Brenda that if she performed she was out on her ear. She ain't ruining my Christmas.'

'But it ain't just about Bren. What about your grandchildren?' Michael argued.

When Brenda began knocking on the window shouting abuse, Queenie ordered Vinny to get rid of her. 'It's all your fault the way that girl's turned out, Albie. Seeing you stagger home all through her childhood has obviously damaged her for life.'

'Don't start on Dad, Mum. Brenda's got worse since she took up with that pisshead from Dagenham. Blame him if you want someone to blame,' Michael shouted.

'Bren inherited your father's bastard genes,' Queenie insisted.

Albie couldn't be bothered arguing with Queenie today. What was the point? In her warped mind, the old witch was always right anyway.

'Well?' Queenie asked Vinny.

'They've gone. I gave the kids their presents and Bren

the money for a cab. I told her to visit when sober to collect her own presents.'

Queenie pursed her lips. 'You shouldn't have given her any money. It'll only go on booze. Good bleedin' riddance.'

Gary Allen was absolutely seething. Every year since he and Meg had moved to this house, they'd invited close friends and family over on Christmas evening, but today they'd had to cancel. Sammi-Lou was upset and complaining of stomach pains, and his younger daughter Millie had been tearful and terrified ever since the argument.

Gary followed his wife into the kitchen. 'I've made my decision, Meg. First thing tomorrow, I'm going round that house and changing the locks. No way is that shitbag upsetting my family any more. Did you see his eyes? His pupils were massive. Definitely a druggie as well as a drunk.'

'Shut up about it now, Gary. You'll upset the girls even more if you keep harping on. Your voice carries, you know.'

'I want him out of our lives for good, Meg,' Gary hissed.

'Mum! Dad! Sammi's wet herself,' screamed seven-year-old Millie.

Meg dashed into the lounge. 'Start the car, Gary, quick! Sammi's waters have broken.'

Hearing the first chords of Chas and Dave's 'Give It to the Girl Next Door', Queenie Butler leapt off the sofa, turned the volume up full blast, then grabbed her sister by the arm. Every time she and Viv played this song they'd stand by the wall that adjoined them to the Bakers and sing at the top of their voices.

'Why is Nan and Auntie Viv dancing like that, Mum? Are they drunk?' Adam asked.

'No, love. They're just enjoying themselves,' Nancy replied, while trying to lip-read what Michael was talking to Albie about. Her husband had been acting strangely these past few days. He'd hardly spent any time at home and when he was there he seemed very distant. Nancy guessed it was because Vinny had been released from prison, as Michael had been fine up until then.

'Mum, me and Lee are bored. Can we go home and play on the machines?' Daniel asked.

Nancy had not been best pleased when the three massive games machines had arrived last night. Her dining room currently resembled an amusement arcade, although Michael had promised to have a cabin built down the bottom of the garden so the boys could use that as a games room. 'No. You'll have plenty of time to play on the machines over the holiday. Christmas is all about spending time with family, Daniel, so wipe that miserable look off your face and go and talk to your nan and granddad.'

'Nan's pissed and Granddad's boring,' Daniel replied.

Clipping her son around the ear, Nancy warned him to behave or she'd wash his mouth out with soap.

'Look, Viv. We got rid of the scumbags. They're going out in the tosspot's van,' Queenie cackled, clapping her hands with glee.

'Mum, turn that music down now. I wanna have a chat with Michael in the kitchen, and I can't even hear myself think,' Vinny complained.

'Where's Little Vinny? I thought you said he'd be here,' Queenie reminded her son.

'I thought he might just turn up. No idea where he is. Twice I've popped round his house and he weren't in.'

'Charming! Not even sent me a card. All the things I've done for him over the years an' all. Even had the ungrateful little sod living with me for Christ knows how long.'

Aware that his mother was on her soapbox, Vinny led

Michael into the kitchen and handed him an envelope. 'Open it then. Your present's inside.'

Michael stared at the formal-looking document. It stated that he now owned seventy-five per cent of the club, Vinny owned twenty-five and there was a box for both their signatures at the bottom. It had already been signed by Vinny's legal representative.

'You taking the piss, or what? Why should you still be coining twenty-five per cent out of me if you ain't even working there?' Michael asked.

'You know the reason why. I bought the gaff with Roy in the first place. This is my final offer, so take it or leave it.'

Michael lit a cigarette, chucked Vinny's offer on the worktop, and sauntered into the back garden.

Staring at the ginger-and-white moggy who was sitting on the fence giving him the evil eye, Michael debated his future. He'd been in touch with a pal of his who worked in the property game and had been advised that the club was worth far more than he'd imagined. His pal reckoned that, because of the size and location, a property developer would snap it up for a small fortune to build one or two blocks of flats.

No way did Michael ever want to see his beloved disco turned into flats. But he didn't want to give in to Vinny's demands either.

Poking his head around the back door, Vinny smirked, 'Oh and by the way, Pete, Paul and Jay have all agreed to work for me. Merry Christmas, bruv.'

His temper finally exploding, Michael flew at Vinny, grabbed him by the shoulders and slammed him against the conservatory door. 'You fucking cunt. After everything I've done for you! If it wasn't for me, your son would currently be locked up for murder, you ungrateful piece of shit. Bet he didn't tell you he killed Alison Bloggs, did he? Silly bastard left a bunch of keys in her house – including the keys to our club. Muggins 'ere was the one who cleaned up after him.'

Vinny was stunned. 'You're kidding me.'

'Do I look like I'm fucking kidding? He killed Alison to get even for Ben, by all accounts. Dosed her up on Temazepam, then slit her wrists. The Old Bill wrote it off as suicide, thank God. Wouldn't have done if they'd have found that bunch of keys there though, eh?'

Face drained of colour, Vinny sank to his haunches. 'When did this happen? Why didn't you tell me?'

Michael was pleased to see his cocky brother looking as if the stuffing had been knocked out of him. 'You had enough on your plate in nick. Unlike you, Vin, I'm not a selfish cunt. I think of others. Anyway, I dealt with it and I promised Little Vinny I wouldn't say anything. So keep it between us. No point confronting the boy now. It's old news.'

Vinny was holding his head in his hands when his mother flung open the door. 'You'd better come quick. The Old Bill are here. They reckon Daniel stabbed the boy next door.'

Sammi-Lou Allen was petrified. The pain she was in was the worst ever, far more horrendous than the tooth infection she'd had last summer.

'You need to push, darling. The baby needs you to push,' Meg urged, squeezing her daughter's clammy hand. When Sammi had first announced her pregnancy, Meg had been just as horrified as Gary, but now things were different. This poor baby was going to be born premature and if her first grandchild was destined not to survive, Meg would be heartbroken.

'I can't push, Mum. It hurts too much. Please ring Vinny. I need him,' Sammi-Lou screamed.

Queenie Butler gave a sigh of discontent as she flopped onto the armchair. Resting her aching feet against the pouffe, she turned to her sister. 'Oh well, that's another Christmas I'd rather forget. What is it with our family? Every year there's drama. Why can't we just eat, drink, be merry and play charades like every other bastard does?'

Vivian chuckled. 'You'd be bored shitless playing charades. You don't even like watching *Give Us a Clue*.'

'Yes I do. When you're not rabbiting all the way through it, that is.'

'Fancy a Babycham?' Vivian asked.

'Nah. Pour me a sherry or a port.'

'But we always have a Babycham at Christmas,' Vivian reminded her sister.

'Go on then.'

Vivian handed her sister the drink, then stood in front of her.

'What the bleedin' hell you doing?'

'Playing charades. Now shush.'

'One,' Queenie shouted, flapping her arms.

'Chicken?'

Vivian shook her head.

'Bird?'

'Duck?'

'Emu?'

'I'm flying, you ignoramus. Emus can't fly,' Vivian hissed.

'One day, I'll fly away,' Queenie screamed, referring to the Randy Crawford song.

Losing her patience, Vivian bellowed sarcastically, 'It's a film!'

'What is it then?'

'*One Flew Over the Cuckoo's Nest*. I thought it was rather apt for our family.'

'It is, very apt. No need to get your knickers in a twist because I didn't guess it, though.'

Vivian burst out laughing. 'Happy fucking Christmas.'

CHAPTER TWENTY-ONE

'Morning, sweetheart. Mummy's going to make breakfast. Would you like your favourite?' Joanna asked her daughter.

Although egg, sausage and beans were tempting, Ava shook her head before pulling the quilt up over her face.

Joanna sat on the edge of Ava's bed. 'What's the matter, darling? You can talk to your mum about anything, you know.'

'Nanny said I haven't got a daddy,' Ava wept.

Lifting the quilt off her daughter, Joanna wiped her tears away and held Ava in her arms. As much as it pained her, after discussing things with Darren last night she knew what she had to do. 'Your daddy is the man you met yesterday, Ava.'

Confused, Ava stopped crying. 'But you and Nanny said he wasn't.'

'Sometimes adults do and say things in life because they think it's the right thing to do. In this case, Mummy was wrong to fib to you. Would you like to see your daddy again?'

Ava's face lit up. 'Will he buy me more nice presents?'

*

'Morning, boy. You're up bright and early. You feeling better today?' Queenie asked. Vinny had been in tears late last night over Molly.

'Much better, thanks. No point wallowing in self-pity. Nothing is gonna bring Molly back, so my aim is to concentrate solely on the future from now on. I was thinking, I know how much you and Auntie Viv loved Kings. How about I treat you to a bungalow or chalet on a different holiday camp? I'll always run yous down there and pick you up. There's another Kings on Canvey Island. I think it's owned by Ray King's brother. That would be half the journey of the Eastbourne one.'

'Thanks, but no thanks. No way will any holiday park match up to Kings in Eastbourne. Can't see Prince Charles and the Three Degrees slumming it in Canvey, can you?' Queenie said bitterly. She'd been devastated when her sons' violent behaviour had got the whole family barred from using the facilities. Both herself and Viv had adored getting glammed up to the nines and watching all the big star acts they'd only ever seen on TV before. 'So what you up to today?' Queenie asked, changing the subject.

'Colin's picking me up at half ten. I'm gonna travel down to Tillingham with him to see what the Prestons have decided. Might even come face to face with that wanker Johnny, but I'm gonna keep me cool if I do. I just wanna see Ava again, even if it's only for ten minutes. There was an instant bonding between us, Mum. I swear I weren't imagining it. I can't wait for her to be a big part of our lives.'

'And what if the Prestons refuse to play ball? I can't see them wanting Ava visiting me somehow.'

'I'll sort it, Mum, don't you worry. Nobody will stop

Ava becoming a big part of our lives. And if that means I have to take drastic measures, then so be it.'

Queenie smiled. 'That's my boy.'

Little Vinny had no recollection of going to bed last night, neither did he recall Ahmed leaving. There was a racked-up line on the bedside table next to an empty bottle of Scotch and Little Vinny felt nauseous just looking at them. Drink and drugs had never really agreed with him and he knew in his heart if his life was to improve he had to knock both on the head.

Self-loathing was an awful feeling, and Little Vinny despised himself right now. Molly's death and Ben's suicide haunted his thoughts, and he couldn't believe he'd messed things up even more with Sammi-Lou by turning up round her house off his face. Why the hell hadn't Ahmed stopped him from mugging himself off yet again?

Wondering if Sammi-Lou had contacted him, Little Vinny ran down the stairs. The light was bleeping on the answerphone. Praying that the caller wasn't his father, or Gary Allen demanding he moved out the house, Little Vinny pressed play.

'Vinny, it's Meg. Sammi-Lou has gone into early labour and is desperate for you to be here. We're at Rush Green Hospital. Don't worry about Gary. I'll deal with him.'

The second message that Meg had left wasn't quite so friendly. 'You've got a son, you useless little arsehole. He's in the special care unit to help his lungs function. Sammi's in pieces, bless her heart. You stay away from her and that child from now on, do you hear me? Oh, and pack your things. Gary will be round the house tomorrow to change all the locks.'

Little Vinny sank to his knees and wept. He was so

relieved that he had a son, rather than a daughter. Knowing that God probably hated him for his past sins, Little Vinny chose to pray to him anyway. 'Dear God, I am so sorry for what I did to my little sister, but please don't take that out on my son. I swear to you, if you let my boy live, I'll be the best dad he could wish for. Amen.'

Johnny Preston was in sheepish mode. He knew he'd disappointed his wife and daughter. 'Look, I'm sorry about going into one yesterday and storming out like I did. I just couldn't believe that bastard had the nerve to turn up here. You have to remember if it wasn't for him killing my mate Dave, I'd never have spent all those years in nick. I hate the geezer with a passion.'

'And so do I and so does Joanna. But throwing all your toys out the pram isn't going to solve anything, is it? We have to be adult about this because nothing is going to change the fact that Vinny is Ava's father,' Deborah said.

'But I can't abide the thought of him having contact with her,' Johnny spat.

'And neither can I, but Ava is Jo's daughter, therefore Jo will be the one who decides such matters. Tell him what you told me, love.'

Joanna squeezed her father's hands. 'Dad, I know this is hard for all of us, but I had a long chat with Darren yesterday and I think he's right. If we keep running, now that Vinny knows Ava exists he will find us wherever we go. Also I'm happy living here. Darren can't just up sticks because of Shane, Mum loves it in Burnham, you have a decent job, and Ava has made lots of friends at nursery. I think we should allow Vinny access, but only on our terms. I don't want him taking her to Whitechapel in case she ever gets caught in the middle of some crossfire, but I will allow him to see her if I'm present. Don't get me wrong, being in Vinny's company is the last thing I want, but Darren has promised to be there too. What do you think?'

'I think you're delusional to consider any form of access. You know what Vinny is capable of as well as I do, Jo. He won't be happy with those terms, then you'll be the one caught in the crossfire, not Ava. The man is a monster.'

Nancy Butler was furious. Michael had just come down the stairs suited and booted, reeking of expensive aftershave and announced he had to go out on business.

'No way are you going anywhere, Michael. I am petrified that the police might turn up again to question Daniel, and I'm sure the little sod is guilty because he couldn't look me in the eyes when I questioned him earlier. I have even had to cancel going to my parents' this afternoon. Can you imagine if the police were to turn up to arrest Daniel in front of my dad and Christopher? I told my mum I had a flu bug rather than face that potential humiliation.'

'Why do you always have to be so overly dramatic about things, Nance? I've spoken to Daniel and he says he didn't do it. Just go over to your mother's as planned. Have a drink and chill out a bit, for Christ's sake.'

'How am I being overly dramatic? Any mother would be worried by the police turning up and accusing their son of stabbing another boy. I don't want you going out today, Michael, and that's final. I want you to talk to the boys again because I know Adam and Lee are hiding something too.'

'I'll speak to the boys again tomorrow, Nance. As I said, I have to go out because I have an important business meeting.'

'With who and where? It must be something dodgy if you've arranged it on Boxing Day,' Nancy screamed.

Knowing his only exit route was a full-scale argument,

Michael let rip at his wife. He called her a nutjob, a drama queen and psychopath before slamming the front door. He did feel guilty as he leapt in his Porsche though. He knew Daniel was guilty and there was a chance of the Old Bill popping back. Yet he was still putting Bella top of his priority list.

Shell Baker thanked the police for their visit, shut the front door and breathed a sigh of relief. She walked into the lounge. 'Well done, boys. You did brilliantly.'

Brad, Shell's youngest son, had tears in his eyes. 'Say more witnesses come forward, Mum? Me and Kurt might end up in borstal and we ain't done sod-all wrong.'

Shell sat between her beloved boys and hugged them. 'Lying to police is better than grassing up the Butlers, trust me. And I promise you faithfully we'll be moving away soon. Then we can start afresh.'

Under Colin's strict instructions, Vinny Butler was left sitting twiddling his thumbs in the car. The ten-minute wait felt like ten hours and when Colin opened the driver's door, Vinny's first question was 'Can I see Ava now?'

Colin started the engine. Vinny Butler wasn't his favourite client of all time, but he paid him top money. 'Ava isn't there, Vinny. Her grandparents have taken her out somewhere. However, I do have some positive news. I spoke to Joanna and her boyfriend Darren and they are willing to allow you to see Ava on a regular basis without involving the courts, providing they are present. Obviously, once you become more familiar with the child, we will ask for you to see Ava on your own and be allowed to spend the whole weekend with her and so on. I really do believe this is the best solution for the time being as you will stand much more chance of gaining equal access to

Ava in a court if you have bonded with her beforehand, so to speak.'

Wanting to smack Colin in the teeth, Vinny instead plastered on a false smile. 'Sounds good to me.'

Relieved that Vinny seemed happy, Colin put his foot on the accelerator. His wife was extremely annoyed that he'd had to work over the Christmas period, but Colin hadn't had much choice in the matter. Vinny Butler was a rather forceful character, to say the least.

Gritting his teeth, Vinny switched the car radio on. In the charts was a geezer called Jim Diamond with a song entitled 'I Should Have Known Better'. How very apt for that to be playing, as that cheeky bitch Joanna should've known better than to throw the rule book at him. As for her new interfering cocktard of a boyfriend, he'd regret sticking his oar in as well. Vinny would make damn sure of it.

Nosy Hilda heard a car engine and discreetly peeped through the net curtain. She'd been a bundle of nerves ever since the police had knocked at the Butlers' last night, and she'd nearly had a cardiac when they'd come back today and knocked at the Bakers'.

Cursing herself for opening her big trap, then accompanying Mouthy Maureen to the phone box, Hilda wondered if there was anybody she could go and stay with until the dust settled. She had a cousin who lived in Plaistow and a niece in East Ham.

The bang on the door made Hilda nigh on jump out of her skin. 'Cooey. It's only me.'

Hilda ushered Maureen into the lounge. 'Did you see the police come back again earlier? Oh, Maur, I wish we hadn't made that phone call now. It's worrying the life out of me.'

'Me too. We were a bit rash. I blame them bleedin'

snowballs we supped. Never mind, what's done is done and at least I had the brains to put me hanky over the mouthpiece so my voice was muffled. I need you to promise me, Hild, that you'll never breathe a word of what we did to anyone. It'll be my head on the chopping block, seeing as it was me who made the call.'

'You have my word, Maur. We'd both be dead meat if the Butlers ever found out. Vinny don't mess about, you know. Rumour has it he's done away with many from round 'ere over the years. Bobby Jackson is common knowledge, but the murderer of Old Jack's boy was never caught and lots of people secretly pointed the finger at Vinny when he was found floating in the Thames. Then Terry Smart and Kenny Jackson both disappeared off the face of the earth after falling out with him. You can bet your bottom dollar they're propping up a flyover somewhere, the poor bastards.'

'Shut your cakehole for goodness' sake, Hilda. Cheer me up, why don't ya.'

Michael Butler was the first to arrive at the restaurant. 'My friend booked a table for two here. Bella, her name is.'

'Ah, the lovely Miss D'Angelo. You are a very lucky man. Come, come,' the waiter ordered, leading Michael to a cosy table in the corner.

When Bella arrived ten minutes later, she was greeted warmly by the staff who spoke to her in their native language. Michael guessed he was the topic of conversation by the waiters gesticulating and glancing, but he stared out of the window, pretending not to notice.

'Hello, Michael. Have you been waiting long?'

Michael stood up, kissed Bella on both cheeks and pulled her chair out. 'Not long at all. You look sensational, by the way. Red really suits you,' he said, complimenting her on the figure-hugging dress she was wearing.

'Thank you. You're not looking too bad yourself,' Bella replied cheekily.

'I take it this is a regular haunt of yours?'

'Yes. I used to eat here when I lived in England before. And now I often bring Antonio here of a Sunday lunchtime. The food is wonderful and the staff so welcoming.'

'Well, at least I know your real surname now, Miss D'Angelo. I'm sure you fobbed me off with a duff one when we first met.'

Bella's pale blue eyes twinkled mischievously. 'My Papa told me never to give out my real name to a man unless I could trust him completely.'

Michael locked eyes with Bella. 'And my Papa told me that one day I would meet this beautiful Italian bird, fall head over heels in love with her and we'd both live happily ever after.'

Vinny Butler slammed his mother's front door. He wasn't in the best of moods.

'Vin, come in 'ere. You've got a visitor,' Queenie shouted.

The last person Vinny expected to see perched on his mother's sofa was his delinquent son. 'Well, well, well, the Scarlet Pimpernel returns. How very kind of you to grace us with your presence.'

'Vin, the boy's got a lot on his plate. Tell your dad what you just told me,' Queenie urged her grandson.

'Sammi-Lou went into early labour, Dad. I've got a son, but I'm not allowed to see him because I missed the birth. Will you come to the hospital with me? Sammi's dad's an arsehole. He hates me. My boy's in some special care unit to help his lungs develop and I really need to see him. If he died and I never got to meet him, I'd never forgive myself,' Little Vinny explained, his voice racked with emotion.

Vinny stared at his son for a moment. He didn't look capable of swatting a fly, let alone killing Alison Bloggs. 'Get your coat on. We'll go now. And don't be worrying about Sammi's old man. This baby is as much yours as it is hers, and I'll deal with that cheeky prick if he starts.'

Back in West London, Michael and Bella had not stopped laughing. They shared a similar sense of humour and Michael could never imagine Bella nagging him constantly like Nancy seemed to these days.

'Come on then, I want to know what this old fortune-teller bird said about me. Did she say I was a handsome bastard who was good in bed?'

Getting a fit of the giggles again, Bella put her hand over her mouth to ensure she didn't spit her champagne out.

Michael smirked. 'Swallow it, babe. I like watching you swallow and it's a waste to spit it out.'

Bella slapped Michael playfully on his arm. 'Stop being so rude. I really don't know where you get some of your expressions from. I didn't even know what a bit of a fluff meant until you used the term to describe me. I thought it was something old ladies got on their cardigans.'

'Well, it does mean that an' all, but you're my favourite bit of fluff. What did this Madam Whatsit tart say about me then? You keep changing the subject.'

'Why are you so interested? Not ten minutes ago you told me you didn't believe in such nonsense.'

'I don't. Your mate's got to be a con-woman. Nobody can see into the future. Madam whatever her name is would be a multi-millionaire by now if she genuinely could.'

Bella chuckled. She knew Michael was dying to know what Madam Lydia had said about him, which was why she had no intention of telling him. 'You men are all the same: scared of what the future might hold. My Papa used to go mad whenever Mamma had tea-leaf readings with a local gypsy lady.'

'I ain't scared, babe. I just think it's a load of old bollocks, that's all. I mean, why hasn't Lydia won the football pools week in, week out if she's that clued up?'

'The only way I will believe you are not a scaredy-cat is if you go to her for a reading. Then we can compare notes, and I will tell you exactly what she said to me about you. It was very interesting, I have to say.'

Michael smiled and squeezed Bella's hands. 'Are you used to getting your own way?'

'Yes. I take after my father.'

'Well, in that case you better book me an appointment to see your old shyster of a mate. I'll prove to you I ain't no wimp, Miss D'Angelo.'

Wondering why her sons and Lee were so quiet, Nancy decided to investigate. 'Where are your brothers?' she asked Adam, who was alone in the bedroom.

'I don't know, Mum. I thought they were playing on the machines.'

Nancy stared at her youngest son. Adam had such a beautiful face and long eyelashes, he truly was the picture of innocence. She sat on the bed next to him. 'Please tell me what happened with those boys who live next door to your nan. I promise I won't shout or get angry, but you really need to tell me the truth now the police are involved. I only want to protect you, Daniel and Lee.'

Unable to look his mother in the eyes, Adam fiddled with his toy. He was still embarrassed that he'd wet himself, and was scared. 'Nothing happened.'

Unconvinced, Nancy hugged her son close to her chest. 'I promise I won't tell Daniel you told me, Adam. It's you I'm more concerned about. You're Mummy's baby boy.'

Furious at the baby boy insult, Adam leapt off the bed. Daniel was always calling him a mummy's boy and a wimp and he hated it. Daniel also said grasses were like rats, and ended up chopped into little pieces once they'd snitched.

'I've already told you, nothing happened, and I'm not a baby any more. Just go away and leave me alone.'

When his mother did as he asked, Adam wept.

Rush Green Hospital had its own maternity unit that specialized in nurturing premature babies. 'It's gonna be all right, boy, I promise. Your son is in the best hands possible,' Vinny said, as he parked the car.

'You find out the score, Dad. The thought of a stranger giving me bad news doesn't bear thinking of. I'd much rather hear it from you.'

The few minutes his father took to return to the car were the longest of Little Vinny's life. 'Well?' he asked anxiously.

Vinny grinned. 'Baby Butler is as strong as an ox. Five pound, he was born, which is a decent weight. His lungs are responding well and within the next day or two the nurse said they're gonna see how his breathing is without the ventilator. Us Butler boys are tough cookies, Vin. I bet he's home within the week.'

Little Vinny held his hands together and tilted his head upwards. 'Thank you, God.'

'I found out what ward Sammi's in. I suggest we see her before the baby.'

'What am I gonna say to her, Dad? I ain't even bought her or our son a present. I feel ever so guilty that I crashed out and didn't hear the phone. Sammi must hate me.'

'Sammi don't hate you, boy. She loves you, which is why she got herself up the duff in the first place. As soon as she realizes you're serious about being a good dad, she'll be putty in your hands. Don't be too apologetic though. Birds see that as a weakness, then play on it. Just say you were pissed. It was Christmas Day and you weren't to know she was going to give birth early, was ya?'

Debating whether to confess he'd turned up inebriated and created a scene at the Allens' on Christmas Day, Little Vinny quickly decided against it. His father would go apeshit if he found out Ahmed had accompanied him, and no way was Little Vinny going to dob his boss in it. Not only did he value his job now he had another mouth to feed, Ahmed knew far too much about him. 'I'd rather face Sammi-Lou and her parents alone. You wait outside and I'll call you if I need you. I need to man up now I'm a father meself.'

For the first time in years, Vinny Butler felt rather proud of his son. Not only had he rid the earth of a loser like Alison Bloggs, he also had the potential to be a good dad. 'OK. I'll wait outside the ward. I dunno who that Gary Allen thinks he is, but he'll fucking know who I am if he starts, that's for sure.'

Michael Butler held Bella's hand as they crossed the road. He'd had a brilliant day. The food and company had been exquisite, and he didn't want it to end. All he really wanted to do was whisk Bella off to a hotel room and fuck her brains out. His groin was pulsating just at the thought of seeing her naked once again.

'I'm only having one drink in this pub, Michael, and then I shall jump in a taxi,' Bella said, dashing Michael's hopes.

'I'll drop you off if you like?'

'No. My parents and Antonio might already be home and I don't want my father interrogating me. I told him I was meeting a girl from work for lunch. If he thought

I was out with a man, he would insist on meeting you first. I have a very old-fashioned papa,' Bella chuckled.

'What's he do for a living, your old man?'

'He owns many different businesses.'

'Like what?'

'Sportswear, clothing. Far too many to mention individually,' Bella replied vaguely. She could hardly tell Michael the truth.

Sammi-Lou was in a small ward with just one other girl whose baby was also in the special care unit, and they both screamed as Little Vinny walked in and Gary Allen lunged at him.

'Please stop it, Dad. Leave him alone,' Sammi cried.

Storming into the ward, Vinny Butler pushed his son out of the way and grabbed Gary Allen by the throat. 'You wanna fucking fight, then you fight me.'

Meg Allen grabbed her husband's arm to stop him throwing a punch. 'For goodness' sake! I'm sick of all this. There's a little boy down that corridor struggling to breathe and he belongs to all of us. Can't we sort this out like adults?'

Little Vinny walked over to Sammi and squeezed her hand. He turned to Gary and Meg and said, 'I'm sorry I wasn't here for the birth. My mind's been all over the place recently. If you want the truth, my little sister's death affected me so bad I was dreading having a daughter in case she reminded me of Molly. I'll step up to the mark now, I promise. I'll be the best boyfriend that Sammi could wish for and a brilliant dad to our son. I want us to be a proper family.'

Vinny Butler wasn't a soft man, but his son's emotional speech brought a tear to his eye. He knew exactly how

Little Vinny felt. He'd been worried that Ava would remind him of Molly.

'I take it you're Vinny's father? Would you please shake hands with my husband, seeing as we now have a grand-child in common,' Meg pronounced boldly.

Vinny and Gary stared at one another, steely-eyed, then very reluctantly shook hands.

CHAPTER TWENTY-TWO

Sammi-Lou grinned when her boyfriend arrived with yet more bags of goodies. 'Whatever you bought now?'

'A proper cool pair of jeans and trainers for our boy. Obviously they won't fit him for ages, but I couldn't resist 'em. And this bag is full of presents for you.'

Meg Allen smiled. Little Vinny had been as good as gold these past couple of days. 'Come on, Gary. Let's pop out for lunch somewhere and leave the youngsters to it. Won't be long, Sammi, and for goodness' sake hurry up and name the poor little soul. He can't remain nameless for ever.'

When Sammi's parents left, Little Vinny gave his girlfriend a kiss. Their son was now four days old and the doctors were going to take him off the machine helping him breathe this afternoon. 'He's gonna be OK, Sammi, so stop worrying.'

'But say he can't breathe on his own? I just want to take him home. I can't go home without him. Even if they discharge me tomorrow, I can't leave him.'

'Sam, these doctors know what they're doing. Look at some of the poor babies in that unit. Our boy looks massive compared to most. He's gonna breathe just fine on his own, trust me. My dad and nan are coming up later. My nan

can't wait to meet him. Now let's choose a name. I know
you think it's tempting fate to choose one before he comes
off that machine, but we have to name him, whatever
happens.'

'I want to call him Oliver.'

Little Vinny turned his nose up. 'Why Oliver?'

'Because a couple of years after Millie was born my mum
fell pregnant again. My dad was desperate for a son and
Mum was having a boy. He chose the name Oliver, but
unfortunately my mum lost the baby, then had to have a
hysterectomy. I know it would mean the world to my
parents if we named our son Oliver. A lovely tribute to the
little brother I never got to meet.'

Unusually for him, Little Vinny felt unable to say no.
He'd been a right bastard to Sammi during her pregnancy
and wanted to make up for his wrongdoings. Plus getting
in her father's good books could only be a positive thing.
Meg had softened towards him already, but Gary still
loathed him. Little Vinny could see the hatred in his eyes.
'I suppose Ollie Butler ain't so bad. Whatever makes you
happy, babe.'

Sammi-Lou threw her arms around her boyfriend's neck.
'Thank you, Vin. I can't wait to tell my mum and dad.
They'll be so chuffed.'

Nancy Butler crept up the stairs. She'd just spoken to the
police, who'd confirmed no further action would be taken
against Daniel unless new evidence came to light.

Having been unable to sleep, relief had seeped through
Nancy's veins until she'd seen her eldest son grinning like
a Cheshire cat out the corner of her eye. Daniel was as
guilty as sin, Nancy knew he was and she was determined
to find out the truth, hence her earwigging.

'Told you the Bakers would be too scared to grass, didn't

I? I overheard Nan and Auntie Viv talking once. Dad beat up Brad and Kurt's uncle and put him in hospital because their mum kept playing her music loud,' Nancy heard Daniel bragging.

'Really?' Adam replied, slightly confused. His dad was quite a gentleman at home, unless he was arguing with his mum, and Adam couldn't imagine him beating up his nan's next-door neighbour so badly that the man had ended up in hospital.

'Yeah, really. Nobody dare upset our dad or family, Adam. We're Butlers, that's why people are so scared of us,' Daniel said, his voice full of pride.

Recoiling from her sons' bedroom door, Nancy felt physically sick as she crept back down the stairs. How had it come to this? Her brother had always insisted that her sons would end up on the wrong road. Said it was inevitable, them being Michael's sons. How Nancy wished the ground could open up and swallow her right now. No way was she going to allow Daniel to get away with what he'd done. He needed to be taught right from wrong and if that meant her telling the police the truth, then so be it.

Madam Lydia lived in Islington, not far from the Angel, and as Michael neared her premises he started to panic. Fortune-tellers had always put the fear of God into him, ever since his mother had told him a horror story about one many years ago. 'We're a bit early, Bella. Let's have a quick drink in that boozer, eh?'

Bella smiled. She could sense Michael's apprehension and was enjoying every second of it. 'OK. But just the one drink. Madam Lydia is not a fan of people drinking alcohol before she stares into her crystal ball. She says it hampers the reading. I know you're a disbeliever, Michael, but you will be shocked at how accurate Madam Lydia is. She has film stars and pop stars visit her from all over the world. I have no idea if this is true, but the friend who first introduced me said Mick Jagger had once flown all the way from Germany to see her while he was on tour.'

Michael dragged Bella into the boozer. The quicker he got this bollocks over with, the better.

'Christ! This is posh. Who you borrowed it off?' Queenie Butler asked, as she stepped into the shiny new-looking black Mercedes. Since Vinny had come out of nick, he'd been driving around in Jay's motor, but this was a bit of a step up.

'It's mine, Mum. Bought it this morning. Only six months old. The previous owner croaked it, apparently.'

'Oh, dear Lord. It looks a bit like a hearse. I hope it isn't cursed.'

Vinny smiled. His mother's superstitious nature never failed to amuse him. 'Did you and Auntie Viv pop down the Roman?'

'No. Too bleedin' cold, so we decided against it. There's a new soap starting in February. Viv showed me the article in the *Sun*. Set in the East End in a fictional area called Walford. I bet it's a right load of old shit. Doubt they'll have proper East Enders acting in it either. What d'you reckon?'

'I dunno, Mum, and to be honest I don't really care. I'd rather stick pins in my eyes than watch soaps.'

Queenie squeezed her son's hand. 'The boy's going to be OK, you know. I've been feeling positive ever since I got up this morning and saw those two magpies staring at me from the conservatory window.'

'Little Vinny won't cope if that baby don't make it, Mum. He isn't strong enough. I didn't realize quite how much Molly's death had affected him until the other day.

He's still really cut up about it and it's obvious he blames himself.'

'And so he bastard-well should. If it wasn't for his inability to stay awake, that dear little girl would still be alive.'

Glancing at his mother, Vinny saw the twisted expression on her face and turned the volume of the radio up. She had no compassion at times. The woman was as tough as old boots.

The last time Michael Butler could remember feeling this nervous was when he and Vinny had kidnapped Trevor Thomas, driven him to East Hanningfield, then tortured the poor bastard to death.

'I see a beautiful dark-haired woman who has stolen your heart. This woman is your soul-mate,' Madam Lydia whispered.

Michael stared at the old bird. She looked about fifty, had red hair and a pleasant face. Michael wasn't silly. If Bella had booked this appointment then of course Madam Lydia was going to describe her. He imagined the diamond stud in her nose and patterned headscarf were all props to make her seem like the real deal.

'I see another woman, blonde, but she is moving towards the background, then completely disappears out of sight.'

'I've never had a reading before. Am I meant to ask questions?' Michael asked awkwardly. He felt like a right plonker, sitting opposite this woman. Vinny would cane him if he ever found out he'd visited her.

'You can ask me questions if you wish. Some I may be able to answer, some I might not.'

'Do you see me with the blonde woman or the dark-haired one in the future?'

Making a strange humming noise, Madam Lydia stared

into her crystal ball. 'The dark-haired woman. But, wait, there is a man, a horrid man who will not allow you to be happy. He is evil. He's watching over you. Watching and waiting.'

Feeling completely freaked out, Michael asked about the blonde woman again.

Madam Lydia was not feeling comfortable. It was very rare for her to stare into her crystal ball and see nothing but tragedy ahead. 'The blonde woman has vanished. I cannot see her any longer.'

'What about my brother? Can you see him?' Michael asked, testing the fruitcake.

'Yes, I can see your brother. Did he take his own life? I have a strong vision of him. He looks similar to you and he is smiling. This is a sign he wants me to tell you he is happy now.'

Michael felt the hairs stand up on the back of his neck. Had Bella told Madam Lydia his past for a wind-up? Or was the old bird for real? Deciding to test her again, he asked 'Can you see my kids?'

Shutting her eyes, Madam Lydia massaged her crystal ball, then opened her eyes again. 'I can see two boys. One is dark, the other blond. They are going to work with you one day. I can see a club with lots of flashing lights.'

'I have three boys, not two.'

Madam Lydia felt herself shudder. She wasn't getting very good vibes from this gentleman at all. 'I am so very sorry, but I must cut this reading short. I have one of my migraines coming on. I will not charge you, but I wish you well for the future.'

'Is he OK?' Little Vinny asked anxiously.

The female doctor smiled. 'Your son seems to be breathing perfectly well all by himself.'

'Cheers, God,' Little Vinny mumbled, holding his girl-friend close to his chest.

Sammi-Lou had tears of utter joy streaming down her face. 'Can we hold him properly now?'

'Yes. Of course you can.'

When a nurse placed her son in her arms without him being wired up to breathing apparatus for the very first time, Sammi-Lou stared at him in wonder. He only had a slight bit of hair, but it was blonde like hers, rather than dark like Vinny's. 'He's so gorgeous, and look at his little chest moving all on its own, Vin.'

Little Vinny planted a kiss on his son's forehead. 'He's absolutely perfect. I can't believe we created him, can you?'

Meg felt very emotional as she witnessed the touching scene. She put her arm around Gary's waist. 'I told you he would be OK, didn't I?'

'We can't keep calling him "he" or "boy". Yous two thought of a name yet?' Gary asked.

Sammi placed her son in her boyfriend's arms. 'Yes. We've decided to call him Oliver, as a tribute to the little brother I never got to meet.'

The tears finally came for Meg. 'Oh, that's such a lovely and thoughtful thing to do. Our Oliver can live on through yours. I'm so happy. Isn't it a wonderful gesture, Gary?'

Gary Allen thought the gesture was anything but fucking wonderful. If his and Meg's Oliver had survived he would have been an Allen, not a poxy Butler. Not wanting to upset his wife or daughter, Gary forced a smile. 'Yeah. Nice.'

Not feeling at all hungry, Michael Butler ordered some food nevertheless, then sat down at the table opposite Bella.

'Well? What did she say? You look as white as a sheet,' Bella commented.

Michael necked his chaser in one, then took a sip of his pint. 'That woman's off her head, babe. Don't be asking me to visit her again, will ya? A proper nutjob if I ever did meet one.'

'Whatever did she say to you, Michael? Please tell me the truth. This was the whole purpose of our visit.'

'Did you tell her about me or you? Or that my brother Roy killed himself?'

'No. Of course not. I told her you were a work colleague of mine, and I swear on Antonio's life I never mentioned anything else about you or your family.'

Michael momentarily froze. No way would Bella swear on her son's life if she wasn't telling the truth, so perhaps that mad old bat did have special powers? 'She just freaked me out, Bella. She spoke about Roy taking his own life and she sort of described you as well.'

'What did she say about me?' Bella enquired.

'You tell me what she said to you about me first. That was the deal we had.'

Bella squeezed Michael's hand. 'Madam Lydia described you to a tee and hinted that we were destined to be together. Is that what she told you?'

'Yeah. Said we were soul-mates, but then started rambling on about some evil geezer who didn't want us to be together.'

It was now Bella's face that turned pale. That was the exact same story Madam Lydia had told her.

Queenie Butler rocked her family's new addition in her arms. She felt far too young and glamorous to be a great-grandma, but the lad was a bonny boy and she'd already fallen in love with him. 'Aw, bless him. He's so gorgeous. Don't look nothing like our side of the family though. Got your looks he has, Sammi. You thought of a name yet?'

Little Vinny slung an arm around his girlfriend's shoulders. He hadn't touched a drink since Boxing Day and felt like a new person. He had a future now. A beautiful girlfriend and a son. 'We've decided to call him Oliver, Nan.'

Queenie Butler sneered. 'Don't like that name, do you, Vinny? Reminds me of the film where that poor little bastard was begging for food. Can't you call him something else?' Queenie asked her grandson.

When Little Vinny explained why he and Sammi-Lou had chosen to call their baby Oliver, Gary Allen stormed out of the ward. Not only did he loathe his daughter's boyfriend. He despised the little git's family even more.

Back in Islington, Michael pushed his barely touched lunch to one side.

'Is your food not nice?' Bella asked.

'I'm just not hungry. I had a big fry-up in the café this morning.'

'Don't be worrying too much about what Madam Lydia said. She isn't always spot on,' Bella assured Michael. She could see how much the reading had freaked him out, so had decided it would be best not to tell him that Lydia had warned her about an evil man as well.

'It's the bit about my boys that scared me the most. How come she could only see two? Makes me wonder if Nancy had a fucking affair and one of 'em ain't mine. She weren't talking about Lee, 'cause she could see a blond boy.'

'You're talking rubbish now, Michael. Of course Daniel and Adam are both your sons. You need to chill out a bit. Having a reading is meant to be a bit of fun, you know. You're not meant to take it so seriously.'

'I didn't like the way she ended it either. It was as though she saw something bad in that ball of hers. I don't believe for a minute that she actually had a migraine.'

'I wish I'd never suggested you visit her now. You sound like my dad did when he used to tell my mum off for visiting that gypsy woman. Just put it to the back of your mind, OK? We hold the key to our future, not Madam bloody Lydia.'

Relieved to be back in Tillingham, Joanna Preston was in the kitchen making sandwiches.

Darren Grant crept up behind her and put his hands around her waist. 'You OK?'

'I feel much better now we're home. My dad harping on about Vinny constantly was doing my head in. What's Shane and Ava up to?'

'Watching *The Wizard of Oz*. I can't believe how well they've bonded, can you?'

Joanna turned around. 'I've been thinking. It's silly you paying rent on your flat when you spend most of your time here. Why don't you move in properly?'

Darren grinned. 'Wait there a minute.'

Returning seconds later, Darren dropped to one knee and opened a small red velvet box. 'Marry me, Jo.'

'Oh my God! When did you buy that?' Joanna squealed excitedly.

'Only recently. I asked your dad's permission first and was going to propose at Christmas, but it didn't seem appropriate after Vinny turned up. If you need time to think about your answer, I'll understand.'

Joanna smiled. Darren was so kind and thoughtful. She'd had no confidence at all during her relationship with Vinny, but life with Darren was the opposite. He made her feel beautiful, desirable, loved and wanted. 'Of course I'll marry you.'

'What you doing, Mum?' Ava asked.

Joanna crouched down and hugged her daughter. 'Darren

and I are getting married, darling. You can be my brides-maid.'

Perplexed, Ava put her hands on her hips. 'But I've already got a daddy.'

Michael Butler smiled as Bella made her way back from the toilet. She was wearing a red leather jacket, red high-heeled knee-length boots, skin-tight faded jeans and a black fitted low-cut T-shirt. She looked incredible and Michael was well aware that virtually every other bloke in the pub had their eyes glued to her as well.

'I got you another drink, babe.'

'Thanks. This will have to be my last though. I need to get home to Antonio.'

'I was thinking. Do you fancy a night or a couple of days away? We could stay in a top hotel, or somewhere in the country?'

'No thanks. I've already explained to you that I will not be your bit on the side again. It isn't fair on me, you, Nancy or our children.'

'Well, I've made my decision. It's you I want, not Nancy, so I'm going to leave her. The boys are old enough to cope with the split now and I will still see them regularly. We can do family stuff together. My boys are great with kids, so they'll love Antonio. We could all go on holiday. I do need to sort out my affairs before I drop the bombshell though. Nancy is sure to want a divorce when I tell her I've met somebody else, so I wanna start shifting some money out my bank and hiding it. She's bound to go for half of all my assets. I was going to buy my brother out of the club completely, but I might have to re-think that one now. Don't get me wrong, I'm no tight bastard and Nance and the boys won't ever want for anything, but I don't see why she should get her hands on half the club.'

Bella was overjoyed, but also shocked. Michael had obviously thought this through and she hadn't expected him to make such an important choice quite so quickly. They'd only bumped into one another again just over a week ago. 'Are you sure this is what you want, Michael? I know it's what I want, but it's much simpler for me because I am single. I would never ask you to walk away from your children.'

'I won't be walking away from 'em, Bell. I'll buy a nice gaff and they can stay over at weekends. A few years down the line they'll be working for me anyway. I know this is what I want. Never been more sure about anything in my life.'

Bella leaned across the table and held Michael's handsome face in her hands. No other man had ever come close in her heart. 'You take as much time to sort your affairs out as you need.'

Michael grinned. 'I'm gonna marry you one day, sweetheart. Bella Butler has a blinding ring to it, don't ya think?'

PART FOUR

My only love sprung from my only hate!
Too early seen unknown, and known too late!
Prodigious birth of love it is to me,
That I must have a loathed enemy.

William Shakespeare

CHAPTER TWENTY-THREE

'Look, Vin. Oliver's laughing again,' Sammi-Lou pointed out.

'I must say that's a beautiful baby you have. Isn't he a happy little soul? How old is he?' a fellow diner asked.

'He's fourteen weeks,' Little Vinny told her, tickling Ollie's tummy.

When Sammi-Lou began a full-blown conversation with the lady, Little Vinny grinned at his son with pride. The boy had been the making of him, he really had, and Little Vinny absolutely adored being a father. Unlike some, he was very hands on. He thought nothing of changing Ollie's nappy or getting up to see to him in the night if he cried.

Having gained weight quickly after leaving the hospital, Oliver was now the same size as most babies his age. His hair was blond, slightly wavy and his eyes had just started to turn from blue to green.

'You really don't have to do that. Please take it back,' Sammi-Lou insisted when the lady stood up and put a pound note on the table for Oliver.

'No. I insist. Put it in that little ray of sunshine's piggy bank.'

'Thanks ever so much. Bye.' Turning to Sammi, Little Vinny said, 'Nice of her, wasn't it?'

Sammi-Lou smiled. Life was absolutely wonderful at present. Little Vinny was a joy to be around these days and they'd not had one cross word since Ollie was born. He'd even changed his work hours and now started earlier and was home by nine every evening. Weekends were spent as a family. They were always going on days out or visiting relatives. Even her dad had finally started to warm towards her boyfriend.

'I'm going to wrap Lee's present up in here. What time have we got to be at his party?'

'It starts at three and finishes at seven, but we haven't got to stay until the end,' Little Vinny explained. It was his cousin Lee's thirteenth birthday today and Michael was throwing a party for the kid at his club.

'Seeing as we've got time to kill, do you mind if I have a mooch round the shops? I don't really like this outfit I'm wearing.'

Little Vinny handed Sammi-Lou a fifty-pound note. 'Go and treat yourself. I'll wait 'ere with Ollie. I'm still hungry. Gonna order another egg-and-bacon roll.'

When Sammi-Lou left the café, Little Vinny grinned as he took the box out of his pocket and showed the contents to his son. 'Look what Daddy's bought, boy. Whaddya reckon, eh?'

Over in Whitechapel, Queenie and Vivian had been glued to Queenie's lounge window for the past hour. The Baker family were moving out and both women were elated.

'State of that sofa, Viv! Looks frowsy, don't it?'

'Hardly surprising. None of that family ever looked too wholesome to me. I wonder who we'll get in there next?'

Queenie shrugged. 'Probably foreigners, knowing our

luck. That's all you get moving in these days. I saw Fat Beryl down the market yesterday. Got Indians either side of her now. Be like walking through the streets of Calcutta round 'ere soon.'

'Oh well, whoever moves in can't be any worse than that motley crew. Be glad to see the back of that bastard moggy an' all. I went to pull up a weed this morning and put me hand straight in a pile of cat shit. Poxy thing was staring at me from the fence. I thought cats buried their turds?'

Queenie burst out laughing. 'They do. I reckon you'll have a win on the Football Pools or Spot the Ball now. Bird shit's lucky, so why not cat's?'

Mary Walker heard the sound of sobbing as soon as she unlocked her daughter's front door. She ran up the stairs. She'd been terribly worried about Nancy lately and so had Donald. The girl seemed to be carrying the weight of the world on her shoulders.

'I'm not going to the party, Mum. Michael never came home last night. I rung the club, and the new manager told me Michael was there but busy, like he always says. So I drove to the club just to catch the bastard out, and surprise surprise he was nowhere to be seen. He was with his other woman, I know he was. I've found traces of her on his clothes before washing them. She wears a strong musky-scented perfume and has long dark hair.'

Mary spoke to her daughter gently. 'Do you remember the last time you thought Michael was playing around? Well, he wasn't, was he? And look how ill you made your-self, worrying about it. You were found in an alleyway in just your nightclothes. Can you imagine what would've happened if that man hadn't found you while walking his dog? You'd have frozen to death and broken my heart, wouldn't you?'

'I'm not ill, Mum. I'm furious. How dare Michael treat me like this? He's not even rung me today to explain where he was, or ask what time I'm going to the party. Our marriage is dead in the water.'

'All marriages go through bad patches, Nance. Look at mine and your father's. I bet I know why Michael isn't coming home at nights. It's because you're constantly at one another's throats. Michael hasn't forgiven you for wanting to shop Daniel to the police, and you haven't forgiven him for threatening to divorce you if you went ahead and did so.'

'No. It isn't that. I know my own husband and I'm telling you now he is seeing another woman. I reckon he met her shortly after we went away for our anniversary. That's when he went ice-cold on me. Between me and you, Mum, I can even see stains and smell their sex on his underpants.'

Mary looked at her daughter in horror. Nancy must be ill if she'd resorted to inspecting Michael's underpants. 'I really think you should ring the doctor's surgery first thing on Monday, love, and book yourself an appointment. I'll come with you of course.'

'And what's the doctor going to do? Does he possess special powers to stop Michael poking his willy in some whore? Or a magic wand to change my eldest son from an unruly, out-of-control pain in the arse into a loving, gentle boy? The man's a GP, Mum, not a fucking magician.'

Johnny Preston drove stony-faced towards the solicitor's office in Maldon. Since Vinny Butler had come back into their lives it had caused nothing but poxy arguments and he'd had enough of it now. 'Go any slower and you'll stop, you wanker,' Johnny yelled, beeping his horn at the car in front.

'For goodness' sake calm down, Johnny. And don't you dare try to overtake on this road. There's too many bends. Look, I know you're upset about the letter, and so am I, but killing us in a car crash isn't the bloody answer.'

Johnny was more than just upset about the letter that had arrived at his daughter's house yesterday, he was fucking enraged. 'I told you as soon as that bastard knocked on our door on Christmas Day that he wouldn't stop until he got what he wanted. I also told you the only hope we had of ridding ourselves of the cunt was fleeing to Spain. But would you or Jo listen? No, of course not.'

Deborah decided silence was better than arguing again. Johnny was always right in his mind, so why waste her breath?

Vinny Butler smirked as he finished counting the previous evening's takings. His new venture was doing very nicely indeed.

Having originally planned to open a wine bar, Vinny had had second thoughts after visiting Ahmed's and a few others. The clientele just wasn't for him and, seeing as he would be running the establishment, Vinny knew it would only be a matter of time before he murdered then disposed of his first yuppie. Unbearable creatures, they were.

A trip to Stringfellows had given Vinny a new idea, and he was now the proud owner of Butler's Gentleman's Club in Holborn. It had cost a fortune to refurbish, but Vinny loved grandeur. Gold and mahogany was the colour theme. Chandeliers hung from the ceiling and the chairs and sofas were made from the finest leather.

Holborn was very much the home of the legal profession, so wanting their custom, Vinny had gone for class. Instead of scantily dressed or topless waitresses he'd opted for the old-fashioned bunny-girl look. There were poles installed on the dance-floor and private booths for gentlemen to enjoy one-to-one dances. There was a no-touching policy, but Vinny generally left that up to the girls themselves. If they wanted to earn a few quid more by letting some old perv touch their tits or snatch, Vinny had no problem with it – providing it was done discreetly.

Judges, barristers, solicitors and even a few Old Bill all frequented the club. Most were as good as gold, apart from one old judge who had a habit of getting his cock out. The geezer spent a fortune on the girls though, so instead of barring him, Vinny had given him a stern warning. The biggest nuisances of all were the yuppie brigade. They would roll in later in the evening when they'd already had a skinful. Pete, Paul and Jay Boy were always on hand to deal with their rowdy behaviour, and even though Vinny despised the tossers he barred very few as they spent mega-dosh on bottles of his finest champagne.

To keep out drunken hormonal teenagers, the club had an over twenty-fives policy. The majority of the music played was from the sixties era, which all of his punters bar the yuppies seemed to enjoy. Shirt, trousers and shoes were a must. No way was Vinny allowing scruffy bastards wearing jeans and trainers in.

'Morning, Vin. Banged out yesterday, eh?' Jay Boy said.

Vinny grinned. 'I bet we're raking in ten times the amount Ahmed does at the wanky wine bar.'

'Dunno why you don't try opening on a Saturday as well. We might get a different clientele, but I bet we'd still be busy,' Jay suggested.

'Nah. I'm coining it in as it is and I like having the weekends free now. Gonna be spending more time with Ava soon, eh?' Vinny chuckled.

Jay Boy smiled politely. He wished he hadn't offered to help Vinny on that particular venture, even though he wouldn't be personally involved because all he'd done was recommend a man for the job. But the job was a bad one.

Vinny wanted his daughter all to himself, which meant Ava's mother had to be disposed of.

Michael Butler hadn't been much older than Lee when he'd shagged his babysitter – at thirteen you were well on your way to being a man – so he'd cordoned off the majority of the club to let the youngsters do their own thing. There weren't many adults invited. Just family and close friends, yet Michael was still astounded when Eddie Mitchell appeared with his wife and children. It had been Vinny's idea to invite them, but Michael hadn't expected them to come. Ahmed had also been invited, along with his wife and kids, but had politely declined.

'Eddie, so glad you could make it. Vinny'll be here in a bit.'

Eddie Mitchell nodded and shook Michael's hand. 'This is my beautiful wife Jessica, and these two are my terrible twins, Frankie and Joey.'

'Why do you always have to embarrass us, Dad?' Frankie Mitchell asked, punching her father on the arm.

Eddie chuckled. 'See what I mean? Where's your wife, Michael? I'm sure she and my Jessica will have plenty to rabbit about.'

Michael felt embarrassed. Keeping up appearances meant everything in his world. 'Nancy hasn't arrived yet. I'll give her a ring in a minute. In the meantime, what would you like to drink? The bar's free and there's plenty of grub. Disco starts in a bit, kids.'

Michael's cheesy grin went down well with Joey, who smiled, but not Frankie. She glared back at him and said, 'We're not kids, we're teenagers.'

Scolding her daughter for being rude, Jessica apologized to Michael.

'Don't worry about it. My three are far worse,' Michael chuckled, before being rudely interrupted by his mother asking, 'What's that wanker doing here?'

Excusing himself from the Mitchells, Michael led his mother over to a corner of the bar. 'Do you always have to show me up? That was Eddie Mitchell and his family I was talking to.'

'I couldn't care less if it was Jesus Christ himself. Who invited Brenda's boyfriend?'

'I did. I invited Bren and the kids and she asked if she could bring him. Please don't start, Mum, not today, for fuck's sake.'

'Well?' Johnny Preston asked as his daughter walked out of the solicitor's office at the top of Maldon High Street.

'Let's talk outside, Dad.'

Knowing by Joanna's face that the news wasn't going to be good, Johnny stamped on a nearby empty can.

Aware that her mum was about to talk to her granddad about her daddy, three-year-old Ava pretended to be asleep as her mother put her in the car and secured her seatbelt. She then waited until her mum's back was turned before opening the window slightly.

Joanna faced her parents. 'To put it bluntly, the solicitor said that if we go to court a judge or magistrate will allow Vinny to spend time with Ava alone. I explained all past history and my concerns like you told me to, Dad, but she said it wouldn't have much impact on their decision. She also said the court would probably side with Vinny even though he'd served a sentence for manslaughter because of the terrible circumstances surrounding Molly's death. In other words, because that evil cousin of mine murdered our daughter, we don't have a leg to stand on.'

Punching his fist into his hand, Johnny turned to Deborah. 'Moving abroad is the only way to rid ourselves of that cunt for good. It's either that or I kill him.'

Startled, young Ava opened her eyes. She hadn't understood most of what had been said, but she understood the end bit.

Back in Whitechapel, Eddie Mitchell was having a couple of sneaky Scotches at the bar with Vinny Butler. Jessica was driving today and hated him drinking Scotch. She said it made him turn nasty, but what she didn't know wouldn't hurt her.

'Can you imagine if one day me and you decided to go into business together? I would love to see the look on all the plastic gangsters' faces if that were ever to happen, wouldn't you?' Vinny chuckled.

Eddie grinned. He knew Vinny was half joking, but the actual idea was a possibility. Eddie could only hide so much of his ill-gotten gains through his scrap yard.

'On a serious note, if you're ever up for doing something between us, just give me the nod,' Vinny urged.

Eddie Mitchell had not got to his level in this life without being thoroughly cautious, so he decided that a change of subject was needed. 'I take it you heard about David Fraser getting banged up? You gotta admire the man's style. Dressed as Old Bill and went for three million!' Eddie said, referring to the son of Mad Frankie.

Vinny chuckled. 'His brother Patrick's banged up an' all now, ain't he?'

'Yeah. And what about Paddy Price? He's bang in trouble, he is. The Old Bill dug up the remains of six dead bodies in the grounds of his property last week. He asked me a while back if I knew anyone to dispose of corpses. Thank

God I'd realized he weren't the full shilling and said I didn't,' Eddie laughed.

'Between you, me and the gatepost, Ed, do you know a trusted contact who disposes of corpses?' Vinny asked.

'Yes, I do. Why? You got problems?'

Thinking of Johnny Preston, Vinny smirked. 'Nothing I can't handle. Just might need a fucking nuisance disposed of in the not-too-distant future.'

Ahmed Zane was in a foul mood. His hotel in Turkey had been shut until further notice because of a fire in the early hours of the morning, and the takings on his wine bar had dipped in the past couple of months since a new one had opened nearby. And if that wasn't bad enough, Vinny Butler's new club was raking it in and Vinny's evil son had sorted himself out and was about to propose to that poor unsuspecting girlfriend of his.

Snorting a fat line of cocaine, Ahmed handed the rolled-up note to his cousin. 'The quicker we do away with Vinny and his horror of a son now, the better. The pair of them dying will lift my mood. Did I tell you Vinny invited Eddie Mitchell to Michael's son's party before he got around to asking me? As for the child-murderer, he is so busy playing happy families these days he seems to have forgotten he throttled his own little sister. I cannot wait to see Vinny's face when he hears my tape. That will wipe away his cocky smile for ever. He will die a very unhappy man, Burak, then go straight to hell with that son of his. We will give him twenty-four hours to wallow in his grief and then kill him.'

Nancy Butler took another of Michael's suits out of the wardrobe and took great joy in cutting it into small pieces with a pair of scissors. If the whore he was shagging could sew, perhaps she could repair them for him?

Placing the remains of Michael's expensive suits into a dustbin liner, Nancy then began packing a suitcase with her own belongings. She'd walked down the road to the phone box earlier and rung Dean Smart. Having been married to Brenda Butler, Dean was the only one who truly understood what she was currently going through, and she could be totally honest with him. Dean was still living in Scotland and only had her best interests at heart.

Lugging the dustbin bags and suitcase downstairs, Nancy rang her mother. 'Do you mind if I move in with you and Dad for a while until I find myself a place? I have to get out of here. Michael and the boys are driving me doolally.'

Relieved when her mother agreed instead of giving her another lecture about making a go of her marriage, Nancy replaced the receiver. She'd told her mum to expect her in the next couple of hours. She had something to do first. If she was going to leave her cheating bastard of a husband for good, then she would do it in style.

Queenie Butler couldn't wipe the smile off her face. She'd been having an awful time earlier. First she'd spotted Daniel drinking alcohol and encouraging his brothers to do the same. Then she'd had to suffer the embarrassment of Brenda and her loser of a boyfriend chucking themselves across the dance floor while all the teenagers laughed at them.

She'd been about to stomp off home when Little Vinny had come up trumps for once and proposed to Sammi-Lou right in front of her. Queenie loved nothing more than a wedding – excluding her own, of course. Sammi-Lou had immediately said yes, and the happy couple had just gone off to tell Vinny the good news.

'Aw, bless 'em and little Ollie, Viv. Don't they make a lovely family?'

Vivian looked at her sister in amazement. 'You've changed your tune, Queen. You told me not long ago he was an arsehole and Sammi and her baby would be far better off without him,' she reminded her sister.

'Yes, I know I did. But I take that all back now. I never thought Little Vinny would be a family man and father material, but he's a changed boy. He's visited me every week since Ollie was born.'

Spotting Nancy storm into the club with two dustbin liners and a face like thunder, Vivian nudged her sister. 'Oh dearie me. I think your Michael might be in trouble.'

Nancy Butler was on a mission. Emptying Michael's mutilated suits at his feet, she screamed, 'Ask your whore if she can repair those, you cheating fucking arsehole.'

Unable to stop himself, Vinny burst out laughing. 'I always told you she was a fruitcake, didn't I, bruv? You should've got rid of her years ago.'

Adam Butler, who'd spotted his mother arrive in a distressed state, ran straight over to her. 'Whatsa matter, Mum?' he asked, throwing his arms around her waist.

Nancy stroked her son's hair. Adam had a caring nature and would be the perfect son if he wasn't so easily influenced by Daniel. He was nothing like the Butlers. 'Mummy's leaving your father and going to live with your nan and granddad for now. Daddy has a new mummy lined up for you, Adam. Has he introduced you to the marriage-wrecking slut yet?'

Nancy was silenced by Daniel, who ran over and shoved her away from Adam, shouting: 'Leave us alone. You've spoilt the party. Dad's right, you are a loony.'

If there was ever a time that Michael Butler wished the ground would open up and swallow him, it was this very moment. Not only was his joker of a brother enjoying every second of the entertainment, the Mitchell family were sitting on the next table with their mouths wide open. 'Get in my office now,' Michael hissed, grabbing his wife by the arm.

Instead of allowing herself to be led away, Nancy snatched her arm free and slapped Michael across the face. 'Piss off. You can give your whore orders from now on, not me. You and I are finished, and if we have to split the kids down the middle, then Adam's mine. The other two are most definitely yours.'

CHAPTER TWENTY-FOUR

'Morning, Queen. I got the papers,' Vivian said, shutting her sister's front door.

'I'm surprised we're not in 'em after that performance yesterday,' sighed Queenie. 'What is it with our family and parties, eh? They never seem to pass without a scene. Do you remember the one when Big Stan started a fight and my glass cabinet and all me ornaments went for a burton? Well, I think Nancy might've upstaged that yesterday. Feel sorry for those boys, I do. Poor little Adam was so upset. Talk about a show-up, eh?'

Vivian nodded. 'I bet Michael weren't too pleased that Nancy cut all his expensive suits up. Do you reckon he has got another woman?'

'Wouldn't surprise me. Born with Albie's womanizing streak, was Michael. We didn't used to call him Alfie for nothing,' Queenie reminded her sister, referring to the charmer Michael Caine had played in the film.

'And what about Brenda and her bloke? Fancy kissing and cuddling like that in front of all them youngsters. Tara and Tommy must've been so embarrassed.'

'Not as embarrassed as me. Disgusting behaviour. Snogging in public at their age should be classed as a crime.

Brought back memories of the odd occasion I had to kiss Albie. Made me feel sick.'

'I bet you wouldn't mind kissing Dirty Den though,' Vivian teased.

Queenie laughed. Both sisters had the hots for Den Watts. He and his wife Angie were landlord and landlady of the pub in that new soap on BBC1 called *EastEnders*. 'I'd like to give Dirty Den a bit more than a kiss, Viv.'

Vivian playfully punched her sister on the arm. 'Hands off, you. I had the hots for him first.'

Michael Butler was deep in thought as he rustled up breakfast for his sons. His assets and finances had now been sorted and he'd hidden plenty. The plan had been to sit down with Nancy this week, come clean with her that he wanted a divorce, then leave her in the house with the boys while he temporarily moved in above the club. Having discussed the situation in detail with Bella, they'd decided it was kinder not to inform Nancy or the boys of their relationship just yet. Bella had been insistent they should allow the dust to settle before going public.

'I like it much better without Mum here, don't you, Dad?' Daniel asked chirpily.

'Shut up, Dan,' Michael hissed. Both Lee and Adam seemed very subdued today and so was he. Nancy storming out and leaving him in charge of looking after the boys had bollocksed his plans right up. 'Answer that phone, one of ya. I've only got one pair of hands.'

'Nanny Mary wants to talk to you, Dad,' Lee said.

Michael snatched the phone out of Lee's hand, listened to what Mary had to say, then muttered, 'OK. See you there.'

'What did Nan want? Is Mum coming home?' Adam asked, his voice tinged with hope.

'Your nan wants to meet me to talk about your mother.'

'Tell her we don't want the nutjob back,' Daniel said, laughing at his own wit.

Clouting Daniel round the head, Michael slammed the saucepan on the hob. He and Bella had planned to start house-hunting soon. Obviously, his sons would've had their own room or rooms for weekend stays, but them moving in permanently had certainly not been part of the equation.

Ahmed and Burak glanced at one another as they surveyed the premises. The location wasn't far from the Circus Tavern, but unlike the others they'd viewed it was off the beaten track. It also had an eerie feel about it, which was rather apt, seeing as they planned to commit two murders there.

'What was this building used for?' Ahmed asked Mehmet.

'A shipping company had their offices here. The guy that owns it wants you to burn it to the ground when your business is finished, so he can claim the insurance money. He's living in Spain, so won't be implicated in any way.'

'No problem. What do you think, Burak?' Ahmed asked.

Burak grinned. He'd been gagging to watch Vinny Butler die a painful death for years. 'It's perfect. Bring it on.'

On the drive to Tillingham to see Ava, Queenie and Vinny Butler were discussing the debacle of a party. 'The BBC should do a soap based on our family. It'd get more viewers than *EastEnders*, that's for sure,' Queenie declared.

Vinny laughed. 'Michael's face when Nancy emptied his chopped-up suits out that bin bag was a picture. I'd have knocked the psycho bitch's spark out if that had been my clobber.'

'Is Michael at it, Vin? Only, if so, I feel sorry for the poor girl. I know what it's like to live with a bloody womanizer. The day I went to visit your father in hospital and Judy Preston was there carrying the dirty old toad's baby was horrendous. Never felt so humiliated in all my life.'

'If Michael has got a bird on the firm, he's certainly keeping his cards close to his chest. I don't see him as much these days, but I'm sure he'd have told me. Changing the subject, I wonder if we're allowed to take Ava out on our own today? The bitch must've had a cardiac when she read Colin's latest masterpiece.'

Queenie pursed her lips. She often travelled to Tillingham with Vinny to see her granddaughter, but the set-up was awful. If Vinny wanted to take the child out for something to eat or to the park or zoo, Joanna and her boyfriend would insist on being at the same destination so they could keep a watchful eye. 'If that cow says we can't take Ava out on our own today, Vin, let's just do it. What the police gonna do if she rings 'em, eh? Hardly gonna send out a search party because Ava's spending a few hours alone with her father and nan.'

'I don't wanna involve the Old Bill, Mum. Let's just see what the slag says. She must've got the letter by now,' Vinny replied. He too hated the current situation, which was why he'd hired Jay Boy's pal to sort it out once and for all. Even though Joanna and her prick of a boyfriend kept their distance whenever he took Ava out, just knowing they were in the same vicinity really grated on Vinny.

'You're not going soft in your old age, are you? You're not even forty yet. Get a grip, Vinny, and stand up to the Prestons.'

Vinny smirked. Little did his mother know, he aimed to do far more than just stand up to the Prestons. Jo would be the first to die, then Johnny. And if that fat bitch Deborah gave him any grief, he'd do away with her as well. As a father, it was his duty to love and protect Ava. That little girl deserved the best in life.

Harry Mitchell was old school. If somebody scratched his back, he'd scratch theirs. As a man of morals, his word was his bond.

'What's occurring then?' Eddie asked. His old man had told him earlier that he wanted a private chat.

Harry glanced at his other sons who were deep in conversation, then leaned forward. 'You remember my old mucker from the Ville? Don't mention names because of earholes,' he said, gesturing towards Ronny.

'I know exactly who you mean. Is he in trouble?'

'Needs a favour, and I want you to sort it. The problem is, it involves the Butlers.'

Michael Butler felt very awkward as he entered Barking Park, then sat next to his wife's mother on the bench. 'Is Nancy OK?'

Mary was in no mood for small talk. 'I'm not going to beat around the bush, Michael, but I need you to be truthful with me. Are you seeing another woman? Or is my Nancy losing her marbles again? I really do need an honest answer, because only then can I work out how to deal with the situation.'

Michael put his head in his hands. How could he lie to Nancy's mother? He'd always had the utmost respect for Mary. She'd stuck up for him in the most difficult circumstances in the past. 'I'm so sorry, Mary, but I have met somebody else. I really wanted to tell Nancy, but her behaviour's been a bit odd lately, to say the least, and I was too scared of pushing her over the edge again. I had the boys to consider and I just wanted everything to be amicable.'

Michael was in complete shock when placid, pleasant

Mary slapped him around the face much harder than Nancy had the previous day. 'You told me to be honest,' he complained.

'Leading that girl on is not honest. Nancy was so happy after you took her away on that romantic anniversary break. Her smile lit up the room when she was telling me all about it. Why do that if you were planning on leaving her?'

Sure he was going to wake up with Mary's hand-print on his mush tomorrow, Michael rubbed the side of his face. 'I wasn't having an affair when Nancy and I went away for the weekend, Mary. And to be honest, neither am I having one now. The lady in question is somebody I met many years ago, but she moved away. We bumped into one another again just before Christmas and, even though we've spent time together, I can assure you there's been nothing untoward going on. She has a son, and I wouldn't do that to Nancy and the boys. But I do love this woman and I can't help my feelings. I'm truly sorry, but that's—'

'And so you should be sorry, Michael. You've broken my daughter's heart. She's in pieces at home, and you can imagine what Donald's saying, can't you? Pointing the blame at me, he is, for sticking up for you from the beginning.'

Michael sighed. 'I'm not gonna keep apologizing, Mary. Mine and Nancy's marriage had run its course ages ago, if you want the truth. We do need to speak and make arrangements, though. I will sign the house over to Nance, providing she takes care of our sons.'

Mary looked at her son-in-law in amazement. 'Nancy is in no fit state to look after herself, Michael, let alone those boys. For the time being, you're going to have to take care of them your fucking self.'

'I can't look after the boys. I'm the breadwinner. I need to work.'

Mary stood up. 'Well, in that case, ask your new tart to help out or employ a nanny. Goodbye, Michael, it's been nice knowing you.'

Ordering his mother to wait in the car, Vinny walked up Joanna's path and pressed the bell.

'Daddy,' Ava screamed excitedly.

'Go in the lounge with Darren, darling, while Mummy has a quick chat with your dad. You can see him in a minute.'

'But I want to see him now,' Ava argued, lip protruding.

'Just do as your mum says, Ava,' Vinny ordered.

When her daughter finally did as she was told, Joanna turned to the man she wished she'd never met. 'I received your solicitor's letter and after much thought I've decided you can take Ava out on your own in future.'

'What about her staying with me for weekends?'

'Not at the moment, Vinny. Let's just take one step at a time and see how you get on spending all day with Ava first. You can pick her up as early as you wish, but it has to be on a Sunday. And bring her home by six. I like her to go to bed early when she has nursery the following day.'

Vinny smirked. 'Fair enough. Expect me first thing next Sunday then, about seven-ish.'

'Ava, you can see your father now,' Joanna shouted out.

'Where we going today, Daddy?' Ava asked, when Vinny picked her up and swung her in the air. She much preferred spending time with her father than her mum's boyfriend. Her dad always spoiled her and bought her nice presents.

'Not sure yet, darlin', but next Sunday we're going to have a party for you at your nan's house in Whitechapel. You'll get to meet your Uncle Michael, Auntie Viv and all your cousins.'

Tears forming in her eyes, Joanna shut the front door

and fell into Darren's arms. 'How am I ever going to relax while she's out with that evil bastard? Say he doesn't bring her back?'

Darren stroked his girlfriend's hair. 'Of course he'll bring her back. Vinny has a business in London and all his family live there. No way is a mummy's boy like him ever going to move away. It'll be fine, trust me.'

'So sorry I'm late, babe. I've had the weekend from hell,' Michael Butler explained as he entered the Italian restaurant.

'Can I sit with you, please, Michael?' Antonio asked.

'Course you can, boy. What you been up to? Been behaving yourself for your mum, I hope.'

When Antonio clambered on Michael's lap and began chatting away nineteen to the dozen, Bella smiled. Her son idolized her boyfriend as much as she did. He was the father figure Antonio had always yearned for. Michael adored Antonio too and was more than happy to spend time with him rather than just wanting her all to himself. They had the potential to be the perfect family and Bella couldn't wait to go house-hunting next week. Perhaps once they moved to Essex, she would even consider giving Antonio a baby brother or sister. She and Michael had agreed that they wanted a child together. They'd even joked that it would be the best-looking baby ever to grace the earth.

'Antonio, Paolo is over there and is waving to you. Go see him and I'll call you when our food is ready,' Bella said. Paolo was the grandson of the restaurant owner and the two boys often played together.

Michael took a deep breath. 'Nancy knows and she's left me, babe. I never said a word to her about you, but I admitted to her mother this morning that I'd fallen for another woman. Obviously, I never mentioned you by name, but Nancy's sodded off and left the boys with me.'

Bella put her hand over her mouth. 'Oh my God! How did she find out?'

'Just guessed, I think. To be honest, I'm quite relieved it's all out in the open, but pissed off that she is refusing to take care of her sons. I always told you she was a shit mother, didn't I? I said to her mum that I'd sign the house over to her providing she takes care of the boys, but she's in one of her moods at the moment and won't see sense. The boys are too old for me to bring in a nanny or au pair. Daniel especially would terrorize the poor woman. So I'm just gonna have to let them fend for themselves while I work at nights. They are quite trustable and there is no way they'd throw wild parties or trash the gaff. What do you think?'

Bella squeezed Michael's hand. She adored her own son but wasn't a massive fan of other people's children. Antonio had impeccable manners and at this stage of her and Michael's relationship, she did not think it fair or appropriate that Antonio would be forced to live with Michael's three much older sons. 'I think we should put our house-hunting on hold for the time being. You can stay at mine whenever you want, but we should wait until Nancy is well enough to take care of her sons before we actually set up home together.'

'Nance won't take care of Lee, Bella, that's for sure. She's not even his mother, so he's definitely going to have to live with us.'

'We will cross that bridge when we come to it, Michael. For the time being, let's just celebrate the fact that we no longer have to hide our relationship.'

Michael grinned. 'Well, at least I'll never have to refer

to you as my bit of fluff again. You are now officially my woman, you lucky lady.'

Having been left to fend for themselves, it was Daniel Butler's idea to take a trip to Dagenham Sunday Market.

Stepping off the District Line train at Dagenham Heathway, Daniel ordered his brothers to run if there was a ticket inspector present.

'But why, Dan? Dad gave us a tenner each,' Adam stated.

'Because it'll be a laugh and we'll have more money to spend on ourselves.'

'Tickets, please,' the inspector bellowed.

Daniel grabbed Adam's arm, before pushing Lee in the back. 'Leg it!' he ordered.

The inspector gave chase to the little blighters, but was soon out of breath. 'I never forget a face you know. I'll have you all arrested,' he yelled.

Daniel burst out laughing as he reached the bottom of the Heathway hill. 'Silly old fucker. We'll wind him up again on the way home.'

'Dad will kill us if we get arrested, Dan. Let's go to a different station on the way back,' Adam suggested.

Daniel flicked his brother's ear. 'Where's your sense of fun? You little wuss. Now come on, let's go spend our dosh.'

Deciding to drive out of Tillingham, Vinny found a great boozer that was very child-friendly with a little family room at the back and a play area.

'Nanny, come and play with me,' Ava pleaded.

'Nanny can't do that, darling. She's far too old. You go and play with the children while me and your dad watch you.'

When Ava happily skipped away from the table, Queenie grinned. 'She's nothing like Molly, is she?'

'It's a blessing in disguise she's nothing like Molly, Mum. We wouldn't be able to deal with it if she was.'

'Who we going to invite to the party next week? We want to make it special for Ava. How old is Jay Boy's girlfriend's little 'un? Lovely girl she is, by the way. Training to be a nurse she told me yesterday. Where did her and Jay meet?'

Not wanting to spoil his mother's perception of Jay Boy's bird or embarrass his pal, Vinny told his mother they'd met in a pub. The truth was Jilly had worked as one of his bunny girls briefly. Jay Boy had fallen in love quickly, taken Jilly under his wing and had forced her to quit the club so he could support her and her daughter. 'I'm not sure how old Jilly's daughter is, but I think she's around Ava's age so I'll invite them. What about Dad? Michael's so up his backside these days he's bound to refuse to come if we don't invite that old bastard too.'

'Let's ask the old goat then. I want Michael there. Don't be inviting Bren and Dagenham Dave though. Poor little Ava would probably hitch-hike back to Tillingham if she saw those two eating one another's faces off.'

'A chip off the old block, Mum. Look! Ava's just clumped that little boy.'

Turning around, Queenie laughed. Her granddaughter was standing with her hands on her hips and wagging a finger at a lad who looked at least a year or two older than her. 'She reminds me of me and Vivian, boy. It's definitely in the genes.'

Vinny smirked. Ava was a Butler all right and he couldn't wait to become her sole parent.

CHAPTER TWENTY-FIVE

The following weekend the weather was lovely, so Michael suggested he and Bella take Antonio to Hyde Park on the Saturday.

Heavily lacquered or messy-looking hair was currently all the rage, thanks to impressionable youngsters copying their favourite pop stars, and Bella hated the look. 'Oh my God, Michael! That woman is far too old for that outfit. She must be at least sixty.'

The woman in question was wearing Lycra tartan leggings, had a mass of dyed-blonde permed hair and to top it all was on roller-skates. 'Jesus wept. I can just see my mum and aunt going out in public like that – not! You do see some sights in London, don't ya?'

When the woman in question began fussing over Antonio, Michael wanted to laugh as she nearly lost her balance. 'Do you wanna sit down for a minute, love?' Michael chuckled.

'No. I'm fine, thank you. What a handsome little boy you have. He's the spitting image of his daddy, aren't you?' the woman grinned.

When the eccentric old bird unsteadily skated off, Michael put an arm around Bella's shoulders. 'How many people is that now who've said Antonio is a ringer for me? You sure he ain't a dwarf and you've lied about his age?'

Bella smiled. 'He looks like me. I think people only say it because he has your eye-colour.'

'What did his dad look like?' Michael enquired.

'Clint was tall and dark with green eyes. He wasn't as handsome as you though, so don't get jealous.'

'Very few men are as handsome as me, babe,' Michael laughed. 'I was thinking, now that I've told Nancy's mother about you, I'd like you to meet my sons.'

'It's a bit too early for that, Michael. You need to give them time to adjust before I am introduced to them. I want them to like me, not blame me for their mum walking out on them.'

'I'm sure they'd be OK, but I suppose you might be right. Adam's a bit sensitive. I am gonna tell my family about us though. Just my mum, dad, brother and aunt. I'm spending the day with them tomorrow, so I'll tell them then.'

'Isn't it a bit too soon to tell them as well? I would hate your mum to see me as some hussy.'

'She won't. My dad and brother knew about you years ago, so it'll be no surprise to them. I told my dad we bumped into one another again at Christmas, and said this time I wasn't gonna let you go. My mum and aunt are as tough as old boots. They won't be too bothered about Nancy. They'll just want me to be happy. You need to chill out. My family are gonna love you, Bella, trust me.'

'Hurry up, Queen. The pie-and-mash shop'll be shut by the time you get ready. Whatever you doing up there?' Vivian shouted out. She knew the Roman would be packed today because of the hot weather and couldn't wait to parade herself up and down the market.

Queenie nearly fell down the stairs in her haste to tell

Viv the news. 'Quick, look out the front. We've got new neighbours!'

Vivian dashed to the window. The council had popped next door on Monday and had obviously done a few jobs because of the drilling. Then on Thursday an Indian family had viewed the property. 'It's just the removal men there, I think, Queen. Gotta be those Indians moving in I reckon, but I can't see 'em. We haven't seen anybody else view it, have we?'

Queenie pursed her lips. She wasn't racist, just preferred her own kind the same as the Indians probably did. She hated the smell of Indian food though. It made her want to vomit. 'Best we stock up on air fresheners while we're down the market. Otherwise our curtains and everything else are gonna stink of curry and whatever other shit they eat.'

Johnny Preston had arranged to meet Black Joe at the Halfway House along the Southend Arterial Road. They'd met in prison and Johnny knew Black Joe could be trusted.

'It's under your seat – don't worry, it isn't loaded. I know your track record when it comes to misfiring, so will drop the ammo off tomorrow. I don't like carrying both together.'

Johnny's hands were shaky and clammy as he put his hand under the car seat. He unwrapped the cloth and stared at the 9mm pistol. Just looking at it scared the living daylights out of him. He'd mugged himself right off when he'd accidentally shot Roy Butler instead of Vinny many moons ago. 'It's perfect for the job,' Johnny said, handing Black Joe the agreed price in an envelope.

'I'll meet you here same time tomorrow with the ammo, OK? Do you want me to bring a sports-bagful, in case you wanna have a little practice first?'

Johnny Preston couldn't help but smile. Black Joe had actually been christened Joseph Jesus Harvey. His mother was a deeply religious woman and Joe was a big believer in God too. 'Piss off you cheeky bastard. Go and pray for your sins.'

Chuckling away, Black Joe zoomed off.

Eddie Mitchell welcomed his dad's old pal warmly. 'Long time no see. You're looking well. Fancy a brandy or a cuppa?'

'I'll have a small brandy, please, Ed. I saw your Gary and Ricky recently. First time I've seen 'em in years. Big strapping lads, eh? You must be ever so proud of the way they've turned out.'

'I am. They're good boys. How's your family doing?'

'The wife and kids are fine. But my brother's not well. Your dad would remember Stan, but I doubt you would. Been diagnosed with terminal cancer. Given him a year, tops. That's part of the reason I need a favour.'

'So, how can I help?'

Eddie listened intently while the situation was explained in detail to him. His ears pricked up when he learned of Vinny Butler's involvement. He wasn't overly surprised. Not much went on in the underworld that he didn't get wind of.

Eddie thought deeply, this was going to be a fucker to deal with but deal with it he would. 'What I want you to do is get your nephew to pen a letter to Vinny. Tell him to keep it short and sweet, hint that somebody was trying to set him up and arrange a meet. Bring the letter to me and I'll hand it to Vinny personally. I'll also have a quiet word in his shell-like saying you're a friend of the family, blah blah blah. I won't mention your name, so don't worry.'

'Do you think Vinny will listen to you?'

Eddie Mitchell chuckled. 'Obviously, I can't promise you anything. But he'd be a silly boy if he didn't. A very fucking silly boy indeed.'

*

Mary Walker was still furious, but doing her best to act normal in front of Nancy and Donald. Her daughter seemed slightly calmer today and she wouldn't tell her about Michael's appalling behaviour until the time was right. Nancy's health and state of mind came before anything else.

'Where did you go when you went out earlier?' Donald asked, peering suspiciously over his newspaper.

'Round the shop to get your bloody papers.'

'But you were gone ages.'

'Gawd blimey, Donald. I thought it was our Christopher who was the policeman, not you. I bumped into a couple of people and had a chat. Is that OK?'

'You didn't go and see Michael, did you?' Nancy asked, concerned.

'No. Course not,' Mary replied, squeezing her daughter's hand while glaring at her husband.

'I'm definitely not going back to him this time, Mum. I've seriously had enough. Obviously, when I'm feeling a bit better, I'll make proper arrangements for the boys.'

'Here we go again. If I had a pound for every time I've heard you were never going back to that villainous husband of yours, I'd be rich,' Donald piped up.

Leaping off the sofa, Mary snatched the newspaper out of Donald's hand and hit him over the head with it. 'Do yourself a favour and go and mow that lawn. Looks like a bloody jungle out there and the Robinses are coming for dinner tomorrow.'

When Donald begrudgingly did as he was told, Nancy allowed herself a little giggle. 'I do love you, Mum.'

'And I love you too, more than words can say. You really have got to move on from Michael this time though, Nance. It'll be better for your state of mind and those boys.'

'It's over, Mum. I've had a gutful and I can't take no

more. I've decided that I'm going to insist Adam lives with me. He's such a sweet boy, and the older two lead him astray. There's still a chance for him in life if I get him away from that environment. Michael's bound to refuse to split the boys up, but he can go fuck himself. You don't mind Adam living here until I sort myself out my own place, do you? I'm sure you'll be able to talk Dad round.'

'I'm not sure it would be fair to take Adam and leave Daniel behind, love. They're ever so close, and both your sons.'

'But I don't want Daniel. He reminds me of a young Little Vinny. I do love him, but I don't like him very much. Does that make sense to you, Mum?'

Desperate to lighten the strange conversation, Mary chuckled. 'It makes perfect sense to me. I feel exactly the same about your father.'

Little Vinny was shitting a brick. He and Sammi-Lou had been engaged a whole week now, yet she still hadn't told her parents. He'd begged her to tell them when they'd popped round the other day while he was at work. But instead she'd taken her ring off and insisted they told her parents today, together.

'I'll unclip Oliver out of his seat, Vin. You take the stuff out the boot.'

Little Vinny nodded. 'Your father will probably put this over me head,' he mumbled, waving the champagne bottle in the air.

'Shush. Mum and Dad are coming,' Sammi-Lou hissed.

Little Vinny handed Meg Allen the big bouquet and kissed her politely on the cheek.

'I wish you'd stop bringing gifts every time you visit, Vinny. It's ever so generous, but there's really no need. I'd rather you spend the money on Oliver.'

'Ollie doesn't go short of presents or anything else, Meg, trust me. I could open a toy and kids' clothes shop with what he's got indoors.'

Hearing the back-end of the conversation, Gary Allen chuckled. He'd been the same with Sammi-Lou and Millie. Had bought them far more than they ever needed, and still did.

'Dad's in a good mood. Tell them straight away,' Sammi-Lou whispered.

'Shouldn't it be you who tells 'em?'

'No. Dad will be far more impressed if you say it.'

Little Vinny felt like a cat on a hot tin roof as he walked inside the house.

'Can I play with Oliver, Vinny?' Millie asked excitedly.

'Course you can,' Little Vinny replied.

Thankfully Sammi-Lou's younger sister no longer freaked him out. It must have been paranoia and guilt that made him think of Molly every time he saw her at the start of his and Sammi's relationship. Since Ollie had been born he'd come to realize that the only real similarity was the blonde curly hair.

Clearing his throat, Little Vinny turned to Meg, then focused on Gary. He was great at lying, but got tongue-tied when it came to telling the truth. 'I asked Sammi to marry me and she said yes. I know I should've asked your permission first, Gary. But it was a spur of the moment thing,' he blurted out.

Having more than forgiven Little Vinny for his past misdemeanours, Meg Allen had tears in her eyes as she hugged the happy couple. 'Congratulations! I'm so pleased for you both, and won't it be lovely for Oliver if his mummy and daddy are legally married, Gary?'

'Can I be bridesmaid? Please can I?' Millie yelled.

Gary grimaced. Little Vinny had surprised him by turning

things around, and there was no denying that he currently made Sammi-Lou very happy. The lad was also a wonderful father and generous to a fault, but Gary still had his doubts. They were teenagers, not adults, and marriage wasn't something to be taken lightly. 'Let's have a man-to-man chat in the kitchen, Vin.'

Feeling like a dog that was about to be put down, Little Vinny followed Gary into the kitchen and then winced as he slammed the door. 'Too fucking right, you should've asked me first! And what do you mean, "spur of the moment"? Marriage is for life, not something you do on a cunting whim.'

'I know that, Gary. If you want the truth, ever since Oliver was born proposing to Sammi had been on my mind. I love her and that little boy so much; I want us to be a proper family. Last weekend we went to my cousin's birthday party and I just sort of blurted it out. I've never been that good with planning stuff or words.'

Gary Allen was a big, strapping bloke and as he approached and put his face just inches away from his own, Little Vinny feared the worst. 'I'm telling you now and I'm a man of my word: you ever hurt Sammi-Lou or my grandson in any way, shape or form, I will fucking kill you with me bare hands. Understand?'

'Totally, Gary.'

Gary Allen slapped his future son-in-law on the back. 'Good, lad. Now let's crack open that bottle of bubbly, shall we?'

Loaded up with carrier bags, two of which contained nothing but air fresheners, Queenie and Vivian stood open-mouthed as they reached their abode. Instead of the finest net curtains like they had, the new neighbours had hung what looked like two old bedsheets that were obviously once white but now looked grey at the windows.

Queenie clutched her sister's arm, then pointed. 'What's that thing poking its head out behind the sheet? Is it a toy?'

Vivian looked upwards. Her eyes were only marginally better than her sister's, but both women were too proud to wear their glasses outdoors, seeing it as a sign of old age. 'Oh my gawd! It's moving! I think it's a cat, Queen. Look, there's another one staring at us an' all.'

Needing a brandy more than ever, Queenie dashed inside her house. She was bemused, to say the least. 'I didn't think Indians had pets. Don't they eat cats and dogs in their country?'

'No, it's them Oriental types who eat dogs – I watched a programme about it once. Not sure if Indians eat cats. I suppose they might.'

Queenie downed her brandy in one. 'Trust our luck, is all I can say. We've either got Indian moggy lovers for neighbours, or those two poor little bastards we saw looking out the window are about to be skinned alive and eaten in tomorrow's curry.'

Elliot's Nightclub was situated along the Southend Arterial Road, and little did Vinny Butler know, as he and Jay Boy drove towards it, that earlier today on the opposite side of the carriageway, Johnny Preston had purchased a gun to kill him with.

'I'm gonna have to frisk this geezer, Jay. I know he's a pal of yours, but this is serious shit. He could have been tagged and put on the Old Bill's payroll for all we know.'

'Gnasher's sound, Vin. Please don't embarrass me by asking to frisk him. You'll make me look a right cunt. Seriously, I've known him since I was about ten. We used to train at the same boxing club. He would rather cut his own arms off than be a snitch for the bizzies. He hates them with a passion.'

'What's his real name? Or have I got to call him Gnasher?'

'Jimmy Williams, but everybody calls him Gnasher. He bit a chunk out of an opponent's chin in one of his early fights, so after that he was known as Jimmy the Gnasher Williams. He got a lengthy ban, but he was even sharper when he came back. Truly was a great boxer. I reckon he could've gone on to become world champion if he hadn't smashed his leg to smithereens in a motorbike accident and had to quit the sport. Honestly, he was that good.'

'So did he become a hitman straight after he retired?'

'Pretty much so. He married some Essex tart. A Page Three bird, so she was high maintenance. He's got three kids with her now.'

'I take it he works as a doorman as a cover then?'

'Yeah, plus it's regular money coming in. It's not every day blokes want their ex and her new fella topped.'

Vinny chuckled. 'You think I'm out of order, don't you?'

'I'm a bit uncomfortable with organizing a hit on a bird, if you want the truth. But I know it's the only way you will get sole custody of Ava, so I totally understand your reasons.'

Snarling, Vinny turned to Jay. 'Don't forget it was that whore's cousin who killed my Molly. And her shitcunt of a father shot my brother. Don't waste your pity on her, Jay. The world will be a far better place without her and any other Preston I choose to do away with. One day, when you have kids of your own, you'll know exactly where I'm coming from. Ava has my blood running through her veins and I like to keep my blood close to me.'

CHAPTER TWENTY-SIX

Queenie Butler was up at the crack of dawn the following morning. She and Vivian had done the bulk of the cooking last night, but there was still plenty to do and prepare. Queenie wanted Ava's first visit to her house to be perfect.

The sun was already peeping through the clouds, so Queenie opened up her conservatory door. She was so pleased that the weather was good as the kids could play in the garden.

About to walk back indoors, Queenie froze. One of the new neighbours was whistling 'Land of Hope and Glory' and then she heard an English voice say 'Look at Prince Charles and Her Majesty rolling on the grass. They love their new home, Mummy.'

Regaining the use of her legs, Queenie ran up the stairs to get a better view. She didn't want to peer over the fence and be deemed nosy. 'Gawd stone the crows!' Queenie couldn't quite believe what she was seeing. Lots of cats, some fat old bird in a wheelchair, and a bald bloke standing in front of her doing exercises.

Queenie couldn't pick the phone up quick enough. 'Viv,

look out your bedroom window. We ain't got Indians living next door. We've got fucking nutters!'

Bella D'Angelo was awoken by her over-sexed lover rubbing his finger against her clitoris. 'Stop it, Michael. Antonio might be awake.'

Michael chuckled. Sex between himself and Bella was intense and magnificent, yet they could rarely let themselves go because of Bella's paranoia over Antonio hearing them. They'd had a fantastic evening at a hotel recently though. Antonio had stayed over at his friend's house and the sex that night had been wild and abandoned.

'Michael, ring your sons to make sure they're OK. It worries me, them being at your house alone.'

'Yes, my lady. Seriously, you needn't worry about my boys. They stick together like glue. The East End's a tough area. Teaches you to man up at an early age. I should know, I was only about seven or eight when I was left on me Jacks.'

'Seven or eight! Where were your parents and brothers?'

'My mum used to clean posh people's houses to make ends meet. The old man would've been down the boozer and I should imagine Vinny and Roy were out trying to earn a crust. Never did me any harm, did it? I'm now a very successful club owner with a bit of fluff to die for.'

Bella laughed as she put her hands around Michael's throat. 'You ever call me that again and I swear I will kill you.'

Daniel Butler shook his brother's arm. 'Wake up. We're getting off next stop.'

Adam Butler rubbed his tired eyes. They'd been playing Pac-Man and Space Invaders until the early hours of this morning, then Daniel had woken him at eight and told him they were going to Dagenham market. 'Why couldn't we have had a lie-in until we had to go to Nan's? I'm so tired.'

'Because I wanna get that Fila tracksuit top. Stop whinge-ing, you tart.'

'What time we gotta be at Nan's, Dan? We'd better get Ava a present, hadn't we?' Lee suggested.

'Dad said to get there by twelve. I think he's bought Ava a present, but if we've got enough dosh left, we'll get her something too. Look, that old bastard who had a go at us last week is working again. Let's run past him and do wanker signs.'

'Can't we just pay the fare, Dan? I don't feel like running. I've got a belly ache,' Adam complained.

'Probably that pizza you ate last night. I said it weren't cooked properly when you took it out the oven. It was cold in the middle,' Daniel reminded his brother.

The ticket inspector was busy giving someone directions as they approached, but as they broke into a run he looked up. Some of his colleagues might have let it go, but Ted Nicholson took his job very seriously. He'd been a train freak as a nipper and landing a job with London Under-ground had been like a dream come true for him. He was furious when he spotted the three boys who hadn't paid their fare the previous weekend, and even more angry when they darted past him yet again.

Despite his arthritis, Ted gave chase, yelling, 'If I ever see your faces again, I will call the police. Hooligans, that's what you are!'

Grinning, Daniel treated the old boy to a hand sign, then urged his brothers to cross the road.

'I reckon we should go to Nan's via Dagenham East, Dan, in case he's still working. Dad'll go mental if we get nicked and miss Ava's party,' Lee said.

Daniel chuckled. 'Nah. I like winding him up. We'll get the train from 'ere. He can barely walk, let alone run. Ain't gonna catch us, is he?'

*

319

Eyes hidden under over-sized sunglasses, Carl Tanner surreptitiously glanced at the other passengers taking their seats. He'd disguised himself well, but it was in his nature to be wary.

Watching the air stewardess explain the safety procedures, Carl clicked his seatbelt into place. After four and a half years living abroad, it was finally time to return to good old Blighty.

Carl sighed as the plane finally took off. Going back to England was a massive risk. One that could cost him his life. Could Eddie Mitchell save his bacon? Only time would fucking tell.

Shirley Preston opened her front door and was surprised to see her son standing there with a gigantic bouquet in his hands. She'd washed her hands of Johnny after Jamie got badly burnt, and a bunch of flowers wasn't going to change that. 'What do you want? Had a row with her indoors, have ya?'

Johnny sighed. After he'd picked up the gun yesterday he'd hidden it, then gone to the pub. Deborah had gone mad when he'd arrived home drunk, but he wasn't about to admit to his mother they'd had a big barney. 'No. I've not fallen out with Deborah. I come offering peace. It's your birthday tomorrow and I wanted to see ya. Any chance of a cuppa?'

Begrudgingly, Shirley waved him inside. The last thing she wanted was the neighbours sticking their noses in. They all knew she'd broken off contact with her daughter Judy and she didn't want them knowing she'd fallen out with Johnny too, else they'd all be gossiping about her.

Following his mother into the kitchen, Johnny put the flowers in the sink and asked how Jamie was.

'Scarred for life, no thanks to you. But he's much happier in Chelmsford. Not getting picked on any more. He's got a new pal who takes care of him. As they say, you can choose your friends but not your family.'

Johnny sighed. 'Mum, he did ring up the Old Bill and hamper the whole investigation. Don't forget all the newspaper clippings that were found in your house an' all. Jamie is hardly a fucking angel.'

'He was a boy back then. A boy who hated Vinny Butler with a passion because of Mark dying and everything else that had happened. You were no angel when you were that age either. You burgled the Shrimptons' gaff and poor old Lily died soon after through the shock of what you'd done. Does that make you a murderer an' all?'

Johnny hung his head in shame. He'd liked old Lily Shrimpton and still regretted to this day what he'd done.

'Want something to eat? I've got a nice bit of bacon in the fridge.'

Johnny smiled. He knew this was his mother's idea of a peace offering. 'Cheers. I'll have a bacon sandwich. So who is this geezer Jamie's palled up with?'

'He's a lot older than Jamie. I've met him on a visit. Lovely bloke. Glen Harper his name is.'

Johnny Preston nearly dropped the cup his mother had just handed him. His boss had often spoken about Glen Harper and his firm. They were the biggest drug barons in Essex and originated from the Basildon area. They also had a reputation of chopping up or shooting any poor bastard who upset them.

'You OK, boy? You look a bit peaky.'

'I'm fine, Mum. Just need that sandwich. I haven't eaten since yesterday morning,' Johnny lied.

Queenie Butler beamed as she opened her front door. 'Welcome to Nanny's house, Ava. This is your Auntie Viv. She's been dying to meet you and give you a big cuddle.'

Vivian bent down and kissed the child. As much as she could never forgive Vinny for killing her Lenny, she would never take her bitterness out on a little girl.

Clocking Nosy Hilda gawping, Queenie waved. 'Come and meet Ava. She's Vinny's daughter.'

'Don't you be telling her nothing, Mum,' Vinny hissed. With what he had planned for his shitbag of an ex and her bloke, the less the likes of Nosy Hilda knew, the better.

Swallowing the last of his cheeseburger, Daniel Butler counted the money he and his brothers had left. 'We ain't got enough. That doll we saw was six quid and between us we've only got four pound odd. I tell you what we'll do. Me and Lee will distract the stallholder by knocking his display over, then you can snatch the doll, Adam, and we'll meet you back 'ere.'

'Why me? Can't you nick it?' Adam asked.

'No. You're smaller than me and Lee, therefore less noticeable. Take my carrier bag. Just slip the doll in there and walk off as soon as me and Lee distract the geezer. You won't get caught, trust me.'

'The man's got cheaper dolls on his stall. Why can't we just buy one we can afford?' Adam argued.

'Because Butlers don't buy crap presents. When has dad ever bought us cheap shit, Adam?'

'But we don't normally buy presents at all. We didn't even buy Mum or Dad a present last Christmas. We spent our shopping money on ourselves,' Adam reminded his brother.

'That is because I had a broken collarbone. Stop being a little prick and grow some balls,' Daniel ordered.

Adam sighed. He'd stolen bits and bobs in the past, but never anything as big as that doll. 'OK. I'll do it,' he said, wishing his dad were here so he wouldn't have to.

*

Queenie Butler was grinning from ear to ear as she watched Ava and young Crystal playing nicely together in her garden. 'Your daughter is beautiful, Jilly. She looks like a tiny version of you. How old is she?'

'She was four in March. Have you got any daughters, Queenie? I did ask Jay Boy, but you know what men are like. He would rather watch the boxing than have a conversation with me,' Jilly joked. Jay Boy was actually everything she'd ever wanted in a man and he was brilliant with Crystal. A massive improvement on her loser of an ex, who'd turned out to be the world's worst partner and father.

Feeling too ashamed to admit to a nice girl like Jilly that her own daughter was an embarrassment and a lush which was why she hadn't been invited today, Queenie was grateful when her new neighbour saved her having to answer by poking his head over the fence.

'Howdy. I'm Norman, the new occupant of this property. I live here with my severely disabled mother. Say hello to our new neighbours, Mother.'

Queenie looked at Vivian in astonishment. Not only was Norman wearing a silly cowboy hat, his mother looked anything but severely disabled as she leapt out of her wheelchair and walked briskly towards the fence. 'Pleased to meet you. I'm Doll.'

'Are you having a party today? Only I'm a very good country and western singer, aren't I, Mother?' Norman beamed proudly.

'What've I told you about being too forward?' Doll scolded her son before smiling at Queenie and Vivian. 'Yes, my Norman is very good. He has all the proper outfits and hats. Entered a competition at the Working Men's Club last year and came sixth. Sung Johnny Cash, he did. I was so proud of him. He got a standing ovation.'

'I do have other hobbies too. I like cats, exercising, the Royal family, old western films and *Emmerdale Farm*. What are your names and interests, if you don't mind me asking?'

Unable to hold it together any longer, Queenie and Viv howled with laughter.

Bella felt she knew Michael well enough now to know when he had something on his mind. 'Tell me what's wrong,' she insisted. 'You've not been yourself since we got out of bed. Have I said or done something to upset you?'

Antonio was watching a cartoon so Michael gestured for Bella to follow him into the kitchen. 'I know you'll think I'm mad when I tell you, but I can't get it off my mind.'

'Try me.'

'It's what Nancy said when she came to the club to tell me she was leaving. She said something like if we want to split the boys, then she'll take Adam because the other two are most definitely mine. That fortune-teller bird said she could only see I had two sons. Why would Nancy say that, unless Adam weren't mine?'

'I imagine she just meant that Lee isn't hers and Daniel is very much like you. "A chip off the old block" – isn't that what you always say? Obviously I don't know Nancy, but she doesn't sound the type to have cheated on you, Michael. I think you've taken her words out of context. As for Madam Lydia, just put her out of your mind. I've visited her every single year for the past eight or so, and even though I think she's good, she does get things wrong from time to time. You must stop worrying about all this.'

'How can you have visited her every year? You told me you were living in New York.'

'Because I used to visit England a couple of times a year to catch up with friends. What is this? An interrogation?'

Michael held Bella in his arms. 'Nah. I'm just upset you never came to visit me, that's all.'

Vinny Butler sat on the doorstep and lit up a cigar. Things had gone very well the previous day with Gnasher Williams. The geezer was straight to the point and Vinny had liked him on sight. Gnasher wasn't cheap, but money wasn't an issue to Vinny. How the job was done was the most important thing. It had to look like a road accident; if bullets were involved fingers would inevitably be pointed his way. No way would Vinny ever chance going back inside. Not even the satisfaction of getting rid of Joanna was worth another long stretch.

'You all right, mate?' Jay Boy asked, sitting down next to his boss.

'Yeah, good. Just mulling over things. Those roads that lead from Tillingham to Southminster are gonna be the best bet, you know. They're very narrow and remote. Loads of ditches for a motor to be shoved into. I know that's the way Jo drives to her parents' from when I had her followed. She gave me her mum's number today and told me to ring her there if I had any problems with Ava. I don't think she'll be able to stand staying indoors while I've got Ava. It'll do her head in. I'll know early next Sunday if her plans are the same. I want you to ring Gnasher tomorrow and arrange another meet.' At the sound of childish laughter, Vinny turned to look down the garden. A smile lit up his face at the sight of his daughter enjoying herself with Crystal. 'Ava's so happy here, look at her. The quicker Mummy dies and she can come live with me permanent, the better.'

Deborah Preston shut the lounge door so Joanna and Darren couldn't hear the conversation. 'Where you been all morning? I've been worried sick. State you came home in last night, you must've still been over the limit to drive.'

Johnny Preston gritted his teeth. He was forty-seven years old and hated nothing more than being spoken to as though he were still a schoolboy. Unable to tell Deborah he'd just popped to the Halfway House to pick up some bullets for the gun he was going to use to shoot Vinny Butler, Johnny came clean about his other visit. 'I went to see my mother, if you must know. It's her birthday tomorrow so I took her some flowers.'

'Why did you bother going to see that old cow? You know what she's like. Rake up the "Jamie is innocent" story again, did she?'

Johnny glared at his old woman. 'You really are a piece of fucking work at times, Deborah. My mother might not be perfect, but neither are you. Don't bother doing me a dinner. I'm going down the boozer.'

'If you walk out of this house, Johnny, then don't bother coming back tonight.'

'Fine! I won't.'

When Michael and Albie arrived, Queenie ushered her family into the lounge to tell them all about the new neighbours.

'Jesus. They sound like a right pair of fruitcakes,' Michael chuckled.

'He's worse than her. She's just a simpleton, but he's completely off his rocker. You should've seen him exercising earlier. His gut was hanging over his shorts and we were lucky we never caught sight of his dingle-dangle. I know people can't help being born ugly but he abuses the bastard privilege. I'd put money on it he's never had his leg over,' Vivian roared.

'What's a dingle-dangle?' Ava asked innocently. She was sat on her father's lap and was thoroughly enjoying being the centre of attention. Her new family had bought her some lovely presents. Her favourite was the battery-operated dog that barked and wagged its tail.

'A dingle-dangle's a toy, darlin'. Bit like a yo-yo,' Queenie lied, nudging Viv as a warning of what she should say in future. She didn't want Ava going back to the Prestons using foul language. 'Young ears,' she hissed.

'Oh, shut up, Queen. They're gonna hear worse when they start school, eh, Jilly?'

Jilly smiled. She found Queenie and Vivian two of the most entertaining women she'd ever met. 'Yous two should have your own TV show.'

Forgetting she'd just warned Viv to tone it down, Queenie poked Albie. 'You're quiet. If you're bored, you can always go and offer the locals a portion of your helmet pie like you did in the old days. That's if your oven still works,' she cackled.

Albie smiled politely. It wouldn't be Queenie if she didn't have a dig at him. These days, rather than bite back he just let the old witch get on with it.

'Can you imagine if my Lenny were still alive. How he would've loved living next door to those two! He'd have been in his element, God rest his soul,' Vivian said, glaring at Vinny. She would never let that bastard forget what he'd done. Not ever.

Feeling awkward, Vinny picked Oliver up. 'How's my gorgeous grandson, eh?' he asked, cradling the child.

Queenie stood up and clapped her hands together. 'Right, who wants some grub? What time the boys getting here, Michael? I've cooked plenty, so they won't starve.'

'I told 'em to be 'ere by twelve. They wanted to go down

Dagenham market first. Can I have a quick word with you and Vin in private before they get here?'

Vinny handed Oliver to Sammi-Lou, then followed his mother and brother into the conservatory. 'What's up?'

Michael briefly explained the Bella situation. 'It isn't just a fling. I love her, and as soon as I divorce Nancy, I intend to marry her,' he revealed.

'Bloody hell, boy. Don't you think you're rushing into things a bit? Be careful she ain't just after you for your money,' Queenie warned.

'I'm not stupid, Mum, and for your information Bella's cakeo. She owns her own modelling company and her parents are also minted.'

Changing her tune immediately, Queenie smiled. 'Bella sounds wonderful. Where did you meet her?'

Michael explained that he'd met Bella years ago, had fallen in love with her then, but hadn't furthered the relationship because of his sons. 'They're older now, Mum. They'll understand. And if you want the truth, I've not been happy with Nancy for a long while. We just drifted along because we had kids together.'

Queenie pursed her lips. 'Tell me about it. Did the same with your father.'

Vinny slapped his brother on the back. 'Good for you, Michael. I always said you could do much better than Nancy. I remember now when you first met this Bella back in the seventies. You were well smitten with her then. You deserve to be happy and I wish you well. She must be something special if you wanna marry her.'

Michael shook his brother's outstretched hand. They'd got on a lot better since he'd told Vinny how he'd mopped up after his son left the keys at Alison Bloggs' place, plus they saw less of each other since parting ways on the work front. It still pissed Michael off that he had to pay Vinny twenty per cent of the club's takings, but he wasn't going to make an issue of it. He had better things to think about now that Bella was in his life.

Ted Nicholson chased the three boys down the stairs of Dagenham Heathway train station. They thought they'd escaped his eagle eye, but they hadn't. 'I've called the police. They're on their way,' he yelled, as a colleague joined him in pursuit.

Realizing they were about to be cornered, Daniel took charge. 'Quick! Dart across the track, and we'll leg it out of 'ere and get the train from Dagenham East,' he ordered.

'There's a train coming, Dan,' Lee warned.

'That's so far away it's probably still at Elm Park. Come on, run now. Quick!'

'Don't you dare do that, you stupid boys. Get away from the platform, at once,' the ticket inspector bellowed.

When his brothers darted across the tracks, Adam stood frozen to the spot. He had done as he was told and stolen the doll, but the thought of running across the train tracks terrified him.

'Leg it, Adam. Drop the doll. Hurry up,' Daniel yelled. The train suddenly seemed to be approaching at rapid speed.

'Stay where you are, Adam. Don't move,' Lee urged, defying Daniel for once.

As one of the men tried to grab him, Adam suddenly took off, still clutching the doll in his arms.

'Oh my God! Do something! He's got his foot caught. Stop the train, for goodness' sake,' a frantic lady screamed.

'Get up, bruv. Please get up,' a panic-stricken Daniel shrieked.

Ted Nicholson and his colleague frantically waved their

arms to try to stop the oncoming train, but there was no sign of it slowing down.

'No, Dan!' Lee screamed, grabbing his brother's arm as he went to jump on to the tracks.

Terrified, Adam tried to get his foot out of his trainer that had somehow got wedged under the track. He could hear the train approaching now and wet himself with fright.

Other passengers were crying and covering their eyes as they feared the worst.

Unfortunately for poor Adam Butler, the train driver had been far too busy reading the *News of the World* to have noticed anything untoward on the line ahead.

'No, no, noooo. Adam, Adam,' Daniel sobbed when he heard the thud followed by the screams of onlookers.

Lee took his hands away from his eyes, sank to his knees and retched.

'Adam's leg's come off, Lee. Look, it's over there,' Daniel screamed.

Vomiting, Lee couldn't speak or move. His brother was not only dead, parts of his body were strewn across the tracks. It was like watching a horror movie.

An old man in a flat cap put an arm around Lee, then Daniel. 'Let me take you upstairs, lads. I'll get you some water.'

Seeing the doll Adam had stolen lying on the track in one piece, Daniel pushed the elderly man in the chest. 'I don't want no fucking water. I want my bruvver back. Adam, Adammm,' he howled.

CHAPTER TWENTY-SEVEN

Queenie Butler was not a woman to be messed with. 'I'm putting the rest of the food out now, Michael. Can't wait no longer, I'm afraid, and if you want my advice, a good hiding might teach those sons of yours some manners.'

Michael looked at his watch. He hated bad timekeeping just as much as his mother did. 'I'll send the little shits straight home when they finally arrive. Let 'em starve and miss the party if they can't be bothered turning up at a decent hour.'

Watching his son and Sammi-Lou both fuss over Oliver, Vinny smiled. Becoming a father seemed to have turned the lad into a man overnight. He'd always had concerns over how Little Vinny would turn out, especially when he was knocking about with that imbecile Ben Bloggs, but the lad had proved him wrong. Having got over the initial shock, Vinny was now proud his son had done away with Alison Bloggs. She was a waste of space anyway and it was good to know his offspring shared his own killer instinct. 'You got a minute, Vin? I wanna talk to you about something.'

Handing Oliver to his fiancée, Little Vinny followed his father up his nan's stairs. 'What's up?' he asked.

Vinny sat on the bed and urged his son to sit next to him. 'I've been doing some thinking and I really want you to jack your job in with Ahmed and come and work with me. It's where you belong, son. In my world, you working for non-family makes me look a proper mug. You get on OK with Jay Boy now, don't ya?'

'I still can't work for you, Dad. Nothing to do with Jay, but I like the hours I'm doing with Ahmed. I get home early evening and that gives me more quality time to spend with Ollie and Sammi.'

'You can do the same hours with me. I'll pay you much more than Ahmed does and you'll be my manager. Just think of all that extra dosh you'll have to spend on Ollie. We're family, and families are meant to stick together, Vin.'

Little Vinny was in a quandary. He was on fairly decent money at the wine bar, but would love to earn more and be classed as management at his dad's posh club. But how could he, when he'd opened his big mouth and blurted out the truth about Molly's death to Ahmed? He'd said he was joking afterwards, but Ahmed wasn't stupid and Little Vinny could never be sure his lie had been believed. There was no way he would ever risk pissing Ahmed off in case he said something to his old man. Much as it hurt to do it, he had no option but to turn the job down.

'Sammi really wouldn't want me working at a lap-dancing club, Dad. It would cause a load of friction in our relationship. Her parents wouldn't be happy about it either. I'm ever so sorry, but the answer has to be no.'

Ahmed Zane slapped his cousin on the back. 'I've come up with the perfect solution to entice Vinny to Purfleet.'

'What?'

'Expensive champagne that has fallen off the back of a ship.'

Burak was slightly confused. He spoke good English, but sometimes found some of their idioms confusing. 'Does that mean the same as if something was to fall off the back of a lorry?'

Ahmed chuckled. 'Yes. But in this case it's a ship. I'm going to pop into Vinny's club tomorrow with a couple of crates of our finest champagne. I will tell him there is a shipment that went astray and it's available at a knock-down price. I'll pretend we're taking half of it and ask if he wants to buy the rest.'

'Say he says no?'

'Vinny is far too greedy to refuse such an offer.'

'Why not say a lorry rather than a ship? I think a ship sounds a bit far-fetched.'

'Because Purfleet is near the fucking docks, Burak. Trust me on this. I know what I'm doing.'

Back at Queenie's, most of the food had been devoured and the not-right neighbours were once again the topic of conversation. They now had nicknames: Norman and Mummy Bates. Little did Vinny know when he'd renamed them, that back in the sixties Johnny Preston used to refer to him and his mother as the same.

When his son began to cry, Little Vinny was relieved. His father hadn't seemed happy or talkative since he'd knocked back his job offer and Little Vinny wanted an excuse to leave. 'Let's make a move now, Sam. I'm tired and so is the boy.'

When Sammi-Lou stood up, she spotted the distinctive vehicle pulling up in front of the house. 'There's a police car outside, Queenie.'

Michael and Albie were having a beer in the garden, so it was Vinny who took charge. 'Yous all stay in the lounge. I'll deal with this,' he ordered.

Yanking open the front door, Vinny asked what the police wanted in his usual blasé manner.

'Are you Michael Butler?' the young female PC asked.

'No. Why do you ask?'

'Because we need to speak to Michael Butler and were told we might be able to find him at this address. The matter is extremely urgent,' the male officer explained.

Ordering the police to stay put, Vinny dashed into the garden. 'Bruv, the Old Bill wanna speak to you. They say it's urgent.'

Guessing that one or maybe all three of his sons had got themselves arrested, Michael followed Vinny inside the house. 'I'm Michael Butler. What the little sods been up to now?'

'Can we come inside?' the female officer asked.

Feeling his legs go to jelly as he saw the sombre look on the officers' faces, Michael nodded dumbly.

Both took their headwear off as a mark of respect, and then the male officer said, 'I am so sorry, Mr Butler, but your son Adam was the victim of a fatal accident earlier today. Your other two sons witnessed the tragic incident and are being treated for shock at Oldchurch Hospital in Romford. Would you like us to drive you there now?'

Michael looked at the copper in amazement. 'Nah. There must be some mistake. Adam only went to Dagenham Market.'

The officer glanced at his colleague. Denial was a common reaction to such news. 'The incident happened at Dagenham Heathway Station.'

Michael sank to his knees and repeatedly punched the carpet.

Vinny crouched next to his brother. 'You'll get through this, bruv. I'll help you, I promise. Poor Adam. I can't fucking believe it.'

Queenie flew out of the lounge. 'What's going on?'

Vinny stood up and held his mother close to his chest. 'It's Adam. He's gone.'

'Gone? Gone where? Michael said he was in Dagenham.'

'Adam's dead, Mum. We don't know the exact details yet.'

'Dear Lord, no! Not Adam. Not another death. Why us?' Queenie howled. 'Why our wonderful family?'

Vinny stroked his mother's hair. 'Everything will be OK, Mum. That cunt God must hate us, but he'll never break us. Us Butlers are unbreakable.'

Donald Walker was carving up the roast lamb and Mary was dishing up the vegetables when their son Christopher arrived unexpectedly.

'What a lovely surprise! Would you like a bit of dinner, son?' Mary asked.

'This isn't a social visit, Mum. Where's Nancy?'

'In the garden, reading a book. Why, what's the matter?' Donald replied, feeling a flutter of panic at his son's grim expression.

Christopher dashed out to the garden, then ordered his sister and parents to sit on the sofa. A colleague had rung him earlier and Christopher had insisted on breaking the awful news to his sister. A cold fish by nature, Christopher delivered the blow in the blunt way he'd been taught as a copper. 'I am so terribly sorry, but there's no easy way to say this. Adam was hit by a train as he was trying to cross the tracks at Dagenham Heathway Station earlier today. He died instantly.'

Donald's complexion went from pink to white. Mary screamed then burst into uncontrollable tears. But Nancy was having none of it. She shook her head. 'There must be a mistake, Chris. It's not my Adam. He's never been to Dagenham Heathway in his life.'

Christopher hated the Butlers and it had put a strain on his relationship with Nancy when she began dating and then married Michael. But now, as he sat next to his sister and held her in his arms, it brought back memories of how close they'd been as children. 'I'm so sorry, Nancy, but it is definitely Adam. Daniel is at the hospital with Lee. They witnessed the accident and are being treated for shock. Would you like me to take you there?'

Screaming like a tortured animal, Nancy began pummelling her fists against her brother's chest. 'Why couldn't it have been Daniel or Lee? Why couldn't they have died instead of my Adam? I only ever loved Adam. Daniel is evil and Lee isn't mine. I want my baby boy back. He belongs with his mummy.'

Tears streaming down their faces, Mary and Donald tried to intervene, reaching out to gently prise their distressed daughter off Christopher.

'Leave me alone! Fuck off, all of you!' Nancy yelled. Seconds later, her legs gave way and she fainted in a crumpled heap on the carpet.

Having refused the offer of a lift from the Old Bill, Michael Butler arrived at Oldchurch Hospital with his father and Jay Boy. Vinny had taken Ava home and said he'd meet them there as soon as he could. Little Vinny had stayed in Whitechapel to take care of his mum and aunt.

'Yous two sit down a minute. I'll find out where the boys are,' Jay Boy ordered. Vinny had taught him leadership qualities while in prison.

Tears in his eyes, Albie put a comforting arm around Michael's shoulder. There was nothing he could say to ease the pain. Adam's untimely death was just another to add to the terrible list of tragedies that had befallen his family.

Head in hands, Michael stared at the floor. He couldn't

stop thinking about Adam and how scared he must have been as that train hurtled towards him.

'Don't you think you should ring Nancy, son?' Albie suggested.

'And say what? That our son popped down to Dagenham Market and ended up under the wheels of a cunting train? How the hell did he end up on those tracks, Dad? Do you reckon he might've been pushed?'

Before Albie had a chance to reply, Jay Boy returned with a woman who introduced herself as Dr Carter. 'I am so very sorry for the sad loss of your son, Mr Butler. Understandably, Lee and Daniel are traumatized. I had to give them each a light sedative to calm them, and would advise they stay in hospital overnight so we can keep an eye on them. If you would like to follow me, I will take you to them now. Be gentle with any questions though. The police can answer those afterwards.'

The moment Michael was led into the small ward, Daniel and Lee both threw themselves into his arms and sobbed like babies.

Joanna Preston was pacing up and down her lounge in a state of panic. Vinny had rung her at her parents' and said he needed to drop off Ava a bit earlier than agreed. 'Something bad's happened. I could sense it in Vinny's voice, Darren. If any harm's come to Ava, I'll never forgive myself.'

Darren Grant held Joanna close to his chest. 'Everything will be fine, sweetheart. At least Vinny rang to let you know.' He looked up at the sound of a car outside. 'There you go, panic over. He's just pulled up, and Ava's with him.'

Joanna dashed out to Vinny's car and grabbed hold of her daughter. 'You OK, Ava?'

'Yes, Mummy. I've got lots of presents,' Ava replied

happily. She didn't have a clue what was going on and had been too excited about her new toys to notice anything amiss.

'Darren, could you look after Ava for a minute while I speak to Jo please?' Vinny asked.

'No. Whatever you have to say can be said in front of Darren,' Joanna insisted.

'Stop talking, Mummy. Look at my doggy that my big brother Vinny bought me,' Ava said, pressing the switch to make the dog bark and walk.

Joanna glared at her ex. Just the mention of Little Vinny brought back terrible memories. 'I hope you never left Ava alone with him,' she hissed.

Vinny sighed. 'I was going to sit you down and try to break this news kindly to you, Jo, but seeing as you're in such a bad mood I might as well just give it to you straight. Adam got killed earlier, and before you start blaming me or my family, he got run over by a train at Dagenham Heathway Station. Ava has no idea about what has happened, I made sure of that. I'll pick her up same time next week.'

Queenie Butler refilled her and Vivian's glasses. Her tears had now turned into anger and bitterness and she couldn't believe yet another one of her family had died an awful death.

'Shall we get a cab and go up the hospital, Nan? I feel so useless,' Little Vinny suggested.

'What's the fucking point? Not gonna be able to sew Adam back together and miraculously make him breathe again, are they? I can't believe the luck of this family. First Roy gets shot and paralysed, then our wonderful Lenny dies, and before he's even had a chance to go cold Roy decides to blast his own brains out and end it all. You'd think that was bad enough and the Grim Reaper would leave us Butlers alone for a bit, but no, poor little Molly gets abducted and strangled, God rest her soul. Now Adam's been sliced in pieces by a bastard train, of all things.'

Vivian squeezed her sister's hand. 'We'll get through this, Queen. We always do, darlin'. Made of strong stuff, us mob.'

Slamming her glass down on the table, Queenie snarled as she pointed toward the ceiling. 'There ain't no God up there, you know. There can't be. This family is cursed. We were born to fucking suffer.'

Carl Tanner read the letter out loud, then shoved it inside the envelope.

It was truly a shit or bust moment in his life. Vinny Butler had two choices: believe him, or kill him.

CHAPTER TWENTY-EIGHT

Bella held Michael in her arms. She could feel his pain and it had upset her greatly to hear him crying in the early hours of this morning. He'd arrived at hers late last night to deliver the devastating news in person. 'Shall I make you some breakfast, Michael? You need to eat, even if it's just a piece of toast.'

'I'm too fucking angry to eat. If that silly little bastard expects sympathy off me when I pick him up, he's got another think coming,' Michael raged. He'd found out the truth of the circumstances surrounding Adam's death yesterday evening. The ticket inspector and his colleague who'd witnessed the whole sorry scene had given the police a statement. Daniel had been the instigator of his brother's death, nobody else.

'Daniel's only a boy, Michael, and he must be feeling terrible. Don't be too hard on him.'

'A boy! He won't live to be a fucking teenager when I get my hands on him, that's for sure. What I can't understand is why they didn't just pay the fare. They get more pocket money than any other kids I know. Thirty quid I left 'em on Saturday before I came to yours. You think that inspector would've had more sense than to chase 'em, but apparently Daniel had taunted him two weeks on the spin, the little shit. And now I'm supposed to go easy on him because he's traumatized after seeing poor Adam—' Michael broke down in great heaving sobs at the thought of his son's final moments as the train bore down on him. 'I can't believe he's gone. How can it be possible I'm never gonna see him again?'

'I will help you get through this, Michael. It's going to be tough, but together we are strong.'

His face deathly white, Michael pushed Bella away. 'That Madam Lydia – she was right, weren't she? She said she could only see two sons of mine in that poxy ball of hers. That woman's not only a jinx, she's a fucking witch!'

Bella's complexion paled too. That wasn't the only worrying thing Madam Lydia had said.

Lee Butler sat on the edge of Daniel's bed. 'Did you sleep, Dan? I kept having nightmares.'

'I tried not to shut my eyes because every time I did, all I could see was Adam's leg lying next to that doll. The doll was still in one piece. Why couldn't that have been chopped up instead of our brother?'

'I kept dreaming about all the blood and gore. It made me feel sick.'

'Don't tell Dad it was my idea to run across the tracks, will you, Lee? Let's say we all came up with the idea because we panicked.'

'OK. I wish Adam was here with us now. It's not the same without his constant chit-chat, is it? I really miss him already.'

Tears streaming down his cheeks, Daniel fiercely wiped them away. 'Let's talk about something else. Adam wouldn't want us to be sad.'

*

'Calm down, Nancy, for goodness' sake. Smashing my house up isn't going to change anything,' Mary pleaded, as her vase shattered into pieces.

With a glazed expression in her eyes, Nancy picked her mother's china fruit bowl up. 'I knew it would be Daniel's fault. He's evil, just like the rest of the males in that family. I wish he was dead. I hate him,' she screamed, as the fruit bowl suffered the same fate as the vase.

Grabbing his daughter in his arms to restrain her, Donald apologized to the policemen. 'I'm so sorry, officers.'

'It's understandable after the terrible shock your daughter's had. We'll leave you alone now. Anything you need, contact me directly,' DC James Maynard said.

Having broken the news of Adam's death, Christopher had left it to the officers dealing with the investigation to inform Nancy how it had come about. He had formally identified his nephew's body though. What was left of it anyway. The train had severed both of Adam's legs and one of his arms.

When Donald saw the officers out, Nancy sank to her knees and sobbed uncontrollably. Her beautiful Adam was gone and she was never going to see his handsome, cheeky face ever again.

Vinny Butler was at his mother's house trying to comfort her when Ahmed knocked at the door. 'I am so sorry, my friend. I rang the club and Jay told me the news. What a tragic accident. Adam was a good kid. It's so very sad.'

'I don't want no visitors, Vinny. Only family. Viv's here with me, so go down the pub with your friend,' Queenie shouted out. She'd heard Ahmed's voice and he was the last person she wanted in her house. She had never liked or trusted that Turk.

The moment he swaggered inside the Blind Beggar, Vinny

was swamped with locals offering condolences and drinks. He waved them all away. 'Thanks, but I just want a quiet drink and chat with my pal today.'

The regulars immediately backed off. If Vinny Butler said he wanted to be left alone, you didn't argue.

Vinny studied Ahmed as he got the drinks. Years ago they'd been inseparable, had even shagged prostitutes together in the same room. But since he got out of prison Vinny hadn't felt the same bond with Ahmed and he didn't really know why. They'd managed to build bridges after the car crash, and he owed the guy big time for tipping him off about Ava's existence, but the old trust wasn't there and he couldn't put his finger on why that should be. Maybe it was because while he was locked up Ahmed had stolen his idea about opening a wine bar, hadn't even offered him a chance to come in on the venture.

Returning from the bar, Ahmed put on his false sympathetic voice. 'How's Michael? He must be in bits. Adam was a lovely kid.'

'To be honest, I don't want to think or talk about Adam while we're in 'ere. It's depressing and sod-all's gonna change what happened,' Vinny said. Molly's death had toughened him up so much that he'd not even shed a tear over Adam's. 'Do you remember the laughs we used to have in those whorehouses? The good old days, they were.'

'They sure were, but you did get us barred from quite a few for being too violent towards the brasses. Do you remember that old madam at reception who chased us down the road with a meat cleaver?'

Vinny laughed. 'That was in Manor Park. If I remember rightly, I broke the prozzie's nose after she refused to let me do her up the arse. That old bird who chased us must have been about seventy, but she couldn't arf run.'

'Hey, why don't we go visit one tonight? It'll be like old times,' Ahmed suggested.

'Nah. Not tonight. Perhaps some other time.'

'Come on, it'll be fun,' Ahmed urged. Since Vinny'd took up with Eddie bloody Mitchell, he never seemed to want to spend time in his company, always coming up with some excuse. 'How many birds you shagged since you came out of nick?'

'About twenty-odd. Remember, I do run a lap-dancing club full of ultra-fit chicks,' Vinny lied. In truth he'd only slept with two birds since being released from prison. Both up-market West End brasses. He ran a classy establishment and would never fuck the staff. He'd made that mistake years ago with Little Vinny's mum, and it hadn't turned out too well. Not for Karen anyway.

Deciding to strike while Vinny seemed to be in a good mood, Ahmed mentioned the champagne that was up for grabs.

'Dom Perignon! You sure it's the real thing? Sounds too good to be true at that price.'

'The guy who has offered it to me is a friend of a trusted friend. Fell off the back of a ship, apparently. I think it's being stored by the docks somewhere, and they need it shifted as soon as. There's five-hundred-odd crates in total. I can only take half. Not got the room in my cellar to take any more. Do you want the other half? I have some bottles in the boot of my car. It's definitely the real deal.'

Vinny's eyes lit up. He could make a fortune at his gaff with such a profit margin. 'Go and grab a bottle. If it's kosher, I'm definitely interested.'

Ahmed smirked as he strolled out of the Blind Beggar. Vinny's greediness had always been destined to end his sorry life.

*

After leaving Bella's place, Michael Butler popped home to change into a black suit. It was a tradition in his family to dress in black until the funeral of a loved one was done and dusted. A mark of respect.

Walking into the house was horrendous. Adam's Nike trainers were by the door, his puffa jacket on the coat stand and his dirty clothes on top of the linen basket.

Dreading the phone call he had to make, Michael took a deep breath as he dialled the number. He should have rung Nancy yesterday, but she'd been the least of his priorities at the time. He'd been in too much shock to call anybody.

Praying that Mary or Nancy would answer, Michael cursed his luck when Donald picked up the phone. In all the years he'd been married to Nancy, he'd never properly met her father. He remembered him from the café in Whitechapel, but Donald had been against their relationship from day one, just because he was a Butler. 'Donald, it's Michael. Can I speak to Nancy, please?'

'No, you can't. You're the last person Nancy wants to speak to right now. And seeing as you've managed to turn Daniel into a monster, I'm sure you'll be quite capable of managing Adam's funeral arrangements alone. Just let us know where and when.'

'Who d'ya think you're talking to? You pretentious old cunt.'

'Nothing but a common spiv. What my daughter ever saw in you I will never know.'

Seeing red, Michael slammed the phone down. He'd rather talk to Donald Walker face to face. See how brave the cocky old fucktard was then.

Vinny Butler grinned as he tasted the champagne. He'd already studied the label and gone over it with a fine-tooth comb to check it was kosher. 'You're right, Ahmed. It is the real deal. I can't believe the geezer only wants two grand for five hundred cases. Does he not realize how expensive this stuff is to buy?'

'I think he just wants a quick sale, Vinny. Not being funny, we own bars that sell this stuff. Not many people are in the market for the quantity he needs to shift. Your average man who runs a local pub isn't going to want to buy it, is he? Neither is your man on the street.'

'I suppose not. Call on the deal then.'

Annoyingly, Burak had gone back to Turkey to attend his grandmother's funeral and wouldn't be returning until Friday. 'I'll call it on for Saturday or Sunday. Which day suits you best?'

'Why wait that long? Someone else might pip us to the post,' Vinny warned.

'They won't. My pal is going to be out of town for the next few days. He gave me his word that as long as we can collect by Sunday, it's ours. I will call him and tell him we definitely want it.'

'OK. Make it Saturday then.'

Ahmed wanted to laugh as he clocked Vinny's glee at the bargain. He could not wait to play him the tape of his son admitting to killing Molly. Neither could he wait to blast his brains out. Ahmed had waited a long time for his revenge. Now that time had finally come.

As soon as Michael led his two sons outside the hospital, he gave Daniel the biggest clout around the head he'd ever given him in his life.

When Daniel fell to the floor, Lee screamed. 'Why did you do that, Dad? Please don't hurt Dan. I've already lost one brother.'

Daniel lay on the floor with his head in his hands until his father dragged him up by the neck of his tracksuit top and marched him towards the car park. 'Crocodile tears don't wash with me, boy. Adam's dead because of your foolish actions. Now get in that fucking car, and I don't wanna hear another word outta ya. Comprende?'

Desperately needing to take his mind off things, Donald decided to tidy up the front garden. He wasn't one to show his feelings like Mary and Nancy, but as he pulled up the weeds he allowed a tear or two to fall. Adam had been his favourite grandson. As awful as it sounded to favour one child over another, he'd always had a much nicer nature than Daniel.

The sound of brakes screeching to a halt made Donald drop his spade, and he was horrified to see Michael Butler leap out of a black BMW. 'I'll call my son. Christopher will have you arrested,' Donald threatened as Michael stormed towards him.

Picking the spade up, Michael slammed it into the ground and had great joy watching Donald cower against the fence. 'Call your tosser of a son. He's a weasel, just like you, so what's he gonna do? Go and get Nancy, now! She has a son in my car who needs his fucking mother.'

Mary flung open the front door. 'Don't you dare threaten my husband, you bastard. I rue the day my Nancy met you. To think I used to stick up for you.'

'Whatever you think of me, Mary, Nancy has a son in that car who needs his fucking mother. He has just watched his brother get mutilated by a bastard train. What type of mother is your daughter, eh? A shit one, that's what. Every time the going's got tough, all she's ever done is run back to Mummy and Daddy. I'm the one who has always been there for our kids. I never dumped them and pissed off, did I?' Michael yelled.

'Oh, don't be giving me your Saint Michael act. Piss off

round your old tart's house and take Daniel with you. You all deserve one another.'

Listening from the bedroom window, Nancy gasped and put her hand over her mouth. 'Old tart'? When she'd tried to tell her mother that Michael was having an affair, Mary wasn't having any of it. She'd accused Nancy of letting her imagination run away with her. Not once had she let on that she knew he had another woman.

Absolutely seething, Nancy put a few belongings into a bag. She couldn't take any more. She'd had enough.

CHAPTER TWENTY-NINE

Jamie Preston acted as lookout as Glen Harper followed Bermondsey Bob into the showers. Glen and Bob had had a massive argument last week, and Glen wasn't a man to forget an insult being aimed his way. Hearing Bermondsey Bob's piercing scream as the razor was slashed across his eyes, Jamie grinned. The geezer was a waste of space anyway.

Glen washed the blood off his hands, put an arm around Jamie's shoulders and strolled down the corridor. Glen virtually ran their wing. Even the screws were petrified of him, which was why they'd allowed the pair of them to share a cell at Glen's request.

Glen sat on his bunk and explained how the blood had squirted upwards out of Bob's eyes. 'Won't be insulting me any more, the cunt. He won't even know if I'm in the room.'

Jamie laughed. Glen had not just become a best pal to him, but also the father figure he'd never had. Glen had no sons, only daughters, and many times he'd told Jamie he was the son he'd never had. 'Shall we celebrate with a spliff, Glen?'

'Sounds good to me, boy. See one day when me and you get out this shithole, we're gonna rule the manor with an iron fist. As a team, we'll be unstoppable. As for all them cunts who have wronged you, watch this space.'

Vinny Butler studied his new gadget. He'd seen a few of the customers in his club using mobile phones, so had invested in one himself. They were new to the UK, had only arrived on the scene earlier this year, but they were very handy. You could talk for a whole thirty minutes before the battery died.

'What time you meeting Gnasher?' Jay Boy asked. He was relieved that, having introduced Vinny to his friend, his involvement in the sordid business of Jo's imminent death was at an end.

'One. Then I'm gonna pop in and see the family. Michael's shut the club until after the funeral as a mark of respect, and I've not really caught up with him since we were at the hospital. Get the door for me, Jay. It's probably Eddie Mitchell. He wanted to talk to me privately about something, so make yourself scarce.'

'Vinny, how you doing? So sorry to hear about Adam. How's Michael bearing up? Life can be so bloody cruel at times,' Eddie said warmly.

'Tell me about it. It's one fucking tragedy after another in my family. Michael ain't doing too bad, but my mum's still in bits. Nothing you can do though, Ed, is there? Just got to pull yourself together and get on with life. How's things your end? Jessica and the kids OK?'

'They're all fine, thanks. Listen, this is a bit of an awkward visit for me. I need a favour from you, Vinny.'

'Name it, pal.'

'I've had a visit from an old family friend. His nephew knew you in the past and reckons he has some important information for you. This is none of my business, so I didn't want to know the ins and outs. But, from what I can gather, it's in your best interests to meet up with this geezer. The only favour I'm asking is you meet and don't harm him. My dad is very fond of his uncle, and he wouldn't be happy if something bad happened to the nephew.'

Vinny immediately felt uneasy. Was Eddie threatening him, in a nice kind of way? 'I've no idea who or what you're referring to, mate. Who is this geezer?'

Eddie handed Vinny the letter. 'See for yourself.'

Michael Butler put all items of Adam's he found lying around downstairs into a bin bag. His eyes welled up with tears as he held his son's discarded T-shirt to his nose, drawing in Adam's scent.

Taking the bag upstairs, Michael plonked it on Adam's bed. He was in no fit state of mind to get rid of his son's stuff yet. Didn't know if he could ever part with his belongings, but the one thing he did know was that he wanted to sell this house as quickly as possible. Everything about it reminded him of Adam.

'Dad, Dan's in a real bad way. He can't eat and keeps being sick. Please talk to him. He didn't know that Adam was gonna get his trainer caught under the track. I'm as much to blame as him,' Lee said.

Michael sighed. Even though he currently hated the sight of Daniel, he had to talk to him at some point and if the boy was ill he needed caring for. 'Dan, get your arse downstairs with Lee. I'm gonna make us all some breakfast.'

'Shall I get it?' Lee asked, referring to the doorbell.

'Nah. I will,' Michael responded, running down the stairs. 'Whatever's the matter?' he said. His brother's expression was one of pure fury.

'I'm fucking livid, bruv. Eddie Mitchell turns up at mine earlier with a letter from this geezer me and Ahmed once did business with. The letter can only mean one thing. That Turkish cunt was trying to set me up.'

'Jesus! Let me read it.'

'I disposed of it. This geezer's asked to meet me on Friday, wants to explain all. I thought the dude's name was Richie Simpson, but in the letter he reckons he'd been told to use that name by the bloke who was paying him to set me up. It can only be Ahmed. Nobody else was involved in the deal. I'll fucking rip his throat out if he has tried to cross me. I just can't believe he'd do that though.'

Michael shrugged. 'I can. He was never going to forgive you for leaving him for dead. What was the deal? Drugs?'

Vinny nodded. 'Cocaine to be precise. Molly going missing was what scuppered it. I then told Ahmed that I wanted out for good. This geezer is called Carl Thompson. You ever heard of him?'

Michael shook his head. 'How come Mitchell's involved?'

'Carl's uncle is a friend of the family. Eddie urged me to meet him and sort of warned me about harming him.'

'Warned you! In what way?'

'He just said his old man wouldn't be happy if anything bad happened to Carl.'

'Fucking cheek! What did you say? I'd have given Mitchell a mouthful if he'd said that to me.'

'No you fucking wouldn't, big man. You'd have bitten your tongue like I did. I ain't afraid of no cunt, bruv, the Mitchells included, but they are the one family I'd rather have as friends than enemies. It wasn't exactly a threat, Eddie asked for a favour. Get it?'

'I'm coming with you to the meet,' Michael insisted.

'No, you ain't. Carl said in the letter he'd only see me alone. I'm meeting him at The Bull car park in Dagenham in broad daylight, so I'll be fine. I reckon Ahmed was planning on me getting caught with a boot full of charlie. Either that or this Carl bloke is spinning me a yarn 'cause he wants dosh out of me.'

'I don't reckon Carl is bullshitting if he's involved the Mitchells, Vin. Sounds kosher enough to me.'

'I'm itching to find out the fucking low-down. Ahmed's called on some champagne deal for Saturday night. We're supposed to be picking up five hundred crates from somewhere in Purfleet. I wonder if that's a set-up an' all. The cunt's probably planning on finishing me off. The champagne sounds far too cheap to me – now I know why.'

'You be careful, bruv, we've got enemies coming out of our arseholes at the moment. I'll always have your back, you know that.' Michael's eyes suddenly welled up. 'I'd better get back to the boys now. They're not coping well. I'm trying to be strong, but it's so fucking difficult. The house just isn't the same without him. It feels empty.'

Vinny thought of Molly. No words were needed as the brothers shared a grief-stricken hug.

Nancy Butler took one last look at her parents' house before firing up the engine of her Golf convertible. The car had been the last present her cheating bastard of a husband had bought her.

Nancy got no further than Barking Park before she had to pull over, the tears streaming down her face till she could hardly see. She and Joanna had spent some wonderful days in the park when their kids were young. Now Molly and Adam were both dead. Why was life so unfair?

It was in this very park Nancy had fallen in love with Michael, back when she was only sixteen. The fair was in town and she'd been standing by the Waltzer with her old school friend Rhonda when he came into view. She'd had a crush on him as an eleven-year-old when her parents owned the café in Whitechapel, but hadn't set eyes on him since they moved away, and couldn't believe her luck when he showed an interest in her and they started dating.

Nancy wiped away the tears, took one last look around, savoured the good memories, then put her foot on the accelerator. Any love she'd felt for Michael seemed to have evaporated overnight. She now hated the bastard with a passion. He'd turned Daniel into a monster, cheated behind her back, and she hoped that after tomorrow, when she realized she was gone for good, the guilt would eat away at him forever.

Vinny Butler got out of his car and climbed into Gnasher's. They'd already agreed a price. Gnasher wanted twenty grand for killing Darren and twenty-five for Joanna. When Vinny had asked why he wanted more to top Jo, Gnasher told him, 'I always find it pricks my conscience more to kill women.'

'Did you have a look at those roads from Tillingham through to Southminster?' Vinny asked.

'Yeah. They're sound. I've already got the vehicle. It was stolen up north. It's had the number plates changed, been resprayed and had bull bars fitted. I've stashed it at a pal's garage in Basildon. What I need to know is, what do you want me to do if Joanna's alone?'

'Just kill her. The boyfriend's not overly important,' Vinny replied, in his usual blasé manner.

'So when do you want the job done?'

'As soon as. I'll be picking Ava up at seven next Sunday morning. I'll find out then if Jo's going to her parents' gaff or not. I've bought a mobile phone, but won't ring on that in case the call can be traced. There's a phone box on the village green not far from Jo's house. I'll leave Ava in the car and ring ya from there. I'll also give my brother a bell at the same time and leave a message on his answerphone. If the Old Bill do suspect me in any way, shape or form, they might just question Ava. You can never be too careful, eh?'

Gnasher nodded. 'You sure she'll definitely take that route to get to her parents' place? Because if she doesn't, the job'll have to wait. I like to make sure I've got the perfect spot, plan everything precisely. I won't just go chasing off after her and do it anywhere.'

'That's the route she always takes when she goes to her parents' – I've had her watched. And she went over there last Sunday when I had Ava. I had to ring her there to tell her I'd be bringing Ava home early after my brother's youngest son had a fatal accident. Got mowed down by a train, God bless him.'

'Fucking hell! That's terrible, Vinny. I'm so, so sorry to hear that. Condolences to you and your family. How old was your nephew?'

'Only ten. Such a waste of life. Adam was a good kid an' all, proper little character . . .'

As the two men chatted away about the circumstances of Adam's death, neither felt the slightest twinge of guilt about the lives they were about to end.

Nancy pulled into the entrance of Kings Holiday Park in Eastbourne, parked up and turned off the engine. She knew she was torturing herself, but wanted to see the place one last time.

She'd spent so many happy times at Kings when the boys were young. Adam, being the youngest, had adored all the activities: the donkey derby, It's a Knockout, the trips to Treasure Island, and he'd loved playing on the machines in the amusement arcade. Nancy could just picture his excited little face when the money used to tumble out of those tuppenny-fall machines.

Daniel had been a much nicer boy back in those days too. He'd never been perfect though, not like Adam. Nancy had always known in her heart that Daniel took after his father's side of the family. He was bolshie, had a temper on him even as a baby, and was always the instigator whenever the boys played her up. Adam had been a gentle soul. Definitely more of a Walker than a Butler.

Staring at the clubhouse, Nancy sighed. She would never forget the talent competition. Adam had got on stage and sung Clive Dunn's 'Grandad'. He'd dedicated it to Albie and the crowd had loved him. He'd have won first prize if it hadn't been for Molly singing 'You Are My Sunshine'. She'd brought the house down, bless her. Then a massive fight had kicked off between Vinny and Michael. That was the night the whole family got barred.

Opening the roof of her car, Nancy shut her eyes. She could smell the chlorine from the swimming pool; hear children laughing and the birds singing. This place held so many memories, and every sound and smell reminded her of Adam and happier times.

Tears rolling down her cheeks, Nancy fired up the ignition and took one last look at the holiday park. It was high time she headed off to her destination.

The British Flag in Canning Town was the Mitchells' stamping ground. They'd used the boozer for many years and it was seen by the locals as their headquarters.

Harry led Eddie to the corner of the bar. 'Did you speak to Vinny?'

'Yeah. I gave him the letter and a gentle warning.'

'How did you word it?'

'I was very diplomatic. Just hinted you would not be a happy man if anything were to happen to Carl, then left the letter with him.'

'Was he OK with what you said?'

'Seemed to be. Although he did give me a strange look. Don't be worrying, Dad. The Butlers won't be wanting to start a war with us. They ain't that daft.'

'I hope you're right, son. Genuinely like the Butlers, I do. But if Vinny cocks a deaf 'un to the little favour we've asked of him, there will be a war. And we'll win the fucker hands down.'

Nancy Butler breathed a sigh of relief as she finally arrived at her destination. She'd never been a confident driver and reaching the top of Beachy Head had been an ordeal in itself.

Darkness setting in, Nancy grabbed her bag and sat down near the edge of the cliff. She switched the torch on and stared at the view. The waves looked fierce, which was perfect.

Aware that this was a very common suicide spot, Nancy took a moment to think about the poor people who'd chosen to end their lives here. She would put money on it that some of the deceased had suffered the heartbreak of losing a child like herself.

Nancy took the framed photo of Adam out of her bag. It was his last school photo and his cheeky grin was so infectious. Such a beautiful boy, whose life didn't deserve to be cut so brutally short. What he went through as that train hurtled towards him really did not bear thinking of.

Aware of a car approaching, Nancy kissed the photograph and laid it on the ground. The thought of the unknown scared the living daylights out of her, but anything must be better than her previous life. It was a case of now or never.

CHAPTER THIRTY

Michael Butler woke up dazed. Had the phone been ringing or had he dreamt it? He hadn't been sleeping well and couldn't stay over at Bella's because now wasn't the time to be leaving Daniel and Lee alone.

Lee burst through the bedroom door. 'Dad, Nan's on the phone.'

Immediately panicking because the clock/radio was flashing 6.45 a.m., Michael snatched the phone out of his son's hand. 'What's up, Mum?'

'I'm not your mother, thank God. You'd have been brought up with better morals had I been,' Mary bravely informed her deceitful son-in-law. 'Is Nancy with you? Only I need to speak to her. Me and her father have been worrying ourselves sick all night.'

Michael sat bolt upright. 'Nancy isn't with me. When did you last see her?'

'Yesterday morning. When me and Donald got back from the café, there was a note on the table saying she was popping round to see you.'

'I was here with the boys all day yesterday, Mary, and I can assure you I didn't see hide nor hair of Nancy. Have you tried Joanna? Perhaps she's gone to visit her.'

When Mary started crying and shouting at him, Michael ended the call. The last thing he wanted to do today was face his wife's parents, but what choice did he have if Nancy was on the missing list? He'd married the girl and, even though he was no longer in love with her, he still cared for her.

Over in Burnham-on-Crouch, Deborah and Johnny Preston were having yet another heated argument. All they seemed to do since Vinny had come back on the scene was row and their marriage was currently hanging in the balance.

This morning's tiff had been caused by Joanna ringing up in tears. Apparently, Mary Walker had just called her to ask if she'd seen Nancy and now Jo was blaming herself for her friend's disappearance because she hadn't visited her since learning of Adam's death.

'When you gonna wake up and smell the coffee, Deb? Roy's dead, Lenny's dead, Molly's dead, Adam's dead and now Nancy's disappeared. How long do you think it's gonna be before either Jo or Ava disappear or die, eh? We've got enough money to move to Spain tomorrow, and I've got a job I can walk straight into out there. Let's just fuck off and get away from the Butler scum before it's too late.'

'It's not that easy, Johnny. Darren can't just up and leave – he's got a son and a job to think about. Jo won't go without him, and we've got all our belongings in this house. I like my home and England. I don't want to live in Spain.'

Johnny Preston put his head in his hands. He'd had a tough time of it ever since he'd purchased that gun. Part of him just wanted to walk into Vinny's new club and blast his brains out. Even if it meant a life sentence, it would be worth it, provided his daughter and granddaughter were safe. The problem was if he killed Vinny there was bound to be retribution from the rest of the Butler clan and he couldn't guarantee his family's safety if he was locked up.

'Do you want a bacon sarnie?' Deborah asked.

Johnny leapt to his feet, eyes blazing with anger. If Deborah was too thick to heed his warnings, perhaps the only way to make her listen was to shock her into doing so. 'You can stick your bacon sandwich up your arse. I've decided I'm going to stay with my mum for a bit. Can't take the arguing and worrying any more, Deb. Be it on your conscience when something bad happens to Jo or Ava – because it will, rest assured.'

DC James Maynard had only just arrived at his desk when his phone rang.

'I'm so sorry to trouble you, but it's Detective Walker's mother here. I tried to ring my Christopher, but his wife said he's out on some undercover job today, so I probably won't be able to get hold of him. I'm ever so worried. My Nancy's not been seen since yesterday morning and I'm scared she might do something stupid. She's had mental health problems in the past,' Mary gabbled.

'Just keep yourself calm, Mrs Walker. I'll be round in fifteen minutes,' James Maynard told her, already getting to his feet and reaching for his coat. Christopher Walker could bore for Britain in his opinion, but the guy was a copper and in their profession you always looked after your own.

The coastguard's buzzer had gone off as soon as dawn broke. His pal who used to man the lighthouse had alerted him to yet another possible suicide.

Peering over the edge of the 530-foot drop, the coastguard could see no body. He picked up the framed photograph and stared at the boy's face. He guessed it belonged to a parent who could no longer face life after the loss of a child.

Feeling melancholy, the coastguard opened the door of the Golf convertible. He'd lived here all his life and Beachy Head was a place he loved like no other. It was such a shame it had become known as a notorious suicide spot rather than for its beauty.

On the passenger seat was a collection of photos, most ripped in half. Putting two halves together, the coastguard stared at the stunning couple. The photo had been taken on their wedding day. The young blonde looked so beautiful and radiant. The man smartly dressed and handsome. They resembled love's young dream, but something had obviously gone dreadfully wrong.

Unzipping the handbag, the coastguard saw what he surmised to be suicide letters. There were four in total, addressed to different people. Opening the purse, he took the driving licence out. Poor Nancy Butler's family were going to get a terrible shock today, that was for sure.

'Bollocks,' Michael muttered, as he pulled up outside the Walkers' gaff. The Old Bill were here already. Knowing that they were bound to want to question him anyway, Michael pounded his fist against the front door.

It was opened by Mary, who was in tears. 'You've got some bloody nerve coming here. This is all your fault.'

'Mary, I haven't come here to argue, I've come to help find the mother of my sons. Any news yet? Did you speak to Joanna?'

'Yes. Jo hasn't heard from Nancy. If anything has happened to her, Michael, I'm holding you responsible.'

'Invite him in, Mary. DC Maynard wants to ask him some questions,' Donald bellowed. He'd just been telling the officer how his villainous son-in-law wanted out of the marriage, and he wouldn't have put it past him to have had a hand in his daughter's disappearance.

Michael walked into the lounge and shook the officer's hand. He'd learnt over the years it was far better to be polite towards the bastards. Tended to get you further. 'I'm Michael Butler, Nancy's husband.'

'Estranged husband,' Mary piped up. 'Michael is now with another woman.'

'Can you tell me where you were yesterday, Michael?'

'Indoors all day with my boys.'

'So you never left the house at all?'

'I popped out for an hour, tops. Why?'

'Where did you go?'

'My youngest son got mown down by a train last Sunday. I went to the funeral directors to order a coffin for him. That OK with you?' Michael replied, his voice laden with sarcasm.

'Are there people who can vouch for your whereabouts?'

'Yes. My sons, brother, dad, the undertaker . . . You're barking up the wrong tree, interrogating me, pal. Nancy's got a history of depression and wandering off alone,' Michael spat. He was no longer in the mood to be polite. This geezer obviously was the cocktard of the police force.

'When Mary rung you this morning to ask if you'd seen Nancy, you told her that you'd been indoors all day,' Donald chimed in.

'D'ya know what, I ain't gotta listen to this shit. I came round here to fucking help. Should've known better. If you wanna ask me anything else, then arrest me. I'm off now. Got better things to do than talk bollocks.'

On that parting note, Michael stormed out of the house and slammed the front door.

Deborah Preston had had better days. Her husband had left her, her daughter had been in tears since showing up at the house and her granddaughter was driving her doo-lally. 'No, Ava. How many more times do I have to tell you, you're too young to have a dog? They need walking regularly and they're bloody hard work. Now go and play with your toy dog in the garden while I try and cheer your mummy up.'

Pouting, Ava picked up her toy dog and threw it against the wall. 'Don't wanna play with this one. Want a real one. Katie's got one and she's only four.'

'I couldn't give a toss what Katie's got. Now get out in that garden before I clout you one. Go on, shoo,' Deborah demanded, raising her hand.

When Ava sulkily did as she was told, Deborah turned to her daughter. 'She's got worse since she's had contact with Vinny. Want, want, want. You're gonna have to have a word and tell him to stop spoiling her, Jo. He'll turn her into a monster if he keeps giving in to her every whim.'

'Ava wanting a dog is the least of my problems today, Mum. Do you think I should drive to Barking and wait with Nancy's parents for news? I feel so bloody guilty. When Molly went missing, Nancy barely left my side. I've let her down. As soon as Mary told me the news, I should've gone straight to her. She needed me.'

Deborah held her teary-eyed daughter in her arms. 'You can't blame yourself, love. You did ring Nancy and she didn't want to talk to anyone.'

'But I should've been there for her, like she was for me. I'd never have coped when Molly died if it wasn't for Nancy. She was my rock.'

Ahmed Zane welcomed his cousin with a hug. 'Happy birthday, Burak. Follow me, I have champagne on ice waiting for you in the office and a wonderful day planned.'

'What are we doing?'

Ahmed grinned. 'Champagne, cocaine and women. Oh, and I thought we'd drop in at Vinny's club, just for the fun of it. It'll be the last drink we ever have with him.'

Burak burst out laughing. 'Fucking brilliant!'

Albie Butler liked Nancy and was very worried when his son told him the news. 'I wonder if she knows about Bella? Did you ask Mary if she'd told her?'

'No. And please don't make me feel any more guilty than I already do. I thought I was doing the right thing, coming clean with Mary. You can't help who you fall in love with, can you? I never meant to hurt Nancy, but our marriage was more stale than a month-old loaf of bread.'

'I understand, boy, and you most certainly aren't to blame. I reckon Nancy's just in pieces over Adam and has gone to clear her head somewhere. She's bound to come back before the funeral. Where are Daniel and Lee? Are they OK?'

'I've said sod-all to the boys about Nancy yet. Daniel's not been eating since Adam died, so I gave 'em some money to go to the Wimpy. They'll go stir-crazy sitting in here. I'm gonna pop to the estate agent tomorrow. I can't go on living in this house. Every time I look round, something reminds me of Adam.'

Albie lifted the curtain. 'The Old Bill have just pulled up outside, boy.'

'Oh, for fuck's sake! If it's that ginger cunt who questioned me earlier, I swear, the mood I'm in, I'll knock him out if he starts again.'

Albie grabbed his son's arm. 'Don't rise to the bait. Keep your cool.'

Michael flung open the front door. There were two Old Bill and thankfully neither was the ginger prick from earlier. 'You come to see me about Adam?' he asked. One of the coppers had been present when he'd learned of his son's death.

With a grim expression, it was the female who replied. 'Is it possible for us to come inside, Mr Butler?'

Michael led them into the lounge.

'I'm afraid I have some bad news, Mr Butler. Your wife's car was found at the top of Beachy Head in Sussex in the early hours of this morning. The police and rescue teams are currently searching for Mrs Butler.'

Michael shook his head repeatedly. 'Nah, nah, nah. That can't be right. Nancy hated heights. I took her up Beachy Head once for a picnic and she was petrified.'

The male officer took a notepad out of his pocket and began scribbling away. 'When did you take Mrs Butler to Beachy Head?'

'Christ, it was a while back. Late seventies, I'd say. The boys came with us. I used to own a bungalow at Kings Holiday Park in Eastbourne and Beachy Head was only about ten or fifteen minutes' drive away.'

'Drink that, boy,' Albie ordered, shoving a brandy in Michael's hand. His son was as white as a sheet.

'I can't believe Nancy would drive up Beachy Head alone. She was a crap driver and uncomfortable behind a wheel. You sure it's her car?' Michael asked. To say he felt dazed was putting it mildly.

'Mrs Butler's car was found by the coastguard, Mr Butler. The doors were unlocked with her belongings inside, including her handbag, photographs and letters addressed to family members.'

'Was there a letter for me?' Michael mumbled.

'Yes.'

'Where is it?'

'The letters will become the coroner's property, for now at least. It's up to the coroner to check the contents before the letters can be released to family members,' the female officer explained.

'Were you having any marital problems, Mr Butler? Only we've been informed that some of the photographs found were ripped in half and we believe these to be your wedding photographs. There was also a framed photo of a child we believe to be your son, Adam, found near the edge of the drop.'

Overwhelmed by memories, Michael put his unshaven face in his hands. Barking Fair, the Waltzer, Nancy's lithe figure, her beauty and innocence back then, and her singing away to 'Chirpy Chirpy Cheep Cheep'. He'd fallen in love with her that day and couldn't believe she'd chosen to end her life. If she'd ripped up their wedding photos, she obviously knew about Bella, which meant he was to blame for her demise.

'Do you want another brandy, boy?' Albie asked, concerned.

Hand over mouth, Michael ran from the room vomiting.

Because of Adam's death, Ahmed had given Little Vinny a week off. However, Little Vinny had left his new leather jacket at work with his house keys in the pocket. Sammi-Lou kept moaning because every time he popped out he'd wake Oliver on his return, which was why Little Vinny suggested they have a romantic date up town today. They'd rarely been out alone since their son had been born and Sammi's mum had offered to babysit for them.

'Vinny! This is a pleasant surprise. I thought you were taking a week off. Couldn't you keep away?' asked Mario, the bar manager.

'Left my jacket here and my keys are in the pocket. Meet my beautiful fiancée. Sammi-Lou, this is Mario.'

Sammi-Lou grinned. 'Hello. Pleased to meet you.'

'Where's Ahmed?' Little Vinny asked.

'In the office with his cousin. It's Burak's birthday and I think they're getting drunk – Ahmed asked not to be disturbed,' Mario chuckled.

'Well, I've gotta nip back there to get me jacket. Get us a drink, Mario. Sammi'll have a Malibu and pineapple and I'll have a Coke.'

As he walked out the back, Little Vinny could hear the laughter. It was raucous and he guessed they were probably on the gear. About to knock on the door, Little Vinny froze as he heard his father's name mentioned. Had Burak really just said he couldn't wait for his dad's funeral, or had he heard wrong?

Ahmed was a loud man, especially when drunk and with cocaine inside him. When Little Vinny heard him say, 'The funeral will be great fun. I might even suggest to Michael that me and you help carry Vinny's coffin,' his blood ran cold.

'Have you forgotten there will be no trace of a body to carry, Ahmed? I cannot wait to see Vinny's face when we play him the tape of his evil son confessing to murdering Molly. What a way to die, eh? Learning your only son throttled your beloved daughter before being tortured your-self. It really is the perfect murder.'

Ahmed roared with laughter. 'Serves the cunt right for leaving me for dead. Rack up another line, Burak, and don't forget, when we get to his club later we have to act normal.'

Little Vinny's legs were trembling so much he had no idea how he crept away from that door.

'Whatever's wrong, Vin? You look like you've seen a ghost,' Sammi-Lou remarked.

'What's up, man? You OK?' Mario asked, concerned.

How he held it together, Little Vinny would never know. 'I just remembered where I left the keys now. Don't tell Ahmed I was here, Mario. He's gonna go mental if he finds out I've lost 'em. Got the bar keys on the same bunch.'

'My lips are sealed,' Mario promised.

Grabbing Sammi-Lou by the arm, Little Vinny all but dragged her from the bar.

'Whatever's wrong, Vin? Where's your jacket?' Sammi-Lou asked, her face full of concern as her boyfriend put his hand over his mouth and crouched in a nearby doorway.

Feeling as though he was about to have a heart attack, Little Vinny took deep breaths before standing up and desperately trying to compose himself. He took his wallet out of his pocket and handed Sammi-Lou a fifty-pound note. 'I want you to jump in a black cab and go home, babe. I need to speak to my dad urgently.'

'But why? I thought we were going for lunch. Please, tell me what's wrong.'

Spotting an unoccupied black cab, Little Vinny stood at the kerb, frantically waving his arm. 'I really need to see my dad, Sammi. Just go home and we'll chat later.'

Queenie Butler was sitting in the garden, planning a eulogy in honour of Adam when the nutter next door started playing and singing along at the top of his voice to Johnny Cash's 'Ring of Fire'.

'Queen, there's a cat shitting in your garden,' Vivian said, nudging her sister's arm.

Chucking her pen and paper on the patio, Queenie leapt up. 'Come on, let's knock there. Had enough of the loonies now. Norman and Mummy Bates will be going head-first in a ring of fire if those cats crap in my garden any more.'

Vivian followed her sister and stood hands on hips as Queenie hammered on the nutters' front door. It was Doll who answered.

'Sorry to bother you, but I'm trying to write a eulogy for my dead grandson, so could you please tell your son to stop singing and turn his music down as it's distracting me? Also, my sister and I are very proud of our lovely gardens, so could you teach your cats to shit in yours in future?' Queenie asked, with a steely expression in her eyes. When it came to sarcasm, she was an expert.

Doll looked at Queenie in horror. 'Norman! Norman! Come quickly,' she yelled.

Norman arrived at the front door at the same time as a chap turned up to deliver a parcel on behalf of Freeman's catalogue. 'Good afternoon, ladies. Which one of you is Mrs Bates?'

'I am,' Doll replied.

Queenie and Vivian stared at one another in pure astonishment, before bursting into uncontrollable laughter. You just could not make that up.

In a pub not far from his father's club, Little Vinny ordered his second pint of cider. He was still in complete and utter shock, but the alcohol had stopped him from shaking. He'd had no idea Ahmed had taped his confession, but now that he knew what a devious cunt his boss was, he was certain there would be more than one copy of the tape.

Little Vinny felt like crying. Now he was a father himself, he truly regretted killing Molly and could not believe he'd been capable of such a callous act. Since Ollie's birth he was a changed person, and the thought of losing Sammi-Lou and his son for ever filled his heart with pain. He was bound to go to prison, unless his father decided to bump him off as payback.

Knowing it was make-or-break time, Little Vinny's mind went into whirlwind mode. He needed to think of a plausible story and he needed to think of one fast.

Desperate to keep occupied while they waited for news, Mary Walker made Donald get the boxes out of the loft.

Nancy had been a bit of a hoarder in her younger years, and had forbidden her mother to chuck anything away. 'Look at all her Marc Bolan posters, Donald. She adored the ground that man walked on and used to get so annoyed with you when you called him a poof because he wore make-up and had long hair. Do you remember the time you told Roger to take her to *Top of the Pops*? T-Rex were top of the charts that week and she wouldn't go because she didn't want to be seen in public with Roger? She was headstrong even back then, wasn't she?' Mary said, bursting into tears again.

Donald sat on the bed and held his wife close to his chest. 'You're torturing yourself looking through these boxes, Mary. Let's go downstairs and have a cup of tea. I rang Tina and all is fine at the café.'

'What did Christopher say when he called?'

'He just asked how things had gone with Maynard. I told him the whole conversation and he said he'll pop round to see us after work.'

The doorbell made Mary jump and she ran to the window. 'It's the police, Donald.'

Reaching the bottom of the stairs in record time, Donald opened the front door. DC Maynard was accompanied by a colleague.

'Have you found Nancy? Is she OK?' Mary asked.

The officers invited themselves in. DC Maynard then urged Donald and Mary to sit down before breaking the tragic news.

'Dear God, no! Not my Nancy. She wouldn't do that. She loved us too much. Tell 'em Donald, tell 'em,' Mary sobbed.

When DC Maynard explained that Nancy had left belongings, photographs and letters in the car, Mary began to wail hysterically.

'Obviously, without a body, we have no firm proof that

Nancy did end her own life, but it certainly looks that way. Grief does strange things to people. Makes them act irrationally. I am so very sorry.'

'Should we travel to Beachy Head to help with the search?' Donald asked, eyes brimming with tears.

'I really think you'd be wasting your time. As awful as it sounds, the chances of finding Nancy alive if she did jump are very remote. I spoke to an officer dealing with the case earlier and he said the tide was high and the sea very choppy yesterday evening. It's probable that Nancy was swept out to sea,' Maynard's colleague explained.

'I cannot believe Nancy would do such a thing without saying goodbye to me and her mother. You mentioned letters. Do you know if one was addressed to us?'

'I guessed you'd probably ask that question, so I checked for you. There was a letter addressed to yourselves and one for Christopher. I'm sure if I kick some backsides, I can ensure the coroner hands them over as soon as possible.'

Hugging his distraught wife, Donald mumbled the words 'Thank you.'

Vinny was in his office, catching up on some paperwork, when Jay Boy walked in. 'Ahmed and Burak have just turned up asking for you. It's Burak's birthday by all accounts and they're already tanked up.'

Snarling, Vinny mumbled the word 'Cunts.'

'You had a falling out with 'em?'

Apart from Michael and Eddie Mitchell, not a soul knew about the letter. Vinny wanted to meet the man who'd written it first to check out his story before telling any other bastard. Part of him still couldn't believe that Ahmed would try to set him up. 'Nah. I just need 'em drunk in 'ere at this time of the day like I need a hole in the head. Tell 'em I'll be out in five.'

When Jay Boy left the office, Vinny poured himself a large Scotch. It was a good job his gun wasn't kept here because it would be so tempting to use it. Saturday was going to be too early to rally his troops, so he'd have to defer the champagne deal. He'd blame Adam's death and Nancy's disappearance. Say he was helping Michael search for her. No way would Michael be up for helping him kill Ahmed and Burak until he'd got Adam's funeral out the way.

Plastering a fake smile on his mush, Vinny bowled into the club.

'Vinny, my friend,' Ahmed grinned, giving his enemy a slap on the back.

'To what do I owe this pleasure?' Vinny asked.

'It's Burak's birthday. He's thirty-five today. We're going whoring later, so thought we'd pop in and whet our appetite by ogling your gorgeous girls first. We wanted to see you as well, of course,' Ahmed chuckled.

Vinny shook Burak's clammy hand. 'Happy birthday, mate. Don't forget it's my fortieth soon. I haven't arranged anything yet because of all the shit that's been going on, but I'll definitely sort something. Probably keep it low key, just close friends and family – which includes you two, of course.'

Seeing the sly grin exchanged between the two men confirmed everything Vinny needed to know.

Two more pints and half an hour later, Little Vinny had his side of the story firmly imprinted in his brain, so rang the club. He'd overhead Ahmed and Burak say they were going there and couldn't face bumping into them.

One of the bar staff answered and Little Vinny told the guy that he needed to speak to his father urgently.

'Vin, it's Jay Boy. Your dad's just popped out. You OK?'

Having originally hated Jay Boy, Little Vinny didn't mind him so much now. 'No. I'm not OK. Where's my dad gone?

It's important I speak to him ASAP. I'm round the corner, in The Lamb.'

Realizing by the lad's voice that something was very wrong indeed, Jay Boy said, 'Stay where you are and I'll pick you up. Give me ten minutes.'

Needing to get away from Ahmed and Burak as quickly as possible, Vinny Butler had blamed Nancy's disappearance for his sharp exit, then drove straight to his brother's.

Michael's day had been awful as well and it felt like old times as they cracked open a bottle of Scotch and shared their troubles. 'I could seriously fucking swing for Mary. How dare she turn up round 'ere, blaming me for Nancy's suicide in front of the boys? I hadn't even had a chance to tell 'em. And she started screaming and shouting about Bella. They knew nothing about her either, so I've tried to cover that up,' Michael ranted.

'She's bang out of order, bruv. I never liked any of that family, Nancy included. They're all wrong 'uns. And no way are you to blame for Nancy chucking herself off Beachy Head. It's obviously Adam's death that sent her over the edge, literally. She was never stable in the mind.'

Michael sighed. 'Nance was a good girl when I first met her, Vin. I really loved her back then, and we had some great times together. It all started to go wrong when we had kids. Don't get me wrong – she loved the boys, but she never really adapted to motherhood. She just couldn't cope.'

'How did the boys take the news? Where are they now?'

'Playing the machines down the bottom of the garden. I built 'em a cabin which they use as their games room. Daniel wants a pool table now. He didn't so much as flinch at the news about Nancy, but Lee cried. You'd think it'd be the other way round, wouldn't ya?'

'I suppose so.'

'Daniel was more bothered about who Bella was than his own mother committing suicide. You've gotta admit, that's very odd. Do you reckon I should take him to see a doctor or something?'

'Don't be daft! The quack'll only send him to a shrink, and you don't want one of them nosy bastards knowing all our family secrets. Dan's bound to be a bit messed up. He's just lost his brother, now his mum's committed hurry-curry. He'll be OK. He's a tough cookie, like us.'

Michael took a swig of Scotch. He only hoped his brother was right about Daniel. 'So what happened with Ahmed then?'

Vinny told him about the cousins' visit to the club. 'Those stupid Turkish cunts were well OTT because they were pissed and had been on the sniff. What mugs! I know that Carl's telling the truth now. Can't wait to meet him and get the full story. You should've seen Ahmed's face when I told him I'd have to put the champagne deal on hold 'cos me and you were spending the weekend in Eastbourne searching for Nancy. Soon wiped the smile off his ugly clock, that did.'

'How did he react?'

Vinny smirked. 'He panicked. That's the gear, ain't it? Got a bit paranoid, stroppy, then pretended to make a phone call to say it was OK to put it on hold for a week, tops. Stupid cunt must think I was born yesterday. I'm so glad me and you don't snort that shit any more. People act like fucktards on it and you can't think straight. I'm embarrassed I ever went through a stage of taking the crap.'

'You and me both. I don't think Bella would be too impressed if she found that out. Proper classy, she is.'

'How's it going with yous two?'

'I spoke to her for an hour earlier. She's blinding, Vin. So supportive. I love her to death. Doubt I'll get much time to see her until after Adam's funeral though. I really can't leave the boys alone at the moment.'

Apart from Jay Boy and Gnasher, Vinny had confided in no one about his plan to kill Joanna. He very much doubted Michael would understand, and Eddie Mitchell would most certainly wash his hands of him. Even his mother would be shocked, truth be known. 'Why don't you spend the day with Bella on Sunday? I'll take the boys out for the day with me and Ava. We'll go to Southend. It might be a bit squashed in the car, but I'll take Mum an' all. I doubt Auntie Viv'll wanna come, she still fucking hates me. But the weather's meant to be nice, and even if it pisses down I'm sure Dan and Lee'll love the old amusement arcades. A bit of fresh air and change of scenery will do them both the world of good.'

For the first time that day, Michael smiled. It had been a long time since he'd felt so close to Vinny. 'Cheers, bruv. That would be blinding, and seeing Bella would proper help me get through the funeral on Monday.'

Vinny grinned too. Not only was he doing Michael a favour, he now had the perfect alibi if all went to plan and Joanna met her maker on Sunday.

Little Vinny had made it clear he didn't want to tell him what was wrong, so Jay Boy ramped the volume up so that Paul Hardcastle's '19' blared out of the car stereo. 'Weird old song this, eh, Vin? I think it's meant to be about the war. I had a cousin killed in the Falklands you know,' Jay Boy said.

Head all over the place, Little Vinny didn't answer. He was too busy going over and over his story to be arsed talking about music or the Falklands.

'Right, here we are and your old man's car's here. I'll come in and have a chat with Michael while you speak alone with your dad,' Jay Boy said.

It was Vinny who answered the door. 'What's up with him?' he asked Jay Boy, as Little Vinny dashed past him and demanded that his father follow him upstairs.

Jay Boy shrugged.

Vinny Butler knew his son well enough to know something bad had happened. 'Whatever's wrong?' he asked as he sat on Michael's bed and put a comforting arm around his son's shoulders.

Little Vinny burst into tears. Guilt, fear, Molly, Sammi-Lou and Ollie flashed through his mind as he tried to form his words properly.

'Is it Sammi-Lou? Has something happened to Ollie?' Vinny prompted his son.

'No. It's Ahmed, Dad. He's planning on killing you. Burak's in on it too. I went to the bar today to pick up my keys and I overheard them talking. I think they're gonna do it this weekend.'

Vinny held his son close and stroked the back of his head as he once had when he was a child. 'It's OK, boy. I already knew. Don't you be worrying. I'm far too clever for those Turkish cunts.'

Little Vinny clung to his father. 'But that ain't all. When you was inside, Ahmed got me on the drink and gear. Then one night, he was proper out of his nut and he forced me to make some stupid confession about Molly's death.'

Vinny's eyes lit up with anger. 'He did fucking what!'

'He was waving a gun about, Dad. We were both out of our nuts. He said he had this big secret about you and told me he couldn't tell me unless I said I was responsible for Molly's death. I swear on your life, he forced me to say it was me and Ben who'd killed her. He held the gun right to my temple. I was shit-scared and couldn't understand why he'd make me act out such a scene. I thought it must be the drugs, but now I know. When I overheard Ahmed talking to Burak today he said he'd taped it and he wanted that to be your dying thought. Why d'ya think I was too afraid to come and work for you?'

'And what was this big secret about me – did he ever tell you?

'He said you'd murdered my mum. That you'd made it look like a heroin overdose.'

Vinny leapt off the bed and smashed his fist against the door. 'I'll fucking rip his brain out of his head and his heart out of his chest with my bare cunting hands. You don't believe I murdered your mum, do you, boy? I would never harm a woman, especially your mother,' Vinny lied.

'Course I don't, Dad. It's as ridiculous as you believing I was capable of killing Molly.'

Vinny kicked the wardrobe. 'I will torture that fucker. In fact, I'm gonna do it right now.'

Hearing a commotion, Michael and Jay Boy ran up the stairs and somehow managed to restrain and talk sense into Vinny. Both were incensed by Little Vinny's revelations, but urged Vinny to hold fire.

'Bruv, we'll sort this together, properly,' Michael insisted.

'I'll be there too, Vin. I'll help you rip both of them to pieces. You don't wanna go back inside though, so just calm down,' Jay Boy urged.

'I wanna be there too, Dad. Now you know the truth, I can work for you. I'm not a boy any more, I'm a man and I can't wait to see Ahmed get his comeuppance.'

When his father ruffled his hair and told him he was proud of him, Little Vinny smiled. It was a massive weight off his shoulders that his story had been believed. He felt as though he'd managed to dig himself out of a bigger hole than the one Molly was buried in.

CHAPTER THIRTY-ONE

At eleven-thirty a.m. on Friday morning, Carl Tanner pulled into the garage opposite The Bull pub. He had a hunch that Vinny might arrive early, especially if he wasn't alone.

The black Merc pulled into the car park approximately twenty minutes later. You didn't see many cars of that quality in Dagenham, so Carl immediately knew it was Vinny. He took the binoculars out of his pocket and had a butcher's. Vinny hadn't changed much and he could see nobody else in the vehicle. There was always a possibility a passenger could be lying on the back seat, but that was a chance Carl was willing to take. He'd borrowed his brother's Triumph TR7 in case he needed to make a quick getaway.

Vinny did a double-take as the car pulled up beside his. He lowered the window. Carl's hair had been much lighter when they'd met previously and the beard had thrown him. 'Blimey, I'd never have recognized you.'

'Case of having to disguise myself, Vinny. Your so-called friend wants me dead as well as you.'

Vinny remained calm. 'Shall we go inside the boozer?'

Carl shook his head. For all he knew Vinny could have told somebody to meet him inside. 'Follow me. There's a pub not far from here where we'll look much less conspicuous.'

Ten minutes later, Vinny and Carl were sat opposite one another in the beer garden of the Farmhouse Tavern. 'Fire away then, and start from the very beginning,' Vinny ordered.

Carl explained how his friend Tarkan Smith had introduced him to Ahmed. He also told Vinny how much Ahmed had hated him, and had devised a plan to get him caught with a boot full of cocaine.

Desperately trying to keep calm, Vinny swallowed his double Scotch in one gulp. 'Let's get this straight. You're telling me you weren't even a dealer?'

'No. Drugs isn't my game. I was a gambler and con-man back then. Ahmed supplied me with the cocaine. He said he was still getting it off your old supplier.'

'Who did the flat and yard belong to?'

'Pals of Ahmed's. He didn't say who and I didn't ask. The only thing he ever really talked to me about was how much he wanted to bring you down.'

'How much did the cunt pay you?'

'We agreed a deal for fifty K, but the shitbag ripped me off. He paid me fifteen up front, then refused to pay me the balance when your Molly went missing. I actually thought it was Ahmed who'd killed Molly. He often joked about her disappearance. Thought it was funny.'

Slamming his fist against the table, Vinny's eyes blazed with anger. 'Why are you telling me all this now, Carl? Because if it's money you're after, you can go whistle for it.'

'All I wanna do is set the record straight, Vinny. I've been hiding out in Spain, but my old man's dying, which is why I've come back to England. Tarkan and Ahmed both ripped me off. They want me dead and I want to take them out before they do me in. I take it that's what you want too? I'm happy to be used as bait to reel the fuckers in. If we work well together, perhaps you can give me a job at the end of it?'

Vinny gritted his teeth, then chuckled. 'I run a tight ship, Carl. Strangers and shysters need not apply. And what makes you think I would trust you anyway? You've already tried to con me once.'

'Because we have friends in common. You don't honestly think the Mitchells would have got involved if they thought I was a wrong 'un, do you Vin? Yes, I've made mistakes and I'm the first to hold my hands up to that. Gambling was always my downfall. But I swear when Tarkan introduced me to Ahmed, I didn't know it was you I'd be expected to set up. I haven't got a death wish.'

Impressed but not fooled by Carl's little speech, Vinny asked, 'How d'ya know the Mitchells?'

Carl took a deep breath. This was his trump card. 'Through my uncle. He and Harry Mitchell grew up together in Canning Town. Best pals, back in the day. Found out only recently that you're a friend of my uncle too. Spoke very highly of you too.'

Here we go, Vinny thought, yawning to show his lack of interest. 'And your uncle's name is?'

'Frank. He's the screw who helped you out in the Ville.'

'What's his surname then?'

'Same as mine.'

Furious that Carl thought he could con him twice, Vinny hissed, 'Don't mess with me 'cause you're messing with the wrong fucking person. You told me in that letter that your name was Carl cunting Thompson. That ain't Frank's surname.'

'It's not mine either. Thompson is my alias. Tanner's my real name, same as Frank. I'll ring him up. Ask him if you don't believe me.'

*

Lee Butler stared at the photo. It had been taken at Kings and Adam was sitting on Nancy's lap.

'What you doing?' Daniel asked.

'Looking through some photos I found in the drawer. I can't believe our mum drowned herself. I wonder if they've found her body yet. I'm really gonna miss her, you know.'

'Why? She weren't even your real mum. I certainly won't miss her. We'll have much more fun living with Dad,' Daniel replied coldly.

Usually ready to agree with anything Daniel said, for once Lee took a stand. 'You shouldn't say bad things about your mum, Dan. She must have been proper sad to drown herself. I wonder if she did it so Adam wouldn't be in heaven on his own?'

'Don't talk bollocks! Mum won't even be in heaven. She'll have been eaten by the sharks.'

Little Vinny swung his pride and joy in the air. Oliver was such a happy baby, always smiling.

'Vin, please tell me what happened yesterday? You promised me, no more secrets. I know it's something bad.'

Vinny sighed and handed his fiancée their son. This must be the tenth time Sammi-Lou had asked him the same question. 'It's just man shit, babe. I swear to you, if it was anything to do with me, I'd tell you. But it's my dad's business, not mine.'

'It must be important to you too, else why would you have been looking like you'd seen a ghost when we walked out that bar? I thought you were going to collapse at one point. I'm not stupid, you know. It's obvious you went to get your keys and overheard something you shouldn't have.'

Not wanting to upset the apple-cart when he and Sammi had been getting on so well, Little Vinny decided to lie. No way could he tell Sammi-Lou the truth and it was obvious she had the bit between her teeth and wasn't about to let it go. 'OK. But you have to swear to me you'll never breathe a word to anybody. This is just between us.'

'You know you can trust me, Vinny.'

'When I went to get my jacket and keys, I overheard Ahmed and his cousin talking about my dad. They said he killed my mum, but I asked my dad and he said they're liars.'

'That's awful, Vin. Why would they say a thing like that?'

Little Vinny shrugged. 'I think Ahmed is a bit jealous of my dad. Don't worry about it. It's all sorted now.'

Adam's untimely death had prompted Michael to purchase a mobile phone. He'd made sure Lee and Daniel both had the number imprinted in their brains, and it was a comfort to know they could contact him wherever he might be.

'Talk outside, boy. You don't want strangers to overhear your conversation,' Albie urged. He and Michael were in the Thatched House pub, and all the customers had looked around when Michael's phone rang. Albie hated unwanted attention and found his son's latest gadget an embarrassment.

Michael returned to the table in less than a minute. 'That was Vinny. He's on his way 'ere. Needs to have a chat with me about something.'

'In that case I'm gonna pop home and have a tidy-up. I told you Bert's coming down for the funeral and staying with me for a week, didn't I?' Bert was Albie's brother who lived in Ipswich.

'You ain't got to go 'cause Vinny's on his way, Dad. His bark's worse than his bite, you know that as well as I do. Have one more drink at least, eh?'

Never one to turn down a freebie, Albie mumbled, 'Just a large brandy then. I don't want another pint.'

Vinny walked in just as Michael returned from the bar.

'Jesus, that was quick. Where was you when we spoke? The graveyard?' Michael joked.

Albie shuddered. Vinny was dressed all in black with dark sunglasses to match, and it wouldn't have surprised him if he had been at the graveyard, gloating over his latest victim. The Grim Reaper had nothing on Vinny. 'I'll leave yous two to it then. Thanks for the drinks, Michael. See you on Monday, Vinny.'

Turning around to make sure nobody was in earshot, Vinny repeated everything that Carl had told him.

'What a complete and utter shitcunt Ahmed is. I don't wanna say I told you so, but I always knew he wasn't to be trusted. Mum never liked him either. As for Carl, he knows too much by the sounds of it. What you gonna do about him?'

'That's a good question. If he weren't Frank's nephew and Frank wasn't Harry Mitchell's mate, I'd put a bullet straight through Carl's skull. Got me hands tied though. I might have to give him a job of some kind so I can keep my eye on him. He can always have a little accident in the future if need be.'

'The Mitchells ain't stupid, Vin. They won't fall for that one. You sure Carl's Frank's nephew? He's already pulled the wool over your eyes in the past. I wouldn't have him working for me. Once a con man always a fucking con man.'

'I ain't stupid, Michael. I thought exactly the same as you which is why I made him ring Frank and put me on the phone to him. Carl's deffo his nephew and Frank also let slip that it was Harry Mitchell who'd told him to befriend me in the Ville. Harry and Frank are Canning Town old school. Harry described me as "one of his own".'

'In that case, best you give Carl a job, sunshine. If you pull a fast one we're gonna be at war with the Mitchells, and that's one war I can seriously do without right now. I don't think I could deal with any more funerals in the family. I still can't believe Adam's gone, Vin. And now Nancy. My luck is well and truly poxed.'

Mary Walker opened the school exercise book and was surprised to see it was actually a personal diary dating back to 1971. Her daughter had left school by then and was working in Woolworths. Mary knew it was wrong to read something so personal, but her need to feel close to her daughter outweighed the guilt.

Nancy had written randomly rather than daily.

March 5th – Went Ilford Palais with Rhonda. Had such a laugh. Snogged two boys from Dagenham. Mine was called Danny and he asked for my phone number. He isn't as gorgeous as my Marc ♥ but I hope he rings. He was a good kisser.

March 11th – Danny still hasn't rung me (bastard). Never mind. Plenty more fish in the sea, including Marc Bolan ♥♥

Mary laughed and cried at her daughter's typical teenage antics and view on life, before gritting her teeth as she reached the month of June.

June 18th – So excited! Mum finally talked Dad round and I'm allowed to go to the fair tomorrow. It's going to be ace. Me and Rhonda are both glamming up. Bound to be lots of hot boys there. Watch this space . . .

June 19th – Oh my God! I am in love! Met the man of my dreams at the fair. Had a crush on him when I was young and cannot believe he asked me to go to his club on Friday night. He has the most amazing teeth, eyes and hair I've ever seen. Sorry Marc ♥ but he's even hotter than you! I seriously need to go shopping before Friday. Help me diary. What am I going to wear?

Tears streaming down her face, Mary put the diary back in the box. Reading intimate details about her daughter's relationship with Michael Butler was something she could never stomach. Nancy had left her side for ever and it was entirely that bastard's fault.

Vinny rallied his troops for a 4 p.m. meeting at the White-chapel club. Usually he wouldn't involve his doormen Pete and Paul in such situations, but this was one occasion he needed all the help he could get.

Much as he was proud of his son for volunteering to take part in Ahmed's demise, Vinny had no intention of allowing him to do so. It was too much of a risk, and Little Vinny wasn't ready to face that kind of danger.

'Where's Michael?' Jay Boy asked Vinny.

'I told him to go home and get some kip. Poor bastard ain't been sleeping properly.'

'First Adam. Then Nancy. I truly feel for him, Vin,' Jay Boy replied.

Vinny opened a bottle of Scotch, poured everyone a drink, then explained briefly what had happened.

Pete and Paul were shocked to the core. Ever since Ahmed had come on the scene, he and Vinny had been joined at the hip – or so it had seemed. 'That's un-fucking-believable! What a Judas!' Pete exclaimed.

'I really don't get it. Why would Ahmed want you dead, Vin?' Paul asked.

For obvious reasons, Vinny had always kept the truth surrounding his cousin's death close to his chest. However, he could hardly ask Pete and Paul for their help without coming clean. 'Because it was me driving the car that killed Champ. It was an accident. I got blinded by oncoming headlights. I'd never have left Ahmed had I thought he was still alive. On my mother's life, I checked his pulse and was positive he was dead.'

'But that was years ago. Why wait until now for revenge?' Pete asked.

Without admitting to his own involvement in drug-dealing, Vinny explained about Ahmed's plan to get him caught by the police with a boot full of cocaine. 'I'd have got a ten stretch for that, without a doubt.' Something else occurred to Vinny as he related the story: 'Ahmed must've been well chuffed when Bobby Jackson croaked it. It was him who wound me up to attack the guy. Said he'd bumped into Bobby and he'd been laughing and joking about Molly dying.' He shook his head, disgusted that he'd fallen for Ahmed's mind games. 'Jackson was an absolute cunt and he got what was coming to him, so I've no regrets on that score, but if it hadn't been for Ahmed getting me so angry I couldn't think straight I would've sorted Jackson out in my own time, covered my tracks.'

'What's the plan then?' Jay Boy asked.

Paul grew tense as he learned what his boss had in mind. He had four kids now and didn't particularly fancy a shoot-out with the Turks. Killing one would've been bad enough, but Vinny wanted three dead.

Jay Boy was more up for it. He'd hated Ahmed and Burak on sight and was furious they'd wronged Vinny. 'When d'ya want the job done?'

'Next weekend. I'll put my thinking cap on over the next few days and come up with a proper plan. Somebody else is disposing of the bodies, so that's one less job for us to worry about.'

'Wouldn't it be wiser for us to dispose of them ourselves?' Pete suggested. He was a big believer that, if you wanted a job done properly, you were better off doing it yourself.

'Nah. I'm paying the pros to get rid. We don't want any unwanted bones or skulls dug up by Fido the fucking dog, do we now?'

Jay Boy, Pete and Paul all chuckled. Only Vinny Butler could crack funnies at a time like this.

CHAPTER THIRTY-TWO

Ava Preston was eating her Rice Krispies when the phone rang. 'Can I answer it, Mummy? Please?' she begged.

'Go on then, quickly,' Joanna urged, hoping it was Vinny and he was unable to come for Ava today. Apart from her mother, nobody else would call this early.

'Daddy, where are you?' Ava squealed excitedly.

'I'll be with you soon, darlin'. I'm going to be a little bit late though.'

'Awww, when will you be here?' Ava asked, lip trembling with disappointment. Every second that she spent with her father was precious to her.

Joanna snatched the phone out of her daughter's hands. 'What's up? Can't you make it?'

'I would never let Ava down, Jo. I'm running a bit late, that's all. Daniel and Lee have been in bits after witnessing Adam's death, so I thought a day at the seaside would cheer 'em up – and me for that matter. The funeral's tomorrow and it's gonna be grim.'

'I don't want Ava anywhere near Daniel,' Joanna hissed.

Vinny sighed. 'My mum and aunt are coming as well, Jo. There's really no need for you to be so dramatic all the time.'

'Your aunt hates you,' Joanna reminded her ex.

'Yes, I'm fully aware of that, thank you. Obviously she doesn't hate me enough to knock back a day out in Southend though, else she wouldn't be coming. Listen, I've bought meself a mobile phone so you can contact me and vice versa whenever I've got Ava. You can write the number down when I pick her up. I don't want you to worry unnecessarily.'

'Give me the number now,' Joanna ordered. She felt much more at ease being able to contact Ava while she was with her father.

Vinny gave his ex the number, then asked her to repeat it back to him. 'Yep, that's it. I'll pick Ava up before eight, OK?'

'Yes. And if you need to get hold of me at all, I'll be here until about ten, then at my mum's until six.'

Vinny smirked. 'OK. Perfect.'

Jimmy 'Gnasher' Williams was just polishing off a healthy fry-up when the phone rang. He hated working on an empty stomach, always had done.

When he'd last met up with Vinny they'd somehow got talking about the TV programme *Only Fools and Horses*. Both men were big fans, which was why they'd decided to use Del Boy and Rodney for their code.

'Is Del Boy there?' Vinny asked.

'Nah. Sorry, mate. You must have the wrong number,' Gnasher replied. Seconds later, he picked up his keys and left the house.

'Michael!' Antonio exclaimed, flinging himself at the man he'd become so very fond of.

Michael picked the child up. 'How's my main man?'

Bella smiled at the touching scene. 'He's going out

and leaving us soon. Got a party to attend, haven't you, Antonio?'

When Antonio excitedly explained it was his friend's birthday and a magician was going to show him how to do tricks, Michael kissed the child on his forehead. Antonio was a smashing boy, but today Michael couldn't wait to be alone with Bella. Making love to her would allow him to forget his woes, for a short time at least.

'Mummy, I don't like this dress. Can I wear the green one?' Ava asked, hands on hips.

Joanna and Darren looked at one another and chuckled. They'd just been talking about Ava's sudden interest in fashion. 'Your green dress is dirty, darling. You wore it yesterday and spilled ice cream down it.'

Indignant as ever, Ava then demanded to wear her pink dress.

'You haven't got time to get changed, love. Your dad will be here any minute,' Joanna insisted.

When Ava started to cry, Darren picked her up. 'Show me what you want to wear and we'll sort it, OK? That's if your mum agrees, of course.'

Joanna nodded, then smiled as her daughter and fiancée left the room. Apart from Vinny being back on the scene, life was so good at the moment. Darren was such a diamond and he was brilliant with Ava. They'd even discussed having a child of their own once married. Their big day was bound to be tinged with sadness as well as happiness though. Molly and Nancy would've been the prettiest bridesmaids ever.

She was just about to pick up the phone to see if Mary had heard any more from the police searching for Nancy when it rang.

'Darren, we need to pick Shane up. His mum's not well,' Jo shouted up the stairs a moment later.

Unaware of what their day had in store, Darren replied, 'No worries. The more the merrier.'

Johnny Preston was in a bar on the Costa Del Sol. He'd flown out yesterday evening, having decided he needed a break to clear his messed-up mind and decide his next move.

Johnny had told nobody he was going abroad. He and Deborah were barely on speaking terms, and he'd informed his mother he was going to visit an old pal from prison. That part at least was true, as he and Balham Clive had met while incarcerated.

Balham Clive looked at Johnny in horror as he explained the situation and his plans. 'You can't just blast Butler's brains out in the middle of a busy street, John. You're bound to get caught and you'll get life this time. Isn't there anyone who can give you a bit of back-up? You stand much more chance of getting away with it if you lure Butler somewhere quiet. He's not at all popular with the Old Bill, so I doubt they'd fall over backwards to find his killer. He has so many enemies; they probably wouldn't know where to start.'

'I tested the water with a couple of pals, but as soon as I mentioned Vinny they didn't want to know. People are shit-scared of the Butlers, Clive, but I fucking ain't. Everything was sound until that bastard turned up on the scene. Now my marriage is in tatters and I can't concentrate at work. I'll probably get the tin-tack when I get home. Never said I was flying out here, just told 'em I was ill.'

'I've said it before, mate, there's a job out 'ere waiting for you. Got a nice little apartment you can rent for peanuts too. Don't go back home. It'll be a fresh start and it's better than a life behind bars.'

Johnny shook his head. 'I really appreciate your offer, but I will do absolutely anything to protect Jo and Ava –

even if I end up with a life sentence. I won't rest until that cunt is dead. I've already bought a gun and I'm determined to pull that trigger – whatever the consequences.'

Queenie was in the passenger seat, Viv in the back with the kids. 'Forgot to tell you, Vin, that Colleen phoned me the other day. She's planning a trip to London in August and is bringing Emily-Mae with her. We must organize a big family get-together. She's thirteen now you know.'

Vinny wasn't impressed. Colleen was his brother Roy's one-time fiancée; Emily-Mae was Roy's only child. But in his eyes, Colleen had moved on far too quickly after separating from his brother. 'I wouldn't bother making a big issue out of the visit. We ain't seen the kid for years and doubt we'll ever see her again.'

'But she's Roy's flesh and blood. If he's looking down, he'd want us to make a big fuss of her,' Queenie insisted.

Vinny glanced at his watch. He had far more important things on his mind than Colleen and Emily-Mae. Joanna's death for one.

Jimmy 'Gnasher' Williams followed Joanna's Ford Fiesta for a mile or so before overtaking. Apparently, Darren was currently on a driving ban, so she always drove.

Putting his foot down on the accelerator, Gnasher headed towards his and their destination. He'd picked the perfect spot where there was a big drop into a ditch. The road was narrow, remote and attracted little traffic. He very much doubted either Jo or her boyfriend would survive. He didn't just intend to tap the Ford Fiesta off the road; he planned to ram the bastard thing.

Vivian grinned as the money tumbled out of the bottom of the machine. She did love an amusement arcade and a decent bit of seafood, which was why she'd agreed to suffer Vinny's company today.

'Daddy, can you win me that doggy?' Ava asked, pointing to the prize she wanted.

Vinny had already decided that, if today went to plan, he would buy his daughter a mutt. She was obsessed with the bloody things and surely owning one would help her get over the death of her mother? 'Dan, you're good on them grab machines. Can you try and get the fluffy dog for Ava?'

'Give me five minutes. I've just gotta beat Lee at this.'

'Good lad,' Vinny replied. He was glad he'd brought his nephews to Southend. To see both Lee and Daniel smiling and having a bit of banter with one another was worth the journey alone.

As soon as Antonio was waved off, Michael Butler slammed the front door, rammed Bella up against the wall and muttered the words, 'I am so horny and desperate to fuck you senseless this very second.'

Bella grinned. She was a lady in public, a great cook in the kitchen and a total whore in the bedroom. 'Then take me by force, if you must.'

Needing no more encouragement, Michael Butler lifted Bella up by her buttocks and carried her into the bedroom. He then tied her hands to the bedposts. Rape was their favourite form of role-play.

Jimmy 'Gnasher' Williams was becoming slightly concerned. He'd overtaken Joanna's motor a good half an hour ago and she still hadn't appeared.

Desperate for a cigarette, Gnasher decided against it. He'd read an article recently in a newspaper saying that in the near future the Old Bill would be able to catch you out by something called a DNA sample. He wasn't sure exactly what that meant, but he'd got the gist. If his mouth had been around that cigarette, there was a possibility he could be traced one day in the future.

Bored shitless, Gnasher switched on the radio. He had leather gloves on; he always wore them when assassinating. 'The Fool on the Hill' by the Beatles was playing and Gnasher took that as a good omen. The Beatles were his favourite group and they'd never let him down yet.

'Daddy, Joanna, can we sing "Row Row Row Your Boat" again?' five-year-old Shane asked.

Darren smiled at Joanna. His son had started infant school last September and his current project was to learn the song and draw a picture of a boat. Darren never usually picked Shane up until later in the day, but his mother had been ill this morning, hence the phone call asking that they pick him up early. 'What do you reckon, Jo? It's your turn to sing it this time,' Darren chuckled.

Joanna sighed, but smiled at the same time. After living with an arsehole like Vinny who'd made her feel so unloved and unwanted, she truly couldn't be happier right now. 'Row row row your boat gently down the stream. Merrily, merrily, merrily, merrily, life is but a dream,' she sang.

About to join in with the second chorus of 'Row Row Row Your Boat', Darren screamed 'Watch out!' as the big red truck hurtled towards them.

Joanna Preston never got the chance to reply. She died within seconds.

Vinny Butler made a point of flirting with the barmaid as he placed the food order. She was a moose, but he didn't care. An alibi was an alibi and she'd be sure to remember him now.

'You took your time. Did you tell her me and Viv want our skate coated in batter?' Queenie asked her son.

'Yes, Mum,' Vinny replied, adrenalin rushing through his veins as his phone burst into life. 'Hello.'

'Is Rodney there?'

'Sorry. You must have the wrong number, pal.'

Ava tugged the sleeve of her father's suit. 'Can I sit on your lap, Daddy? I really do love you.'

'Do ya love me more than you love Mummy?' Vinny chuckled.

Ava couldn't decide, but said yes as he bought her better presents.

Vinny smirked as he lifted up his daughter and hugged her. Ava finally belonged to him, and him alone.

Deborah Preston was in a right old state. Joanna had been due to arrive hours ago, yet there was still no sign of her.

Debating whether to ring the police, Deborah decided to call Johnny first. 'Hello, Shirley. It's Deborah. Is Johnny there, please?'

'No. He's gone to stay with a friend.'

'What friend? Do you know when he'll be back? I need to contact him urgently.'

'I ain't got a clue where he is or when he'll be back. Just said he was visiting an old prison pal. What's the matter?' Shirley asked, in the usual sharp tone she used when speaking to her son's fat, miserable wife.

'It's Joanna. Her and Darren were due at mine hours ago. Jo always rings me if she's going to be late. My stomach's in knots. Something's happened to her, I know it has, Shirley.'

Shirley Preston pursed her lips. Her son had had a few too many one night and told her all about his falling out with Deborah. 'You've only got yourself to blame if something bad has happened to that poor girl. My Johnny warned you, didn't he? Wanted you to move abroad. You've never been able to see the wood for the trees, you. Please God, Jo turns up safe and sound, because if she doesn't that'll be the end of my son.'

Vinny knocked at Joanna's door in Tillingham and as expected, nobody was home. He leapt the small fence and pressed a neighbour's doorbell. 'So sorry to bother you, but have you seen Joanna at all?'

'No, love. You're Ava's dad, Vinny, aren't you? I think we spoke once before.'

'We sure did. Never one to forget a pretty face, me. Could you do me a favour, please? I have my mum, aunt and nephews in the car, so I can't hang about for Jo. When you see her, will you tell her that Ava will stay with me tonight and I'll bring her home tomorrow? Just tell her to bell me.'

'Will do. I'll keep an eye out for her.'

Aware that the old bird fancied him, Vinny kissed her on the cheek. 'You're a darlin'.'

The woman smiled. Vinny oozed charisma and she couldn't understand why Joanna would swap him for Darren. 'My pleasure. I will definitely look out for Jo and pass your message on.'

Ava was beside herself with excitement. She had never stayed with her father before. 'Let's go, Daddy,' she demanded, trying to drag Vinny back to the car before her mum turned up.

Vinny picked his daughter up and smiled at the neighbour. 'I don't even know your name.'

'It's Ruth.'

Vinny winked. 'Thank you, Ruth. Hopefully see you again soon.'

*

Deborah Preston was in a paranoid frenzy by the time her best friend Sandy arrived. As soon as Deborah had told her Jo was missing, she'd driven straight over from Tiptree.

'Johnny was right,' Deborah sobbed. 'He said Vinny would kill her, and now he has, I just know it.'

Sandy held her sobbing friend in her arms. 'Shhh, calm down, Deb. I'm sure there must be some simple explanation, but since you're so worried why don't we drive over to Jo's place and if there's no sign of her we can call the police to—'

'The police won't do nothing yet,' Deborah said frantically. 'I rang them earlier and they said it's too soon to file a missing person report on Jo. I told them how reliable she was, but they wouldn't listen.'

'They'll listen to me, Deb. Get in my car and we'll call by Jo's and then if there's no sign of her we'll go on to the police station. People don't just disappear into thin air.'

'Pass me the phone, Mum,' Vinny Butler ordered. He dialled Joanna's parents' number and it went to answerphone. 'It's Vinny. Just to let you know I took Ava back to Jo's, but she wasn't there. I hung about for a bit, but couldn't wait for ever as I had my family in the car. Anyway, Ava's gonna stay with me tonight at my mum's house. Tell Jo to give me a bell and I'll arrange a time to drop Ava off tomorrow.'

'Strange Jo wasn't at home eh, boy? She usually can't wait to snatch Ava back off us,' Queenie said.

'I thought the same, Mum. She said she was going over to her mother's for the day. Perhaps she broke down on the way home or something? Not being funny, but I've given her my mobile number and she could've called if she was anywhere near a phone box.'

Staring at her nephew's evil eyes through the interior mirror, Vivian kept her opinion of what had happened to Jo to herself. That poor girl was bound to be dead and Vivian had no doubt in her mind Vinny had organized it.

Darren Grant's eyes flickered open. He wasn't sure of his surroundings, but could feel immense pain. 'Jo, Shane, where are you?' he mumbled.

'Daddy, I'm hurting. My foot hurts and my arm,' Shane whimpered.

'Hang on in there, son. I'll be with you,' a disorientated Darren replied.

'Help me now, Daddy. Please help me now,' Shane screamed.

There was no reply. Unfortunately for poor Shane, his father's heart had stopped beating.

CHAPTER THIRTY-THREE

After the escape from reality the previous day, Queenie Butler woke up feeling thoroughly depressed. Today Adam would be laid to rest, and all she could think of was his cute little face.

Hearing voices, Queenie opened the curtains. The sun was shining, thankfully, and the loony next door was doing his morning exercise routine while Mummy looked on from her wheelchair.

Instead of watching them and cackling as she usually did, Queenie walked away from the window. She had a eulogy to perfect, then read out, and was determined to do so with a stiff upper lip. Anything less would be a sign of weakness.

Little Vinny gave Sammi-Lou a peck on the cheek. 'I'll give you a bell when I want picking up. Have a nice day out with your parents.' His fiancée had wanted to attend Adam's funeral to support him, but he'd told her there was no need. His dad and Michael were bound to get on the piss afterwards and there were important things to discuss. Such as killing Ahmed.

'You scrub up well in a suit. You should wear 'em more often. You OK?' Vinny asked his son.

'So-so, Dad. I hate funerals, but who doesn't?'

'You spoken to Ahmed at all?'

'No. But I'm due back in work on Wednesday. I was thinking of telling him I've got the flu or something. I can't face having to look at the bastard.'

Vinny led his son out into the back garden. 'I need you to man up. I want you to go into work and act totally normal. The cunt's coming to the funeral today, and we all have to act as though nothing's wrong. You get me?'

Little Vinny nodded. 'I'm worried about that tape, Dad. He's bound to have made more than one copy. Say the Old Bill ever get their hands on it? Can't we tell the police what he forced me to do?'

'Don't talk bollocks. This time next week, Ahmed will have disappeared off the face of the earth. The Old Bill ain't stupid, boy. Don't worry about the tape. If it ever comes to light, I'll sort it. If you had a gun at your head, it's hardly likely to be a heartfelt confession. The police have experts for that kind of stuff. They'll know you were forced to say what you did.'

Little Vinny bit his lip anxiously. If the Old Bill ever got their hands on that tape, he was definitely in shit-street.

Deborah Preston was in pieces. She hadn't slept, couldn't eat and had a constant churning of dread in her stomach.

'Do you want another cup of tea?' Sandy asked. After they'd come back from the police station last night, having secured a promise that someone would come out and see them in the morning, Deborah had been in such a state she didn't dare leave her alone.

'No. I just want the police to bloody well hurry up. She'll have been missing twenty-four hours soon. That girl's my world, Sand. Life without her wouldn't be worth living. I hope Ava's OK too. She's never stayed with her bastard of a father before. She must be missing her mum. I hope he brings Ava back today.'

Sandy tried to offer reassurance, but with each hour that passed she had grown more convinced that something untoward must have happened. She'd lost count of how many times she'd gone to the window in the hope of seeing Jo's car coming down the street. This time when she got up to look, she saw a panda car pulling up. 'The police have arrived, Deb. I'll let them in.'

The two officers showed little sense of urgency as they began asking questions. Appalled when the older officer suggested that Joanna might have gone somewhere without telling her, Deborah immediately put him straight. 'I can assure you that isn't the case. Joanna is totally reliable. She's a mum herself and would never want me to worry. We're very close. We speak at least twice a day.'

'Are you positive Joanna's boyfriend was with her yesterday?'

'I can't say for definite, but I should imagine he was. He's with Jo every Sunday, and she said he was coming for dinner.'

'Was Joanna having any relationship problems?'

'None whatsoever. Jo idolizes Darren and vice versa. They're engaged to be married.'

'Do you know where the mother of Darren's son lives?'

'She lives in Bradwell. I don't know the address though. Her name's Lorraine and Darren's son is called Shane Grant.'

'We'll find out the address. Is there anything else you can tell us? We already have the model and registration of Joanna's car.'

'Yes. My daughter's ex is the notorious gangster Vinny Butler. He's Ava's father. I'll play you a message he left on my answerphone last night. The man is evil and will go to any lengths to get what he wants. If any harm has come to my daughter, Vinny Butler is behind it.'

Knowing the Old Bill were bound to listen to Joanna's messages, Vinny rang her again. 'What the fuck you playing at, Jo? Do you not want to be a mother to our daughter any more? Ava's gonna have to come to Adam's funeral with me now, and I can't drop her at yours after because of the wake. I'll bring her back in the morning, if you can be arsed returning my calls, of course.'

'Leave that bleedin' thing 'ere. You can't take a phone in a church. It's disrespectful,' Queenie told her son.

'I'll leave it in the limo. I need it with me, Mum, because Jo still hasn't been in touch. I've just left a stinking message on her answerphone. What sort of mother is she? Good job you shot out earlier and bought Ava something to wear today. Poor little cow had chocolate all down the front of that dress she had on yesterday.'

Queenie wasn't stupid. Joanna was a bloody good mother. If something bad had happened to the girl, Queenie wouldn't put it past her son to have arranged it. She would never ask Vinny outright though. She'd rather not know the answer. Ignorance is bliss, so they say. Besides, it would be lovely to see more of Ava.

Douglas Jones had a prostate problem. He could no longer hold his urine in like he'd once been able to, which was why he'd just had to stop his car and flop his todger out.

Zipping his trousers up, Douglas's eyes widened at the sight of the rear end of a blue car poking out of the ditch.

Douglas decided to investigate. There was a road not far from here known to the locals as the 'Dengie Straight'. It was a magnet for boy-racers and there'd been a fatal accident there not that long ago. Two cars had collided while racing and both drivers and one passenger had died.

Cursing as he slipped on his backside, Douglas picked himself up and tottered down the slope. He knew his cars and could see it was a Ford Fiesta.

Nothing could have prepared Douglas for the horror he was about to encounter. Blood, gore. Two dead adults and a small boy in the back crying his eyes out.

Mary Walker put the phone down. 'That was DC Maynard, Donald. The search for Nancy has now officially been called off, and he's promised he'll deliver her letters to us in person in the next day or two.'

Donald held his wife in his arms. 'I'll pay the vicar a visit, as Christopher suggested. I'm sure he'll be happy to hold a short service in Nancy's honour. We can word it as a celebration of her life, rather than a memorial. We'll invite family and close friends and have a drink somewhere afterwards.'

'Donald, will you do me a favour? I want to go to Adam's funeral. We still have plenty of time to get ready. Please come with me?'

'No, Mary. Christopher forbade us to attend. Let's pay our respects at the graveside tomorrow, as previously agreed. I could not think of anything worse than being in close proximity to that vulgar family. Nancy would be here with us now if it wasn't for them.'

'I know all that, but our grandson is lying in a small coffin as we speak. We should say goodbye to him properly. We'll leave as soon as the service is over. It's terrible that nobody from our side of the family is going.'

Donald wasn't a brutal man, but for once he knew he had to be. 'Mary, our grandson was chopped into pieces by a train. His soul is already in heaven, my darling. All that is left in that coffin is his body parts.'

*

Michael Butler had never felt at home in Barking. He'd always kept himself to himself there, spoke to very few of the neighbours, which was why he'd agreed to his mum's suggestion that Adam's funeral leave from her house. It made sense. Whitechapel was where his heart belonged, and his business. He knew all the locals would want to pay their respects too.

Done up to the nines, Queenie and Vivian hugged Michael. Both knew exactly how he was feeling, having lost sons themselves. The hearse and funeral cars weren't due for another hour, but people were already gathering along the street.

Nosy Hilda ran across the road. 'How are you, Michael? So sorry for your loss, lovey. Adam was a dear boy. May he rest in peace.'

'Not now, Hilda. Come and look at the beautiful flowers, boys,' Queenie urged her sons and grandson.

Little Vinny walked inside his grandma's house. He couldn't bear to look at floral tributes. They reminded him of his sister's funeral.

'From the Frasers, this one, bruv,' Vinny said.

Michael crouched down. 'That Turkish cunt has just turned up,' he hissed.

Seething inside, Vinny stood up, plastered a fake smile on his face, walked over to Ahmed and shook his hand. 'I thought you were going straight to the church?'

'I was. But I wanted to be here for you and Michael. It's tough days such as these when you need your true friends by your side.'

Resisting the urge to slit Ahmed's throat there and then, Vinny instead gritted his teeth and gave the Turkish turncoat a pat on the back. 'You're a good 'un, mate.'

*

Adam's service was to be held at St Leonard's Church in Shoreditch. The same vicar had delivered a lovely sermon at Roy's, Lenny's and Molly's funerals. The burial would then take place in Plaistow, where Adam would be laid to rest in a plot near to his deceased relations.

Two stunning black horses took Adam on his final journey. The streets of Whitechapel weren't quite at a standstill and neither had as many shops closed as they had for Molly's funeral, which angered Queenie immensely. 'I'm never shopping in Cliff's butchers again or buying another item off Ginger Bill, the ignorant bastards,' she hissed.

Vinny squeezed his mother's hand. Molly had been murdered, while Adam had died in an accident; those were two different things, but he didn't want to say that in front of Michael. 'It's a sign of the times, Mum. The area's changed and so has the culture. There's a lot of outsiders working on the market now and selling stuff for peanuts. I doubt Cliff and Ginger Bill could afford to take a day off work.'

'Shame we can't be transported back to the fifties or sixties, Queen. I'd go back in a heartbeat if I could, wouldn't you? They were the good old days, all right,' Vivian said solemnly.

Surprised that his aunt had even joined in a conversation that he was involved in, as she usually blanked him nowadays, Vinny took the bull by the horns. 'A lot of your generation have moved out to Essex now, Auntie Viv. It's lovely there. I'm sure you and Mum would like it. Just say the word and I'll buy you a nice house you can share.'

'I don't want fuck-all off you,' Vivian spat.

Lee bursting into tears brought the conversation to an abrupt end.

'Can't yous lot stop arguing, even on a day like this? We're in a funeral car following my brother's coffin,' Daniel piped up.

Agreeing with Daniel totally, Michael gave both his sons a hug.

At the mention of Vinny Butler's name the two police officers in Deborah Preston's living room had suddenly begun taking her daughter's disappearance very seriously. After asking a lot of questions about Joanna's relationship with her ex and taking a look at the correspondence with Vinny's solicitor, they had asked Deborah to accompany them to Joanna's house so they could search for clues to her whereabouts.

'They're wasting their time looking here,' Deborah told Sandy as they waited in Jo's kitchen while the police officers checked the rooms upstairs. 'They won't find anything – if there was anything to find we'd have seen it last night. I'm telling you Sandy, this has Vinny Butler stamped all over it. I was mad not to listen to Johnny. He warned me over and over,' Deborah wept.

Sandy didn't know what to say. Her gut told her Deborah could be right, so she said nothing.

At that moment one of the police officers entered the kitchen. 'I've just had a call on my radio, Mrs Preston. It appears your daughter's car has been found. I'll take you and your friend back to your house. An officer will be waiting there for us.'

'Where was the car found? Is Jo OK?' Deborah asked, complete panic in her voice.

'I really don't know any more details, I'm afraid. Let's make tracks, shall we?'

When Deborah stood up, her legs felt like jelly. Joanna was dead. She could feel it in her bones.

Queenie's opinion of the local community took a turn for the better when the entourage reached St Leonard's. There was an enormous crowd waiting outside the church, including many familiar faces. She even spotted Jeanie Thomas, which was remarkable considering the poor woman must know in her heart that Vinny had ended her son Trevor's life by setting fire to him.

Wearing big black hats with veils covering their faces, the sisters climbed out of the limo, Queenie holding Vinny's arm while Vivian held Michael's. Both women liked to glam up even more than usual for a funeral and had worn higher stilettos than usual.

The church wasn't big enough for all the mourners, so anybody who was a somebody barged past anyone who was a nobody to ensure they were inside rather than out.

The vicar began his sermon by telling the congregation what a lovely boy Adam had been and how he'd brought joy to all those around him.

'All Things Bright and Beautiful' was one of the hymns Michael had chosen. He remembered Adam singing it at home as a nipper, having learnt it at infants' school.

Lifting her netted veil, Queenie made her way to the front of the church to give the first eulogy. She praised Adam to the hilt, then told the congregation some funny stories about him, including the time he'd found a frog in the garden and put it in her bed. 'I squealed like a pig when I heard that bleedin' frog croak as I got under the covers. How I stopped myself launching Adam out the window after it, I'll never know.'

Michael was the next to stand up and he managed to hold back the tears as he spoke about his son's love of life in general and the things he'd done and adored doing the most.

Albie Butler was far weaker than his son and sobbed when Michael mentioned the talent competition at Kings when Adam had got on stage and sung 'Grandad' in his honour.

'The Lord's My Shepherd' was then sung by all.

Unexpectedly, the moment it finished, Daniel insisted he wanted to stand up and say something.

'Go on, boy. Do your bruvver proud,' Brenda slurred from the pew behind.

Queenie turned around with hatred in her eyes. Her daughter was nothing but an embarrassment to the good name of her family and she truly wished Brenda had never been born. Tara and Tommy, her grandchildren were nowhere to be seen, and Queenie knew the gossip-mongers would have a field day speculating on their absence, not to mention Brenda turning up at the church pissed with her similarly pissed arsehole of a boyfriend in tow.

'Shut up, you fat moose,' Queenie hissed.

Brenda had had the brains to wear black, but had put on at least another two stone since the last time Queenie had seen her. She looked like a beached whale in an ill-fitting dress.

'Don't talk to Bren like that,' the arsehole boyfriend intervened.

Vinny turned around with fire in his eyes. 'I'll deal with yous pair later, and you're barred from the wake,' he hissed.

'Shush. Daniel's about to speak,' Michael ordered.

'Lee, do you wanna stand up and say a few words with me?' Daniel asked.

Lee started to cry and shook his head emphatically.

'You do it, Dan. Your brother's too upset,' Little Vinny piped up. How he'd got through reading that poem at Molly's funeral he'd never know.

Dressed in a smart black suit, Daniel held his head high as he addressed the congregation. 'Adam wasn't just mine and Lee's bruvver. He was our best mate too. We were inseparable when we weren't at school, did everything together, and life ain't the same without him. As my nan always says, "Only the good die young" and that couldn't be more truer with Adam. Love you for ever, bro. Rest in peace.'

Vivian stared at Daniel. He'd delivered his short speech fully composed and had not shed one tear, even though it was his bloody fault Adam was dead.

The vicar said a few more words, then the service ended with the Vera Lynn song 'We'll Meet Again'.

'You OK, Mum?' Vinny asked.

'Yep. Case of having to be. Another one bites the dust, but life goes on for the rest of us.'

Deborah Preston's hands were trembling so much, she couldn't put the key in her lock.

'I'll open it, Deb,' Sandy said. Two plain-clothes officers had been waiting outside the house and had asked to talk inside.

Deborah was told to sit down.

'I'm DS Birch and my colleague is DC Cooper. I'm so sorry to be the bearer of bad news, but we have found your daughter's car and we strongly believe the two dead bodies inside the vehicle are Joanna Preston and Darren Grant. Obviously, we will need formal identification, but Mr Grant's son Shane was in the back of the car. Thankfully the boy was still alive.'

Deborah put her hand over her mouth. The news was surreal and she couldn't take it in.

'My husband was right. He said Vinny Butler would kill her. You need to arrest him and lock him up for life,' Deborah sobbed. She honestly felt as though she was in the middle of a bad dream, and prayed she would wake up soon and Jo would still be alive.

'Where was the car found?' Sandy asked.

'Asheldham, not far from Tillingham. I'm not sure if you're familiar with the stretch of road known as the Dengie

Straight? It's notorious for cars and bikes racing. Joanna's car was found in a ditch not too far from there. I fear she might have collided with or tried to avoid one of the boy-racers heading to or from the Dengie Straight.'

Deborah shook her head vehemently. 'No. You don't understand. Vinny Butler has done this. Jo has a daughter with him, Ava, and he obviously wanted the child all to himself. Don't be fooled by the messages he left on my and her answer machines. The man is a known villain and killer. I need you to collect Ava and bring her home to me. No way is he and his evil family bringing my granddaughter up. The Butlers have no scruples whatsoever. Please get Ava away from him. She's all I have left,' screamed Deborah.

Adam's wake was held at the club in Whitechapel. Michael had spared no expense. He'd hired a company who special-ized in weddings, christenings and bar mitzvahs to decorate the inside of the club and do the catering and waitress service. They'd managed to put drapes up to cover up the walls he'd had professionally graffitied and the gaff no longer resembled a disco at all. It looked more like a wedding venue.

'Ahmed's talking to Little Vinny. Go over there,' Michael ordered his brother. He knew his nephew could be a bit of a hot-head at times.

'All right, boys? Nice send off, weren't it?' Vinny said.

'Very nice. A wonderful send-off for a top lad. Speaking of top lads, I'm looking forward to your son being back at work on Wednesday. The wine bar hasn't been the same without him,' Ahmed said, putting an arm around Little Vinny's shoulders. Ahmed knew it must piss Vinny off that his son worked for him.

'I was telling Ahmed how bored I've been, stuck at home. I love my job,' said Little Vinny, managing somehow to sound as if he meant it.

'I'm gonna steal your top lad for a bit, Ahmed. I wanna introduce him to the Mitchells properly. Why don't you come with us? Eddie's a good guy. So is his old man Harry. I'm gonna sit with 'em for a while.'

Ahmed was not a man to be scared of anybody, but there was something about the Mitchells that unnerved him. He'd heard many a tale about Harry and Eddie in particular, and instinct told him not to get involved with them. 'I'm afraid I must leave soon, Vinny. Without Little Vinny, I am quite short-staffed at my bar. I'll give you a bell tomorrow to see how everything went. And don't forget about the other thing on Saturday. I'll drive and will pick you up about ten.'

'I meant to have a word with you about that. I need to shoot down to Eastbourne in the daytime. Michael's taking Dan and Lee to Beachy Head to lay some flowers for Nancy. He's staying down there overnight. Gonna make a weekend of it, but I don't wanna miss out on the deal, so I'll drive back. You'll have to tell me where the gaff is and I'll meet you there.'

'But I have no exact address. Our goods are being stored in a disused office building which is off the beaten track.'

'Well, just give me directions then. It can't be that off the beaten track if it had offices in it, Ahmed.'

Deborah Preston could not stop crying. It had now sunk in that she would never see her beautiful, vibrant daughter again and it was the worst feeling she'd ever experienced. She'd never imagined that anything could break her heart more than Molly's death, but this had. The pain she felt inside was excruciating.

'Deb, you're gonna have to let Johnny's mum know, and Johnny Junior.'

'Johnny's mother is an old cunt – and how the hell am

I meant to let Johnny Junior know when he's in the middle of the ocean somewhere?' Deborah shrieked. Her son was now a chef on one of those posh cruise ships.

'The company he works for will be able to let him know, Deb. I'll give them a bell tomorrow, and Johnny's mum. You can't deal with this alone. Jo's body will need to be identified and all sorts will have to be arranged.'

'The police are fucking useless. Why didn't they arrest Vinny and bring Ava home like I asked them to? How is the poor little mite gonna feel when she learns her mum is dead? She needs me, Sandy.'

The police had not long left the house. They'd heard Deborah out, making notes as she levelled accusations at Vinny, and had promised to pay him a visit. They'd said Joanna's car would need to be analysed and they'd appeal for witnesses if evidence proved Joanna hadn't simply lost control but had been involved in a collision with another vehicle. Shane was currently mute as a result of the shock and had been taken to hospital. DS Birch said he could prove to be a key witness in the case, but it was too soon to begin questioning the child.

'I thought the bloke was a bit drippy, Deb, but that DS Birch seemed clued up. Her old ears pricked up when you were saying all that stuff about Vinny, and she wrote loads in her notebook.'

'She never went and rescued Ava for me like I begged her to though, did she?' Deborah screamed, necking her brandy and slamming the glass against the coffee table with such force it smashed.

'Deb, it's not as easy as that, mate. In the eyes of the law, Vinny hasn't abducted Ava. He's her father.'

Queenie felt nothing but relief as she shuffled down the stairs in her fluffy Marks and Spencer slippers. Those stilettos she'd bought from Panache down the Roman had almost crippled her.

'Ava asleep?' Vivian asked.

'Went out like a light, bless her. Weren't she well behaved at the funeral?'

'She still not asked about her mum?' Vivian enquired.

'No. Just seems pleased to be able to spend a bit of extra time with us and her dad. It's weird Jo hasn't been in contact though, isn't it? Perhaps Nancy going missing has sent her a bit doolally and she fancied getting away or something?'

Having absorbed a skinful of sherry, Vivian couldn't contain her sarcasm any longer. 'Queen, it's me you're talking to, not one of the divvy neighbours. You know as well as I do Joanna will either turn up dead or never be seen again. Speaking of which, strange nobody mentioned Nancy at the funeral. I thought Michael might mention her in his speech.'

Queenie explained that Michael had purposely left Nancy's name out of his speech because he was worried Mary and Donald would turn up and Mary would kick off. 'As for Joanna turning up dead or never being seen again, I dunno what you mean. Vinny was in Southend all day on Sunday with us, so he can't have done away with her – if that's what you're insinuating,' Queenie replied shirtily.

'How very convenient. I don't wanna argue with you, Queen, so let's change the subject. How handsome is that Eddie Mitchell, eh? He even knocks spots off Dirty Den. I would, given half the chance, wouldn't you?'

CHAPTER THIRTY-FOUR

It was two days after Adam's funeral when Vinny was awoken by a fist pounding against his front door. He and Jay Boy had rented a flat not far from the club, although Jay Boy was rarely there these days as he spent most nights at his bird's gaff.

Guessing it was the Old Bill, as the only other person who knew where the flat was was Michael, Vinny yelled, 'Give us a minute. I need to put some clothes on.'

Vinny splashed his face repeatedly with cold water. He needed to be alert to face the filth. He put on his suit and peeped through the spy-hole before opening the door. 'Hello. How can I help you?'

DS Birch and DC Cooper flashed their badges, introduced themselves and asked if they could come inside.

'Would you like a cup of tea or coffee?' Vinny asked politely.

'No, thank you. We just want to ask you a few questions.'

Vinny slouched on to the armchair. 'Fire away then.'

DS Birch did the talking while her colleague put pen to notebook. 'We need to know your whereabouts on Sunday, Mr Butler.'

'I stayed at my mum's on Saturday night. Got up crack

of dawn, then took my mum, aunt, nephews and my daughter Ava to Southend for the day.'

'And what time did you leave Southend?'

'Just after five. My daughter doesn't live with me and I have to get her home by six. Her mum wasn't there though, so I hung about a bit, then brought Ava home with me. Once Ava had gone to bed, I popped round to the Blind Beggar for a couple of hours, then went back to me mother's. I stay at hers most weekends. Why? What's the problem?' Vinny asked, as cool as a cucumber.

'Where's your daughter now, Mr Butler?' Birch asked.

'At my mum's house. She's been looking after Ava while I'm at work. Her mother Jo's gone on the missing list, you see. Her best mate committed suicide recently and I think it might have sent Jo a bit funny. Grief does strange things to people. I've rung her about a dozen times and she hasn't replied to any of my calls. Do you mind telling me what this is about now? Only I have a club to open.'

'Joanna is dead, Mr Butler. It seems her car was involved in a fatal collision with another vehicle before plummeting into a ditch. Her boyfriend, Mr Darren Grant, also died in the accident. The only survivor was Shane, Mr Grant's son.'

Vinny was about to feign shock, but the mention of Shane made his reaction genuine. 'You're fucking kidding me! When did this happen? I can't believe it,' Vinny said, putting his head in his hands.

'We believe it happened on Sunday morning. Joanna was due to visit her mother, but never arrived. Obviously, we will need to check out your alibi.'

Vinny stood up and poured himself a brandy. 'Why would you think I had anything to do with it? Me and Jo weren't exactly Romeo and Juliet, but I would never hurt a woman, especially the mother of my child.'

'We are not accusing you of any wrongdoing, Mr Butler.

It is our job to investigate such cases and check out alibis.'

'I bet Jo's vindictive mother has been sticking her oar in and stirring the shit about me. Did she also tell you that her husband Johnny once tried to kill me? He accidentally shot my brother instead and paralysed him, which resulted in my bruv taking his own life. She hates me because her old man was banged up for shooting Roy. Well? Did she tell you all that?'

'I'm afraid I'm not at liberty to answer such questions.'

'You don't need to. I can guess. In future, when you listen to any of Deborah's poppycock, you really should check out your facts before you start accusing me of stuff.'

'Nobody is accusing you of anything, Mr Butler,' Cooper piped up.

Vinny smashed his fist against the door. 'I can't believe Jo's dead. How am I meant to tell Ava she ain't ever gonna see her mother again? I don't know what to say to her.'

'Actually, Mrs Preston has offered to break the news to Ava. She feels it would be more appropriate for her to take care of the child for the time being.'

'Over my dead body,' Vinny spat, his eyes blazing. 'Ava is my daughter. She stays with me.'

Mary Walker stared at the envelope. 'Will you read it to me, Donald?'

'I can't, Mary. You read it, darling.'

'Do you mind reading it to us? We spent yesterday at our grandson's grave, and it's all been a bit too much for us,' Mary said.

DC Maynard took the letter from Mary and read it out:

Dear Mum and Dad,
    By the time you read this letter I will hopefully have succeeded in ending my life. I'm so sorry to have put

you through such an ordeal, but life without Adam was too unbearable for me to even consider. When he died, part of me died with him and I just wanted to be with him. He needs his mum to look after him in heaven.

'Oh, Donald,' Mary sobbed.

'Do you want to read the rest yourselves?' DC Maynard asked. Most grieving parents preferred to read such letters in private, but this wasn't the first time he'd been asked to read one aloud.

Donald dabbed his eyes with a handkerchief. 'No. Please continue.'

Maynard cleared his throat.

Dad, I'm so sorry for not listening to you about Michael. You were spot on about that bastard from the very beginning, and I hope you'll forgive me for being too stupid to take your warnings seriously. You were only looking out for me, I know that now.

Mum, you were the most wonderful mother I could've ever wished for. Kind, supportive, generous. Simply the best.

I didn't want either of you to have to go through the trauma of my funeral, neither did I want you to spend hours at my graveside. That's why I've chosen Beachy Head.

I must end this letter now as I'm crying too much to continue. But always remember, even though I won't be with you in person, I'll always be with you in spirit.

Until we meet again.

All my love,

Nancy

'She put five kisses at the end as well,' DC Maynard said awkwardly.

Sobbing uncontrollably, Mary put her hand over her mouth and bolted from the lounge.

Ashen-faced, Jay Boy grabbed Vinny's arm. 'We need to talk. It's urgent.'

Vinny closed his office door. 'What's up?'

'Gnasher isn't happy, Vin. He had some local radio station on this morning and they were appealing for witnesses to come forward about you-know-what. There was a fucking kid in the car, and Gnasher don't mess with kids' lives. He said he told you that.'

Vinny held his hands up, palms facing outwards. 'I know. I only found out myself this morning when the Old Bill turned up at the flat. I swear to ya, that kid weren't at Jo's when I picked Ava up. I even asked Ava, making a bit of chit-chat, to be sure it would just be her and the boyfriend.'

'Well, Gnasher's going ballistic. He wants me to drop the balance of his money off. Said it's far too dangerous for you and him to meet up at the moment.'

'Shane's only about fucking five, Jay. He's hardly gonna be a credible eyewitness, is he? The kid's bound to have been sat in the back, so what's he gonna have seen? The car must've been in the ditch seconds after Gnasher clumped it.'

'Gnasher's more worried that the kid might die, Vin. Said he'll never forgive himself. They said on the radio the boy's in hospital.'

Vinny walked over to his safe, counted out another ten grand and put it in an envelope with the other he'd already checked. 'There's an extra ten grand in there to cover Gnasher's upset, OK? And you tell your pal none of this is my fucking fault. They must've picked the kid up on the way or something. It really isn't my problem.'

'When do you want me to take it to him?'

'Now. It might help ease his pain,' Vinny replied sarcastically. 'Oh, and hurry back. I've gotta meet Carl later to discuss the Tarkan situation. Then I'm taking a little drive out to Purfleet to check out the Turkish wonder's directions. You'll be OK locking up tonight, won't ya? I wanna spend some time with Ava later.'

'Of course, boss.'

Sandy let the police in, then went out the back garden to have a cigarette. She hadn't been able to leave Deborah's side, and was relieved Johnny Junior was flying home tomorrow. Sandy worked cash in hand on Pitsea market and couldn't afford any more time off.

Deborah's moods had been fluctuating between total despair and acute anger. Today was no different. 'Well? You arrested him yet? Where's Ava?' she spat at DS Birch.

'We cannot arrest Vinny Butler or anybody else, for that matter, with no evidence. What I can tell you is we've had a couple of phone calls today in response to our radio appeal, and a certain vehicle is of particular interest to us. It was apparently parked near where the accident occurred. The colour described to us also matches some paint forensics found on Jo's Fiesta. The scenes-of-crime officers believe that Jo didn't lose control but was hit with possibly quite some force by an oncoming vehicle.'

'Vinny drives a black Merc, but he wouldn't have used that. You need to check the whereabouts of all his associates as well as him,' Deborah insisted.

'Myself and my colleague paid Vinny a visit this morning. He's given us an alibi, which we're currently checking out.'

'Was Ava with him? How is she?'

'Ava wasn't there. Vinny said she was at his mother's house.'

Picking up a framed photo of Ava, Deborah hurled it against the wall. 'Queenie is nearly as evil as Vinny. You can't leave Ava with her. You need to get her away. The whole family is rotten to the core.'

'I'm so sorry, Deborah, but Vinny is Ava's father so we have no power to take her away. If you're seriously worried about the child's welfare then you should have a chat with Social Services, or perhaps a solicitor who will be able to help you get custody.'

Before meeting Carl, Vinny had an hour to kill, so he popped round his mum's to break the news. He'd already warned his mother that the Old Bill would probably be in touch asking if she was with him and where they were on Sunday, but he was careful what he said on phones, so told her just to be truthful and he'd explain all later.

'Where's Ava?' Vinny asked, as he let himself in.

'In the garden, playing. She was a bit bored, so I invited Stinky Susan's little girl in as company for her.'

'I don't want her knocking about with scum, Mother. She'll probably catch nits off that child.'

'Beggars can't be choosers, Vinny. There's not many kids her age live nearby for her to play with. Anyway, they're having a whale of a time. So what's going on?' Queenie asked, although she was sure she already knew the answer to her question.

'Have the Old Bill been round?'

'No. And I've been in all day.'

'Where's Auntie Viv?'

'Popped indoors for a nap.'

Relieved that his aunt wasn't about, as he knew she

would give him that knowing look, Vinny told his mother about the police knocking on his door this morning and Joanna's death.

'What a shock for you, boy,' Queenie said, hugging her strapping son.

'I've gotta go out in a bit, so I need to break the news to Ava now. If the Old Bill turn up and I ain't told her, they're gonna think it weird. They seem to view me as a suspect as it is, the arseholes.'

'How can you be a suspect? You were out with us all bloody day. I'll send young Destiny home and tell her to come back in an hour, OK?'

'Destiny! Is that her name?'

'Yes, love. Strange, isn't it?'

'Too fucking right it is, with that sow next door but one as her mother. The only destiny that poor kid'll get is being knocked up at fourteen or the dole queue.'

'Ava, Daddy's here, love. He needs to speak to you about something. Destiny, you pop home to your mum and I'll get Ava to give you a knock in a bit. Would you like to have your tea here with Ava later? How does sausages, chips and beans sound?'

Destiny beamed from ear to ear. Her mum rarely cooked and she usually lived on either jam, Marmite or fish-paste sandwiches. 'Yes, please!'

'Off you go then,' Queenie said, ushering the child out the front door. Ava would most certainly be shocked and upset after the bombshell Vinny was about to deliver, but Queenie hoped some company of her own age might help her through the grief.

'Daddy,' Ava squealed excitedly as she threw herself at Vinny. She loved spending time with her new family, but wished her dad wasn't at work so much as he was her favourite person in the whole wide world at the moment.

Vinny hugged his daughter. 'I've got some bad news for you, sweetheart.'

'Can't I have a real doggy one day?' Ava asked innocently.

Vinny wasn't the most compassionate man in the world, so he just came straight to the point. 'There's no easy way to say this, Ava, but Mummy has gone to live with Molly and the angels.'

Ava was confused. Her mum rarely spoke about Molly, but her dad and nan did and they had shown her loads of photos of her. 'But Mummy lives in Tillingham.'

'Help me out, Mum,' Vinny pleaded.

Queenie kneeled down in front of her granddaughter. 'Mummy's dead, love. She had an accident in her car. The police told Daddy today.'

When Ava began to sob, Vinny held the child close to his chest and stroked her hair. 'I'm sorry, Ava. But everything's going to be OK. Daddy and Nanny Queenie will look after you now.'

'But I want to see Mummy too,' Ava sobbed.

Shrugging, Queenie looked at Vinny. Seeing Ava so upset was awful, but both were thinking the same thing. She was only a nipper; therefore it wouldn't take her long to forget about her mother. The younger they were, the quicker the memories faded.

Michael Butler opened the letter and stared at the contents in horror.

Dear Unfaithful Husband,

I rue the day I ever met you and I mean that with all my heart. Not only did you and your family's lifestyle make me feel like I was going mad at times, Daniel is now off the rails thanks to you, and my beautiful Adam is dead.

I so hope you're proud of what you've achieved in life. Notoriety, money, a successful disco, a flash car, etc.

Good luck to the new lady in your life is all I can say. Because by jove she's going to need it.

Thanks for the life of misery,

Nancy

Instead of being angry, Michael cried his heart out.

Vinny Butler met Carl Tanner at the Albion pub in Rainham. It was a big old boozer and not one they looked particularly conspicuous in. Some of the pubs around Rainham and Dagenham were very cliquey. Vinny had arranged to meet somebody in the Cross Keys once and couldn't have been more stared at had he been an alien.

'Have you thought any more about what we spoke about? I promise I won't let you down,' vowed Carl.

Vinny sipped his Scotch. Frank had assured Vinny that he'd never mentioned him to Carl until recently and even then it had only been a fleeting comment. Carl had then confided in his uncle about the set-up and Frank had urged his nephew to allow him to warn Vinny via the Mitchells. 'I've decided to give you a chance, Carl. But I need you to prove yourself first. Call it initiation.'

'I'll do whatever it takes, Vinny.'

'I want you to phone Tarkan Smith tomorrow. You tell him you've got his dosh and arrange to meet him on Saturday night at eight in the car park of the Farmhouse Tavern. You tell him what you told me in that letter: if he breathes a word to anybody or brings anybody with him, then he won't see you. The lads will be waiting in a blue Transit van. Park as close to it as you can. You'll be driving a white Cortina. As soon as Tarkan gets out of his car and walks towards you, the lads are gonna leap out the back of the van and bundle him in. You jump in with 'em. Both motors are hooky, but make sure you wear gloves.'

Carl nodded. 'You gonna give me a job if all goes well?'

Vinny smirked. 'All depends how much bottle you've got. Only it'll be you killing your pal Tarkan, not me.'

Vivian wasn't one bit surprised when Queenie told her the news about Joanna's unfortunate accident. Why would she be with Vinny's track record? However, she did feel sorry for poor little Ava, who seemed very confused and upset. 'How about you help me and your nan make some fairy cakes? Have you ever made fairy cakes before?' Vivian asked, cuddling the child.

Ava shook her head. 'Is heaven far? Daddy said that's where Mummy's gone. Can we visit her there?'

Wanting to reply, 'Daddy won't be going to heaven when his time's up, he'll be going to hell,' Vivian bit her tongue and looked despairingly at her sister.

Queenie was worried about Ava. She hadn't wanted to play with Destiny again. Neither had she eaten the sausages, chips and beans she'd cooked her. Not knowing what else to say to cheer her granddaughter up, Queenie mumbled the words, 'How about Daddy buys you that real dog you've always wanted?'

For the first time since the news of her mother's death had been broken, Ava smiled.

Ahmed's directions were a bit sketchy, to say the least, so knowing the area like the back of his hand, Eddie Mitchell had offered to accompany Vinny. Eddie had been pleased when Vinny contacted him and asked for help in disposing of the bodies. That spelled no hard feeling between the families, which had reassured his father too. Vinny had also agreed to give Carl a chance to prove himself and

Eddie saw such a gesture as a mark of respect towards the Mitchells.

'Nice gaff you've got there, mate,' Vinny said, as Eddie got in the car. He hadn't even known Eddie's address until he'd rung him earlier to ask for help with Ahmed's badly drawn map.

'Yeah. Me and Jess like it round 'ere. It's quiet down these lanes. Only them pikey cunts the O'Haras lower the tone of the area.'

'Didn't your family have agg with that mob years ago?' Vinny enquired. He'd not had many dealings with gypsies himself, but the Mitchells' feud with the O'Haras was the stuff of legends.

Eddie Mitchell pointed to a house they happened to be passing, then the deep scar on his face. 'Jimmy O'Hara lives there. He's the cunt who gave me this, back in the day. I'll tell you all about it another time. Let's have a look at that map.'

Fifteen minutes later, thanks to Eddie's expert navigation skills, Vinny and Eddie stepped out of the car.

'Well, well, well. Your so-called Turkish pal certainly did his homework,' Eddie Mitchell said. Ahmed had chosen such a remote spot that even Eddie hadn't known this disused building existed until he'd worked it out via the map.

'Fucking desolate, ain't it?' Vinny said, taking a good look around.

'Definitely the perfect setting for a murder.'

Vinny grinned at Eddie. 'And a bit of torture.'

CHAPTER THIRTY-FIVE

Adrenalin pumping through his veins at the thought of wiping out Ahmed later that evening, Vinny Butler was up with the larks on the Saturday morning.

'Frightened the bleedin' life out of me, hearing that door creak open. What you doing here at this unearthly hour?' Queenie asked her son.

'I thought I'd take Ava out and get her that dog this morning. You sure you're OK with it?'

Queenie was far too house-proud to want to share her lovely home with a mutt. But Ava was missing her mum and if a dog cheered the child up, Queenie was willing to suffer it. 'Just make sure it's a little dog, Vin. I couldn't handle one of them big slobbering Alsatians like Fat Beryl's got. The smaller the better, and it's barred from the lounge. That's human domain only.'

Vinny nodded. 'I'll tell Ava. Proper put a smile back on her face, this will. Thanks, Mum, for everything.'

Daniel Butler scowled when his dad knotted his tie. 'I don't even wanna go, let alone wear this stupid thing,' he complained.

Michael sighed. Mary had rung him the other day and

coldly announced that a local church was holding a special service in honour of Nancy. She'd made it clear that he wasn't welcome, but said the boys were. 'It's one day out your life, Dan, and you're going out for a meal after the service.'

'Would rather eat beans on toast,' Daniel mumbled.

Michael put his hands on his son's shoulders. 'You're not a little kid no more, Dan. You'll go there today and do me and your mum proud. OK?'

'But I don't want to go, and neither does Lee. Mum's been eaten by the sharks and that was her choice. End of.'

Michael pointed a finger near to Daniel's face. 'You better learn some respect soon, boy, else me and you are gonna fall out big time. Your mother was a good person who loved you very much and today is about her, not you. Now do you fucking understand?'

Face like thunder, Daniel had little option other than to nod.

Jay Boy Gerrard was worried as he pulled up outside Elliot's nightclub. Gnasher had asked to meet him. If he was planning on starting a war with Vinny, Jay Boy already knew where his allegiances lay.

Gnasher was chomping on a sandwich and thankfully smiled as Jay Boy clambered inside his car. 'Thanks for coming. I didn't want to talk on the phone, nor leave things as they were. I've heard through the grapevine that boy's going to be OK. Bound to be left with mental scars, but there's sod-all we can do about that now. Tell Vinny I do believe his side of the story that the kid was picked up on the way. That would certainly explain the delay. The truck's been dealt with. Burnt out, then crushed. Are the bizzies still sniffing around your end?'

'Vinny's not heard from them since they checked his alibi out.'

'Good. We're probably best to keep our distance from one another for a while. Better to be safe than sorry. Only contact me if it's urgent, and do so from a call-box. I can always meet you here if necessary.'

Jay Boy shook Gnasher's hand. He was relieved his old pal had calmed down. The reason being, he'd have sided with Vinny if push came to shove. Jay Boy wasn't daft. He knew where his bread was buttered.

After visiting two pet shops where the dogs were all unsuitable, Vinny Butler drove his disappointed daughter to Aveley. When he'd been out with Eddie Mitchell the other day, he'd spotted a sign with an arrow saying 'Jack Russell/ Shih Tzu pups for sale'. Vinny was no expert on dogs, but he knew a Jack Russell was only small. He had no idea what a Shih Tzu looked like, but it could hardly be big if it had been mated with a Jack.

'Why couldn't I have that spotty dog, Daddy?' Ava whinged.

'Because it was a Dalmatian and they grow to the size of a horse, darling. We'll get you a doggy here instead,' Vinny promised, before mumbling the words 'For Christ's sake.' The sign advertising the dogs led to a gypsy site.

'Daddy, why aren't you stopping the car?'

'We can't buy a dog from here, sweetheart. I'll take you somewhere else.'

Already upset because of falling in love with the puppy in the pet shop, Ava pleaded with her father and cried.

Vinny put his handbrake on. 'OK. Seeing as we're here, we might as well take a look at the doggies.'

The first thing Johnny Preston did when he came through customs at Gatwick was ring his mother. 'Everything OK? I'll be home in a couple of hours.'

Shirley Preston couldn't bear to break the awful news to her son. 'Johnny, you need to go straight home to Deborah. She needs you and so does Johnny Junior.'

'What the hell's happened? And why is Johnny Junior home?'

'I can't talk right now. Deborah will explain all.'

Forced to sit in the front pew with his grandparents and Uncle Christopher, Daniel Butler felt his lip start to tremble. His mum committing suicide had happened so soon after Adam's death that he'd not really allowed himself to think about her.

When the vicar remarked how Nancy had cherished her sons, Daniel couldn't hold the tears back any longer. It had finally dawned on him that he would never see his mother again and he was so bloody angry with her.

Mary took a tissue out of her clutch bag and handed it to her grandson. She'd initially been fuming with him when the details of Adam's death had come to light, but had softened a bit now. Daniel was only a kid himself and unfortunately kids did stupid things such as running across train tracks. He was also the closest thing to Nancy she had left.

Lee squeezed his brother's arm. 'You OK, Dan?' he whispered.

Seething he'd been made to feel this way and show himself up by crying, Daniel interrupted the service by shouting out 'No, Lee. I ain't fucking OK. My mother chose to be eaten by the sharks rather than be our mum any more, so why are we sat 'ere mourning her? She's nothing but a selfish cunt.'

Appalled and humiliated, it was Donald who apologized to the shell-shocked vicar and marched his unruly grandson from the church.

*

Queenie and Vivian were perving over Dirty Den on *EastEnders* when Vinny arrived home with Ava and the puppy.

'Urgh, get it away from me,' Vivian insisted, as the new member of the family made a beeline for her.

'Vin, I said it ain't allowed in the lounge. What breed is it?' Queenie asked. The puppy was tiny. It had tan-and-white colouring and a strange comical face.

'It looks like a cross between a rat and a piglet,' Vivian squealed, as the puppy sank its needle teeth into her little finger.

Vinny picked the mutt up and placed it in his daughter's arms. 'It could be anything. Came off a pikey site. How weird is this, Mum? Do you remember Molly wanting a dog and saying she wanted to call it Fred?'

'Yes. How could I ever forget anything Molly said? I think she came up with that name because me and Viv kept talking about Freddie Starr when he appeared at Kings.'

'Well, we gets back in the car and I say to Ava, what you gonna call him? Her reply: Fred.'

Queenie smiled. 'That truly is fate, son.'

Vivian was less impressed by the strange-looking creature. 'Should've called it Ratpig,' she mumbled.

Young Shane Grant had been so traumatized by his ordeal, he hadn't spoken for days after the accident. The hospital staff had deemed him as unfit for questioning up until now, which was why DS Birch was currently pacing up and down the corridor.

Inside the small ward, Shane's mother stroked her son's hair. She and Darren hadn't seen eye to eye on most things, but she'd been as upset as anyone to learn the father of her child was dead. Shane had been through an awful experience and she just hoped her son wouldn't end up scarred for life. The thought of him alone and crying in the back of that car while Darren and Joanna were dead in the front was too awful to even think about.

DC Larcham studied Shane playing with the cars she'd given him. He seemed relaxed enough now, which was a good sign.

DS Birch put her ear to the door. Her team had now received six calls about a red truck that had been spotted close to the spot where Joanna and Darren had died, and Birch was certain this wasn't the type of vehicle that would have been racing along the Dengie Straight. She sensed some kind of foul play was involved, but unfortunately, the truck had not been traced, neither had anybody come up with a description of its driver.

Desperate for promotion, Birch wanted answers. Vinny Butler's calm denials and alibis hadn't fooled her. She actually believed Deborah Preston's theory could be true. Proving it and locking up Butler and his hitman would do her career prospects the world of good. That was why she'd assigned Larcham to the task of questioning Shane, rather than doing it herself. DC Larcham had a knack for getting information out of abused and shell-shocked children, patiently gaining their trust and having them tell her what had happened using toys or by drawing pictures.

Unable to hear the conversation and aware of a nurse keeping a stern eye on her, Birch moved away from the door. Five minutes later, her hopes of promotion were well and truly dashed. 'But he must remember something?' Birch prompted her colleague.

DC Larcham shook her head. 'The only thing Shane remembers is singing "Row, Row, Row Your Boat" before the impact. He has no idea of how the accident actually happened, I'm certain of it.'

*

Johnny Preston's heart was beating rapidly as he paid the cab driver. He'd convinced himself on the journey back to Burnham that either Johnny Junior was in trouble or Deborah had experienced some kind of mental breakdown.

Johnny's worst fears were confirmed the moment he walked through the door and his sobbing wife flung herself at him. 'You were right all along. I'm so sorry for not listening to you. Please forgive me.'

Shaking Deborah by the shoulders, Johnny asked, 'What the fuck you on about?'

'Joanna's dead, Dad. Her and Darren were killed in a car crash,' Johnny Junior explained bluntly.

Shaking like a leaf, Johnny grabbed his wife by the neck. 'Where's Ava?' he hissed.

'With that murdering bastard. He killed our princess, Johnny. I know he did. We need to get Ava back. She belongs to us now.'

Instead of comforting the stupid woman he'd twice married, Johnny slammed her head against the wall, then ran out the house.

Vinny and Michael Butler arrived at the disused building just after seven. They'd driven to Purfleet in a hooky van, and instead of their usual Savile Row suits both were wearing hooded tracksuits and gloves. 'Get all our tools out the back, Michael. We'll break in through a window round the side.'

'You were right when you said this was the perfect location. I wonder how the Turkish cunt found it?' Michael replied.

'Knowing that slippery bastard, he hunted high and low for somewhere to top me before choosing this gaff. Can't wait to see the look on his face when he realizes the boot's on the other foot. He told me yesterday he's borrowed a van off a pal to pick the bubbly up. You can guarantee Burak will be waiting in the back ready to jump out. Just shoot that cunt immediately, Michael, in case he's armed. I'm not too worried about torturing him. I do hope he dies a slow, painful death though. With a bit of luck, we can drag him inside and he'll be in agony as he watches me cut his cousin into pieces. I dunno whether to cut his tongue out first or chop off his cock. Whaddya reckon hurts the most?'

Michael winced. His brother was a sadistic bastard and never did anything by halves. 'Probably the cock, Vin.'

Having been a cool, calm and collected con-man most of his life, Carl Tanner felt no nerves whatsoever as he pulled up in the Farmhouse car park next to the blue Transit van. He already trusted Vinny implicitly, thanks to his Uncle Frank's views on the man. It was amazing in a way how fate had set up this situation. Frank was the only member of his family Carl had trusted enough to invite over to Spain and it had been after a few beers one night that Vinny's name had cropped up in conversation.

Carl had told Tarkan what vehicle he would be in and as soon as the slick green Mercedes-Benz swept into the car park just after eight, Carl flashed his headlights.

Peering through the side mirror, Jay Boy yelled the words 'Go, lads.'

Seconds later, a suited and booted shocked Tarkan Smith was bundled into the back of the blue Transit van.

Back in Whitechapel, Queenie Butler had started to bond with the new member of her family. So much so, that the ban on entering the lounge had already been lifted. Fred had frightened the life out of a couple of the not-rights' cats earlier and Queenie had clapped her hands with glee watching the nuisances scarper from the garden.

433

'Nanny, please can Fred sit on the sofa with us? He's crying,' Ava pleaded.

Queenie stroked her granddaughter's hair. Ava hadn't stopped smiling today, neither had she mentioned her mother. 'Whaddya reckon, Viv? I think Fred deserves a cuddle after chasing away Her Majesty and Prince Charles, don't you?' The nutters had named their six cats in honour of their idols. The other four were Johnny Cash, Willie Nelson, Patsy Cline and Dolly Parton.

Vivian locked eyes with Fred. She didn't like him at all. He kept staring at her and he'd bitten her twice already. She was sure he had an evil streak, just like Vinny. 'Up to you, Queen. But he won't be coming in my lounge or sitting on my sofa.'

'Pick Fred up then, Ava,' Queenie said.

Vivian squealed as the puppy lunged straight towards her and playfully sank his needle teeth in the end of her nose.

When Ava roared with laughter, so did Queenie. Fred was no ordinary mutt, that was for sure. He had character about him. A definite Butler.

Tarkan Smith was shaking like a leaf in a hurricane. What man wouldn't be, if they knew they were about to die? He cursed himself for not trusting his instincts. The moment Carl had contacted him, he'd thought about telling Ahmed. The only reason he hadn't was because he'd wanted to get his hard-earned dosh back before arranging to end the shyster's life.

All that had backfired now though. Here he was, tied up in a van with Vinny Butler's henchmen plus Carl and he had no idea where he was being driven to. His last roll of the dice was to plead with Carl's better side. 'How could you do this to me? I gave you that money to set yourself up in Spain, and I saved your life,' Tarkan said.

Knowing that Pete, Paul and Jay Boy would report every word to Vinny, Carl casually kicked Tarkan in the head. 'Then you tried to rip me off. Shut it, you cunt.'

Ahmed and Burak Zane chuckled as they listened to Little Vinny's confession again. Both were buzzing at the thought of Vinny's face when he heard it. 'What a way to die, Burak. Learning your son killed your beloved daughter before being beheaded yourself. Biding my time has not been easy, but it will be worth the wait to see him suffer such a fate. Leaving me for dead, then trying to blame me for Lenny's death is the biggest mistake Vinny Butler ever made.'

'I disagree,' said Burak. Then when his cousin's head whipped round in surprise, he grinned and added, 'Being a greedy, stupid Englishman who arranged to buy cheap champagne will be Vinny's biggest mistake. It's a shame we can't keep his head as a souvenir. I would like to have it stuffed and put on the wall next to my deer's head trophy.'

Sitting with his back to the wall, Vinny Butler was whiling away the time by reminiscing about the good old days.

'We look a right pair of muppets dressed like this, bruv. Remember the last time we got all dolled up in our tracksuits and went on a little ride in a van? I'll never forget that cunt Trevor Thomas squealing like a pig when I pulled his gnashers out with pliers one by one. And the sight of you, sawing his bleedin' hand off. We did good that night. He was still alive when we set him on fire,' Vinny chuckled.

Michael grimaced. Vinny's sense of humour truly left a lot to be desired at times. Unlike Ahmed, who actually deserved to be tortured, Trevor's only crime had been eloping with Vinny's first love, back in the early sixties. 'I still can't get over Nancy writing those terrible letters, bruv. I can understand her bitterness towards me, but you'd think she'd have said a proper goodbye to the boys.'

'You never told me you'd opened the boys' letter. What did it say?'

'It was short and none too sweet. Just told Daniel and Lee to make something of their lives and not end up like me. She didn't even say she loved them. I'm not letting 'em see it.'

'Good riddance to the fucking fruitcake. Just wipe her from your mind and start a new life with Bella. How's it going with you and her? Any plans to move in together?'

The sound of a vehicle approaching stopped Michael from replying. It was time for action, not small talk.

Tears rolled down Johnny Preston's cheeks as he read the local rag. His daughter and Darren had made the front page for all the wrong reasons. The Old Bill were appealing for witnesses and trying to trace the owner of a red truck. 'Useless bastards,' Johnny mumbled, before unscrewing the lid on the brandy bottle. Back in the sixties, Vinny had stabbed his best pal Dave Phillips in broad daylight and got away with murder. The filth had no chance whatsoever of convicting him for Jo's death. Vinny was far too cunning to have got his own hands dirty this time around. The driver of the red truck would most definitely have been a hitman, hired to carry out an act of such evil while Vinny was elsewhere making sure he had a rock-solid alibi.

Swigging the brandy as though it were water, Johnny started the engine of Deborah's car. He had her spare key on his own bunch and had driven off like a maniac after leaving the house. The car-lot would most certainly be deserted at this hour. It was time to make use of the gun he'd bought.

*

Vinny Butler grinned at the state of the jibbering wreck known as Tarkan Smith. The coward had already wet and crapped himself. 'Not very manly, are you, Tarkan? Only, I know if I was about to die, I'd like to go out in style.'

Tarkan was on his knees, sobbing. All he could think about was never seeing his wife and children again. 'Please, Vinny, don't kill me. I swear to you I'll do anything you ask. I will even kill Ahmed if you want me to. None of this is my doing. I didn't even know you.'

'Which is exactly why you shouldn't have got involved in business that had fuck-all to do with you, Tarkan. Hiring Carl's services for Ahmed to set me up is the biggest error of judgement you'll ever make,' Vinny said, kicking the man hard in the face.

'Our van's hidden, bruv. Pete, Paul and Jay Boy are all in position. Jesus! It's chucking up in 'ere. Has he shit himself?' Michael asked.

'Yes. The sign of a bold man, Michael. Please remind me, if we're ever in a similar situation, to keep my arse cheeks clamped together,' Vinny joked. He loved scaring people, especially ones who had wronged him, and Tarkan was a bigger coward than he could ever have imagined.

'Just finish him off, Vin, and we'll stick him in the back of the blue van before the other pair arrive,' Michael ordered. That had been the original plan.

Vinny handed Carl the machete. He wanted to test the man's nerve. 'Cut off his left foot, then slice him straight through the neck. You should be able to chop the head right off with that. Call it a test of strength.'

'Carl! Please don't do this. I helped you. Saved your life, you know I did,' Tarkan wept.

Carl Tanner had never actually killed anybody before, but as he carried out Vinny's orders, he could honestly say he felt no remorse whatsoever. Tarkan had taken liberties over the repayments due from their joint business venture and would no doubt have delivered him into Ahmed's hands to endure a fate like the one he was about to suffer, therefore he deserved to die.

Johnny Preston stared at the photos on his work desk in the car-lot office. One was a snap of him and Deborah celebrating their second wedding. The other, a wonderful shot of Joanna and Ava, both grinning and looking adorable.

Throwing the snap of him and Deborah on the floor, Johnny stamped on it until it was no longer recognizable. He'd loved her with all his heart, especially when she'd stuck by him in nick. But she was dead to him now. It was all her fault his beautiful daughter had been murdered.

No fight left in him, Johnny downed the rest of the litre bottle of brandy, then laid on the floor and placed his daughter and granddaughter's photo against his heart. Without them in his life, there was no point in going on. Ava was Vinny's property now, and that bastard would never allow him to see her again, that was a certainty.

Alcohol and grief clouding his judgement and urge for revenge, Johnny Preston placed the gun against the right-hand side of his head. 'You won, Vinny. But you won't in the next life,' he mumbled.

Smiling at the thought of seeing Joanna again, Johnny Preston pulled the trigger and blew his own brains out.

As expected, Ahmed Zane arrived at the disused building an hour before their appointment. Vinny was more than ready and waiting for him. All his troops were in place and, like a colonel addressing the ranks, Vinny had given them a final pep talk.

'Burak,' hissed Ahmed, 'the scum is here already. Just stay in the back until I give the word.'

Realizing Vinny was waiting for him to make the first move, Ahmed plastered a smile on his face as he stepped out of the van. 'You're early.'

Grinning like a Cheshire cat, Vinny replied, 'I decided to leave my motor at home and take the van to Eastbourne. Bloody thing's filthy and stinks of diesel – that's why I'm wearing this clobber. No way was I gonna ruin one of me designer suits.'

'How is Michael?' asked Ahmed.

'Devastated. So were Dan and Lee. Meself, I couldn't wait to get away from Beachy Head. As you well know, I was never that fond of Nancy. So I fucked off early and did a bit of shopping. Got some proper nice gifts for your little 'uns and Ava. Take the presents out my van now before we start loading the bubbly up.'

Slightly bemused to see Vinny in a tracksuit, yet still having no idea whatsoever that he was on to him, Ahmed happily trotted over to Vinny's van. What a nice surprise it would be for Vinny when they opened the door of his van to load the gifts and Burak leapt out and pointed a gun at his head.

Ahmed had never been more shocked in his life when the back doors swung open to reveal the sight of Tarkan Smith's severed bloodied head lying on the floor. 'Burak,' he yelled, gagging.

Michael Butler was in the perfect position to blast both of Burak's kneecaps to pieces. A submachine gun was a far better shooter than your average.

Deborah Preston had always considered herself a strong woman, but recent events had made her doubt her ability to cope any longer. 'I'm ringing the Old Bill, son. Your father's gone to kill Vinny, I know he has. I need to stop it before it happens. He can't go back to prison. I need him by my side.'

Johnny Junior snatched the phone our of his grieving mother's hands. He had never been that close to any of his family, which is why he'd chosen a career that took him as far away from them as possible, travelling the world. 'Mother, you're not thinking straight. If you ring the police and start spouting shit, you will make things a hundred times worse. Just go to bed for an hour or two and we'll decide what to do when you've sobered up.'

When his mother started crying, then screaming how much she loved his father, Johnny Junior put his head in his hands. Right then he'd have given anything to be back on a cruise ship instead of spending time with his dysfunctional parents.

Vinny Butler had to give credit where it was due. Apart from his initial shock at the sight of his beheaded friend, Ahmed had since acted with nerves of steel. Burak, however, had writhed and squealed in agony before passing out. 'Try and wake that shitbag up, Michael. I would hate him to miss out on all the fun,' Vinny ordered.

'Why don't you just get on with it, big man? You've already left me for dead once, so you might as well finish the job off. I don't know who is more of a coward. You, for trying to blame me for killing your cousin, or your evil son for throttling his own little sister. You must listen to his confession, Vinny. It will be music to your ears. Like father, like fucking son,' Ahmed goaded. He knew his time was up and was determined to die as he'd lived his life, with pride.

'I can't wake him up. I think he might've bled to death,' Michael said, having no joy in arousing Burak.

Vinny picked up the gun and without flinching blasted

Burak in the head. 'If he wasn't dead before, he sure is now. Drag him into the van, lads. Then start tidying up. Me and Michael'll be with you soon.'

When Jay Boy, Pete, Paul and Carl dragged his cousin's body from the building, Ahmed kept a stiff upper lip. Burak had been right all along. He should have dealt with Vinny years ago. Too late for regrets now though.

Once his troops had left the building, Vinny knelt down next to his enemy. 'Little Vinny never killed Molly. You know that as well as I do. He told me all about you forcing him into a confession. He also said you'd told him I killed Karen, you Judas cunt.'

'If you believe that, then I'm fucking Allah. Yes, I did tell your warped son about Karen, but only to get the truth out of him. I'd known he'd been harbouring some massive secret. Like it or not, Vinny, your son murdered your daughter. Listen to the confession, then you'll believe me.' Seeing the look on Vinny's face, Ahmed chuckled. 'I actually think he is more evil than you. You wronged him by wiping out his mother and he's wronged you twice as much by killing your perfect little Molly. Fact!'

'Where's the tape?' Vinny spat.

Cool as a cucumber, Ahmed replied, 'In the van. It was actually the same equipment I used to tape my conversations with Christopher Walker. He was going to be the one who made the drugs bust that would put you away. But then your son killed Molly and put paid to our plans. Go on – listen to the tape, listen to it in front of me. That's my dying wish.'

Michael Butler was horrified. Not only did Ahmed's story about Karen ring true, but he had somehow roped Nancy's brother into all this – or so he claimed. He had to be lying though, surely? No way did his nephew throttle his niece. That was absurd.

'Go get the fucking tape, Michael,' Vinny ordered. He was fuming that Ahmed wasn't blubbering and begging for forgiveness the way he'd envisaged.

As soon as Michael returned with the recording equipment, Vinny smashed it to smithereens. His son was no angel like Molly had been, but no way could he have killed her. Jamie Preston had done that. The Old Bill had him bang to rights.

'Finish him off, Vin, and let's get out of 'ere. Time's ticking on,' Michael urged. He'd started to get the heebies now. Ahmed was far too cool for his liking and he wondered if he had back-up on the way.

Ahmed's hands and legs were tied up with rope. 'Poke that lying tongue of yours out, cunt,' Vinny ordered.

'Make me,' Ahmed hissed.

Trying to pull Ahmed's tongue out of his mouth was no easy task, so Vinny unzipped his enemy's trousers instead.

Ahmed's cool persona left him as his penis was sliced off. His screams were that horrific, Michael picked up the gun and ended the man's misery immediately.

'Whaddya do that for? I hadn't finished with him yet,' Vinny growled.

'Which is exactly why I shot him. Knowing you, Vin, you'd have been here until midnight chopping every limb off. Let's clean up and get the fuck out of here.'

CHAPTER THIRTY-SIX

'Happy Birthday, boy. I cannot believe at this very moment forty years ago I was in bleedin' agony trying to push you out. How time flies, eh?'

Vinny Butler grinned and held the woman he loved so dearly close to his chest. She'd given him the same speech every birthday he could remember, but this year she'd forgotten to add that his useless arsehole of a father was pissed and out whoring at the time. 'Bless ya, Mum. Where's Ava?'

'Where d'ya think? Out in the garden with her furry friend. That little sod's getting naughtier by the day. Chewed my Marks and Spencer slippers up yesterday. Might have to take him to Battersea Dogs Home soon,' Queenie joked. She was actually just as besotted with the funny little mutt as Ava was.

Vinny chuckled. His daughter was obsessed with Fred and thankfully seemed to be well over her mother's death. She'd rarely mentioned Joanna recently, nor Nanny Deborah or her dead Granddad Johnny. What a moment that had been when Vinny had learned Preston had blown his own brains out. He and his mother had celebrated into the early hours in honour of Roy. 'You're gonna have to enrol Ava in a school soon, Vin. I know you don't want her going to one round 'ere, but I think your idea of a private school is an awful one. She'll be like a lost sheep amongst all those posh kids. She's not one of them, she's one of us.'

'This area's gone so far downhill, Mum. I just want the best for Ava.'

'I understand that. But Ava will be far more comfortable starting at the local infants' with Destiny. I know you don't like Stinky Susan, and neither do I, but them little 'uns get along so well. You can always consider sending Ava private once she reaches Juniors. She's gonna be devastated to be parted from Fred in the daytime as it is, and you have to remember all the other kids are gonna have their mums taking them to and from school. Bound to bring back memories of Jo. And we don't want that, do we? At least if she goes to school locally, I'll be able to take her and pick her up with Fred.'

'You do have a point, but let's discuss this another time. I woke up with mixed emotions this morning and kind of wished I hadn't arranged a do for meself. I couldn't stop thinking of Molly. It don't seem right to be celebrating without her, Roy, Champ and Adam present.'

Queenie stroked her son's cheeks. 'The past is the past, boy. We can't change that. But we have plenty to be thankful for and to look forward to. Far more than most. Let's celebrate your birthday in true Butler style. Even your Auntie Viv has agreed to attend. Told you she'd come round one day, didn't I?'

Michael Butler ordered Daniel and Lee to sit on the sofa. He knew he should have said something beforehand, but these past couple of weeks had been manic and it just never seemed to be the right moment to break the news. Especially

444

after the fiasco Daniel had caused at Nancy's remembrance-of-life service.

'What's up, Dad? We're still going to the party, aren't we?' Lee asked.

'Yeah. Course we are. Actually, it's the party I wanted to speak to you about. I've invited a lady friend of mine and she's bringing her little boy. I want you to be nice to them. You OK about that?'

'You got a new bird, Dad?' Daniel asked bluntly.

Michael chose his words carefully. 'Bella's a lovely lady and very special to me. She's helped me cope with what happened to Adam and your mum.'

'How old's her son? What's his name?' Lee enquired.

'Antonio's four. He's a nice kid.'

'Bella's definitely your new girlfriend, Dad. I can tell,' Daniel said cockily.

'It's too early after your mum for me to have a proper girlfriend, Dan. But I do really like Bella. The future all depends on if you and Lee get on with her and Antonio. I'll always put yous two first, you know that.'

'As long as Bella ain't a nutter like Mum was, I'm OK about it. What do you reckon, Lee?' Daniel asked chirpily. Since he'd embarrassed himself in front of his mother's parents, who had severed all contact with him as a result, Daniel had put Nancy totally out of his mind.

Lee shrugged. Unlike his brother, who didn't seem to care that his own mother was dead, he still missed Nancy. However, he wanted his dad to be happy too.

'I'm OK about it,' he mumbled.

Bella D'Angelo wasn't usually a woman to suffer from nerves. She had strutted up and down catwalks all over the world, brimming with confidence. However, the thought of meeting Michael's entire family today for the very first time was making her feel nauseous. So much so, she'd spent an hour on the phone to a friend earlier discussing outfits and the big occasion. What if Michael's sons hated her? Or his mother? Where would that leave the relationship with the only man she'd ever truly loved?

'Why do I have to wear this, Mummy? It hurts my neck,' Antonio complained. He didn't mind the suit and shirt he was being forced to wear, just hated the tie.

'Because we want to make a good impression in front of Michael's family,' Bella explained. She'd chosen to wear a long red halter-neck dress. It was less provocative than her usual choice of clothing. She'd bought it especially for the occasion, as she would hate Michael's family to see her as some tart. As her father had always drummed into her, first impressions truly count.

Anna Zane smiled as the last of her belongings were loaded into the removal van. Three weeks had gone by since her husband had disappeared into thin air and Anna knew in her heart he was dead. It was too much of a coincidence that both Burak and Tarkan had gone missing at the same time for there to be any other explanation. That's why Anna had decided to put the house on the market and rent a smaller property. There were far too many bad memories for her and the children to stay here.

Ahmed had never been a great husband, or father. He'd spent most of his time away from his family and Anna knew without a doubt he'd messed around with other women. She'd smelled their scent on his clothes and Ahmed had rarely wanted sex with her. He'd been a good provider though, which was why Anna had suffered him. Her children would always come first and they had loved their father on the odd occasions they'd spent quality time with him.

'You OK, Anna?' her mother asked.

Anna Zane was more than OK. She was now a very wealthy woman and glad to be rid of the vile man she'd married. Unbeknown to him, he'd even once given her a sexually transmitted disease.

Anna took one last look around before shutting the front door. What she didn't realize as she trotted down the huge driveway was that Ahmed had kept a secret safe inside the abode. And not only did that safe contain a huge amount of money, it also contained the truth about Molly Butler's death.

Vinny Butler was savouring his first Scotch of the day. His mother was right. The past couldn't be changed, but he still had plenty to be thankful for. Which was why he was now determined to enjoy his birthday.

It had been a hectic month. The biggest killing spree he'd ever been on in such a short spell. The police had never returned to interrogate him about Joanna, which was hardly surprising since he'd had the perfect alibi. They had checked it out thoroughly, asking for the name of the boozer where his family had eaten lunch in Southend and even questioning Ava, Daniel and Lee. It got them nowhere, the mugs.

The Old Bill didn't seem anywhere near as bothered about Ahmed, Burak and Tarkan's disappearance. They'd paid Vinny only one visit, saying they knew he and Ahmed were good friends and asking when was the last time he'd seen Ahmed. Vinny had told the police they were still good pals but, since opening their separate business ventures, they didn't see one another anywhere near as much as in the old days. Vinny had also informed the police that he'd never met Tarkan, neither had he ever socialized with Burak except in Ahmed's company.

Michael's arrival snapped Vinny's thoughts back to the

present. 'Happy birthday, bruv. I didn't wanna take this to the restaurant in case it got lost among all the other gifts.'

Vinny was bowled over by the Rolex watch. It was a beauty. 'Fucking hell! I weren't expecting that. It's mint,' Vinny said, taking his old watch off and putting the new one on. After being at one another's throats for years, it was a good feeling to have all their differences sorted and behind them.

'You're the only brother I've got now, Vin, and forty is a special birthday. Just make sure you're as extravagant when I reach your ripe old age,' Michael chuckled.

Vinny grinned. 'I've got a present for you an' all. And it's just as extravagant,' Vinny said, handing his brother an envelope.

Michael's eyes widened as he read the official document. Vinny had signed away his percentage of their old club, so he was now the sole owner. 'I dunno what to say. Why now?'

'Because the time felt right. Ahmed put a lot of obstacles between us, and you're the clever bastard who sussed out he was a wrong 'un long before I did. You also made a major success of turning the gaff into a disco, so I know it's in good hands. Most of all, you've backed me whenever I've asked for your help. All in all, you're a top fucking brother, Michael Butler, and I love ya to death.'

Tears in their eyes, Vinny and Michael shared a brotherly hug. They also vowed never to let anybody or anything come between them ever again.

'Viv, you look stunning! Peach don't 'arf suit you,' Queenie gushed, admiring her sister's dress.

'Thanks. You look beautiful too,' Vivian replied lamely. She wasn't looking forward to the party at all. She had only agreed to go for Queenie's sake. Albie was dreading it as well. Viv had bumped into him down the market yesterday and they'd commiserated, as they always did before a family event involving Vinny.

'I can't wait to meet Michael's new girlfriend. Little Vinny's bringing his future in-laws too. Plus our handsome Eddie Mitchell's gonna be there.'

For the first time that day, Vivian cracked a smile. 'Let's hope Eddie doesn't bring his wife with him. I want him all to my bleedin' self!'

Vinny Butler had decided to organize his own fortieth bash for a reason. He'd guessed that, if he didn't arrange something, his family would surprise him. And if there was one thing Vinny hated in life it was being surprised. Neither did he want people attending who he had no desire to socialize with.

Nick's restaurant in Stratford was the venue Vinny had chosen. He and Ahmed both owned a stake in the business after buying it for Nick to run in the first place, so to celebrate his birthday there appealed to Vinny's warped mind. Ahmed screaming as he'd chopped his penis off was a moment Vinny would cherish for ever.

'The venue looks the nuts, Vin. I've escorted your family inside. Funny pair, your mum and aunt. Never fail to make me laugh,' Carl Tanner said.

'Tell me about it,' Vinny mumbled, checking his appearance one last time. His hair Brylcreemed back as always, Vinny had treated himself to a new dark-grey Armani suit. Accompanied with a crisp white shirt and shiny electric-green tie that matched his eye colour, Vinny couldn't help but think what a handsome bastard he was.

'You ready to make tracks?'

'Yep,' Vinny replied, slapping the new member of his workforce on the back. Carl now worked at his club in the same role as Pete and Paul. Vinny actually liked the guy, but had made it clear to the Mitchells that if Carl ever fucked up, he wouldn't be given a second chance.

Vinny had been well impressed with Carl on the night of the cull. Not only had the guy sliced Tarkan up as calmly as a butcher slaughtering a cow, he'd also driven the van with the dead bodies to its pick-up point.

Vinny had no idea of the name of the geezer who'd disposed of the Turks, but Eddie Mitchell had assured him all had gone smoothly and not so much as a chip of bone or a tooth would ever come to light. Vinny had settled up via Eddie. Ten grand per body, the mystery man had charged.

The DJ Vinny had hired for the occasion had been tipped off that he'd arrived, so as he walked into the restaurant Vinny was greeted by Stevie Wonder's 'Happy Birthday' belting out the speakers. Lots of clapping, cheering, pats on the back and handshakes followed.

Waiters were walking around with trays of champagne plus alternative beverages, and Nick and his chefs had organized a wonderful array of food.

'Happy birthday, Dad. This present is from me and Sammi, and the smaller one's from Ollie,' Little Vinny said. He'd been a bit miffed at first when he'd found out his father had dealt with Ahmed without telling or involving him, but now he was just relieved it was all over. He'd been told no details of what had occurred on the night, but his dad assured him that Ahmed and Burak wouldn't be seen again and that his forced confession had been destroyed without him even bothering to listen to it.

Obviously, Little Vinny was still concerned that Ahmed had made copies of the taped confession, but those could be anywhere and there was nothing he could do about it. Instead of worrying about that, he'd made up his mind to forget about the past as best he could and concentrate on the future. He and Sammi-Lou had booked their wedding for next June and they'd already discussed having another child soon afterwards. Working for his father was another bonus. Little Vinny loved his new job and it paid far more than his previous one.

'Come and say hello to Sammi's parents and sister, Dad. They've got a present for you too.'

'I'll be over in a bit, boy. Just give all the gifts to Nick. He's gonna keep 'em safe out the back for me.'

Vinny grinned as he did the rounds, shaking the men's hands and politely kissing the ladies. He'd kept the numbers down, only invited the elite. His sister Brenda wasn't one of those. No way did Vinny want her there, spoiling the good family name.

Pete, Paul and Jay Boy had brought their other halves and nippers. The Mitchells were also there with their families, including Eddie's older sons, Gary and Ricky, and Jessica's brother Raymond who was part of the Mitchell firm.

Greeting his loyal cleaner Edna, Vinny then moved over to the Kelly brothers, who were chatting to his brief Colin.

'Daddy, Fred just bit Auntie Viv again,' Ava said, tugging her father's trouser leg in a fit of giggles. Ava had been heartbroken at the thought of Fred being left at home all alone, so Vinny had allowed her to bring him to the party with her.

Vinny picked his daughter up and swung her in the air. 'That's 'cause Fred is a legend, just like your daddy, angel.'

Vivian sidled over to Albie clutching a handkerchief to her little finger. 'That mutt's as evil as Vinny. Just nipped me again. Only he could've chosen that bastard ratpig. You bought golden boy a present?'

'Just a bottle of Scotch. You?'

'Nothing. Not even a card. Can't believe I agreed to come. My Lenny's never gonna reach forty, thanks to him, so what am I doing 'ere?'

Aware of the anger in Vivian's voice, Albie patted her on the back. 'I'm not sticking up for Vinny, Viv. As you well know, I'm no fan of my own son. However, he did idolize your Lenny. Made a stupid decision to drive a car drunk and drugged up, but he would never have harmed that boy purposely, like he did me that time.'

'I'm hardly gonna forgive him though, am I, Albie?'

'No. But bitterness eats away at you, Viv. I should know, I've been there. Just eat, drink and be merry with Queenie today. No point going home now you're here, is there? I might even get up and sing "Spanish Eyes" later. How's that grab ya?' Albie winked.

Vivian chuckled. 'Even when I hated you back in the day, Albie Butler, I always said you had a smashing voice. You sing it like Al Martino and I'll definitely stay.'

'Where's Michael, Mum? Daniel and Lee are sat with Eddie Mitchell's twins, but I can't see me bruvver anywhere. Perhaps he's out the back giving his bit of fluff a sneaky one? Whaddya reckon?' Vinny chuckled.

Queenie nearly choked on her sherry. 'Stop being so rude! And don't you dare tell Bella that we used to call him Alfie,' she insisted.

Vinny strolled over to his nephews and smiled as he overheard Daniel ask Frankie Mitchell if she had a boyfriend. 'Sorry to interrupt. Where's your old man, lads?'

'Gone to pick his new bird and her son up. We're cool about it, ain't we, Lee?' Daniel replied, in a grown-up manner.

'So how did yous two get here?' Vinny enquired.

'We was gonna make our own way 'ere, but Pete offered

452

to pick us up so we snapped his hand off,' Daniel replied brazenly.

Vinny Butler laughed as he walked away. His nephew was a chip off the old block, all right. What's more, it looked as if he had his first major crush in life, and of all the girls to hit on, he'd chosen Eddie Mitchell's daughter.

Bella D'Angelo was even more edgy now than earlier. Antonio had only ever been travel-sick once before, but today he'd managed to vomit not just over himself, but also over her new red dress. Hence Michael had had to drive them all the way back to Chelsea to get cleaned up and changed. 'I'm so sorry, Michael. About your car and making you late for your own brother's party.'

'Bella, calm down. I've never seen you like this before. My family are cool, they're gonna love ya. I'll explain what happened. Antonio's not the first child to be sick in one of my motors, you know. Adam, God rest his soul, did it regularly.'

'Are you sure you feel OK, Antonio? Give Mummy plenty of warning if you think you might be sick again,' Bella gabbled. Madam Lydia had once told her if she ever started a journey and a vehicle broke down or something went wrong, it was an omen and that journey should not be continued.

'Yes, Mummy. I'm fine. Stop asking me.'

Bella smiled at her son. He now had a dark suit on and looked so grown-up and handsome. She had changed into an electric-blue number that suited her eye colour. 'Are you sure I look OK, Michael? I much preferred the red dress.'

'You look beautiful. How could you look anything but? Now read that,' Michael urged, showing Bella the deeds to the club Vinny had given him this morning.

'That's brilliant, Michael. So it's all yours now?'

Michael winked. 'Yep! And half yours, when I get to marry you one fine day.'

The DJ Michael had recommended wasn't much cop in Vinny's eyes. He was playing too much recent chart crap. Madonna's 'Into the Groove' was the final straw, so Vinny marched over to him. 'Make the next record your last, then Ted's gonna finish the party off, mate.'

'I know Michael said you wanted some older tunes played, but I was gonna save the likes of Elvis and the Beatles for later. You have to cater for the youngsters too,' the DJ replied.

Vinny glared at the fat bastard. 'If you play Elvis it will upset my Aunt Viv because he was her son's idol and her son is now dead. And I never liked the Beatles; I was more of a Rolling Stones man. So just do as I say, OK?'

Scared by the vicious look on Vinny's face, the DJ nodded.

Within minutes, Teddy Brown stood at the other end of the restaurant and began his set with Sinatra's 'That's Life'. Ted had been one of Vinny's regular crooners back in the good old days at the original club. He used backing music and allowed others to get up and sing as well.

Vinny walked over to his mother, who was busy taking photographs. 'I remembered you and Auntie Viv loving Ted singing at the club back in the sixties, which is why I booked him. He might be knocking on a bit now, but he's still got it, ain't he?'

'Definitely! Oh look, there's Michael.'

'So sorry I'm late, bruv. Bella's little 'un spewed up all over himself, her and my motor, so we had to shoot back to West London to clean up. Only ever been travel-sick in his life once before, by all accounts. Trust my fucking luck!' Michael laughed.

Queenie stood up. 'Where is Bella then?' She was desperate for a first glimpse of the woman who had stolen Michael's heart.

'Gone to the toilet to powder her nose. You know what women are like, Mum.'

'I'll be back in a tick. Little Vinny's waving at me. I've made the fatal mistake of forgetting to greet the future in-laws,' Vinny grinned. After dreading his party earlier, he was having a great night now.

'Oh my lord, Michael! She's absolutely beautiful! Vivvy, what an angel, look!' Queenie exclaimed, as the striking dark-haired woman gracefully walked towards them.

'Stunning!' Vivian agreed, as Michael put a protective arm around Bella's waist before formally introducing them.

'I'm so very pleased to meet you,' Antonio said, before standing on tiptoes to kiss Queenie and Viv on both cheeks.

'Oh, bless him. What a gorgeous, polite boy. He's adorable, Bella,' Queenie gushed.

Bella smiled proudly. She'd taught her son the art of good manners from the moment he'd started to walk and talk. Her father always insisted that the younger a boy was taught how to behave impeccably, the better a man he would become.

Sidling over towards her grandmother, Ava grinned at Antonio and he grinned back. 'This is my doggy, Fred. Would you like to play with him?'

'And what's your name, sweetie?' Bella asked, crouching down.

'That's Ava. My brother Vinny's daughter,' Michael explained. He could tell his mother and aunt were already as besotted with Bella as he was. So far so good, he thought.

Aware that Fred seemed to be sniffing around and hovering as though he was about to have a dump, Queenie leapt out of her seat and clapped her hands. 'Take Fred outside to play. Quickly!' she screamed. She'd hate to be shown up in front of Bella, and knew there was a small yard at the back of the restaurant that was enclosed and safe.

'Is it OK if I go outside and play with Ava and Fred, Mummy? Please?' Antonio pleaded.

'The yard's perfectly safe, Bella. There's a six-foot fence with barbed wire along the top. However, I can tell my mother and aunt are already bowled over by you. So I'll keep an eye on the kids and leave them to give you a good old grilling,' Michael chuckled.

Bella had no idea what a good old grilling meant, but her earlier nerves had now completely disappeared. Queenie and Vivian had given her such a warm welcome, one she hadn't expected after Nancy's death. 'Shouldn't I meet your sons first, Michael?'

As Fred crouched down to do his business, Queenie had no option but to kick the dog up the arse to stop him from fouling next to Bella's expensive-looking shoes. 'Plenty of time to meet the boys later, lovey. Take the dog and children outside now, Michael!'

When her son did as he was told, a relieved Queenie sat back down and patted the seat next to her for Bella to sit on. Trying to make herself heard over Ted singing Tom Jones's 'Delilah' wasn't an easy task. 'So tell me and Vivvy all about yourself, my dear. You have a beautiful accent, may I say. Where is it exactly you come from? And what do your parents do? I can already tell you're a fabulous mother. Antonio is a credit to you. What did his father do? And are you still in contact with him?'

Jokingly, Vivian yawned at Queenie, then winked at Bella. 'Please excuse my sister. When she gets on the sherry, she has a terrible habit of asking too many questions at once.

I've always told her she'd be great on *Mastermind* if Magnus ever decided to retire.'

Bella burst out laughing. Now she knew where Michael got his one-liners and sense of humour from. It was weird. She had only just met Michael's family, yet already felt part of the clan.

'Can we have the birthday boy up 'ere for a speech?' Ted announced over the mike.

'He's sodded off somewhere, probably talking skulduggery with my brother,' a drunken Ronny Mitchell shouted back.

'Shut your trap, son,' Harry Mitchell ordered. Ronny was the bane of his life. Never failed to embarrass him.

'OK, in that case, let's have Albie Butler up to sing.'

'He do sound like Al Martino, Queen. I know you hate him, but he could've been a professional singer,' Vivian said.

'No, he couldn't! The man is a drunken tosspot, Viv,' Queenie hissed.

Bella couldn't stop smiling. She had been to many events and parties in her time, but never one like this. It had such a cockney feel to it and had given her a wonderful insight into the man she loved so much. She had even tasted jellied eels for the first time ever, and learnt some of the words to 'Knees Up Mother Brown'. Antonio was having a ball as well. He, Ava and Fred the dog had been inseparable since the moment they had met.

Michael's sons had been polite to both her and Antonio when introduced, and Bella had taken to Albie instantly. She could tell Queenie hated him, but the whole family was hilarious and reminded Bella of something out of a comedy show.

'You OK, babe?' Michael asked, squeezing Bella's hand.

'I'm having a fabulous time, Michael. Your family are wonderful.'

'Let's grab another glass of champagne and stand near Ted. Vinny's gonna give a speech in a minute and little does he know I'm gonna jump up, grab the mike and cane him with my own speech afterwards. You been introduced to him yet?'

'No.'

'And so the wanderer returns,' Ted joked, as he spotted Vinny Butler. 'Come and give us a speech, birthday boy.'

About to do so, Vinny locked eyes with the stunning woman holding his brother's arm. He then dropped the mike in shock. She'd told him her name was Izzy. He'd not only fucked her senseless, but she'd asked him to take her in a brutal manner. The games they played that night still made him hard. He'd never forgotten her. How could he? No woman had ever made him come like she had.

'Whatever's wrong?' Michael asked, as his girlfriend vomited and seemed unsteady on her feet outside the restaurant. She had just bolted from inside, with her hand over her mouth.

How Bella held it together she did not know, but she had no option other than to lie. 'I was nervous about meeting your family and I've obviously drunk far too much champagne. Please put Antonio in the car, Michael, and pick me up from here.'

'Do as the lady says, Michael. I'm Vinny, your beau's brother, by the way. I'll look after you.'

Once Michael had darted off to find Antonio, Vinny Butler smirked. 'Well, well, well. I wasn't expecting you to be the famous Bella. You told me your name was Izzy.'

'My real name is Isabella. Please don't tell Michael about us, Vinny. It was a drunken one-night stand. I love your brother so very much and it would destroy him if he found out.'

Having supped far too many Scotches, Vinny shoved Bella against the wall, stuck his tongue down her throat, then put his hands around her neck. 'Memories, memories. I've never forgotten that tight little pussy of yours. Nor your mouth around my cock. Wanna suck it again now, do ya?'

Pummelling her fists against Vinny's chest, Bella screamed, 'You fucking bastard.'

Vinny chuckled. He actually had a slight erection. Goading her made him feel horny. 'Don't you be worrying that pretty little head of yours, sweetheart. Your dirty secret is safe with me. Only just got back on track, me and Michael. No way will I allow a whore like you to come between us. I'm warning you, though. You ever hurt him, I will stick a knife up that precious cunt of yours and slice your insides to shreds. Understand?'

When Vinny Butler released his grip on her, Bella crouched down and sobbed her heart out. Madam Lydia had warned her of an evil man who would come between her and Michael. Now she knew who. He was standing right in front of her.

CHAPTER THIRTY-SEVEN

Michael Butler kissed Bella, then waved her and Antonio goodbye. Bella's grandmother had fallen seriously ill, hence their trip back to Italy at such short notice.

Driving away from the airport, Michael's mobile phone rang. 'You OK, bruv? Mum's offered to cook us a roast, so I said we'll be there. Dan and Lee are coming,' Vinny informed him.

'Yeah. Fine by me. I've just dropped Bella off at the airport. She's been a bit weird with me since your party, Vin. Did you ask around to see if anybody upset her?'

'Bella obviously feels embarrassed because she got drunk, Michael. She must have been nervous about meeting us all. I asked around and nobody said sod-all to upset her.'

'You're right. It's a lot to take on, meeting all the family at once, especially the boys. And I was plying her with champers like it was going out of style. My battery is about to die. What time's Mum cooking dinner for?'

'Three.'

'OK. See you there.'

Vinny Butler flopped on the armchair, put his hands behind his head and reminisced.

It was the end of August 1980 when he'd met Izzy, or Bella as she was now known. He remembered the timeline so well, because not only had he got into a fight down at Kings the weekend he'd met her, it wasn't long afterwards that Molly had been murdered.

He and Ahmed had been on a proper bender in some glitzy West End club. They'd been planning on ending the evening at a whorehouse, until they'd met these two fit birds. Bella had looked jaw-droppingly gorgeous and, unusually for Vinny, he hadn't been able to take his eyes off her. Apart from Yvonne Summers back in the day, Vinny could never remember a bird having such an effect on him.

The experience that followed was explosive and mind-blowing. Vinny was not a man with your average sexual taste. He liked it brutal, which was why he usually shagged brasses. However, Bella had a warped mind to match his own. She'd demanded he pretend to be a rapist and take her by force the moment they'd entered the hotel room.

Vinny had no hesitation in participating in such role-play and Bella had fought back hard. She'd bitten, kicked and punched him, which had turned him on no end. He'd finally restrained her by tying her arms to the bedposts, before shoving his throbbing cock in her mouth, then fucking her senseless. His orgasms that night had been truly memorable. So much so, Vinny had debated whether to return to the West End to try and track Bella down. He would've definitely asked to see her again had she not crept out the hotel room when he'd drifted off to sleep.

Thinking back to his party, Vinny smirked. Bella's face when he'd kissed and threatened her outside had been a picture. He'd guessed that the whore would give Michael some cock-and-bull story, then scarper. She could hardly stay with a man whose brother she'd shagged, could she? It wasn't morally right.

*

461

Isabella D'Angelo was greeted by her parents as she and Antonio arrived in Sicily. She'd hated her name from an early age, and had called herself Bella ever since. The only time she used Izzy was when meeting people she had no desire to see again.

When her mother began to pry, Bella assured her all was OK. What else could she say? That she'd met the family of the man who she loved and wanted to marry and was upset because she'd once fucked his brother's brains out?

Clutching Antonio to her chest in the back of her father's Limo, Bella allowed her mind to wander back to that fateful night.

She'd been on a short trip to London. New York had been her home at the time. She and her friend Patti were tipsy, and as soon as Bella had laid eyes on Vinny, he'd reminded her of Michael. The way he dressed, his mannerisms and his voice were so similar. Bella had never forgotten Michael, hence why she'd ended up in bed with Vinny.

Giovanni D'Angelo kept a dignified silence. Bella was his pride and joy, yet the bane of his life at times. He worried about her immensely, yet knew she could hold her own. She was headstrong, took after her Papa.

When his wife began asking more questions about Michael Butler, Giovanni sighed. He'd had such high hopes for Bella, had wanted to her to marry Marco Rossi, the son of a very well-respected friend. But Bella had other ideas. She'd led poor Marco a dog's life before deciding she wanted to travel the world working as a model. A big success she had become, but in Giovanni's eyes her poxy taste in men left a lot to be desired.

'Are you crying, Mummy?' Antonio asked.

'No, sweetie pie,' Bella replied, quickly pulling herself together.

'Why couldn't Michael come on holiday with us?'

'Because Michael's busy. He has his club to run.'

'We will be seeing Michael again soon though, won't we, Mummy?'

Bella couldn't reply because she had no idea of the answer. That was why she had come away, to clear her head and work out her next move. The thought of ending her relationship with Michael was unbearable. But what choice did she have?

'Have you heard anything from Clint, Bella?' her mother enquired.

Bella sighed before mumbling 'No.' Clint didn't even exist. She'd invented him and their imaginary long-term relationship because anything was better than telling her parents that Antonio was the result of a drunken one-night stand with a man whose name she could not recall.

She knew who that man was now though. Antonio's father was a nasty piece of work. An evil, sadistic, psychotic bastard who answered to the name of Vinny Butler.

Bella's father stared at his daughter via the interior mirror. Clint didn't exist. He knew that much. He'd even sent a man over to New York to find him. He'd also done his homework regarding Michael Butler. Had sent the same man to watch him in London. Having studied the photographs, Giovanni D'Angelo was sure that Michael was Antonio's father. Little did he know that his beloved grandson was actually conceived by the satanic sperm of Vinny.

'You OK, Papa?' Bella asked, aware that his eyes were focussed on her.

Giovanni smiled. He was more than OK. Being the boss of the D'Angelo family meant that he could wipe out a man in a split second. Including Michael Butler, if he ever wronged his daughter again. The Butlers might be classed as big fish in London. But in Sicily and Giovanni's world, they were nothing but mere tadpoles.

CHAPTER THIRTY-EIGHT

Christmas Eve 1985

Mary Walker could barely contain herself. 'How much longer, Donald?'

'I don't know, dear. Like yourself, I'm unfamiliar with the area. Ah, hang on. I think we're in the right street. Look at the numbers on your left.'

'Number forty!' Mary squealed.

Slowing down, Donald pulled up outside a four-bedroomed detached house. 'I'll get the presents out the boot. Go and knock then.'

Mary didn't need telling twice. She ran up the path and straight into the arms of her stunning daughter. 'Nancy!' she cried. 'I've missed you so much.'

When Christopher had first told her he was going to help Nancy fake her own death, Mary had been appalled by the idea. Not only was pretending Nancy was dead so very wrong, but how the hell was she meant to lie to people? Christopher had convinced Mary to go through with the sham. Said it was the only way to free Nancy from a life of misery. 'Don't be so ridiculous. Nancy'll end up in prison and you'll be slung out the police force,' Mary had argued.

Donald had a different view. 'Christopher is talking sense, Mary. Nancy's only chance of happiness is to rid herself of Michael Butler for good. I know this is difficult and we'll miss her dreadfully, but Nancy has a chance to start again. Raise another family with a decent man instead of that scoundrel.'

The decent man Donald referred to was Dean Smart. Dean had met Nancy at Beachy Head, and had even helped her write her suicide notes before driving her to his home in Glasgow.

Christopher had sorted false documentation for his sister. He'd hated breaking the law, but sometimes you had to put family first, and what his superiors didn't know couldn't hurt him.

'Dean, how are you, lovey?' Mary asked, hugging the man who had put a smile back on the face of her daughter.

'I'm very well, thanks, Mary. Your daughter takes good care of me. So much so, I asked her if she would do me the honour of becoming my wife.'

'And I said yes!' Nancy exclaimed.

'We're getting married in Gretna Green on my birthday and we'd love you and Donald to come. Can't exactly invite anybody else, can we?' Dean chuckled.

'Congratulations,' Donald said, shaking his future son-in-law's hand. 'Mary and I wouldn't miss your big day for the world.'

Mary was crying tears of joy. Nancy looked so radiant. Sitting through her daughter's remembrance-of-life service had been one of the hardest things Mary had ever done, but Christopher had insisted she go through with it. 'I'm so happy for you both, and wouldn't your nan be delighted too, Dean?'

'Me nan's probably looking down, grinning as we speak. Just before she died she told me never to give up on Nance.

Reckoned we were made for each other – and she was right.'

Watching the happy couple gaze lovingly into one another's eyes, Mary smiled. Lying to friends, neighbours and customers at the café had been awful. But seeing Nancy so happy made it all worthwhile. Her daughter had sacrificed a lot to be with Dean, and had finally found the peace and happiness she truly deserved.

EPILOGUE

Father Patrick had heard many a confession in his lifetime. But as Queenie Butler finally stopped speaking about her dysfunctional family, he was shocked to the core.

'You OK, Father?' asked Queenie, shoving another large brandy into the man's visibly shaking hand. 'You better drink that.'

'Saint Michael, the archangel, defend us in battle. Be our protection against the wickedness and snares of the Devil,' Father Patrick rambled, closing his eyes.

'Oh, for fuck's sake, Queen, shut him up. Silly old bugger is as pissed as a fart,' Vivian hissed.

Smiling politely, Queenie snatched Father Patrick's drink out of his hands, grabbed him by the elbow and edged him into the hallway. 'Lovely to meet you, Father. And thank you so much for ridding my family of evil spirits,' Queenie said, as she all but pushed the shocked priest out of the front door, slamming it behind him.

'Do you reckon his prayers will work, Queen?' Vivian asked, bemused by the whole affair.

'How the hell should I know? I'm not a Catholic!

Ask God. On second thoughts, don't bother. That bastard hates us. Stop feeling fucking sorry for yourself, Queen. The past is the past. Sod all we can do to change it, so harping on about it is pointless. It's time to move on. Concentrate solely on the future.'

Taken aback by Viv's little speech, Queenie glared at her. 'You've changed your bloody tune. Does forgetting the past and concentrating on the future include you forgiving my Vinny, then? Loves you that boy does. Breaks his heart you still won't talk to him.'

Vivian chose her words carefully. 'I'm not ready to forgive, but I am ready to try to forget. Bitterness eats away at your insides like cancer. I don't wanna be bitter no more.'

Queenie poured two glasses of sherry and handed one to Viv. 'So what's brought on this change of heart then? And don't say "nothing" as you were acting weird earlier.'

'I had a dream last night. Lenny was sat on the edge of my bed, urging me to make things right. Mum was with him an' all, holding his hand. They both said they were happy, and told me to be happy too. So vivid it was. I cried when I woke up. But not with sadness. I felt comforted.'

Eyes welling up, Queenie squeezed her sister's hand. 'Fat Beryl reckons spirits can visit us in our sleep. I reckon Mum and Lenny came to talk to you. Probably to bang our bleedin' heads together. You're right. It is time to leave the past behind.'

Vivian held her glass aloft. 'To new beginnings.'

Queenie chinked glasses and smiled. 'New beginnings.'

The Butlers will return

in the explosive new novel from

Kimberley
CHAMBERS

Look out for
TAINTED LOVE

Coming early 2016